Karen C

DANCING WITH

A York Ladies' Detec...

Dancing with Dusty Fossils

© Karen Charlton 2022

Visit Karen Charlton's website to learn more about her historical novels and sign up for her occasional newsletter for the latest news about her writing and public events.

www.karencharlton.com

Published by Famelton Publishing.
Cover design and illustration by Lisa Horton.
Cover photograph of the museum by Lorena Muscai

ALSO BY KAREN CHARLTON

The York Ladies' Detective Agency Mysteries
The Mystery of Mad Alice Lane (short story)
Smoke & Cracked Mirrors
Dancing with Dusty Fossils

The Detective Lavender Mysteries
The Heiress of Linn Hagh
The Sans Pareil Mystery
The Sculthorpe Murder
Plague Pits & River Bones
Murder on Park Lane
The Willow Marsh Murder

The Mystery of the Skelton Diamonds (short story)
The Piccadilly Pickpocket (short story)
The Death of Irish Nell (short story)
Death at the Frost Fair (short story)

Other Works
February 1809 (short story)
Catching the Eagle
Seeking our Eagle (non-fiction)

Chapter One

The old wireless in the corner of the Dunns' sitting room crackled as Britain's new prime minister, Mr Winston Churchill, gravely told the nation about the tremendous battle raging on the Continent.

Maud Dunn clutched the threadbare arm of her chair until her arthritic knuckles turned white as Mr Churchill explained how the Germans had broken through the Allied defences and were ravaging the open and defenceless countryside of France and Flanders.

Maud groaned and turned her pale, lined face towards her husband. Her voice cracked with emotion. 'Our lads are in trouble, Charlie!'

On the other side of the hearth, her husband's jaw clenched around the stem of his pipe as he fought back a wave of nausea. He'd seen it coming for days; the newspapers had been full of dire warnings. 'Steady, love,' he said, 'they'll be all right. The Green Howards have trained them well.'

Maud shook her head and her voice rose hysterically. 'They're surrounded! They're runnin' for their bloomin' lives!'

Charlie rose stiffly, crossed the hearth rug, and put a comforting hand on his wife's shoulder. 'Aye, well, in that case it's a good job they're fast runners, ain't it? No one can ever run faster than our lads…'

His voice trailed away helplessly, and his anxiety was replaced with a flash of anger.

How the devil had it come to this? Didn't their family suffer enough last time around?

He'd lost a brother in the aerial bombardment on the Somme and Maud had lost one in a hail of machine-gun fire at Ypres. It was only by sheer luck that Charlie himself had returned unscathed after two years in the trenches. Apart from their two sons, they also had two nephews fighting with the British Expeditionary Force in France.

Fighting? No, Maud was right – they were running for their bloody lives. How many of them would come back? He held his wife tighter.

Maud shook her shoulder free from his grip. 'You're hurtin' me, Charlie.' She leant forward as the sonorous tones of Winston Churchill sought to reassure the nation.

Outside in the hallway, the telephone rang.

'Who the hell is that?' he snapped. 'Tonight – of all nights?'

Maud dabbed her eyes with her apron. 'You'd better get it. It must be important.'

It was important. It was Clifford Street police station.

'Mr Dunn?' the officer said. 'We understand you're the caretaker at the Yorkshire Museum. We've had a report that a group of young lads have scrambled over the wall into the Museum Gardens at the bottom of Marygate.'

Harry rolled his eyes and swore under his breath. 'Not again! I'm sick of telling them they've got to repair that damn wall. Bloody young scamps!'

'Our witness thinks it might be more serious than just trespass, Mr Dunn. They're carrying a crowbar – it looks like they intend to break

6

into the museum. Have you got the keys? We'll send down a couple of officers.'

Harry sucked in his breath and thought of the Hospitium, filled to the rafters of its medieval roof with Roman, Viking and Saxon treasures. He didn't want to leave Maud right now, but he had no choice.

'Meet us with the keys at the Abbey Gatehouse entrance on Marygate in ten minutes,' the officer continued. 'With any luck we'll catch the little beggars in the act.'

Aye, and I'll tan their bloody hides for them when we catch them, Charlie thought. He grabbed his coat and hat.

Despite his stiff joints and the dangers of the uneven pavement, Charlie strode angrily down the quiet blacked-out streets towards the museum, cursing the old gentlemen who'd planted the botanic garden around it. Created one hundred years ago on the site of the ruins of one of the country's grandest abbeys, the sprawling ten-acre site, with its swirling islands of exotic and mature shrubs and thick-trunked old trees, provided far too many places for the trespassing youngsters to hide.

Two officers waited at the Abbey Gatehouse entrance. There was no police car parked nearby. They must have hot-footed it from Clifford Street to get here before him.

The Abbey Gatehouse, home of the elderly keeper of the museum, was already in darkness. This didn't surprise Charlie. Mr Collinge was nearly seventy, frail and always retired to bed early, exhausted with the responsibility he carried for the gardens, the ancient ruins and the vast treasure trove of priceless antiquities and fossils under his care.

'Evening, officers.'

One of the policemen was a rough-looking chap with a scowling face and hands like hams that toyed with the truncheon dangling from his belt. His uniform was too tight, and the brass buttons strained over his stout, muscular body. *He's the kind of fellow to scare the living daylights out of the thieving little sods*, Charlie thought with a grunt of satisfaction.

But his anger flared again when saw the face of the other officer in the moonlight. The fellow was under thirty. *Why hadn't he signed up?*

'Thanks fer comin' out, Mr Dunn. Have yer got the keys?' the younger officer asked.

Charlie ignored him and turned to his companion. 'I know one of yer inspectors,' he told him. 'Clever chap. Inspector Gabriel Roxby. D'you work wi' him?' He pulled the heavy iron key ring out of his pocket and unlocked the gate.

'Yeah, we know the archangel,' the older officer replied, smirking.

Discomfited by their lack of respect, Charlie pushed open the spiked wrought-iron gate. It screeched on its hinges in protest. A noise loud enough to wake the centuries-dead monks in the graveyard of the ruined abbey.

'Needs oilin',' the older officer commented gruffly.

'Yeah, the whole damn place is goin' to rack and ruin,' Charlie admitted.

The officers strode ahead, beneath the medieval stone arch that linked the Abbey Gatehouse with St Olave's Church.

Charlie hesitated, unsure whether to shut and lock the screeching gate behind them. There were now four air bases with thousands of airmen surrounding the city and most of these chaps spent their time off getting drunk. The last thing Charlie needed was to round up the trespassing youngsters and then find a squadron of intoxicated airmen had sneaked inside the grounds to sleep off the drink beneath the exotic magnolias and chestnuts.

In the end, he just pulled the gate shut and quickened his pace to catch up with the policemen. He'd never liked this place after dark. There were too many ghosts haunting the abbey ruins, for a start. Apart from the dead monks, they said King Henry VIII had once stayed here – at the old abbot's house – and had nailed the heads and dismembered body parts of honest Yorkshire rebels above the gates. He scurried beneath the straggly overhanging branches of a Scottish Dawyck beech tree. It rustled eerily in the wind.

Why did they grow this foreign stuff? he wondered. *What's wrong with a good old English oak?*

The officers had already turned the corner of the path by the time he'd caught up with them.

'How many of them are there?' he asked. The solid black mass of the medieval Hospitium loomed into the dark sky ahead, obscuring the stars. Charlie heard its ancient timbers groan in the wind.

'How many what?' asked the older officer.

Charlie glanced at him, frowning. 'Kids. In the grounds.'

'Oh, them. Half a dozen, we think.'

The wind dropped and for a moment the Hospitium stood silent and – apparently – undisturbed. The moonlight glinted off the glass in the mullioned windows. None of them were broken or appeared to have been forced and the heavy oak doors were firmly closed.

'Wait here,' said the older officer. They left him shivering on the path and disappeared into the gloom to check out the sides and rear of the building.

Charlie's ears strained to catch a sound of the intruders. Any sound.

His eyes squinted and peered into the darkness, trying to pick out movement. *Who'd have thought there were so many shades of black in the world?*

The older officer suddenly appeared out of nowhere and made Charlie jump. 'Can't see anythin',' he said. 'We'd best go inside and check.'

Sighing, Charlie led the way up the twisting wooden exterior steps towards the main entrance of the Hospitium. If there wasn't any evidence of a break-in here, they'd have to go round the main museum building too, which was far bigger. It was going to be a long night.

The second officer joined them on the platform outside the main entrance. As Charlie unlocked the door, the sound of boyish laughter and shouting drifted towards them on the breeze.

He spun round, glanced up the slope towards the main museum building and saw several lithe shadows flitting across the path among the trees.

'There!' he said, pointing. 'There's the little bastards!'

He opened his mouth to holler at the kids… then his world went an even darker shade of black.

Chapter Two

Amelia Edwards' eyes lit up with delight as her fiancé, John, led her inside the dining room of the Dean Court Hotel. Her feet sank into its thick carpet and her nose wrinkled in anticipation at the delicious smell of the exquisite food wafting around the high-ceilinged restaurant. Everything was perfect, from the soft flickering light emitted by the lamps in the centre of the tables to the pristine linen of the dusky rose tablecloths. Absolutely perfect.

It was the ideal place to celebrate their engagement and John's business success, and to forget about the beastly war raging outside. John was so thoughtful.

They reached their table next to the tall window. John waved aside the waiter and pulled out a chair for her. She sank gracefully on to the soft velvet cushions of her seat.

Laughter lines crinkled around John's wonderful blue eyes. 'For the future Mrs Leyland,' he said. 'The most beautiful woman in the room.'

Her heart melted.

'Will this be all right for you?' John asked. As always, his handsome face was etched with concern for *her*.

'It's perfect,' she murmured. 'Beautiful.'

'You didn't want to go somewhere livelier to celebrate?'

In the far corner of the restaurant, a pianist struck up a gentle ballad.

She smiled and waved her thin wrist and fingers in the pianist's direction. 'This is lively enough for me.'

For the next few minutes, John was busy with the waiter, ordering their food and champagne, and she was able to enjoy the magnificent view from the window of the towering Gothic minster across the road. The evening light was fading, and they'd draw the blackout curtains soon. She tried to etch the view in her memory so she could describe it later to Sonia in a letter.

The thought of her childhood friend filled her with a little unease. She was unsure what Sonia would make of John, who was many years her senior. Sonia was mean about how people looked and would focus on John's deeply furrowed brow and the crinkled skin around his eyes – not the love shining out of them. John's face reflected the hard life of sorrow and disappointment he'd had to endure, caused by swindling business partners and the faceless women who'd taken advantage of his soft heart and generous nature and let him down.

Amelia's heart hardened. She'd already defied her grandfather over John, and if Sonia persisted in being mean and jealous, well… it would be the end of the friendship, wouldn't it. Amelia was filled again with a burning desire to make John happy and to single-handedly banish the disappointments of his past.

The waiter left and John squeezed her hand in his long, sensitive fingers. 'You belong in a place like this,' he murmured. 'I promise you, darling – once the business gets on its feet, we'll dine here every night. No more fish and chip suppers for us in my cramped flat!'

Amelia smiled. 'Once a year on our anniversary would be enough for me,' she said. 'This should become our "special place", John. Just visited for special occasions. Besides which,' she added, in what she hoped was a mature and practical manner, 'we need our money for the new business.'

'I'm not sure a mere sixty trips over a lifetime will be enough. Because that's how long we'll be together, Amelia – sixty glorious years. We'll celebrate our diamond wedding anniversary here – just think of the children and grandchildren we'll have!'

She laughed in delight at the thought – then blushed. Her cheeks always burned when he mentioned children. To cover her embarrassment, she asked him how his day had been.

'Fantastic! I met a new chap today – Reynolds. He thinks artificial nitrogen is the way forward for agricultural fertiliser and wants to invest. Obviously, because I own the patent, I'd still be the main partner in the scheme.' Inspired, he chatted away for some time about crop yields and the incredible ability of his product to increase agricultural fertility and reduce starvation across the globe.

The waiter arrived with the champagne and John toasted her: the woman of his dreams, the future Mrs Leyland. Then his mind turned back to his venture. 'You can't imagine what it means to me, Amelia. I want to give something back to the world, to society and the country I adore.'

'You're so noble, John,' she murmured.

'By the way, Reynolds told me about a new scheme he's invested in – it sounds promising but I don't have the spare cash…'

'I can help, John. I still have loads left of my inheritance.'

He patted her hand. 'I wouldn't dream of it, darling. You've already given me so much for the plant in Dringhouses.'

'I do wish you'd let me visit your new premises.'

'Want to check up on your investment, do you, Amelia?'

'No,' she said hastily. 'This means so much to you – you're so passionate about everything. I just want to become more involved – a part of it.'

'But you are part of it, my darling. You're the reason I do everything. It's the thought of coming home to you every night…'

He broke off as a brassy woman in a low-cut blouse and tight black satin skirt sauntered casually over to their table. Her swaying hips attracted the attention of every diner in the room – especially the men. Beneath her heavy foundation and lipstick, she looked a bit like the actress Vivien Leigh. Albeit a more voluptuous and bushy-haired Vivien Leigh.

To Amelia's horror, she came straight up to John. 'Hello, my lover. I'm so glad I've found you at last.'

'What the devil …?' John spluttered.

Unperturbed by his shocked reaction, the woman pulled over a vacant chair from the next table and sat down. 'What are you doin' here with this little lass?'

'Who are you?' John snapped. 'What on earth do you want?'

The woman leant across the table, exposing the depths of her ample cleavage. 'I warned you, darlin', that I'd find you if you didn't play fair – and pay me what you owed.' Her voice was quiet, husky and sensuous – but the threat was ominous. The conversation died at every surrounding table as the other diners turned to watch.

John's voice was shrill. 'I don't know you, madam. Waiter!'

The woman smiled a slow, knowing smile, then picked up John's glass and took a sip of his champagne. 'You don't know me, lover? You don't know your own wife?'

'Wife?' Amelia glanced in horror at the cheap wedding ring on the woman's finger.

'Ooh, nice champagne, John,' the woman said. 'What are you celebratin' – and who paid for this?'

'This is ridiculous,' John snapped. 'Amelia, I've no idea who this woman is. I'll get her removed. Waiter!'

The woman laughed and turned her languid, sultry gaze in Amelia's direction. 'Amelia, is it? So, *you're* his latest floozy.'

'I beg your pardon! I'm John's fiancée!' Amelia's voice squeaked with indignation.

'Not unless I divorce him first, you're not,' the woman said, with a wink. 'Been touchin' you up for money, has he? Wants you to invest in his crazy old nitrogen scheme, does he?'

Amelia's mind swirled; she felt like she was about to faint. Her world was falling apart.

'How dare you, you bitch! Waiter! For God's sake, where are the staff?' John was red with anger, ugly with rage.

The woman ignored him and leant across the table towards Amelia. Her voice was low, her gaze direct. 'That's his favourite line, sweetheart. But it's a lie – the nitrogen stuff never existed – neither does the factory in Dringhouses.'

'Don't listen to her, Amelia – this is poison, pure poison!'

The woman continued, unfazed. Her voice was low, her gaze direct. 'Took a hundred off me to get some damn patent, he did. But it was a lie. I told him to sling his hook and give me back what he owed.'

'You'll regret this impertinence – you bitch!'

Amelia swallowed hard. 'If she's not your wife, how does she know so much about you?'

'I've no idea. The tart's probably been sent by one of my competitors!'

Amelia glanced between them. John wouldn't look her in the eye and there was something about this vile woman's audacity and calmness that made her more believable.

The waiter finally arrived 'What's the problem, sir?'

'This woman is bothering us. Remove her.'

The waiter reached out and grabbed the woman's shoulder as if to haul her away. 'On your feet, you! Out! Your type don't belong in here.'

'Oh, but I do belong here,' she said calmly, tapping her wedding ring. 'A woman always belongs by the side of her husband.'

The waiter's hand fell away in confusion. Evicting the occasional cheeky prostitute from the hotel bar was part of his job but refereeing in a marital dispute wasn't. He turned on his heel. 'I'll fetch the manager.'

'If you won't bloody remove her, I will.' John whipped his napkin off his lap and rose to his feet.

Terrified at what he would do, Amelia also stood up, knocking over her glass in the process. The crash and sound of splintering glass stopped John in his threatening advance towards the interloper.

Amelia flushed with shame and picked up her purse. 'Leave her, John. I'm going. It's over.'

'There's no need, Amelia,' he pleaded. 'Once they get rid of this bitch we can carry on, there's so much more I need to tell you… about Reynolds and this new investment.'

Tears flooded down her flaming cheeks as she pulled her engagement ring off her trembling finger and slapped it down on the tablecloth. 'It's ruined. Everything's ruined.'

'One day you'll thank me for this, sweetheart,' the strange woman said, 'especially as he takes his teeth out before he goes to bed.'

Amelia's eyes widened with horror, and she turned and fled. John hurried after her, calling her name. The waiter followed.

The woman's laughter followed them out of the restaurant.

Once they'd gone, the brassy woman ignored the hostile glances of the other diners and the tuts of disgust and reached out for the bottle of champagne. 'Don't mind if I do,' she said to no one in particular, as she topped up her glass and took a generous swig.

'Disgraceful!' someone hissed.

'You should be ashamed of yourself!' a male diner muttered from the next table.

The waiter returned and wrestled the bottle of champagne out of the woman's grasp. As he did so, he leant over her and whispered: 'I stayed away for as long as possible, Bobbie, to give you more time.'

'Yes, I know. Thank you.'

'But you need to get out of here – my manager has sent for the police.'

But it was too late. The outraged and indignant restaurant manager finally made an appearance – with a burly police officer in tow.

The next moment she was manhandled out of her seat and only just managed to grab her coat from where she'd hidden it behind an aspidistra before she was frogmarched towards the exit.

'Yer under arrest for disturbin' the peace,' hissed the officer. 'Yer comin' wi' me t'police station.'

'Lead on,' said Bobbie, grinning.

Chapter Three

The custody suite in Clifford Street had greasy walls stained yellow with nicotine, and high barred windows. A single light bulb dangled from a wire in the ceiling. Bobbie was told to sit down on a scuffed wooden bench next to a thin, crumpled little man in handcuffs. The duty sergeant was already busy with a drunk and noisy airman at the desk.

'You wait 'ere,' her arresting officer snarled, 'while I process yer.'

'Don't bother.' She reached into her purse. 'Is Inspector Roxby here?'

When he nodded, she handed him a small, printed card. 'Just give him this and save yourself the paperwork.'

The policeman eyed it suspiciously. '*Smoke & Cracked Mirrors*? What the devil's this?"

'My get-out-of-jail card.'

'This ain't a game of Monopoly. You're in deep trouble, lass.' But he took the card anyway and disappeared with it into a back office.

Bobbie sighed with relief and sat back on the uncomfortable bench to wait, wrinkling her nose at the unpleasant reek of male body odour. She hoped Gabriel Roxby, Jemma's brother, was in a good mood. He was a grumpy beggar at times and would probably roast her for wasting police time. But at least he wouldn't lock her up.

Bored with the wait, she glanced curiously at the miserable, hunched little man beside her. He was staring gloomily down at the toes of his scuffed shoes through black horn-rimmed spectacles. The handcuffs seemed unnecessary on someone so thin and weedy – a strong gust of wind would blow him over. He was about fifty years old; his thinning hair barely covered his bald patch and his complexion was sallow and unhealthy, the skin drawn tight across his cheekbones. His spectacles were hooked round a pair of extremely large protruding ears, which seemed at odds with such a narrow face. All in all, he was a peculiar-looking little fellow.

'What are you in for?' she asked.

The man blinked but refused to abandon his study of his toes.

'Why have you been arrested?' she persisted.

'Assault,' he muttered.

'Good grief! You don't look like you've got it in you!'

He didn't bother to look up. 'I didn't do it,' he said wearily. 'I didn't attack him. I'm innocent.'

'Of course you are,' Bobbie said cheerfully. She was still excited after the success of her evening's work. 'What's your name?'

'Gill. Anthony Gill. My name's Anthony – not Tony,' he added automatically, as if he'd spent his life pointing this out to people.

'Well, don't you worry, Mr Gill. England's police cells are full of innocent men.'

He finally glanced up at her and disapproval settled in his brown eyes. But it wasn't the sarcasm that had roused him; that had gone straight over his head. 'You're wearing too much make-up. Are you a tart?'

She laughed. 'No, I'm a guardian angel – a private detective in disguise as a trollop.'

She had his attention now. 'Why?'

'I've just stopped a seventeen-year-old girl from making the biggest mistake of her life. That's what we guardian angels do – help people.'

He sighed. 'I could do with a guardian angel right now. They don't believe me.'

'I'm sure if you just tell them the truth…'

'I'm not telling them anything,' he snapped. 'It's their job to find evidence of guilt – and there isn't any.'

'Oh?'

'Silence!' snarled the sergeant across the room. 'No talking among the prisoners.'

Bobbie shrugged. Her partner-in-sin resumed his miserable contemplation of his toes.

Five minutes later, her arresting officer returned and gestured her to follow him down the corridor towards Gabriel's bland and cluttered office. His desk overflowed with piles of paperwork and his head of white curly hair was bent low over it. His cap dangled from the hat stand in the corner.

When he glanced up, his eyes rolled to the ceiling in shock. 'Good God, Bobbie! Heaven help Jemma if I ever see her dressed like that!' He waved away the other officer and Bobbie slid into the chair on the other side of his desk.

'I'd never let Jemma take on a role like this. She couldn't pull it off. She'd still look like a blonde angel even dressed as a harlot.'

'What the hell have you been up to?'

'I've been preventing a crime. I've just saved a naive young heiress from the clutches of a con man. Amelia moved to York about six months ago from Beverley and met this cad, John Leyland. Her grandfather asked us to make discreet enquiries about him. The man's a love rat; he has a history of taking money from vulnerable women on the pretence of investing it in lucrative schemes, which turn out to be spurious. Amelia has already given him a thousand pounds for his non-existent plant in Dringhouses.'

Gabriel gestured with his pen towards her clothing. 'And it was necessary to dress like this and cause a major disturbance at the Dean Court Hotel in order to save this young woman from herself?'

Bobbie sighed. 'This was Plan B. Plan A was to sit down with Amelia and tell her the truth, but her grandfather said she wouldn't listen. He tried to pay Leyland off and gave him another £200 to leave the girl alone.'

A wry smile twitched at the side of Gabriel's mouth. 'Let me guess what happened next. Leyland took the money but carried on with his seduction?'

'Exactly. I warned the grandfather it wouldn't work, but he's a stubborn old man. Anyway, this little charade was our last chance to split them up. It was time for desperate measures.'

'Did it work?'

She shrugged again. 'I hope so. She looked pretty devastated when I mentioned Leyland's false teeth.'

Gabriel struggled to hide his smile. 'You're a cruel woman, Roberta Baker. Young love stands no chance with you around.' He pulled a pile of papers towards him. 'Right, now leave me in peace to get on with some work. I'll let you off this time.'

'Thanks, Gabriel.' She stood up to leave. 'By the way, have you heard from Jemma?'

Gabriel's smile faded. 'She telephoned last night to let me know she'd arrived safely in London. She planned to see one of Michael's air force friends today, and his landlady. Tomorrow she's going to Bletchley.'

Bobbie hesitated at the door. 'You don't think she'll find Michael, do you?'

Reluctantly, Gabriel shook his head. 'Michael's been missing since January and, wherever he is, he doesn't want to be found – even Special Branch have failed to locate him. But Jemma won't rest unless she tries herself.'

Bobbie nodded sadly. 'By the way – how's Maisie's father? Is the wedding still going ahead on Saturday?' Gabriel and his fiancée, Maisie, had already had to cancel one marriage ceremony due to the ill health of her elderly father.

He glanced back up from his paperwork. 'Yes, he's much better, thank you. Will you be there?'

'Yes, I'm looking forward to it. Maisie must be relieved he's on the mend.'

He sighed heavily. 'She is – but she's also worried about her sons – especially Harry. He's in the thick of this chaos across the Channel.' He glanced at Bobbie sharply. 'I don't suppose you've heard from your own brother?'

Bobbie grimaced and shook her head. She didn't particularly like her older brother, Frank, but she'd give anything right now to see his ugly mug walk through the door. There were rumours the British Expeditionary Force were trapped on the northern French coast and were retreating towards the beaches. The thought of defeat was galling but this was overshadowed by fear for their men; everyone in Britain was desperate for news about their sons and brothers.

'There's nothing any of us can do – except wait. Your honeymoon in Scotland will do Maisie good – and young Tom will be quite safe with Jemma.'

'It's not Jemma who's the problem – even my scatterbrained sister couldn't mess up the care of a ten-year-old boy. It's Tom himself. He's been rather… difficult… recently.'

'Tom?' Bobbie was genuinely surprised. Maisie's younger son was one of the most polite and easy-going lads she'd ever met. 'It's probably just all the change – moving house etcetera. Plus, he'll be worried about Harry as well. I'm sure it'll come right in the end.'

'Thanks, Bobbie. Oh – and by the way—' Gabriel called after her as she turned to leave, '—if you turn up at my wedding dressed like that, I'll arrest you for soliciting.'

24

Chapter Four

Friday, 24th May 1940

York

Bobbie saw Anthony Gill in the dock at the magistrates' court the next day.

Prior to joining Jemma full time in their agency, she'd worked as a store detective at Grainger's, York's most prestigious department store. Giving evidence against shoplifters in court had been part of her job. The wheels of justice were turning slowly in York since the outbreak of the war; the magistrates' court had been overwhelmed with cases of blackout infringement and this outstanding case had only just come to court.

As she approached the imposing red-brick Victorian building on Clifford Street, she saw a large group of photographers and reporters milling around on the steps leading to the arched entrance. There was a palpable buzz of excitement in the air as they waited for something – or someone.

Among them was a familiar figure in a short tweed jacket with shapeless and stained flannel trousers, a Leica II slung round his neck on its leather strap. It was Ricky Wilde, a freelance photographer with the *Yorkshire Evening Press*, who'd helped the women out several times with tricky cases. She pushed her way through the crowd to his side. 'Hello, Ricky, what's going on? Are we expecting royalty?'

An enthusiastic grin lit up his long face. 'The next best thing – we're waiting for a murderer.'

'A murderer!'

'Well, almost. One of the curators at the Castle Museum had his head bashed in yesterday. He's unconscious and not expected to survive. The cops have already arrested his attacker and he's due for his first hearing in the magistrates' court.'

Bobbie frowned, glanced down the road to where the police station adjoined the court and thought of the little man she'd met in the custody suite. *Was it Anthony Gill?* 'Is this something to do with that robbery when the museum caretaker was attacked by a couple of guys disguised as police officers? I thought he was recovering in hospital.'

'No! That was at the other museum – the Yorkshire Museum. These guys – both the victim and the suspect – work at the Castle Museum.'

'Good grief! Another assault? Staff at *both* the city's museums have been attacked within the same week?'

'Yep,' he confirmed. 'The world of dusty old fossils has never been so exciting.'

'That's appalling! But why are you waiting out here?'

'No one's allowed inside unless they're on official business. If the bloke's charged, they'll bring him out and put him in a prison wagon to take him to Armley Gaol. It's our best chance for a photo.' He rubbed chemical-stained fingers over his stubbled jaw and smoothed down his short-clipped moustache. His eyes were already on the street and the position of the sun, working out the best angle for his beloved Leica.

'Gosh.' Bobbie glanced around at the expectant and unsympathetic crowd of journalists and photographers, laughing and smoking on the steps. She knew they were only doing their job, but she felt a twinge of sympathy for the shy, hunched little fellow who'd have to face this onslaught.

Ricky's intelligent hazel eyes narrowed. 'Why are you here, Bobbie?'

'Official business.' She pulled her subpoena out of her handbag and turned to enter the imposing building. 'I'll let you know if I discover anything,' she added hastily, before he pestered her to spy for him.

Her court appearance as a witness was mercifully short. The shoplifter was found guilty and led away to serve time in the local women's prison at His Majesty's pleasure. Bobbie left the grim wood-panelled courtroom to find a large crowd of court dignitaries and lawyers in suits standing around on the elaborate mosaic floor in the corridor. She heard Gill's name mentioned in hushed tones.

She knew she was supposed to vacate the premises immediately, but Anthony Gill intrigued her. Moving stealthily to the edge of the crowd, she positioned herself between a marble pillar and a tiny middle-aged woman with a black coat and hat and tearful eyes.

When a court official glanced, frowning, in her direction, she fished out her handkerchief and offered it to the woman beside her as if she was there to support her. The woman declined her offer, but the action was enough to fend off the suspicious official, who turned away. When the woman moved up the stairs into the public gallery, Bobbie quietly followed and joined her on the hard wooden bench.

Anthony Gill shuffled into the courtroom in handcuffs, his eyes downcast. The woman beside Bobbie groaned at his appearance and clutched the handbag on her lap so hard her knuckles turned white.

Gill only spoke a few times to confirm his name and address and to plead 'not guilty' to the charge of assaulting Lance Richards. The lawyers then spent several minutes arguing about bail. The prosecution told the magistrates this had been a singularly vicious attack on Mr Richards, who wasn't expected to survive the assault. The defendant had given no alibi for the crime and the evidence against him was overwhelming. Mr Gill, the lawyer added, had also been uncooperative with the police.

Both Bobbie and the magistrates raised their eyebrows at this news. She remembered Gill's determination last night when he'd said: *I'm not telling them anything.* Stubbornness like that wouldn't endear him to the court.

Beside her, the tiny woman groaned again and Bobbie suddenly realised she had the same sallow complexion, prominent cheekbones and thin face as the man in the dock. She was also roughly the same age.

Meanwhile, the defence lawyer argued that Mr Gill was a man of exemplary character, who'd never been in trouble with the police in his life and had no prior convictions.

It didn't help. The magistrates decided Gill should be remanded in Armley Gaol pending his trial. The bail application was dismissed and Gill was taken away.

The woman beside Bobbie remained in her seat, fighting back her tears as the public gallery emptied.

Bobbie offered her handkerchief again and this time it was accepted. She squeezed the woman's hand sympathetically and made a lucky guess. 'You're Anthony's sister, aren't you?'

The woman's swollen eyes blinked. 'Yes, he lives with me. How do you know? Oh God, you're not another reporter, are you?'

'No. I'm a private detective and my name's Bobbie Baker. I work for a ladies' detective agency called Smoke & Cracked Mirrors. I've met Anthony.'

'He's never mentioned you.'

'We don't know each other very well but I know him well enough to know he doesn't like his name abbreviated.' She fished a business card out of her handbag and gave it to the startled woman. 'Look, for what it's worth, I don't think Anthony did this thing. If there's anything I – or my company – can do to help prove his innocence, please contact us.'

The woman hesitated, confused.

'Defence lawyers often use P.I.s to help gather evidence, Miss Gill – especially if their client has no alibi. Just pass this to Anthony's lawyer and let him decide.'

The woman gave a small nod and slid the card into her own handbag. 'Any port in a storm…' she whispered. 'Thank you, Miss Baker.'

'Bobbie. Call me Bobbie – although your brother knows me better as a *guardian angel*.'

Miss Gill's eyes widened but she didn't ask why. She sat up straighter and sniffed back her tears. 'I'm Dora.'

Bobbie remembered the reporters and photographers lurking like vultures outside and silently cursed Ricky for being part of the pack. 'Do you want me to walk out with you and take you home, Dora?'

Dora shook her head and rose to leave. 'I'll be fine. I'm hoping they'll let me see Anthony before they… take him away. Thank you, again.'

Bobbie nodded sympathetically and watched her leave. She'd no idea what she'd just committed herself to – or what the devil was going on in the dusty and archaic world of the city's museums – but instinct told her there was a mystery here worth exploring.

Chapter Five

Friday, 24th May 1940
London

Jemma picked her way carefully through the heaving crowd in the Great Hall of Euston station, clutching her small suitcase in one hand and her ticket and newspaper in the other. The noise reverberating beneath the high smoke-stained glass roof was deafening.

Jemma had never seen so many people crammed into one place. Passengers and khaki-clad soldiers scurried past with suitcases and kitbags, dodging round the overloaded barrows pushed by the porters. No one smiled and everyone looked exhausted. She was glad to leave behind the grim-faced crowds, the horrendous traffic and the unnerving sense of imminent danger that hung over London like its smog.

Naively, she'd hoped she might find someone – a porter, perhaps – who remembered Michael. But no one in this crush of people would have the time to stop and answer her questions or remember a lone traveller catching the Inverness train back in January.

Disillusioned, she wound her way through the crowds to where her train waited, hissing steam. She climbed aboard one of the maroon carriages and squeezed her way down the narrow corridor, past a couple of soldiers and a blond man in a tan coat and a brown hat. He gave her an unwelcome and appraising glance out of his pale-blue eyes.

She chose a wood-panelled compartment that contained a couple of middle-aged ladies and a woman with a sleeping baby in her arms. The deafening noise of the station outside was muffled in here and the floral perfume of one of the older women masked the stale cigarette smoke and the stuffiness of the carriage.

She placed her newspaper on the seat while she lifted her case up on to the luggage rack. Once in her seat by the window, she pulled her copy of Bradshaw's 1940 *Guide to British Railways* out of her handbag and double-checked her calculations.

This was the same train she assumed Michael took – or was due to take – on the fateful day he vanished. They'd arrive in Bletchley at 8.35 a.m., which would have given him plenty of time to take the short walk to Bletchley Wireless Manufacturing and report, as instructed, at 9 a.m. Michael hated being late for anything. He was obsessive about punctuality. *Is* obsessive, she reminded herself; he's missing, not dead.

Her mind wandered back to those dreadful months when, thanks to a mistake by the air force, she'd been sent the wrong telegram and had believed him to be '*missing in action*'. Gabriel had played hell with Special Branch when the error came to light and forced them to help her to try to find Michael herself. Embarrassed, they'd agreed. Yesterday, she'd met both Michael's pal, AC Freddie Tidsworth, and his landlady, Mrs Sutton.

They were kind people and she sensed they'd both liked her husband in the short time they'd known him. But she heard the disappointment in their voices when they talked about his disappearance; they'd both now accepted the sickening idea that her husband was a deserter.

But none of it made sense.

Freddie had studied with Michael at the polytechnic. He told her how excited Michael had been about his mysterious posting to Bletchley

Wireless Manufacturing and how he'd looked forward to doing something useful for the war effort. They'd gone out for a drink a few days before Michael left.

Mrs Sutton was staying with her pregnant daughter on the day Michael left his lodgings but earlier that week she'd lent him her own copy of Bradshaw's Guide to plan his route. Apparently, he'd pored over it for hours.

None of this was the behaviour of a man who planned to run away.

The carriage door slid open and a businessman in a bowler hat walked into the compartment. He placed his briefcase up on the luggage rack, took his seat and buried his nose in *The Times*.

Did he – or any of the women in this compartment – travel regularly on this train? Jemma wondered.

She remembered Michael's photograph in her handbag and felt a desperate urge to pass it around. Her travelling companions may have been his.

But the thought of confiding in strangers, once again, held her back. She hated watching those alternate waves of sympathy, disgust, suspicion – and sometimes anger – settle on the faces of the people she told about Michael's disappearance.

Outside, the station inspector shouted 'All aboard!' Carriage doors slammed shut with the rhythm of falling dominoes. The guard gave a piercing shriek on his whistle, and the train eased forward and gathered speed.

The baby murmured in its sleep then settled again, lulled by the sway of the carriage.

They travelled through a tunnel and sat in silence for a while in the unreal, pallid light of the compartment lamps. When they emerged, the two older women resumed their quiet conversation and the ticket inspector arrived. By the time he'd examined and punched a hole in her ticket, they were travelling across open countryside.

This was a journey of fifty miles that would take them from London, through Middlesex and Hertfordshire to Buckinghamshire, with several stops along the way. Special Branch had checked the hospitals and morgues in London and Buckinghamshire in case Michael had had an accident en route.

But what about the hospitals in those other two counties? Michael might have left the train at any point along its route and got into difficulties.

The train slowed down to stop at Watford Junction. She craned forward in her seat to peer at the platform but jerked back as a southbound train screamed past on the other line, blocking her view.

Sighing with frustration, she picked up her newspaper to distract herself. An article on page seven caught her attention:

York City Police Retrieve Stolen Museum Antiquities

This was welcome news. Earlier in the week, two criminals had coshed the poor caretaker of the Yorkshire Museum, stolen his keys and ransacked the Hospitium. To add insult to injury – and much to the embarrassment of the local police – the shameless thieves had hired costumes from York's theatrical supplier and pretended to be police officers to gain the caretaker's trust.

But despite this audacious impersonation, it had been a bungled, ill-planned robbery. The most valuable antiquities in the Hospitium had already been dispatched to the safety of the countryside, far away from the threat of German bombers. The random items the thieves stole were worth little and would be hard to sell on the black market.

Gabriel had made a point of leaking this last piece of information to the *Yorkshire Evening Press*, who'd followed up their report of the crime with another article under the headline *Yorkshire Museum Robbery: Thieves Take Worthless Items.*

If this London newspaper in her lap were to be believed, Gabriel's ploy had worked. Apparently, a member of the public had found the green holdall used by the thieves dumped down a back alley, containing all the stolen items.

Jemma frowned. *What green holdall?* Gabriel hadn't mentioned anything about a large bag.

Then all thoughts of York went out of her head when she heard the ticket inspector shout, 'Bletchley! Bletchley station!' The train slowed with a squeal of its brakes.

According to Bradshaw's Guide, Bletchley was a small rural town of only ten thousand inhabitants, but it had a large Victorian station with half a dozen platforms beneath its towering, soot-blackened glass roof. Dozens of passengers waited to board their train and many more disembarked, including a large group of uniformed Wrens and the insolent man in the tan coat and brown hat who'd looked her over. Everyone moved briskly towards the exit, sidestepping piles of sandbags, the loaded barrows and the rows of parked bicycles.

But Jemma hesitated. Her eyes scanned the platform for railway staff. This was her last chance to ask about Michael. A young porter of about fifteen, with an oversized black jacket hanging off his shoulders and a smattering of freckles across his nose, stood talking with the guard at the rear of her train. A moment later they were joined by an elderly white-whiskered man with the gold-braid trimming on his jacket and cap that denoted an LMS stationmaster.

Another porter walked the length of the train, slamming the doors shut. The guard waved his green flag and gave a piercing blast on his whistle. The steam train heaved into motion and rolled away towards Scotland with a final belch of sulphurous smoke.

Nailing her courage to her mast, she approached the group of men and showed them her photograph of Michael.

They shook their heads at the image.

'We've thousands of passengers come through here every year, madam,' the stationmaster told her.

The young porter pushed back his black cap and scratched his greasy head. 'Mind you, sir – Michael James – the name's familiar…' He had quick, intelligent eyes. 'Weren't someone else askin' about him a while back?'

There was a short silence, then Jemma saw the stationmaster's eyes flick up to the left as he recalled the memory.

'Yes, it were those blokes from the military police…'

He broke off as a southbound goods train on the other line drowned out his voice. While they were distracted, Jemma beat a hasty retreat, away from their accusing eyes.

She blinked against the sunshine when she emerged from the brick-pillared portico of the gloomy station and into the forecourt. It was bordered on three sides by the station, the Post Office depot where men were unloading vans, and a large area of mature woodland. Blackbirds chirped in the trees and the noxious fumes of the station were replaced with the country smells of hawthorn blossom, manure and warm soil.

She straightened her shoulders and set out on the last stage of her journey. A journey that had turned into a fool's errand. She might as well finish what she'd started.

Her walk to Bletchley Wireless Manufacturing only took her a few minutes. A large wooden sign with peeling paintwork at the entrance to a side road announced she'd reached her destination – and the end of her quest. The buildings of the mysterious establishment that had recruited Michael were hidden by the trees.

A liftable metal barrier blocked the entrance to the site. It was guarded by two soldiers with rifles slung over their shoulders. They eyed her warily as she hesitated on the other side of the road.

It didn't take a genius to work out something top secret was happening behind that innocuous and battered sign. But whatever it was, it wasn't her concern. Nor Michael's. Because the one thing she knew for certain was he'd not turned up and reported for duty on that bitter winter's day.

She sighed with disappointment. She'd discovered nothing new over the past two days. Everywhere she'd been, Special Branch and the military police had been there before her. Every question she'd asked, they'd already asked it.

Then a thought struck her like the smack of an icy snowball on the side of her face.

The weather.

Oh, my God. She'd forgotten to factor in the terrible weather.

Last winter had been atrocious. The heavy snow in January had downed telegraph wires across the country. It had blocked roads and disrupted travel on the railways. The police were called out many times to rescue stranded travellers.

Her brain raced as she tried to calculate if it would have made any difference to Michael.

It was only a short walk from the station to his new posting, but would her conscientious and punctual husband have risked being late due to the disruption caused by the snow? So many trains were late or cancelled. Did he travel the night before and stay somewhere in Bletchley?

She thought back to what Freddie and Mrs Sutton had told her. Freddie and Michael had had their farewell drink on the Monday night. Mrs Sutton had left her boarding house on the Wednesday to stay with her pregnant daughter. Michael was supposed to travel to Bletchley on the Friday. But what if he'd decided to leave London a day earlier – on the Thursday – and had booked a room in the town for the night?

If so, there would be a record of this somewhere. It was a slim chance. Her last hope. But it was worth exploring.

She pulled out her copy of Bradshaw's Guide and scanned it for advertisements for local hotels, knowing Michael would have done the same with the copy he'd borrowed from Mrs Sutton. There were several hotels in the town. She decided to retrace her steps to the Station Hotel.

She turned sharply and was just in time to catch the flash of a brown hat and a tan coat as a man leapt off the road into a small copse of trees about twenty yards behind her.

The back of her neck prickled with fear. It was the man who'd brazenly looked her up and down when she'd boarded the train in London. Acutely conscious that she was a woman alone in a strange town, panic flared. Was he following her? Did he mean her some harm?

Then her common sense kicked in. It was broad daylight. She was on a public road with two armed guards standing less than twenty feet away. If he planned to confront her – or harm her in any way – it wouldn't be here.

A more likely explanation flashed through her mind, and she shook her head in frustration. Special Branch knew of her trip. At one point they'd suspected Michael of using her to pass information to the enemy. Did they still have doubts? Was she was being shadowed by one of their operatives in case she led them to her Russian-born husband?

She set off back to the station, with her head held high and her eyes fixed on the path ahead. If he wanted to follow her, let him; she'd nothing to hide.

The manager of the Station Hotel shook his head when he checked the register for the eleventh of January. But he did recommend she tried the Eight Belles on the Buckingham Road, which had stayed open throughout the bad weather.

There was no sign of her mysterious stalker when she took the short walk to the large half-timbered public house. But when she passed through its arched brick entrance, the back of her neck prickled again; he was still with her.

The proprietor was a friendly woman with a soft lined face, frizzy grey hair and a brisk, choppy way of speaking. Thankfully, she didn't question Jemma's unusual request and led her straight to the reception desk in the wood-panelled hallway. She pulled out a dog-eared guest ledger, turned a few pages and stabbed a bony finger at an entry.

'Yes, 'e done booked a room fer the eleventh, see? *Mr Michael James* – it's written here.'

Relief swirled through Jemma with such force it caused her to stagger.

Michael had booked a room. He wasn't a deserter.

The woman was still speaking. Jemma clutched the edge of the reception desk for support and strained to listen.

''E done sent me a postal order fer the deposit. Of course, 'e never turned up. But we weren't expectin' 'im to – not after the accident.'

'Accident?'

'At the station, dearie. Terrible it were. Nasty train crash. Didn't you 'ear about it?'

'No, I'm… I'm not local.'

'I guessed as much. From the north, are yer? A man were killed – there were a dozen injured.'

Jemma's blood ran cold. 'What happened?'

'The 12.37 from Lunnen never saw the signals. Blamed the blindin' snow, the driver did. Went straight into the back of another train. Terrible mess. The line were blocked fer the rest of the day while they done cleared it.'

'So, Michael – Mr James – never arrived here?'

40

'Wouldn't 'ave been able to if he came by train. The line were blocked till midnight, see? Are yer all right, dearie? Yer look a bit queer.' The woman came round and led her towards a chair. 'Sit down a while.'

Jemma sank down gratefully and blinked back the tears. 'Michael James is my husband. He's not been seen since that day.'

The woman patted her arm. 'Well, 'e ain't dead, dearie. There were only one poor fellow killed in the accident, and he were an elderly gent. It were in the paper, see?'

'Where did they take the injured passengers?'

'Our doctor done patched up the walkin' wounded, and the rest were taken to the hospital in Aylesbury.'

Jemma rose to her feet. She had to get to Aylesbury. If Michael was injured, there'd be a record in the hospital admissions. She might just have enough time to do this before she returned to York. 'Thank you, thank you so much,' she called as she hurried out of the door.

Chapter Six

Back at the station, Jemma was crushed to discover there wasn't a train to Aylesbury for another hour.

Frustrated and still shaking with shock, she staggered into the crowded tearoom and bought a cup of tea from a cheerful W.V.S. volunteer. She found herself a small table and sat down to think.

She's been elated to discover the hotel booking. It was clear evidence that Michael wasn't a deserter. But her initial flush of joy had been replaced with alarm at the news of the train crash. Was he one of the injured? And if so, how badly had he been hurt?

Her stalker suddenly appeared at the entrance and scanned the tearoom. His cold blue eyes didn't linger on her, but she knew he'd seen her. She bristled with irritation, then her common sense reasserted itself. She'd have to report her discovery to Special Branch anyway. She raised her arm and beckoned him over; this was no time to be coy.

He hesitated, then approached. His square, good-looking face with its firm jawline and short-clipped blond moustache was expressionless. 'Can I help you, madam?' He was in his early thirties and had a strong London accent.

'Yes, you can. I know who you are – and I know you're following me. Please get yourself a cup of tea and sit down. I've some news for you.'

The expression of innocent surprise on his face would have earned him a screen test in a Hollywood movie. 'I'm sorry, madam, but I don't believe we've met.'

'I'll give you a tip. When you're shadowing someone, never look them directly in the face if they pass by you in a cramped train corridor. They tend to remember you.' She paused to let her words sink in, before adding: 'I know you're Special Branch and you've been following me since Euston station.'

A range of conflicting emotions flickered in his eyes, then he shrugged. 'They warned me about you. They said you were smart. Private detective, aren't you? I'll get a drink. Don't leave the room while my back's turned.'

When he returned, he sat down and raised a quizzical eyebrow. 'So, what's this news?'

'Introductions first. You know I'm Mrs Jemima James but I'm at a disadvantage.'

'I'm Marlowe. D.S. Marlowe from Special Branch.'

'Your first name's not Christopher, is it?'

'No. Why should it be?'

'Something I learnt at school. The dramatist who did a bit of spying on the side.'

He frowned. 'Just tell me what you've discovered. I saw you dashing between those hotels.'

'My husband booked a room at the Eight Belles for the night of the eleventh of January – the day before he was due to report at Bletchley Wireless Manufacturing.'

He sipped his tea and shrugged. 'So what?'

Jemma bit back her anger. 'It was the day of the fatal train crash here at Bletchley station. Michael might have been on that train and may have been injured.'

44

'He wasn't.'

His arrogant assurance made her gasp. 'How do you know?'

'Because during their investigation into his disappearance, the military police heard about the accident. They interviewed the doctor who'd dealt with the minor injuries and checked out the admissions at Stoke Mandeville Hospital in Aylesbury. He wasn't there and never had been.'

Jemma deflated like a punctured barrage balloon. Special Branch were one step ahead of her again. 'It's too much of a coincidence,' she insisted. 'That accident has to have something to do with his disappearance.'

'That's if he was ever here in Bletchley.'

'But he'd booked the room at the Eight Belles on the night of the train crash!'

'So what? He might have been laying a false trail before he went AWOL.'

Jemma had a strong urge to slap his insolent face. 'Nonsense!' she spluttered. 'You don't know my husband, sergeant. He's an astute businessman. He wouldn't have sent a postal order with the deposit for a room he had no intention of using! He's a Yorkshireman, for heaven's sake!'

Amusement flitted across Marlowe's face. 'That's supposed to be significant, is it?'

'Michael is a decent and honest man who loves his country.'

'Which country? Britain or Russia?'

'He had every intention of reporting for duty,' she hissed through gritted teeth. 'Something awful must have happened to prevent it. You people need to try harder to find him. It *has* to be something to do with the train crash.'

'As my superiors have already told you and your brother, we've looked everywhere.'

'Obviously *not*. You've not looked everywhere because you've not found him.'

He leant forward across the table and lowered his voice. 'Look, Mrs James, I know how tough it must be for you to accept your husband has vanished, but interfering like this doesn't help. Go back to Yorkshire and let us do our job.'

She reached for her handbag with a shaking hand. 'You need to try harder to find him.'

He never got the chance to reply because they were suddenly joined at the table by the young porter she'd spoken to earlier.

A cheerful grin lit up his freckled face. 'Hello again, missus, I thought I saw you come in here. I've remembered somethin'. Can you come wi' me? It's in the lost property.'

Marlowe rose to his feet. 'If it's to do with AC Michael James, I need to come too.'

Jemma scowled but was powerless to stop Marlowe. The young porter led them out on to the platform and into the parcel office and cloakroom.

'It were found up the track, which were odd. That's how I remembered it,' the boy said. 'Mind you, it's surprising sometimes the things that fall from them trains.'

'What's your name, son?' Marlowe asked.

'Bainbridge, sir. Jack Bainbridge.'

Behind the desk at the back of the parcel office, a door led to a large storeroom. It was lined with shelves of bags, clothing, children's toys, umbrellas and the other sundry items passengers regularly left on the trains. Jack removed a tennis racket, rummaged through the clutter, and returned with a brown leather suitcase.

Jemma recognised it immediately, gave a small cry and dragged it towards her. But even in her moment of elation her eyes spotted the dark, ominous stains on the handle and the outside of the case…

A childish hand had scrawled *Mr James* on the label dangling from the handle.

'Is it his?' Marlowe asked.

Jemma nodded, unable to speak, her fingers fumbling with the catch.

'There weren't no label on it when it were brought in,' Jack said. 'My stationmaster said to open it and look for clues. I found some letters addressed to a *Mr James* inside. So, I put the label on it in case he came back for it when I weren't here.'

'Thank you, Jack,' she whispered, 'that was clever of you.'

His chest swelled with pride.

Jemma clicked open the case and pulled out the packet of letters lying on top of the clothes. They were her letters to Michael. He'd kept every one of them. Tears welled in her eyes; she grabbed one of his shirts and pulled it to her face.

His scent was faint, but it was still there. Unmistakably Michael.

Marlowe pulled the case towards him and shut the lid. 'You can keep the shirt, but I need this case. It's evidence.'

'Those are my private letters to my husband!' she protested.

'Not any more they're not. They're evidence relating to the disappearance of AC James.'

Jack's eyes flicked nervously between them as they glared at each other. Jemma blinked, fighting back the tears. All she wanted was a few minutes' privacy in a quiet room with the case, immersing herself in what remained of Michael.

But a brute like Marlowe wouldn't understand this.

She swallowed hard. This was no time to let emotion get the better of her; they had to keep looking. 'You need to get those dark stains analysed in your laboratory.'

'I know how to do my job, Mrs James,' he snapped.

'You don't understand. They weren't there when he left home. This suitcase was brand new. I think they're bloodstains.'

Marlowe glanced at the marks on the leather before turning back to the young lad. 'Where was this found and when did it turn up?'

'It were sometime last winter.'

'Who handed it into lost property?'

Jack turned to a ledger on the counter and flicked through the pages. 'I'll check in the book. One of the plate layers brought it in – but I can't remember when. It were found down the London line when they were doing some maintenance.'

'Now do you believe me?' Jemma hissed at Marlowe, as the boy scanned his ledger. 'I told you Michael had every intention of reporting at Bletchley for duty.'

'Nothing's changed,' he snapped back. 'He's still absent without leave.'

'It were the fifth of February,' the boy told them.

48

Jemma searched her memory. By February, the worst of the winter snow had cleared across the country. *Had Michael's case lain buried beneath it since the train accident?*

'Where was this case found?' Marlowe asked.

'By the bridge.'

'Can you show us the spot?'

Alarm flashed across the lad's face. 'Members of the public aren't allowed on the track. It's dangerous.'

Marlowe pulled out his identification. 'I'm an officer with Special Branch – not a member of the public. Show me.'

'And I'm with him,' Jemma said firmly. 'I'm going too.'

The bewildered young lad headed for the door. 'I'll have to ask my stationmaster.'

They followed him out on to the platform, blinking at the sudden glare of sunlight. The day was turning out warm.

Marlowe gave her a sideways glance. 'Mrs James, I think you should leave this with me. Catch a train back to Manchester and get a connection to York. I'll let you know if anything turns up.'

Oh, my God. He thinks we'll find Michael's decomposing body…

'I want to see where Michael's case was found. I need to see this through until the end.'

He observed her calmly and with a flicker of compassion. 'Very well – but I'm not responsible for the consequences.'

'No, you're not. It's my decision.'

He grunted and shifted his gaze to a pile of sandbags on the opposite platform. They had a truce.

A red-faced and indignant inspector approached them. He had a bulbous nose and was already perspiring with the heat. 'I've been sent by the stationmaster. I'm told you want to walk up the track to the bridge. This is irregular, most irregular. It's against LMS company rules and downright dangerous.'

Marlowe pulled out his identification again and explained what he wanted. 'AC James has been missing since January and this is a matter of national security. This is his wife and she's helping me with the investigation. She comes too.'

'Very well,' snapped the inspector. 'But you walk behind me and keep away from the tracks.' He pulled out a round metal pocket watch. 'We've still got thirty minutes before the 10.50 to Crewe. We'll walk on the ballast and face the oncoming trains. Leave those cases in the luggage office.' He cast a glance at Jemma's comfortable slacks and sensible flat shoes. 'Good job you're not in heels, missus.'

They took Jemma's small case and Michael's larger one back to the luggage office, then walked to the end of the platform, down the ramp and on to the track.

Several lines came into Bletchley station. They kept to the right-hand edge, stepping carefully over the point rodding and the signal wires. A southbound express thundered past on the far side of the station, blasting its whistle in warning. A man peered at them curiously from the signal box.

Jemma soon realised why the inspector had commented on her footwear. Walking on the ballast was hard work. The chippings were deep and edged with ash. They crunched uncomfortably beneath her feet, and she felt their sharp edges beneath the soles of her shoes. The whole area was open and elevated above the town and the road and contained no bushes or vegetation scrub where anything unpleasant – like a dead body – might be concealed.

'That's Water Eaton Road below us,' the inspector said, as they approached the parapet of a bridge, 'and this is as far as we go. His suitcase was found here – abandoned by the side of the bridge.'

Jemma glanced around and peered over the parapet. An army dispatch rider on a motorcycle zoomed along the road below and a woman stood with her shopping bag at the bus stop. There was an overgrown and steep bank leading down from the bridge to the road. It was possible for a fit and able man to climb – or slither – down from here on to the road below.

She turned and stared back at the station, which she estimated was about a hundred yards away, and tried to imagine the scene in a blizzard. 'How long was the 12.37 from Euston? How many carriages did it have?'

The inspector glanced at her curiously. 'The bad weather meant fewer passengers. So the train was shorter than usual – thankfully. Otherwise, there'd have been more injuries and fatalities.'

'I understand it crashed into a goods train at the station?'

'Yes. As I told the inquiry, the goods train was about seven yards short of the north end of platform three.'

'Where did the last carriage and the guard's van of the express stop?'

The inspector scratched his head. 'They were both derailed and jutted out at the end of the platform towards us.'

'So, there's no reason to suppose Michael's suitcase was thrown out of the carriage due to the impact – the distance between here and there is too great.'

The inspector shook his head. 'None of the wreckage was this far away.'

'So, in order for the suitcase to get *here*—' she said thoughtfully, '— Michael – or someone else – must have carried it from the train.'

'I can see what you're thinking, Mrs James,' Marlowe said, 'but it doesn't make sense. If your husband *was* on that train—'

'Which he was.'

'—and he was injured—'

'Which we know from the bloodstains, he was.'

'Then he'd either wait for help in the carriage or make his way forward towards the station to get help. No one wanders off after an accident.'

'Unless it was a head injury and he was disorientated,' Jemma said quietly.

'What was the visibility like?' Marlowe asked.

'Dreadful,' the inspector confirmed. He'd been watching them closely. 'The snow was blinding but the station was well lit. If anyone staggered out of the last carriage on to the track, they'd have known which way to go for help from the shouting alone.'

There was a sudden hiss and the signal wire pulled taut through the pulleys. The signal arm came down with a rattle.

The man in the signal box came out to the top of the wooden stairs and yelled: 'Watch out! Crewe train coming on the down fast near you!'

The inspector hurried them away from the bridge and back towards the station.

Marlowe looked perplexed as he crunched over the chippings beside Jemma, and less sure of himself.

'Do you still think Michael went AWOL?' Jemma asked. 'Knowing now that he'd made it to Bletchley?'

Marlowe frowned and shook his head. 'It seems unlikely,' he conceded. 'But it's still a damn mystery. I'll organise a proper search of this area and reopen our investigation.'

He's still looking for Michael's dead body, she thought.

Once they'd clambered back up on to the platform, she handed him her business card. She'd reached the end of the line – literally – and she knew it. 'Here's my office phone number. If you discover anything – *anything* – please telephone me immediately.'

He nodded and gave her his number in return. 'Thank you for your help, Mrs James.'

Jemma managed a wry smile. 'Help? A few minutes ago, I was accused of interfering.'

'I was wrong about that,' he said with a wink. 'What are you going to do now?'

'I'm going to leave you to it and go home. My brother's getting married tomorrow.'

Chapter Seven

Gabriel was nineteen years older than Jemma but in the hour before his wedding, she found herself assuming the role of the calmer, more experienced older sibling. He stomped round the kitchen in his best dress uniform, waving his arms in agitation.

'What if Maisie changes her mind?' he asked, over and over again. 'She's already cancelled the wedding once.'

'That was because her poor father was ill. Of course she won't change her mind! Please stop pacing and sit down. You're wearing a hole in the rug.'

'She might have second thoughts.'

'Oh, for heaven's sake! Why would she do that? She *loves* you.'

The front door opened, and their sister, Cissy, breezed into the house with her family. Only a couple of years younger than Gabriel, Cissy was bossy, abrupt and accustomed to the role of the family matriarch. She ushered them into the parlour and took charge.

Gabriel was inspected, found passable, and promptly told to calm down. 'Of course Maisie will turn up!' Cissy announced. 'This is a great match for a woman like her. There's no way she'd miss this opportunity to ensnare you.'

Jemma grimaced and Gabriel's face flushed with anger. But their brother-in-law, Gerald, took Gabriel aside and poured him a whisky to steady his nerves. Cissy had always made it plain she didn't think

Maisie was good enough for Gabriel, especially after she'd learnt about young Tom, Maisie's illegitimate son.

Meanwhile, Jemma's nephew, Jack, sat on the sofa with the family's two evacuees. All three boys were tugging at their stiff shirt collars. Every time Cissy's back was turned, they tried to loosen their ties. Their faces had been scrubbed until they shone like round moons.

'Can we go out to play?' asked Jack.

'No, you can't,' his mother snapped. 'It's taken me ages to get the three of you clean. You sit there until it's time for the service.'

The boys scowled in sulky silence.

'What a gorgeous hat!' Jemma said. 'Did you send for it from London?' Her sister spent hours poring over London fashion magazines.

Cissy touched the brim of the grey felt hat and its tiny blue flowers with her beautifully manicured fingers and gave a brittle smile. 'Of course it's from London. I sent for it from Madame Derringer's on Bond Street.' Then she frowned, leant closer and lowered her voice. 'But tell me the truth – is that your wedding dress you're wearing?'

'Yes, I dyed it peach and added the voile sleeves to get more use out of it. *Make do and mend* etcetera.'

'Yes, but considering what's happened to you and Michael, don't you think it's bad luck to wear *that* dress on Gabriel's wedding day?'

Jemma blinked. She'd been rather proud of her handiwork. Her revamped gown had received many compliments when she'd worn it before, especially for its voluminous flared sleeves, which shimmered when she moved. 'I usually wear it with a short-sleeved cream bolero jacket.'

'Yes, do. Keep it covered up. It's bad enough they've chosen the same church as you and Michael. We don't want history repeating itself.'

'They didn't have much choice. There's only one parish church in Clifton.'

'Why didn't they turn Methodist for a day and use their church instead? People will draw comparisons all day between the two weddings.'

Jemma wondered vaguely who these 'people' were. She smiled, leant towards her sister, and whispered, 'Then it's a good job they don't know Gabriel's taking Maisie to the same hotel Michael and I used for our own honeymoon.'

Cissy's face was a picture of horror. 'Why on earth is he doing that?' she spluttered.

'Because I recommended it.'

'Doesn't he have *any* imagination of his own?'

'I guess not,' Jemma said, enjoying the moment.

'And don't forget—' Cissy added, lowering her voice, '—if people ask you about Michael, stick to the story that he's "*missing in action*". We don't want anyone to know he's a deserter. Oh, the shame he's brought on us!'

Jemma was saved from the necessity of correcting her sister by a loud rap on the front door.

Gabriel's best man, Chief Constable Herman, had arrived with his wife.

After the introductions were made, the party set off for the short walk across the village green to the church. Cissy walked with Mrs Herman and followed the three men. Jemma trailed behind with the three boys.

She didn't mind and welcomed a few minutes' peace to dwell on her own thoughts. In her tactless bossy way, Cissy was right. It was inevitable Gabriel's wedding would draw comparisons with her own. She herself couldn't stop thinking about it.

Last spring, she had taken this same walk across the green, past the ancient horse trough with its tiled canopy roof, leaning on her father's arm. She'd been a hopeful and excited bride. Some of the neighbours had come out of their houses to wish her good luck. The church bells rang, the sun had blazed down from a cloudless sky and the gardens they passed were blooming and fragrant with roses, elegant delphiniums and ruby-red peonies.

Now the bells had been silenced for the duration of the war and her neighbours were growing cabbages and beans in their front gardens. Her poor father had died quietly in his sleep – and God only knows what had happened to her handsome bridegroom.

Sadness swamped her and she hesitated at the bottom of the steps of the church, blinking back the tears.

Gabriel, always more in tune with her moods than their sister, fell back from the group and joined her.

'Don't flake out on me now, Jemma,' he whispered. 'I need you. Especially if Maisie doesn't show up. You'll have to slap a muzzle on our Cissy. I don't think I can stand to hear her say "I told you so"!'

Jemma laughed and they went into the cool interior of the church with its pale Gothic stone arches and lofty hammerbeam roof. As they walked down the aisle, they paused to greet Gabriel's other guests, who mostly consisted of police officers and their wives and his motorcycling chums.

The pews on the other side of the aisle were already full with Maisie's family and friends.

'Gosh, aren't there a lot of them!' Cissy commented in disapproval to no one in particular.

Tom, Maisie's son, sat with his mother's relatives. His freckled face had been scrubbed with the same vigour as those of Cissy's brood, and his thick thatch of red hair was still damp with the water used to flatten it. He looked thoroughly miserable in his formal shirt and tie. Jemma gave him a warm smile, but he barely responded.

A flicker of anxiety went through her about the next week.

Maisie had wanted Tom to stay with her sister and his cousins in Acomb during her honeymoon. But Tom had refused and demanded to stay with Jemma in Clifton, near his school and his own pals. *Was he regretting his decision now?*

Gabriel and Chief Constable Herman took their places in the front pew on the groom's side. Mrs Herman, Cissy and Gerald sat immediately behind them with the boys.

Jemma slid into the third row and glanced at the lovely display of wild meadow flowers in the large vases near the altar. *Someone's gone to a lot of trouble*, she thought. It was virtually impossible to get hold of hothouse blooms these days.

Suddenly, Bobbie slid into the seat beside her and squeezed her hand. Her friend looked both stylish and fashionable in her green patterned tea dress and her new brown belted jacket. Her unruly hair had been captured and tamed in a jewelled chignon, and an elegant brown hat with a sculptured felt bow sat at a rakish angle on her head.

'Good morning, Cissy,' Bobbie said. 'It's a lovely day for a wedding, isn't it?'

Cissy turned stiffly and nodded. 'Good morning, Roberta.' She gave Bobbie's hat an envious glance before resuming her conversation with Mrs Herman.

'How are you bearing up?' Bobbie whispered. Jemma had telephoned Bobbie from Manchester station the previous afternoon while waiting for her connection to York and had updated her about her search for Michael.

'All the better for seeing you,' Jemma said, 'My sister thinks I'm the spectre at the feast – an omen of bad luck. And poor Gabriel! He's a bag of nerves.'

Bobbie glanced at the front of the church where Gabriel was now twisting his cap round and round in his hands and casting nervous glances down the aisle. 'Ignore Cissy – and Gabriel will relax the minute Maisie arrives. Do you think you can trust this Marlowe fellow to search properly for Michael?'

Jemma shrugged. 'I don't have much choice.'

'Well, thank God you went down there – you definitely made a difference. Don't worry, Jemma, they'll find him soon.'

Jemma shuffled in her seat. 'I need a distraction. What's happened at the office?'

Bobbie's dark eyes gleamed. 'We've got two new cases.'

'Two?'

'Yes. Firstly, our fairy godfather phoned yesterday afternoon.

'Terence King?'

'He needs our help with a high-profile divorce case. He wants you to go to his Leeds office first thing Monday morning to discuss it.'

Jemma was delighted. Terence King was the owner of Yorkshire's largest private detective agency and the work he'd sent them when they'd first launched their own agency had been a godsend. But she'd never met him in person. 'Who are the unhappy couple? And which spouse are we working for?'

Bobbie's grin broadened. 'It's Baron Stokesley, one of the county's wealthiest aristocrats, and Jodie – his starlet wife. Lord Stokesley is the one who wants the divorce.'

'Jodie! Isn't she the actress who doesn't use her last name?'

Bobbie grinned. 'Yes, she's the darling of the West End and Broadway – and Yorkshire's most famous daughter. They married about three years ago in a blaze of publicity and from what I can gather have been avoiding each other ever since.'

'I remember it vaguely but I'm not a great one for the gossip columns and magazines. What's the second case?'

Bobbie seemed to grow even taller in her seat. 'It's even better. It's murder!'

'Murder!'

Cissy turned round and gave them a withering look. 'That's not an appropriate topic of conversation, girls.'

Jemma hid her smile. As most of the guests were from York City Police, the irony of Cissy's misplaced concern hadn't escaped her.

Bobbie lowered her voice. 'While you were away in London, one of the curators at the Castle Museum, Lance Richards, was found unconscious with life-threatening injuries. The police arrested one of his co-workers for the crime, a clerk called Anthony Gill.'

'Good grief! More trouble at the city's museums! It's not connected with last week's robbery, is it?'

'No. There's lots of incriminating evidence against Gill and he doesn't have an alibi. Unfortunately, Richards died yesterday afternoon, so now Gill will be charged with murder. His solicitor phoned me just before I left the office yesterday. He wants us to help find evidence to prove Gill is innocent.'

'Who's the officer in charge of the police investigation?'

'D.S. Fawcett.'

Jemma grimaced. Fawcett, with his oily slicked-back hair and a pair of eyes that rarely laughed along with his mouth, was her least favourite of her brother's colleagues.

'You do realise what this means, don't you, Jemma? If Anthony Gill didn't kill Lance Richards – and I don't think he did – we've got to find out who did and why. We've got a murder case to solve!'

Jemma opened her mouth to ask more questions, but there was a sudden flurry at the end of their pew. Every head in the church turned as an elderly woman, swathed entirely in black and with bright mischievous eyes, shuffled into a seat beside them. Her pale, lined face crinkled into a broad smile beneath her black net veil. 'Jemma! Thank goodness I've found you – I thought I'd missed the service!'

'We're running a little late, Fanny,' Jemma confirmed with a glance at her watch. 'Bobbie, you remember our neighbour, Fanny Rowland, don't you?'

Bobbie grinned. 'Of course I do! How are you, Fanny?'

'And more to the point,' hissed Cissy from the pew in front, 'why on earth are you dressed in full mourning, Fanny? This is a wedding – not a funeral!' Beside her, the chief constable's wife smiled kindly at the eccentric old lady.

'I'm in mourning,' Fanny announced loudly, 'because I've waited for years for that gorgeous young police officer, Gabriel Roxby, to propose to me—'

'Fanny! Keep your voice down!' Cissy hissed.

But Fanny already had the attention of the entire congregation and deliberately spoke louder.

'—but that ravishing Maisie Langford has bewitched him! She's stolen my beau!'

The congregation erupted into peals of laughter – even Gabriel smiled. 'I'll tell you what, Fanny,' he called over, 'if Maisie doesn't turn up in the next five minutes, step up to the altar and I'll marry you instead.'

'Gabriel!' Cissy shrieked. 'Behave yourself!'

Everyone was laughing now. Mrs Herman leant towards Fanny, smiling. 'You're Frances Rowland, the artist, aren't you?'

'That's right – and I've been a friend of the Roxby family for years. I was particularly close to Gabriel's mother.'

'We've got one of your gorgeous landscapes in pride of place over our sitting-room mantelpiece. You're a talented artist.'

But before the delighted Fanny could reply, the church organ launched into Wagner's *Bridal Chorus*. Everyone scrambled to their feet and turned around.

Maisie and her frail elderly father had begun their slow walk up the aisle.

Relief washed over Gabriel's face like a tsunami.

Chapter Eight

Maisie wore the wedding dress Jemma had designed and sewn. She looked stunning. It was high-waisted, with a wide band of delicate lace, decorated with tiny seed pearls and diamante. The ivory silk flared out smoothly over Maisie's ample hips before dropping to the floor. The short veil over her flaming auburn hair was held in place by a satin band decorated with seed pearls, diamante and silk orange blossom. Her bouquet was made entirely of the same delicate wildflowers that decorated the church. Happiness and love radiated from her smiling face. She looked ten years younger than her forty-four years.

Gabriel fluffed his lines during the vows, of course, much to the amusement of the congregation. But the laughter was kindly meant.

The reception they attended afterwards at a local hotel was one of the pleasantest social occasions Jemma had known for a while. For a few short hours, the damn war was forgotten. Jokes were made during the speeches about Maisie's skill in persuading York's crustiest old bachelor to finally embrace married life, but everything was done with good humour and the affection for the couple was genuine.

Fanny gave the bride a big hug and was heard to mutter, 'I concede, I concede – the better woman has won!'

A few hours later, the bride and groom changed into their motorcycle gear and everyone went outside to watch them leave on Gabriel's beloved Vincent Rapide. With the First World War flying goggles that had belonged to her first husband, Maisie looked more like the aviator Amy Johnson than a bride. After a final hug with her young son, she climbed up behind her new husband and the vehicle roared into life.

They sped off in a shower of paper confetti, with a 'Just Married' cardboard sign flying behind them on a piece of string.

The guests began to leave. Jemma gathered up the bags of wedding presents she needed to take back to the house and went in search of Tom. She'd been vaguely aware of him during the reception, racing around and playing with the other boys. But when she found him, he was alone at the rear of the hotel, moodily kicking the wall. 'There you are, Tom. Are you ready to come home now? Can you help me carry these bags?'

'It's not my home.'

Jemma hesitated. She'd only known Tom a few months but normally he was pleasant company and they got along well. Maisie had warned her he'd been 'difficult' recently.

She smiled and said lightly, 'I beg to differ, young man. That cottage is now your forever home. Your mum and Gabriel have worked hard to make the bedroom you'll share with Harry perfect for you both. This is your new life, Tom – and it'll be fun.'

'Our Harry is going to die, isn't he? The Jerries will shoot him.'

She gasped and reached out a comforting arm, but he stepped away.

A warning voice in her head said: *Don't lie to children.*

'I won't pretend things aren't difficult for our soldiers,' she said gently. 'But there's no reason to suppose anything bad will happen to your brother. Harry's tough, isn't he? He'll look after himself. Have you ever known anyone beat your Harry in a fight?'

He stood up straighter with pride. 'No. Once he beat up Bert Grimshaw.'

Jemma had no idea who Bert Grimshaw was, but it didn't matter. 'There. See? Harry can look after himself.'

Mollified and slightly reassured, he grabbed one of the bags and let her lead him home. He sat quietly in the kitchen while they ate a few leftovers from the reception for their supper.

'I've managed to get a bit of pork from the butcher's. I'll cook you a proper Sunday lunch tomorrow with Yorkshire puddings,' Jemma promised.

He gave her a wary sideways glance. 'Uncle Gabe has warned me about your cooking.'

She laughed. 'Fair enough – but I'll do my best. By the way, you can call him "Dad" now if you want. I know he'd like that. He's really fond of you, Tom.'

A flush of pleasure rose from his neck to his face, but he didn't comment.

She wondered how hard it must have been for Tom, growing up without a father of his own. His older brother, Harry, was the legitimate son of Maisie's first husband, who'd died during the last war. But poor Tom was the result of an unfortunate relationship Maisie had tried about twelve years ago. Her lover had abandoned her when she became pregnant, and Tom had grown up with the stigma of bastardy. Other children – and some adults, like Jemma's own sister – were cruel to illegitimate children.

'Are you my big sister now?'

'No. Officially I'm your step-aunt. But I don't want you to call me *Aunty*. Jemma will do.'

'That sounds more like a big sister.'

'Fair enough. I'll be your big sister. I'm good at being a sister – I've had lots of practice.'

'Are you Harry's step-aunt as well?'

'Officially, yes.'

'But it doesn't make sense! He's older than you!'

'Exactly. That's why you must both just call me Jemma. Anyway, I'll do my best not to poison you tomorrow. We'll eat lunch after church.'

'Church?'

Jemma was flummoxed and suddenly felt the weight of her new, if temporary, parental responsibilities.

Did his mother take him to church?

She had no idea. 'We Roxbys have always gone to church,' she added lamely.

'Am I a Roxby now?'

'Of course you are!'

He mulled that over while chewing his food and she sensed the thought pleased him.

'If you're tired, perhaps we can give church a miss for once,' she conceded. 'We've had a long, busy day.'

He nodded and with a quiet 'good night', took himself up to his room.

Am I supposed to tuck him in? she wondered. *Check he's settled?* There was a lot more to parenting than she'd anticipated.

Sighing wearily, she tidied up the kitchen and prepared a flask of cocoa in case of an air raid, then went upstairs to her attic bedroom.

It *had* been a hectic and emotional few days. And by the sound of it, thanks to Bobbie's resourcefulness, next week would be busy too.

Banishing her gnawing anxiety about Michael, she relived the best moments of the wedding and drifted into sleep, smiling.

She was woken by a loud scream.

Staggering down the attic stairs in her bare feet and nightdress, she found Tom sitting bolt upright in his bed, staring wide-eyed with terror at the wall.

She hurried to his side and put her arm round his shoulders. 'Tom! Whatever's the matter? Have you had a nightmare?'

He pushed her off, gave a gulping sob and threw himself back down on his pillow. 'Go away! Leave me alone!' He turned his back towards her.

'If you're sure. Do you want me to make you some warm milk?'

'Just go, can't you!'

Reluctantly, she retreated to the landing and pulled the door closed behind her. The unmistakable sound of pillow-muffled sobbing drifted through it and her heart twisted with distress. *What was wrong with him? Was he missing his mother?*

Shivering with cold and conflicted, she made her weary way back to her attic. She was desperate to help him, but she knew she had to respect his privacy.

She pulled out Michael's shirt, hugged it close and slept fitfully for the rest of the night.

Chapter Nine

Monday, 27th May 1940

Bobbie grimaced as she and Gill's solicitor, Mr Pearson, walked up the steep incline towards the forbidding façade of Leeds's notorious Victorian prison, known as Armley Gaol.

Mr Pearson had agreed to bring her to Leeds so she could talk with Anthony Gill, but she hadn't expected the bad memories this visit would evoke.

Built on a ridge overlooking the small textile town of Armley, the prison dominated the skyline – a grim, sprawling and brooding reminder to the inhabitants of Leeds of the perils of breaking the law. It had a castle-style entrance with turrets either side of a high arched doorway, but there was nothing romantic about this soot-blackened building with its barred windows, unsmiling guards, and the intimidating castellated perimeter wall.

Despite the early-morning warmth, Bobbie shivered.

'Are you all right, Miss Baker?' Mr Pearson asked. 'I appreciate it's an unpleasant place.'

'I'm fine,' she lied. 'I've been here before – to visit a prisoner convicted of assault.' She didn't mention it was her father. There was no need to share that.

A quiet, greying man with a deeply furrowed brow, Mr Pearson had been a silent companion for the first few miles of their journey; but eventually, she'd drawn him out. He'd admitted he was a long-time family friend of the Gills and had doubts about his own competency to take on this case. 'To be frank, Miss Baker, I'm not a criminal lawyer. Property conveyancing and dealing with probate are my specialist fields. But Dora insisted I took on this case because of our, er, long association.'

Bobbie gave him a sly glance, saw the flush creeping up his neck, and came to her own conclusions about the nature of his 'association' with Dora Gill.

'We're both concerned about the impact this arrest and trial will have on Anthony,' the lawyer continued. 'I don't know how well you know him, Miss Baker—'

'Hardly at all, to be honest.'

'He's a very particular, sometimes rather strange fellow. He's forty-five years old and has never shown any interest in leaving the family home, which he shares with his sister. He has the same routine every morning before he leaves for work and every evening when he returns.'

'What do you mean?'

'He insists his meals are served at exactly the same time. The house is immaculate – he can't stand anything being out of place – and his only social interest is his modelling club. He builds model cars. His father was a garage mechanic. They built model cars together before his death. Anthony loves his cars.'

Mindful of the alibi issue, Bobbie asked, 'What's his evening routine?'

'When he returns home from work at a quarter past five, he eats his tea, reads his paper, walks the dog for half an hour and then settles down with the wireless to work on his models. Dora, his sister, works four nights a week as a nurse at York City Hospital. She says he never varies from this pattern.'

'Was she at the hospital the night Lance Richards was attacked?'

'Yes, unfortunately. Things would have been so different if she'd been at home to give him an alibi. But she says everything was normal that evening. Anthony ate his tea and was home with the dog before she left for work. He wasn't agitated about anything and seemed content with his models.'

'Does he become agitated easily?'

'Yes – especially if his routine is interrupted. Neither of us can understand why he went out in his car that night. But the police are adamant they've got a witness – a neighbour called Elgin – who saw him drive off just before nine o'clock.'

'Did he see Anthony return?'

'No. But he was definitely in the house at 7 a.m. when Dora returned from her shift.'

'What about the dead man? Who was the last person to see him alive?'

'His landlady, Mrs Rainbow. Richards left his lodgings about eight o'clock. No one saw him again until he was found dying the next morning in a back alley, a few streets away from the Gills' home.'

'Was Richards unmarried?'

'He was separated from his wife, Ida. She moved back to Heslington to live with her elderly and wealthy father. I don't know what happened to the marital home, but Richards lodged in a cheap boarding house down by the station.'

'Did Richards have money problems?'

The lawyer nodded. 'He was overdrawn at the bank. His room was full of discarded betting slips and football pools coupons, which suggests a gambling habit. I've no doubt the departure of his wealthy wife left him short of cash.'

'Does Mrs Richards have an alibi for the night of the murder?'

'Yes, a cast-iron one. She spent the evening with her father, Mr Yardley. It was the first thing the police checked.'

Bobbie nodded. Most murders were committed by someone close to the victim – often a spouse. But there was no such thing as a cast-iron alibi according to her hero, Lord Peter Wimsey; he'd made his career breaking difficult alibis. 'I'll need Mrs Richards's address – and that of his landlady. I'll talk to them both. I need to build up a picture of his movements, and his friends and acquaintances. Someone among them is a vicious murderer with a grudge.'

Mr Pearson took his eyes off the road for a moment to give her an approving look. 'You seem convinced Anthony didn't do it.'

'I am. I told Dora this when I met her. But I don't understand why he's being so stubborn and uncooperative if he's innocent. Do you know why?'

The lawyer shook his head and sighed. 'I've no idea. He's always been rigid in his opinions and views. He's also an intensely private man and doesn't like questions. I can only hope,' he added grimly, 'that a few unpleasant nights in Armley Gaol have shocked some sense into him.'

'I assume the police are obliged to share their evidence with you. What's the full extent of the evidence they hold against Anthony?'

The solicitor rolled his eyes to the roof of his Morris car. 'Apparently, Anthony and Richards had a blazing row at work earlier that day, which was overheard by one of their colleagues. During the argument, Anthony threatened to kill him.'

'Oh. That's not good.'

'Exactly. This, combined with the fact the police know he lied about being at home that night and won't explain his whereabouts, has led to his arrest. The inquest into Richards's death is tomorrow morning. You'll attend, I hope?'

'Yes, of course.' She frowned. The close location of the dying man to Anthony's home was purely circumstantial and a good lawyer would argue the same about the death threat spoken in the heat of anger. The fact Anthony had been arrested on such flimsy evidence suggested that D.S. Fawcett was desperate for a conviction.

The inside of Armley Gaol was even more intimidating than the exterior. Its high Victorian ceilings and flaking plastered walls echoed and boomed with the shouting and raucous laughter of the inmates and the slamming of metal doors. The prison guard led them along a narrow iron gantry lined with cells. The air reeked of desperation, fear, anger and male sweat. Keeping her eyes lowered, Bobbie ignored the catcalls, lewd comments and wolf whistles that followed her.

Gill was already in the interview room, sitting under the watchful eye of a burly guard. The first few minutes were taken up with introductions. The little man now sported a nasty black eye behind the cracked right lens of his glasses. When his lawyer asked how he acquired the injury, Gill merely shrugged. 'I upset someone. It's fine.

The guards gave me an aspirin for the pain. But you need to ask Dora to send me my spare spectacles.'

Despite his nonchalance, Bobbie knew Gill was rattled. His hands shook and his eyes flitted uneasily around the room.

But Mr Pearson's hope that a few nights in jail would make Gill more cooperative had been too optimistic.

When the lawyer asked him again where he'd gone on the night of the attack, he dismissed the question with a wave of his hand and informed them his whereabouts were irrelevant, and their job was to find out who was with Richards that night. Because, he added sharply, the police weren't going to bother to try and find the killer.

Bobbie leant forward and rested her elbows on the cracked Formica tabletop. 'So, tell me about Lance Richards. What kind of a man was he and who disliked him enough to want to kill him?'

Gill blinked and frowned, as if he'd expected her to know the answer to those questions already. 'Well, nobody liked him, of course. He was a lazy scoundrel, untidy and untrustworthy. He took great delight in leaving his tea mugs and litter on my desk and rifling through my drawers for stationery. I only had to leave my office for one minute and when I came back, he was in there!'

Bobbie blinked. She knew Gill was a fastidious man but none of this was any help to her.

'Poor Miss Rodgers was always kind to him,' Gill continued, 'but I knew she was disappointed with his workshy attitude.'

'Who's Miss Rodgers?'

Gill seemed to grow a little taller. 'Miss Violet Rodgers is the Deputy Curator at the Castle Museum. She helped Dr Kirk open the museum in 1938 – and has been running it virtually single-handedly since he died. The younger curators left last year to join the forces. Richards was experienced, and the only replacement Miss Rodgers found. Desperate times lead to desperate measures, I'm afraid, Miss Baker.'

Bobbie remembered the opening of the Castle Museum and the fanfare of publicity surrounding it. Dr Kirk was a social historian, a visionary and an avid collector of antiquities and a miscellany of things from a bygone era. His remarkable collection included items as diverse as nineteenth-century children's clothes and toys, pharmaceutical measuring scales and complete Victorian shop fronts. The disused women's prison in the centre of York had been converted into a museum to house the collection, whose pièce de resistance was a Victorian cobbled street complete with nineteenth-century shops, an old police cell and a stuffed horse pulling a hansom cab. Bobbie wasn't a huge fan of museums and found some of the exhibits a bit creepy.

'Besides which,' Anthony continued, 'I think the staff at the Yorkshire Museum were keen to get rid of him and they put pressure on her to take him. But you'd have to ask them.'

Bobbie's ears pricked up. Five minutes into the interview and she'd already found a connection with the city's older, more prestigious museum.

'He was previously employed at the Yorkshire Museum?'

'Yes.'

'Do you work closely with their staff?'

He frowned. 'I don't. I was moved to the Castle Museum by York Corporation to manage the accounts and the clerical side of things. But Miss Rodgers has spent a lot of her free time helping them pack up their antiquities, to be sent to the country for safety. Richards was supposed to help too, but he didn't bother.'

'What else did he do to annoy everyone?'

Gill's frown deepened. 'It's difficult to explain. He had a sneering, leering way of talking, was foul-mouthed and crude. He often sneered about his previous employers, the Yorkshire Philosophical Society, who run the Yorkshire Museum. He claimed they were ignorant and conceited small-town nonentities. He said the society was made up of sacked members of the committee from Bootham Park lunatic asylum, who'd brought with them their tradition of incompetence and were tainted with madness themselves.'

'He sounds thoroughly unpleasant. Had he angered anyone in particular?' she asked. 'Did anyone else – besides you – threaten to kill him?'

'I've no idea.'

Mr Pearson leant forward. 'Anthony, please will you tell us why you were arguing with Richards?'

Gill stiffened and averted his eyes. 'It was a private conversation. I'm not prepared to divulge its contents. I uttered that threat in the heat of the moment.'

'It wasn't private if Miss Rodgers overheard you,' Pearson said firmly. 'She's now a police witness.'

Shock flashed across Gill's face. 'Miss Rodgers overheard us – and she's talked to the police?'

'She only heard raised voices and the bit where you threatened to kill Richards,' Pearson explained. 'Naturally, she had to reveal this to the police when they questioned her.'

This seemed to mollify Gill. 'Yes, of course… of course… it's her duty.'

'Was anyone else around at the time of this argument?' Bobbie asked. 'Did anyone else overhear you threaten Richards? Someone who might have used this to frame you?'

'I've no idea. I don't think so.'

'Do you know anything about Richards's private life?' Bobbie continued. 'Whom he mixes with outside of work – or what he does in his spare time?'

'I've never been interested enough to enquire. I assume his mates are scoundrels. No doubt it's one of them who murdered him. Can't you find out? Isn't that why we're paying you, Miss Baker?'

Bobbie smiled. 'Yes, it is – and I will.'

They left shortly afterwards. When they climbed back into the car, Mr Pearson gave her a sympathetic glance. 'That wasn't helpful for you, was it?'

'It was a good starting point.'

He pulled out into the traffic on the main road. 'What will you do now?'

'Speak to Miss Rodgers and the staff at both the city's museums about Richards,' Bobbie said. 'Then I'll track down his estranged wife, his landlady and any pals – or cronies – he hung around with. If we're right, the real killer is still out there somewhere. It seems to me D.S. Fawcett is after an easy solution to this murder and he's not looking hard.'

'Well, good luck, Miss Baker. I have to confess, I was sceptical when Dora first came to me with this idea of employing a private detective to establish Anthony's innocence. But I've changed my mind. If he won't help himself, we've got to do it for him. The police evidence against him is circumstantial at best. But what he doesn't seem to realise is that if he's found guilty – he'll hang.'

Chapter Ten

King's Private Inquiry Agency was situated on the third floor of a towering Victorian building on busy Albion Terrace in the centre of Leeds. It consisted of two suites of rooms, with glass panels that looked out onto a bland corridor. About a dozen staff, men and women, were busy at their desks or on the telephone. They glanced curiously at Jemma as she walked towards her meeting with their boss.

King's secretary led her into a brightly lit and functional office, devoid of the personal touches they'd added to their own cosy office back in York.

An extremely tall, well-built man with dark curly hair sat at a huge mahogany desk by the window. His office may not have been welcoming but the dark-brown eyes of their fairy godfather gleamed with warmth and humour, which distracted Jemma from the jagged scar that snaked up his chin to the left-hand corner of his generous mouth. Without that scar, he'd have been very good-looking.

'Take a seat, Mrs James, and thank you for coming to see me. I hope you'll agree in a few minutes that this journey was worth your time.'

She sat down and pulled her notebook and pen out of her handbag. He had a surprisingly empty desk for such a busy and important man. Apart from the black telephone, it only contained an ashtray and a thick buff-coloured file. Confidentiality and secrecy were vital in their line of work. She herself always tidied everything away out of sight if she expected a visitor to the office. But she had the sense that anything that landed on King's desk was swiftly delegated to someone else.

He cast a professional and appraising glance over her appearance, pulled out a silver cigarette case and offered her one. She politely declined.

'You don't mind if I do? Good. Now tell me, Mrs James, what do you know about the glamorous Lord and Lady Stokesley? Especially Baroness Stokesley, the actress, otherwise known as *Jodie*.'

Despite his welcoming smile, he was watching her closely. She was being interviewed; their involvement in the case wasn't a done deal. She would have to work to gain his trust.

She sent up a silent prayer of thanks for Bobbie, who'd turned up at her home yesterday afternoon with an armful of old magazines and newspaper cuttings. They'd spent two hours poring over photographs of the beautiful blonde actress and reading about her life and career.

'There's a lot written about Jodie – some of it contradictory – but from what I can gather she's about twenty-eight years old. Born in York, she became a dancer and chorus girl at the Leeds City Varieties during her teens. She moved to London, and after several small roles in short-lived productions she had her first major success as the leading lady in an adaptation of Evelyn Waugh's *A Handful of Dust* at the Palladium. The company toured the United States with the play to great acclaim. Apart from her theatre success – in the West End and on Broadway – she's appeared in three British movies, all comedies.'

Jemma remembered watching Jodie in a musical love story called *The Midnight Girl* at Clifton picture house. There'd been a lot of fog, melodrama and dark alleyways in the film – and the singing was only just passable. But the actress had an expressive face, and her dancing was enchanting. She had a great sense of comic timing.

King smiled. 'I see you've done your homework.'

'She holidays in Biarritz, mixes with the show business elite and multimillionaires and knows the younger brothers of the king. But she gave up her career in 1936 when she married her wealthy aristocrat in a blaze of publicity.'

'On the rebound.'

'Pardon?' King's interruption had been softly spoken and she thought she'd misheard.

'She was on the rebound from a failed love affair with Arthur Kerner, the motor-racing driver who's also the heir to the Kerner diamond mines in South Africa. They got together when she was twenty, but Kerner and his wife are Catholics, and Kerner's wife wouldn't divorce him. Jodie waited for three years, then she left Kerner and dug her beautifully manicured claws into Stokesley. She told friends she wanted to add the title of peeress of the realm to her other accolades.'

Jemma stiffened. This image of a heartless social climber was far removed from Jodie's public persona as the talented and warm-hearted Yorkshire lass who'd made her own way in the world.

'Lord Stokesley, meanwhile, had recently buried his first wife, who'd died in a tragic boating accident off the coast of Malta. He was lonely and still reeling with grief. He was on the rebound too.'

'I, I didn't know about Kerner…' Jemma stammered. *Had she shown too much sympathy and respect for Jodie?* After all, it was the baron who was their client. 'But I did know about Alicia Finton, Lord Stokesley's first wife,' she said. 'Wasn't she a society beauty and the only daughter of James Finton, the millionaire owner of the Finton Grocery Shop empire?'

'Yes. Everyone in this story is worth a few bob. Stokesley has spent his life collecting beautiful objects and artworks – and beautiful women too. So, if you ever meet him – you've been warned,' he added with a wink.

Jemma smiled at the compliment and relaxed.

'Let me fill you in on what happened next,' King continued.

Jemma sat back in her chair, braced herself for a barrage of sordid details about the breakdown of the Stokesley marriage and wished she'd accepted a cigarette.

Scrape off the glamour and gilt and most of us are flawed, damaged and a writhing mass of irritating habits, she thought. A successful marriage only ever survives through tolerance and unconditional love – and it sounded like the Stokesleys had very little of either.

'Naturally, Jodie was expected to leave her showbiz life behind her and settle down as Lady of the Manor…'

Naturally? Jemma bristled at the word. *Why was it expected?*

'It quickly became apparent that a life of grouse-shooting, brogues and tweeds didn't suit Jodie,' King continued. 'Even being presented at Court wasn't enough. Nor was the rambling medieval pile known as Castle Stokesley, his yacht in the Mediterranean or their swanky London flat. She defied Stokesley's instructions to cut herself off from her theatrical pals and embarrassed him repeatedly in front of the servants and his circle of friends with her constant references to her life as a chorus girl.'

Jemma tried to imagine what it must be like to give up the people and the world you know and love, to live in a draughty ancestral pile, in the shadow of the dead, idolised first wife… It reminded her of Daphne du Maurier's novel *Rebecca*.

Another thought struck her. If she ever did find Michael, would he *naturally* expect her to quit Smoke & Cracked Mirrors and settle down once more as a housewife?

'She finally left him in January 1938. There were unsubstantiated rumours that she'd rekindled her relationship with Arthur Kerner. Whatever the truth of this, she flatly refused Stokesley's attempts at reconciliation – or to let him divorce her on grounds of adultery. She claimed being labelled an adulteress would ruin her career and demanded that he "went away with an actress" to a hotel for a few days so she had grounds to divorce *him*. Naturally, he refused.'

It was that *naturally* again.

'Why? she asked. 'I thought it was considered the "gentlemanly thing to do" in cases of an irretrievable breakdown of a marriage.'

King laughed, stubbed out his cigarette in the glass ashtray and promptly lit another. Jemma was glad the window was open behind him to let in the breeze. It also let in the muffled roar of traffic on the busy street below.

'Being branded an adulterer has consequences for peers of the realm as well as for actresses,' he said. 'Their invitations to regimental dinners tend to dry up and since the affair of the last king with that American divorcee and the scandal of the abdication, our queen is prejudiced against divorcees at court. The baron intended to bide his time until he found grounds for divorcing her. That's when he first approached my agency for help.'

'How has your investigation progressed?'

'Not well, to be honest. Jodie may be a dancer, but she's also a smart woman. She quickly became wise to my operatives shadowing her. She has a whirlwind social life and is always surrounded by men. We persuaded her personal maid to spy on her for us – but Jodie soon got wind of this and sacked the girl. Then we bribed her chauffeur to spy on her, but Jodie soon found out about that and sacked him too.'

'So, the Stokeleys had reached an impasse?'

'Yes. Word leaked to the press about their separation and she struggled to find work in English theatres. So, she pawned some of her diamonds, booked a stateroom on the *Queen Mary* and sailed to New York.'

'You must have enjoyed that part of the job – following her across the Atlantic.'

He smiled. 'Unfortunately for us, the baron decided to employ some agents from Pinkertons, the famous New York agency, to watch her at this point.'

'How did she support herself?' Jemma braced herself for another revelation about some besotted American sugar daddy.

'Fortunately for her, not a whisper of their separation had leaked through to the American public. She used her American contacts – especially an impresario called Max Glazer – to find her a lucrative role in a flagging Broadway musical and she changed her stage name to *Jodie, Baroness Stokesley.*'

Jemma spluttered with laughter. 'I'm sorry – it must have been devasting for the baron when he saw that up in lights! But I bet the Americans loved it!'

King smiled and rolled his eyes to the ceiling. 'Yes, they did. They'd never known anything like this before; one of the snobbish and revered British aristocracy treading the boards on Broadway? They flocked in their droves to see the damn play, revived its flagging fortunes and its run was extended. She had moderate success in America on her previous tour but now she was an overnight sensation. By the time the show closed in April '39, she was living in a suite in the Waldorf Astoria and socialising with the Astors, the Rockefellers and the Vanderbilts.'

Good for her, Jemma thought.

'Her next venture was less successful. She moved to Beverly Hills in California and tried to get into the movies. By now, the news had leaked out about her separation. She was linked romantically at this time with Hollywood's latest golden boy, Budd Martin.'

'I saw Budd Martin's last film,' Jemma confessed. 'He's quite a dreamboat. Gorgeous eyes and a beautiful sexy southern drawl—' She stopped abruptly when she saw King raise an eyebrow. 'Did Pinkertons find any evidence of adultery between them?'

'Not as such, but she spent six weeks in Reno, Nevada. We think she'd gone there to try to acquire an American divorce from Stokesley. We think she planned to marry Martin.'

Jemma frowned. 'Would such a divorce be recognised in Britain?'

'No. If she'd married Martin and tried to get back into her home country, she'd have been arrested on the docks for bigamy. Anyway, war was about to be declared in Europe. The next thing we knew, she'd split up with Martin and sailed back to England. She's been kicking her heels in London ever since.'

'I'm surprised she came back. I think I'd have sat out the war in the States. How does she support herself now?'

'She penned a mini autobiography for the *Daily Mail*, which they printed in instalments. Lord Stokesley nearly had a seizure when he found out.'

Jemma nodded sympathetically but she knew there'd been nothing in those articles for his lordship to worry about. Bobbie had brought round some of them yesterday. Jodie had focused on her career and her glittering lifestyle and had peppered her story with harmless bits of information about her famous and well-heeled friends. She'd shied away from mentioning her marriage.

'The *Daily Mail* paid her well and she's also sued a couple of magazines who stupidly – and libellously – linked her to other men. But she's on the move again – this time back to her hometown of York.'

'Ah, so this is where I come in?'

King sighed wearily and leant back in his leather chair. 'I sincerely hope so, Mrs James, because this investigation definitely needs new blood. She runs rings round my own men, half of whom are in love with her. At least you ladies in Smoke & Cracked Mirrors won't be swayed from your duty by her pretty baby-blue eyes. Lord Stokesley is running out of patience, and I'm worried he might try a shot in the dark and embarrass himself – and us – with a false accusation of adultery in the courts.'

'Why has she come back to Yorkshire?'

'She's bought her family a new home on the outskirts of York, and she's come up north to oversee the interior design herself. She's staying in a suite at the Royal Station Hotel. How many operatives do you have these days, Mrs James?'

Jemma's first thought was Little Laurie Tipton, the young man with the growing disorder who operated the lift at the hotel. They'd wheedled information out of him in the past, but he had a huge crush on Jemma and she wasn't comfortable with using him.

'Well, apart from myself and Miss Baker, we've taken on another woman part-time, called Hannah. Like Miss Baker, she's a former store detective. There's a photographer with the *Yorkshire Evening Press* who helps us out occasionally.'

'He'll be useful,' King said. 'The damn woman loves publicity. She never shies away from a press photographer. Look, here's what I propose. I'll send up a couple of my blokes to work alongside your team. Jodie knows their faces, so she'll expect to see them. She might not notice the rest of you if they're still hanging around. Between you, you need to watch Jodie in shifts around the clock. Try and get another informer into the hotel. You know the score. I'll send my blokes, Irton and Emmett, to your office at ten tomorrow. They're good blokes – former police officers.'

He opened the file on the desk and slid a sheet of typed paper across the desk towards her. 'I had this contract drawn up with the terms and conditions I'm prepared to offer for your assistance.'

Jemma scanned it quickly and tried to hide her delight at the financial remuneration he'd proposed. Lord Stokesley was one of the richest men in England and was obviously prepared to pay a lot of money to get rid of his irritating wife. 'Who are we watching out for? Who's the latest man in Jodie's life?'

'Ha!' King waved his hands in the air in mock defeat, then reached for a pile of photographs. 'It's like sticking a pin in a list. She travels with a large entourage, and these are just a few of them.' He spread photographs of several men out on the table in front of her and jabbed his finger at each of them in turn. He was left-handed and didn't wear a wedding ring.

'Meet Max Glazer, the American impresario, who's back on the scene, allegedly trying to get her to return to the States for a new show. Here's her ex, Arthur Kerner, who's still sniffing around. And this is Nigel Lansdowne, a British film producer who wants Jodie to sign for a series of inspirational short films he's making for the War Office. I'm not sure how that'll work out when we finally drag her into the divorce courts and charge her with adultery, but the government must know its own business.'

She smiled at his cynicism. 'Budd Martin's not here?'

'No – sorry to disappoint you, Mrs James, but the American golden boy is in California resting in between films. He's definitely out of the picture.' He replaced the photographs and pushed the whole file across the desk towards her. 'There's a lot more information in there. I trust you'll read it and get your team up to date.'

She nodded, put the file in her bag and said, 'What a tangled web we weave through life.'

He sat back and lit another cigarette. 'Yes, we do. And I'm sure most of us would never contemplate marriage if we knew how damn hard it was to escape from it.'

'I take it you're not married yourself, Mr King?'

'Alas, I'm one of those men whose wife is hoping I'll do the *honourable thing* – as you so quaintly put it.' He watched her reaction carefully through a haze of cigarette smoke.

'Oh. You're separated. I'm sorry.'

He dismissed her embarrassment with a wave of his hand. 'We were married too young, and it's run its course. Our separation is quite amicable, thankfully, which is a good thing for our daughters. But we need to finalise it – I need to finalise it. Unfortunately, I'm loath to let one of my own men photograph me taking a prostitute into a seedy hotel.'

'Is there anything I can do to help?'

He burst out laughing and his broad and pleasant grin distracted Jemma from the scar. He was attractive when he relaxed. 'That would be even worse, Mrs James – having a beautiful and respectable lady like you witness my shame.'

His honesty encouraged her own. 'I'm not as respectable as I appear, Mr King. My own husband is missing.'

His eyes filled with compassion. 'In action?'

'No. He's just missing. Vanished. Disappeared.'

'He's abandoned you?' He leant forward across his desk, intrigued. Like her, King was a mystery-solver.

She told him the full story, culminating with her own recent efforts to find Michael. He stopped her a couple of times to ask questions and to check his understanding.

'That's an alarming and distressing tale, Mrs James. I take it you've no choice except to leave the search for Michael in the hands of Special Branch?'

91

'No, none. D.S. Marlowe promised to go back to Buckinghamshire and look again.'

'He might have to look further afield if your injured and confused husband clambered aboard a bus.'

'A bus?'

'Yes. You mentioned the bus stop down on the road below the bridge. What if he slithered down there and boarded a bus? I can't think why he would have done that, but there's so much in this story that doesn't make sense, everything should be explored.'

'But the terrible weather!'

King shrugged. 'If there were trains still running, why not the buses?'

'My God! You're right!' Startled, she rose to her feet, suddenly desperate to get back to the office. *Was it possible?*

She only just remembered her manners in time and reached out her hand towards King. 'Thank you, Mr King – thank you for everything!'

His grasp was warm and his smile friendly. 'You're welcome, Mrs James. I'll send my boys over to your office in Grape Street at ten tomorrow. And good luck with your search for Michael.'

Chapter Eleven

It was just before lunch when Bobbie and Mr Pearson returned to York. She asked him to drop her off at Gill's home, which was on Baile Hill Terrace in the south-west corner of the old medieval city. This neat row of terraced houses looked across the road on to a grassy bank that led up to the city walls. A group of laughing children were rolling down the mound, the site of a motte-and-bailey castle built by William the Conqueror.

She reached for the door handle, then turned back. 'Where does the neighbour live? Mr Elgin – the man who saw Anthony drive off on the night of the attack.' Apart from the neighbours either side, it was a quiet street with the privacy someone like Anthony would relish.

'The Elgins live two doors down. Mr Elgin works a night shift in a factory. He was leaving for work when he saw Anthony drive off.'

Bobbie thanked him and climbed out of the car.

'Please tell Dora I'll come round tonight before she leaves for work.'

Bobbie smiled, said goodbye and wondered exactly how close Mr Pearson was to the Gills – especially to Dora.

Dora Gill led her into the sitting room and made a pot of tea. The room was immaculately tidy and dominated by two comfortable leather chairs either side of the rug in front of the electric fire. Next to one of the chairs was a table with Anthony's spare reading glasses on top of a neat pile of newspapers and magazines. Bobbie mentioned Anthony's need for the spectacles.

Dora winced in distress when Bobbie described his black eye and broken glasses.

To distract her, Bobbie pointed to a beautiful model of an old Bentley with gleaming chrome and a sleek green bonnet, which took pride of place on the mantelpiece. 'That's lovely. Did Anthony make it?'

'Yes, it's a perfect replica of his own car. His Bentley is his pride and joy. Personally, I think it's draughty and noisy and those roll-back roofs leak.'

'It's also distinctive,' Bobbie said thoughtfully. 'Where's the car now?'

'The police took it to examine it. They know Lance Richards's body was moved after the attack. Not enough blood where they found him, apparently.'

Bobbie nodded. All this would come out at the inquest tomorrow morning. 'Do you have a photograph of this car, by any chance?'

Thankfully, Dora didn't question why she wanted it. She leant over to the pile of magazines and rummaged through them. 'I don't think so – but I know there's a drawing of it in one of these magazines.'

'He's very talented,' Bobbie said, as she compared the artist's drawing in the magazine with the model.

Dora smiled and her nervous hands finally lay still in her lap. She was dreadfully thin and had dark circles beneath her soft brown eyes. 'He always pays painstaking attention to detail. Occasionally, Miss Rodgers asks him to repair one of the broken museum exhibits and he takes intense pride in the job.'

'I thought he was a clerk at the museum – a bookkeeper?'

'Yes, but things have been so chaotic since Dr Kirk died and war was declared. They're short-staffed and everyone helps out with whatever needs doing. Besides which,' she added with a wan smile, 'he's devoted to Miss Rodgers and would probably walk off a cliff for her if she asked.'

'How did he get along with Lance Richards?'

Dora sighed. 'Not well. Mr Richards was careless and slapdash in his habits and seemed to take a perverse delight in teasing Anthony. He often referred to Anthony as *Mr Gill, from the York Society for the prevention of lewdness and profanity.* Mr Richards was close to retiring and Anthony said he just didn't care any more about his job.'

'I had no idea Richards was in his sixties. Was he fit and healthy?'

Dora gave her a sharp look. 'You mean, was he capable of fending off an attack from my puny brother?'

'It's something the prosecution – and the defence – will need to consider.'

'Yes, Lance Richards was as fit as the proverbial butcher's dog. He often went hiking, mountain climbing and caving. He hated the war because it stopped him touring the Austrian Alps. He adored that part of the Continent and made Anthony feel uncomfortable when he talked about his trips there and how much he liked the people. Richards admired everything Austrian and German, from their fascist politics to their fanatical approach to outdoor exercise and their sporting prowess. None of us are supposed to like anything German any more, are we?'

Bobbie shook her head sympathetically.

'He also shocked Anthony by describing in detail some of the seedy cabaret shows he'd seen in Berlin, full of women in stockings and black corsets.'

'I can see how this would have been uncomfortable for Anthony. Richards sounds a thoroughly unpleasant man. Have you any idea why Anthony threatened to kill him?'

Dora shook her head. 'I know he disliked him, but such a threat is out of character. Anthony is obsessive and gets upset if things don't go the way he wants, but he's a gentle soul at heart.'

'Have you any idea where he went on the night Lance Richards was attacked?'

'None whatsoever. I was surprised to find out he'd left the house. To be honest, Miss Baker, Anthony's nervous about the air raids and the threat of bombs. He's made our Anderson shelter in the back yard comfortable and cosy – despite the damp – and prefers to be close to it at night. If he does go out, he always makes a note of the nearest air-raid shelter first.'

'You work a night shift at the hospital, I understand?'

'Yes, I do four shifts a week. They're rather gruelling at times.'

The sound of childish laughter drifted down the street outside. Dora's head swivelled towards the window. A woman with a perambulator and small group of children were walking past. 'That's Mrs Elgin, our neighbour. Her husband saw Anthony leave the house just before it got dark.'

Bobbie rose. 'I'm sorry to dash out, but I think I'll have a quick word with her. Please excuse me.'

Mrs Elgin was a tiny woman in her mid-thirties, wearing an ill-fitting coat with a turban pulled down over her frizzy hair. Once Bobbie explained her business, the woman was keen to chat. 'Dora's a lovely

96

neighbour,' she volunteered. 'Her brother's a bit odd – but Dora's kind. She works too bloomin' hard at the hospital, though.'

'Dora says her brother rarely leaves the house at night. Have you ever seen Mr Gill go out when his sister is at work?'

Mrs Elgin's mouth set in a wry smile. 'Oh, yes. He's always poppin' out. Dora don't know the half of it, I reckon.'

Bobbie frowned. 'How often does this happen?'

The woman shrugged. 'Several times a week, perhaps? Mostly on the nights she's at work. I'm usually upstairs puttin' the little uns to bed and watch him through the window. I often see him goin' to his car with his thermos flask and drivin' off. He's been at it for months.'

'Have you any idea where he goes?'

'Well, it's a woman, i'nt it? Someone he don't want his sister to know about. It's got to be.'

'And you've not mentioned this to Dora?'

'No, 'tain't my business if he's got himself a fancy woman. Good luck to them, I say.'

'Did you tell the police?'

She shook her head. 'No, they just wanted to know if he were at home last Wednesday or not.'

'Did you see Anthony leave the house last Wednesday?'

Mrs Elgin shook her head. 'I didn't – not that night. My husband did, though. My youngest were snufflin' with a cold last week and I had trouble gettin' her to sleep. I didn't see owt.'

Bobbie's frown deepened as she watched the Elgin family disappear into their house. The man she was paid to protect and prove innocent was turning out to be quite an enigma. Refusing to co-operate with the police was one thing – but deliberately lying to his own sister?

Chapter Twelve

Jemma was already back in their office and hammering away on the typewriter when Bobbie returned.

Bobbie hung up her coat and hat and glanced around at the warm and cosy room. Jemma had taken her own furniture out of storage and used it to furnish the office when they'd acquired the premises. The soft carpet, the potted aspidistras and the comfy easy chairs made it a pleasant and comfortable place to work.

'I've got some great news!' Jemma said. 'Mr Edwards in Beverley has telephoned – Amelia has dumped her love rat, John Leyland, and returned to the family home. I'm just typing out the final bill now. You did well there, Bobbie.'

Bobbie chuckled as she walked into their kitchenette to put the kettle on. 'I'm now banned from the Dean Court Hotel for life – but it's good to hear it was worth it.' She made them both a cup of tea and they shared a plate of fish-paste sandwiches while they exchanged news.

'So, Anthony Gill is not as innocent as he makes out,' Jemma said thoughtfully.

Bobbie nodded. 'I'd love to know what the devil he was up to on the night of the attack.'

'Don't do the police's job for them,' Jemma warned. 'We need to find out who else had a motive – and the opportunity to attack Richards.'

'I agree. The problem is, no one knows where the attack took place or when. The dying man was moved and dumped down an alley. I've also discovered that Anthony has a serious crush on his employer,

Violet Rodgers, at the Castle Museum. What with Dora and their solicitor, there's a lot of middle-aged mooning going on in this case.'

'Was Anthony sneaking out at night to see Miss Rodgers? York Corporation frowns on love affairs among their employees.'

Bobbie shrugged. 'I don't know.'

Jemma smiled. 'Meanwhile, no one seems to know the identity of Jodie's latest lover – but we're paid to catch her out in an adulterous clinch anyway.'

Bobbie shook her head sadly. 'I know divorce cases are the bread and butter for P.I.s but it seems such a shame to hound her.'

'That's rich, coming from you,' Jemma observed. 'You're the one who's always telling me not to get sentimental – or personally involved with the people we work with and shadow.'

'Yes, but this is *Jodie* we're talking about. Yorkshire's darling.'

'If we don't take on the case, someone else will. Baron Stokesley is determined to get rid of her. You're star-struck, Bobbie.'

'No I'm not.'

Jemma raised a cynical eyebrow and pointed towards the novel peeking out of the top of Bobbie's handbag. 'That's Josephine Tey's *The Man in the Queue*, isn't it? If I remember rightly, it's about a man obsessed with an actress who was murdered in a queue outside a London theatre. You're immersing yourself in the theatrical world.'

'Ha! Nothing escapes you, does it, Miss Sherlock. Well, for your information, I'm only reading it while I wait for Dorothy to write another Lord Peter Wimsey novel. It's been almost five years since the last one.'

'There's some short stories.'

'Not the same. I like to get my teeth into a full-length book.'

'*Gaudy Night* is a hard act to follow,' Jemma conceded. 'It's Dorothy's most perfect novel. But stop changing the subject.'

Bobbie laughed. 'Oh, fair enough. Guilty as charged, ma'am. I feel sorry for Jodie. It's probably just as well if I stick to the murder and let you and the others grub about in our starlet's life.'

Jemma nodded. 'The information you brought me about Jodie was helpful. Thank you. I was able to talk about her with Terence King without sounding like a complete idiot.'

'What's he like in the flesh?'

Jemma hesitated for a moment. 'Charismatic, charming and surprisingly open about his business and his personal life.'

Bobbie raised a curious eyebrow. 'Is he attractive?'

Jemma changed the subject. 'I've already telephoned Ricky and Hannah and invited them to join us in the case. They're delighted – especially Ricky. I want him to be himself and work as a photographer for the *Yorkshire Evening Press*, while watching her closely.'

Bobbie snorted. 'He'll love that – being paid by the newspaper *and* by us at the same time.'

'It gives Ricky the perfect cover story. He'll be hiding in plain sight. Hannah has a friend who works in the kitchens at the Royal Station Hotel. She's told her they're desperate for chambermaids. Hannah's volunteered to apply for a job.'

'It'll be good to get a few people on the inside – and don't forget we've got our bellhop Little Laurie if we want to use him. By the way, I've also discovered that the staff at the Castle Museum are *very* friendly with those at the Yorkshire Museum – and Richards used to work there. He left under a bit of a cloud, or something.'

Jemma's large, pale-blue eyes became thoughtful 'There's a few things about the robbery at the Yorkshire Museum that don't make sense.'

Bobbie recognised the look on her friend's face and smiled to herself. 'I planned to visit Violet Rodgers at the Castle Museum this afternoon. Do you want to come with me?'

Jemma glanced at the old grandfather clock in the corner of the office. 'I can do – if we're quick. I need to get back for Tom and cook his supper. I promised him I wouldn't be late.' She rose and took the dirty plates into the kitchen.

'How's it going with Tom?' Bobbie called after her. 'Has he had any more nightmares?'

'No. And he was as good as gold yesterday and came home before dark. But I don't want to leave him too long in an empty house. It must be strange for him without his mum.'

'By the way,' Bobbie said, as they put on their coats, 'you didn't answer my question: is Terence King an attractive man?'

'He has a scar on his chin. I think he runs his operation with an iron hand and would be ruthless if crossed.'

Bobbie laughed and winked. 'So, he *is* quite attractive?'

Jemma pushed her out of the door. 'Get away with you, crazy woman.'

The maze of medieval streets in the city centre was crowded. Above their heads, the spring sunshine filtered down through the jutting upper storeys of the timber-framed buildings.

'King said something about Michael's disappearance that got me thinking,' Jemma confided as they walked. 'He reminded me about the bus stop beneath the bridge where we found Michael's suitcase.'

Bobbie glanced at her sharply. *How does she cope?* she wondered. *Inside, she must be churning with grief and anxiety.*

'I know it's clutching at straws,' Jemma continued, 'but I telephoned D.S. Marlowe when I returned to the office and shared the idea that if Michael *was* dazed and confused after the accident, he *may* have boarded a bus. He's going to look into it – check out the bus timetables and routes connected with the bus stop.'

'That's good. And don't worry about clutching at straws. They're all you've got left to hang on to.'

'Marlowe also confirmed that the blood on the suitcase was the same blood group as Michael's.'

Bobbie squeezed her arm. This was less welcome news. 'It's good you and Special Branch are working together. Between you, you'll find him, my love.'

'I sincerely hope so,' Jemma said wearily. 'Because someone spat in the street after I walked past them this morning. I think the gossipmongers have been working overtime. Word has got out that I'm married to a deserter.'

Chapter Thirteen

They left the narrow shopping streets and entered the area known as the 'Eye' of York. Allegedly, this was the geographical meeting point between the three historical ridings of Yorkshire. It was a vast open space with a huge circular lawn. Surrounding it stood three of the city's grandest eighteenth-century buildings: the County Crown Court, the debtors' prison and the former women's prison, now the Castle Museum.

At first glance, the museum mirrored the auspicious court building opposite, with its elegant steps and porticoed entrance. But there were no decorations carved into the stone and no statues on the roof. The metal grilles on its high arched windows were a gruesome reminder of its former use.

'Visiting two prisons in one day,' Bobbie said cheerfully. 'There's never a dull minute in this job, is there?' They climbed the broad steps in front of the museum.

'Michael and I came here when we were courting,' Jemma said. 'The Victorian street is amazing.'

'I've been too,' Bobbie admitted, 'but I thought it was a bit gruesome. I didn't like those old-fashioned toys and dolls from the last century. The children who played with them are now dead. I think it's creepy to display dead children's stuff.'

'I think you're a bit of a philistine, Bobbie Baker.'

Bobbie grinned and shrugged. 'History was never my favourite subject at school.'

'Well, I think the museum is fascinating. My favourite exhibit is the glistening array of poisons in the jars behind the counter of the Victorian chemist shop.'

'And you think *I'm* weird? You're just a frustrated arsenic poisoner!'

A cash desk stood on the right at the entrance to the museum. They handed over their business cards to a custodian and asked to speak to Miss Rodgers.

Bobbie didn't know what she'd expected a female museum curator to look like. A greying, bespectacled and slightly dusty old woman in tweeds and pearls, perhaps?

Violet Rodgers couldn't have been more different. Aged somewhere in her mid-twenties, she wore an elegant and tight-fitting black dress and heeled shoes, all of which enhanced her slim figure and shapely legs.

She had a heart-shaped face and a little pointed chin that gave her an elfin look. Above her high forehead, her glossy black hair was rolled back in the latest style and held in place with tortoiseshell combs. Beneath her perfectly arched eyebrows, her brown eyes twinkled with warmth. It was easy to see why Anthony Gill was captivated with the woman. But his adoration was futile; she wore a diamond engagement ring on her left hand. Clearly, their first theory that the two were involved in a clandestine love affair was wrong.

Violet greeted them warmly and led them through a maze of corridors that still bore an unpleasant resemblance to a gloomy prison. The plaster was cracked and had fallen away from many of the walls, exposing the crumbling stone and brickwork beneath. There were exposed pipes and electric wiring everywhere and the few windows they saw were barred.

Violet's office appeared to be in a former cell. It didn't have a window and smelled of damp masonry. Cramped and cluttered, there was only just enough room for her desk and a couple of chairs. The floor-to-ceiling shelving at the back of the room was stacked with boxes, metal cylinders and a pile of nineteenth-century military sabres.

'Thank you for finding the time to see us,' Bobbie said. 'We're here on behalf of Mr Gill's solicitor.'

Violet raised her elegant hands and opened her arms wide. 'If there's *anything* I can do to help either the police or yourselves get to the bottom of this tragic affair, I will. It's so awful!'

'It must be difficult for you,' Jemma murmured. 'You must feel caught in the middle.'

'Absolutely! One of my staff has been murdered in the most brutal fashion – and another arrested for the crime. I'm reeling, to be honest with you, Mrs James. I still can't believe poor Lance is dead – or how he died. No one deserves a death like that.'

'And what about the arrest of Anthony Gill?' Bobbie asked. 'Did that shock you too?'

'Gosh! Yes! Anthony – a murderer? What nonsense! And I feel so guilty. I'm sure the only reason they arrested the poor man was because I told them about the argument I overheard.'

'What happened?'

Violet pointed towards the door. 'I was working in here and my door was slightly ajar. Unbeknown to me, Lance was in Anthony's office across the corridor. I became aware of raised voices – or rather,

Anthony's voice raised in anger. I'd never heard Anthony shout before, and I knew it must be something serious. I got up to intervene, but Anthony's door burst open, and Lance came out, laughing. As he left, Anthony shouted after him "I'll kill you – you bastard!" Lance just laughed again and walked off.'

'Did you ask them what the argument was about?' Jemma asked.

'Yes, but neither of them would say. Lance just shrugged and told me it was none of my business. Anthony was terribly agitated and wouldn't speak. I decided to leave them to calm down until the next day and try again. But by then,' – she hesitated, her eyes clouded over with grief – 'by then, it was too late.'

Bobbie nodded sympathetically. 'Did they argue often?'

'Not like that. Lance used to tease Anthony sometimes. He often called him a prude.'

'Were they arguing about work?'

Violet shook her head. 'I doubt it. They've different areas of work and expertise. Anthony deals with the paperwork and finances for the museum – the business side of things. Lance's job involves cataloguing, displaying and storing the exhibits.'

'Did anyone else overhear this exchange besides you?' Bobbie asked.

Violet shook her head. 'No. The other staff were busy in different parts of the museum.'

'Is Anthony a good employee?' Jemma asked.

'Gosh, yes. He's very efficient. Lance was... less so. He knew the job inside out and could be efficient, resourceful and productive when he wanted. But most of the time he couldn't be bothered. He was just biding his time here until his retirement.'

'How long did he work here?' Jemma asked.

'About six months.'

'Why did he leave his job at the Yorkshire Museum?' Bobbie asked.

For the first time in the interview, Violet broke eye contact with them. It was only for a split second, but it was enough for Bobbie to recognise that her next statement would be a lie. 'I don't know. Mr Collinge, the keeper at the Yorkshire Museum, may be able to tell you.'

'When I spoke with Anthony this morning, he seemed to think there was some sort of problem at the other museum – and you were pressured into employing Lance.'

Her eyes still avoided Bobbie. 'After several younger members of our staff left to join the armed forces, I was just grateful for the extra help.'

'It can't be easy doing your job during a war,' Jemma said. 'And for a woman, too. I've never heard of a female museum curator before. You've done well, Miss Rodgers.'

Violet smiled. 'Oh, you're behind the times, Mrs James. There's several of us. Mary Kitson Clark is the curator of antiquities over at the Yorkshire Museum. However, her position is "honorary" – they don't pay her.'

'They don't pay her?' Bobbie was shocked. 'Do her bosses think it's some kind of hobby, or something? I was paid half the wage of the male store detectives in my previous job – but at least I got something.'

Violet's eyes twinkled with amusement. 'Yes, it seems to me that provided we gals don't ask for a fair wage, men don't mind women in the workplace, do they? Fortunately, Mary has family money and income from her publications. She's a specialist in the archaeology of the Romano-British culture. She's highly respected.'

'Still,' Jemma said calmly. 'With or without remuneration – it's an impressive achievement you've both risen to your positions in our male-dominated world.'

Bobbie opened her mouth to try to bring the conversation back to Lance Richards, but Jemma seemed to be shooting off on a tangent. 'Are you local, Miss Rodgers? Do you live in York?'

'Yes, I live in Haxby.'

'It doesn't seem like much of a change for Lance Richards to me,' Bobbie persisted. 'Moving from one museum to another, less than a mile away.'

'Ah, but that's where you're wrong, Miss Baker. York's two museums are *very* different. While the Yorkshire Museum houses prehistoric fossils and the region's priceless antiquities – some of them dating from Roman times and the Saxon era – we're more of a folk museum, with an emphasis on social history. Thanks to Dr Kirk and his beautiful collection, we've created a wonderful exhibition to safeguard the history of the lives of ordinary people in the more recent past. Do you have time for me to show you around?'

Bobbie froze in horror.

Jemma came to her rescue. 'I'm afraid we don't – but thank you for the offer. Regarding the Yorkshire Museum, I understand you and your staff have helped them pack up their antiquities for removal to the safety of the countryside.'

'Yes. It's terrifying to think of those priceless artefacts in danger of being destroyed by the Jerries. We help them out whenever we can, but their task is mammoth! They've tens of thousands of irreplaceable items – and it's so hard to prioritise which of them need removing to safety.'

Bobbie frowned. 'But what about your own exhibits here?'

Violet stubbed out her cigarette in the glass ashtray and smiled. 'I love our museum – and so do the public – but I'm not blind to the fact that in terms of historical value, our exhibits are not in the same league as those belonging to the Yorkshire Museum. The Yorkshire Philosophical Society can call on many volunteers from their membership to help with the removal, of course, but even then, the process is slow.'

'Anthony mentioned this society earlier,' Bobbie said. 'Who are they?'

To her surprise, it was Jemma who answered her. 'Don't you remember? We learnt about them when we went on that school trip with Miss Colbeck. The Yorkshire Philosophical Society have run the Yorkshire Museum since it was built back in 1830. They're a dedicated group of historians, archaeologists, scientists and naturalists with specialities in many fields.'

'You're well informed, Mrs James,' Violet said with a smile. 'So, you two have known each other since school, have you?'

'Yes,' Bobbie said. 'But Jemma always paid more attention in class than I did.' She leant forward across the desk. 'Can you think of anyone who disliked Lance Richards sufficiently to want to kill him?'

Violet sat back in her chair and frowned. 'No, I'm afraid I can't. I don't know much about Lance's life outside of work. And the same goes for Anthony. Both men kept their private lives private. I can only assume there's someone in Lance's past who held a dreadful grudge against him. It's frightening to think the real murderer is still walking around York somewhere,' she added.

'Yes, it is.' Bobbie put her notebook away in her bag. 'We won't bother you any further, Miss Rodgers. Thank you for your help.'

Bobbie was grateful for the fresh air after the damp stuffiness of the museum and she breathed in deeply. The pink blossom on the trees was a cheerful and welcoming sight after the gloom of the museum. 'Well, that was a right blooming history lesson! I think I need a cup of tea to rinse the crumbling antiquities out of my mouth.'

Jemma smiled. 'You'll survive.'

'She was helpful. But I think we might have to look a little further to find out who Anthony meets when he sneaks out at night. She might be his type – but I can't see such an attractive and ambitious woman falling for Anthony. Besides which, she's engaged to someone else.'

'I agree. But don't forget to add Violet Rodgers to your list of potential suspects for the murder.'

'What?'

'As Dorothy and Agatha often show us – it's usually the least likely suspect. Violet Rodgers is charming and professional, but from what I've heard about Richards so far, I suspect he was the kind of man who resented having a lady boss – especially such a young one. I'm sure there was some friction between them. We need to know more about her.'

'Is that why you tried to find out her address?'

'Yes, although I didn't want to make it obvious.'

'Fair enough. Can I take the car? I'll pop over to Haxby tonight and have a snoop around.'

Jemma nodded.

Bobbie fell quiet for a moment while she thought about Jemma's suggestion. 'I can't imagine Violet Rodgers as a violent murderer, but she was lying when she said she didn't know why Lance Richards transferred across from the other museum. Something happened there.'

'You need to go to the Yorkshire Museum and talk to the staff.'

Bobbie groaned. 'That place always leaves me feeling intellectually inadequate when I come out – and dusty.'

Jemma smiled. 'I've got to go home to Tom now, but I'll come with you tomorrow once we've met Mr King's operatives and set up a rota for shadowing Jodie. Beside which, I want to know more about the robbery at the Hospitium. Out of the two contracts, the divorce case will be the more lucrative – but there's more of us to handle that and I can help you with this murder case.'

Bobbie gave her friend a knowing glance. 'It's the mystery that attracts you, isn't it?'

Jemma smiled. 'Yes, the museum murder is definitely the more intriguing case.'

Chapter Fourteen

Tom wasn't at home when Jemma arrived back at the house, but she didn't worry unduly. She picked up the post from the doormat, made herself a cup of tea and prepared their meal.

There was still no sign of Tom at half past six. Ignoring her rumbling stomach, she went to the bookcase in the front parlour to look for a novel. Her hand instinctively went to her old copy of *Lord Edgware Dies* by Mrs Christie.

She smiled to herself when she reread the summary on the back. This was Agatha's story about a famous actress who married an aristocrat and then was accused of his murder. Bobbie wasn't the only one being sucked into the glamorous but fraught world of Baron Stokesley and Jodie.

Settling down on the sofa, she enjoyed a few peaceful minutes with her book. But as the old clock over the mantelpiece ticked its way towards seven o'clock, she became uneasy. Maisie had warned her that Tom had developed a habit of staying out late – but surely the lad was hungry by now?

She pulled on her coat and tried to remember where his friends lived. He had three special friends: a pleasant young lad called Kenneth Newby, whose father was away with the Yorkshire Regiment – and the more boisterous Wright twins. The twins lived on Burton Stone Lane. She'd start there.

Mr Wright greeted her in his slippers on the doorstep and told her Tom wasn't there. A gruff, well-built chap with a strong accent, he eyed her with concern. 'Is everythin' all right, lass?'

'I'm worried,' she confessed. 'I'm looking after Tom while his mother is away with my brother and there's no sign of him tonight.'

Mr Wright turned his head and hollered down the hallway. 'Jim! Davy! Get out 'ere – now!'

A pair of identical and grubby curly-haired boys of about ten materialised behind him. Both were chewing and one held a large slab of buttered bread in his hand.

'What's up, Da?'

'Where's Tom Langford?'

The boys shrugged. 'We ain't seen him since school.'

'Do you think he might be with Kenneth?' Jemma asked.

One of the boys shook his head. 'Naw, Ken's ma took him t' dentist tonight, straight from school.'

'Did Tom mention where he was going tonight?'

The twins looked at each other, then one of them said: 'He might be at the barn.'

'The barn?'

'It's the old barn on the allotments,' Mr Wright informed her. 'Their grandad owns it. He lets the lads store their bits of salvage there.'

Salvage. That made sense. Tom and the other boys were collecting scrap metal and paper for the war effort – and taking part in a competition organised by the W.V.S.

'Hold on, I'll get me coat,' Mr Wright said.

'Oh, I don't want to cause you any bother…'

'It ain't no bother, lass. I've got four lads. I know better than most, I reckon, what a bloody worry they can be.'

Jemma soon found herself hurrying beside Mr Wright towards the allotments down by the river. Prone to flooding, this area had always been agricultural land and it was dotted with dilapidated old farm buildings. The wooden barn he led her towards had greyed and warped with age and was surrounded by nettles and weeds. Some of the lower planking had been replaced with rusty corrugated iron and several wooden beams leant against the building at an angle to brace it.

'I've got the key to the padlock,' Mr Wright informed her. 'The lads only use it for their salvage, but they keep it locked.'

'Why?'

He laughed. 'To stop the others from stealin' their hoard. Half the city's kids are collectin' this stuff for that damn competition and they ain't above filchin' it from each other.'

As they drew nearer, they realised the door was ajar.

'Someone's here.'

'Tom!' Jemma shouted. There was no reply.

'Bloody hoodlums!' Mr Wright snapped. 'They've forced the lock!'

Jemma's eyes followed his to the broken padlock at their feet and the damaged staple on the door. Someone had used a crowbar to snap off the padlock.

They hurried into the gloomy interior. Despite the thin slivers of light streaming through the gaps in the wooden planks of the walls, it was dark. Jemma's eyes took a moment to adjust.

The end of the barn was stacked almost to its cobwebbed roof with piles of old newspapers, books and sheet music tied into bundles with string. Beside her was a mountain of metal: old cooking pots, rusty garden tools, bits of piping, bird cages – and even a couple of old bikes with damaged wheels and twisted frames.

Tom lay unconscious on the lower edges of the sloping newspaper pile.

Mr Wright swore, and Jemma screamed.

They dashed towards him. Jemma fell to her knees beside the child and gathered him into her arms. His red hair was matted with blood from a weeping gash on the back of his head. 'Tom! Tom! Can you hear me, darling? Wake up – please!'

His round freckled face was deathly pale. So innocent. So vulnerable. It broke her heart.

'Is he still breathing?'

She nodded, gulping back her panic.

'We need to get him to the hospital.' Mr Wright reached down and lifted the stocky boy up into his own arms like he was a feather. 'I'll carry him home and we'll telephone for an ambulance.'

Jemma staggered to her feet. *How had Tom hit his head? Had he fallen on something?* She glanced around but there was nothing obvious that might have caused the accident.

She scurried beside Mr Wright as he strode back to the house.

The twins were waiting outside for them on the street.

'Open the bloody door!' yelled their father.

The boys leapt at his command, and they burst into the house.

'Edna! We need help!'

Mr Wright carried Tom into their shabby but scrupulously clean front parlour and laid him on the cushions of a faded sofa. 'I'll call the ambulance.'

Edna Wright appeared a moment later with a bowl of warm water and a cloth and the two women bathed Tom's head.

Jemma grimaced when the water turned pink. *How much blood had he lost?*

The twins hovered behind them, their grubby faces stricken with shock. 'Is he dead?'

'No. Be quiet, lads,' their mother replied.

But one of the twins wouldn't be silenced. 'Were it an accident? Did he fall?'

'I don't know,' Jemma replied. *Was it an accident? Weren't lads of Tom's age as sure-footed as mountain goats?*

Then she remembered the broken padlock and ice flooded into her veins. 'He may have been attacked,' she stammered.

Mr Wright returned to the room. 'The ambulance is on its way.'

Jemma turned to him. 'I need you to secure the barn, Mr Wright. If this is an assault, then the barn is a crime scene and the police will need to examine it. No one must go in there.'

The Wright family froze around her.

'We don't want no coppers here!' one of the twins protested.

'The police won't come here,' she reassured them. 'But if someone bad has done this to Tom, they'll want to see the barn – intact.'

'Has some bugger filched our stuff?' the other twin asked in horror.

Mr Wright ignored his son and nodded. 'I've got another padlock. I'll sort it out.'

She exhaled with relief when she heard the distant clanging of the ambulance bell.

The next hour passed in a blur.

She was dimly aware of the bumpy ride in the ambulance, the endless hospital corridors, their glaring white lights and the bitter smell of antiseptic. While a grim-faced doctor examined Tom, a nurse whose crisp white apron crackled with starch, took Tom's details. And Jemma realised once again how little she knew about the child in her care.

The nurse regarded her coldly from beneath her voluminous white cap as she struggled to remember his date of birth.

'Are you his sister?'

'No, I'm his step-aunt.'

'Where are his parents?'

'They're away on their honeymoon.'

The nurse blinked, unsmiling, and told Jemma to sit in the public waiting room while they examined Tom further.

She sank wearily on to an uncomfortable hard-backed chair with the other injured and miserable wretches who were waiting to be seen and wrung her hands. *Dear God. How on earth was she going to find the words to tell Gabriel and Maisie about this?*

'Jemma?'

A man stood before her in the smart blue uniform of the Royal Canadian Air Force, his attractive dark eyes full of concern. It was Flight Lieutenant Don Hudson, who lodged in the same building as Ricky.

'Don!' Relief flooded through her at the sight of a friendly face. Staggering to her feet, she threw herself into his arms and burst into tears. 'Oh, Don! I'm so pleased to see you! It's awful!'

'What the devil's happened, ma'am?' Gently, he disentangled himself and they sat down.

Gulping and stammering, she told him about Tom.

'He'll be fine, Jemma. Young boys always get into scrapes – but they're tough and soon bounce back. I should know – I've got two of them.'

'But what if he doesn't? He's too young to die.' Her voice cracked as she whispered, 'God help him!'

He squeezed her hand but turned away at the same time. The slight tic returned to the corner of his left eye and his long black eyelashes fluttered. She suddenly realised how stupid she sounded. It was war. Children were dying all over Europe – and it was the men in aeroplanes like Don who were killing them.

'He'll pull through, Jemma. I'm sure he will.'

A shrill female voice interrupted her thoughts. 'Don? Who's this?'

A thin, brassy-haired blonde woman in a tight skirt and ridiculous heels hovered beside them. Her stockings were muddy and torn. Her right wrist was bandaged and suspended in a sling. *She's fallen off her shoes*, Jemma decided.

'We can go now,' the woman said. 'The doc says it's nowt. Just a sprain.'

Don rose to his feet. 'Gina, this is Jemma, a friend of mine. Jemma's nephew has just been admitted following a nasty accident.'

The two women nodded to each other. Gina's eyes were close set and gleamed with hostility. She reached out and grabbed Don's arm in a possessive gesture. 'Well, I'm sorry to hear this, lass, I'm sure. But we need to get goin'.'

'Please don't let me stop you. It looks like you've been in the wars yourself.'

In any other circumstances, Jemma would have been amused by Gina's jealousy. When she first met Don, she'd thought she was a widow and they'd enjoyed a light flirtation. It stopped abruptly once she found out Don had a wife and family back home in Ottawa. He'd obviously moved on now – and Gina wasn't so fussy.

The grim-faced doctor appeared at their side. 'Mrs James? Can you come this way, please? I need to talk to you about Thomas Langford.'

'Has he woken up?'

'No, not yet.'

Don sat down and pulled Gina into the seat beside him. 'We'll wait for you, Jemma – and I'll drive you home afterwards.'

The doctor led her into a bland interview room with a tiled floor and walls. He spoke too quickly, and she struggled to understand what he was saying. Her heart sank as she registered the words: 'a fractured skull', 'swelling' and 'maybe a bleed on the brain'.

'Has Tom got all these? How bad is he?'

'It's impossible to tell – yet. The X-ray shows a small fracture, but we'll have to wait and see about the rest. The next twenty-four hours are critical. We'll monitor him overnight. He's comfortable on the ward now. The best thing you can do, Mrs James, is go home and contact his parents to come back from Scotland.'

'Is Tom going to die?'

The doctor hesitated for far too long. 'It's impossible to tell with youngsters like him. He's had a nasty head injury, but he's got youth on his side. I've seen children bounce back from far worse than this.'

'Can I see him before I leave?'

'You're not supposed to. Visiting hours are between one and four in the afternoon.'

'I... I just want to kiss him goodnight.'

He nodded curtly and led her through more bland tiled corridors to a male ward. The little boy looked even more vulnerable lying among a row of unshaven men with tortured faces. The nurses had bandaged Tom's head and dressed him in a pair of hospital regulation pyjamas with a faded blue stripe, which were far too big for him.

Jemma held on to the iron bedstead as she leant down to kiss him. 'Mummy will be here soon, darling.' Her tears dripped on to his pallid cheeks, and she pulled herself away in embarrassment.

She stumbled back to the waiting room, where she was surprised to find Don still there, with Gina cuddled up next to him. Don must have promised the woman something special because she was far pleasanter and more sympathetic towards Jemma now. She didn't even make a fuss when he gave Jemma his handkerchief and guided her gently outside to the car. Jemma slid wearily into the back seat and closed her eyes for most of the journey home.

'Do you want us to come in with you?' Don asked, as he pulled up outside the house.

'No. Thank you – but no. I've got to phone my brother.'

'Do you know where they are? I thought newlyweds usually kept the location of their honeymoon a secret.'

She gave a wan smile. 'Yes, I know where they are. My brother doesn't have much imagination.'

'Take care, Jemma – and try not to blame yourself.'

She stumbled into the house and sorted out the blackout curtains. Shivering with cold in the chilly hallway, she looked for the telephone number of the Scottish hotel where she knew Gabriel and Maisie were enjoying themselves, blissfully unaware of the bombshell she was about to drop.

Her mouth was parched with thirst and her stomach growled with hunger. Taking a big breath to steel herself, she reached out a shaking hand and lifted the receiver to make the hardest telephone call of her life.

Chapter Fifteen

Tuesday, 28th May 1940

Because of the blackout and the dangers of travelling at night on unlit roads, Maisie and Gabriel planned to set off for York at first light.

Jemma had no idea what time the sun rose in Scotland, but she herself was up with the Yorkshire larks. She'd slept badly, waking constantly and worrying about Tom. She feared the worst and desperately wished Michael was here to support her and Gabriel.

Then her misery was replaced with a flash of anger. *Where the hell was Michael? How dare he disappear like that?* It took her a few moments and two cups of tea to calm down and think rationally again.

Just after nine o'clock, her exhausted brother and sister-in-law burst into the house. Gabriel must have thrashed the engine of the Vincent Rapide and driven at top speed to get home this fast. Beneath the road dust, he was white with anger. Maisie's hair was a wild and tangled mess, and her eyes were red from crying.

She handed them a cup of tea each and gave Maisie the telephone number of the hospital. Maisie ignored the tea and hurried towards the telephone.

Gabriel gulped down his drink and slammed his fist down on the table. 'How the hell did this happen, Jemma? We leave you alone for five minutes with the child and he ends up dangerously ill in hospital!'

'Gabriel!' Maisie called from the hallway. 'We talked about this – it's not Jemma's fault.'

'Of course it's Jemma's fault!' he yelled. 'She was in charge, wasn't she? What happened, Jemma? Too busy working, were you? Too busy to take care of Tom? You're hopeless, Jemma – bloody hopeless!'

'Gabriel, I don't think it was an accident.'

'You're just too bloody busy these days with that damn agency of yours to care for your family... what did you say?'

'I think he was attacked.'

Quickly, she explained about the forced lock on the barn door and the lack of an explanation for an accident. Gabriel's face was as grey and immobile as granite while he listened, his pale-blue eyes glinting with rage.

'There wasn't anything lying around that could have caused his injury. I think someone coshed him on the head. Maybe he disturbed a thief? You need to—'

'I know what I need to do.'

Maisie reappeared, blinking back fresh tears. 'The hospital said Tom's had a comfortable night but is still unconscious. There's no change.' Her face crumpled with distress. 'They won't... they won't let us visit him until this afternoon.'

'Like hell they won't!' Gabriel stormed out of the kitchen. 'I'm a bloody police inspector – nobody bars me entry! Get changed, Maisie – we're going to that damn hospital.'

Jemma reached for her coat and handbag, grateful Gabriel had found another outlet for his fury. There was nothing more she could do, and the sight of her would only irritate Gabriel further if she stayed.

It was time to go to work, meet Terence King's men and plan the surveillance on Jodie. Never in her life had she been so grateful for the distraction she knew she'd find at her office.

Jemma was sticking the photographs of Jodie's entourage on to a noticeboard when the rest of her team arrived.

Hannah, who'd worked with Bobbie as a store detective, was the first one to appear. A quiet, greying, middle-aged widow with unremarkable features, a shabby coat and a shopping bag, she looked like a harmless old grandmother. Jemma had heard her muttering to herself sometimes and suspected she talked to her dead husband. She rarely spoke to anyone else, unless what she had to say was relevant. Beneath her bland expression, she hid a surprising amount of initiative and the tenacity of a bulldog; she never let go and always saw the job through to the end.

Jemma greeted her and they went into the kitchenette together to make a pot of tea for the rest of the team.

'I'm goin' to the Royal Station Hotel this mornin', to apply for that job as a chambermaid,' Hannah told her.

'That's great, Hannah. Your friend did us a real favour when she told us about the vacancy. Do you think she'll feed us information too, about Jodie, if we pay her?'

'Maybe. She also told me Jodie caused a real kerfuffle when she first arrived by changin' rooms. She turned down the best suite the hotel had to offer and asked for a smaller one at the back instead.'

Jemma paused, with the kettle held in mid-air. 'Why did she do that?'

Hannah shrugged. 'Dunno. Maybe it were cheaper or she just fancied watchin' the trains come and go at the station.'

'Can you get me a map of that floor of the hotel? What do they call it? A floor plan?'

'Yes. They're all over the place with fire escape routes marked on 'em. I'll nick one.'

Ricky sauntered into the office wearing his Leica slung around his neck and a cheeky grin. 'Mornin', Miss Marple.'

'Hello, Ricky – you know Hannah, don't you? Make yourself comfortable. The rest will be here soon, and we'll have tea.'

He paused in front of the noticeboard. 'What's this? A rogues' gallery?'

Jemma crossed the carpet to join him. 'It's Jodie's entourage and her family. Here's three of the men she may be dallying with: Max Glazer, an American impresario; her ex-lover, Arthur Kerner; and Nigel Lansdowne, a British film producer. That's a photograph of her family: her mother and younger siblings. I thought we should familiarise ourselves with the people around her.'

Ricky stroked his short-clipped moustache thoughtfully. 'What about her staff?'

'I need photographs of them too. Both her personal maid and her chauffeur are new – their predecessors were removed for spying on her for Terence King.'

He patted his Leica affectionately. 'I'm onto it.'

'We also need images of her secretary and her agent – and any of her local friends.'

'I'll get as many decent photographs for you as I can – and replace these grainy cuttings with decent mugshots.'

'Thank you.'

The door opened and two burly middle-aged men strode confidently into the room.

It was Irton and Emmett, Terence King's men. Hard-faced, with dark rings beneath their eyes and prominent red veins on their noses, they looked like they indulged in late nights and heavy drinking. Irton's muscle was in danger of turning to flab and Emmett had a small scar beneath his right eye. Neither of them looked pleased to be here and Jemma sensed she might have trouble controlling them.

'Well, I say!' Irton exclaimed, in a faux posh accent, after they finished the introductions. 'This is a nice gaff, i'n't it, Emmett. Look – they've even got a carpet!' They threw themselves down into the armchairs, the two comfiest chairs in the room, took off their hats and unbuttoned their coats. Irton was bald and Emmett's hair looked like it hadn't seen a comb in weeks. Hannah silently handed them a cup of tea.

'Aye, very warm and cosy. And posh china too,' Irton added, tapping the cup with his fingernail.

'We'll have a word with the boss when we get back. We need posh china and carpets in Leeds.'

'And a couple of armchairs,' Emmett added.

'You've met him, have you, lass?' Irton asked. 'You've met the King?'

Jemma smiled and sat down at her desk with her own tea. 'Yes, I've met Mr King.'

Irton nudged Emmett in the ribs. 'She's met the King.'

'Aye, I know. I heard.'

'Did yer like him?' Irton didn't wait for her to reply. 'Most of the lasses do. A real ladies' man is our Terry – and you're just his type. They swoon at his feet like wiltin' violets.'

'Did you swoon?' Emmett asked.

'I've never fainted in my life.'

'Miss Marple here is made of sterner stuff,' Ricky volunteered. 'I think you're goin' to be pleasantly surprised once you get to know her.'

'Who the devil is Miss Marple? I thought yer name were Mrs James?'

'It's a nickname. Miss Marple is a famous female detective,' Ricky informed him.

Irton scowled. 'Never heard of her.'

'She's with the Bradford City Police,' Ricky added casually. 'She'll be their next Chief Constable.'

Jemma nearly choked on her tea with suppressed laughter.

'Lasses get everywhere these days,' Emmett said with a tragic sigh. 'It'll be the knacker's yard for us blokes soon, Irton.'

Bobbie arrived and her friend took in the scene in a flash, especially the nonchalant attitude of the two burly men sprawling in the armchairs. Jemma knew by the set of Bobbie's jaw that she'd got their measure.

'Good morning, everyone. I'm Miss Roberta Baker – but you can call me Bobbie. I'm the co-founder of Smoke & Cracked Mirrors.' She unpinned her hat and put it on the stand.

'Ooh, *two* lady bosses,' Irton said. 'The King never said nowt about that, did he, Emmett?'

'He never said nowt to me.'

Jemma introduced Irton and Emmett.

'Yer late, Miss Roberta Baker,' Irton said with a smirk.

'I've been out on another case.' Bobbie slid into the seat next to Jemma, leant towards her and whispered, 'I've something to tell you later.'

Jemma nodded and cleared her throat. 'Let's get this schedule drawn up. Mr King wants Jodie watched round the clock and *I* want us to record and photograph everyone she meets.'

'We already know who she hangs about with,' Irton said, yawning. 'We know her mates and her staff.'

'Not in York you don't. This is her hometown and there's a whole new bunch of old friends, family and old flames floating about. I assume you and Mr Emmett have pocket cameras and a car? You do? Good. I want a photograph of everyone she meets or visits. Ricky will develop them, and they'll go up on this noticeboard with labels. It'll be updated regularly, so you need to study it.'

'She knows who we are,' Emmett said. 'Sometimes she waves and calls out to us. "Hello, Adolf!" she says. "Nice day for spying, isn't it?" Always calls us *Adolf*, she does.'

'Ooh, that must hurt your soft little hearts,' Bobbie drawled sarcastically.

'Cuts me to the bone, lass,' Emmett replied. 'Gutted, I am.'

'It doesn't matter if Jodie knows you,' Jemma said. 'She knows her husband won't give up and will expect to see you two around. But she doesn't know the rest of us work for her husband and I want it to stay that way. It's important you're not seen with us. We'll meet here every morning at eight thirty for a briefing and share information. Once we think we've got a promising lead about her latest lover, we'll refine our tactics—'

'*Refine*?' Irton interrupted, in mock horror. 'D'you hear that, Emmett, lad? She's gonna refine us!'

'Already begun,' Emmett said, tapping his teacup. 'We've got real china.'

'Familiarising ourselves with the people in Jodie's world is our current priority,' Jemma continued. 'And good communication is important for the success of this operation. We need to work as a team – not alone. Here's the telephone number of this office.' She passed some of her business cards across the table to the men. 'If she's on the move, try and phone in her whereabouts so someone else can take up the chase. And here's some spare keys to the office. Please feel free to use it as your base.'

'Don't mind if I do,' Emmett said smugly. 'This is good char, this, lass. I don't suppose there's any biscuits to go with it?'

'Any breakages come out of your wages,' Bobbie snapped.

'We'll take turns manning the office,' Jemma continued. 'I hope you men know how to answer the telephone politely in case any of our other clients phone us?'

Irton snorted and his face turned ugly with anger. For a brief second, Jemma saw a frightening glimpse of the brute beneath his mocking exterior. 'Of course we do, lass! We've been trained by the biggest and best private inquiry agency in Yorkshire.'

'Good. And whoever mans the telephone is also responsible for completing this logbook. We'll track her movements about town and record whom she meets. We need to know what she's doing – and who she's with – twenty-four hours a day. We've got Hannah working for us inside the hotel. The rest of us will shadow her in the wider world.'

'I saw Little Laurie Tipton this morning,' Bobbie interrupted, 'we could ask him to help us.'

'I'll think about it,' Jemma said warily.

'Who's this Tipton fellah when he's at home?' Irton asked.

'The bellhop at the hotel.'

'We need someone on her staff,' Irton protested.

'Terence King tried that, and it didn't work. We're going to do it my way for now.'

Emmett laughed, then leant towards Hannah. 'You're quiet, missus. What do you think?'

Hannah stared at him blankly before saying: 'Laurel and Hardy.'

'Eh?'

'She called us Laurel and Hardy,' Irton reminded him.

'Yeah, I heard. She's a deep one. Very profound.'

Jemma brought their attention back to the job in hand and they talked for another fifteen minutes, while she drew up a rota for the surveillance. Hannah left to see the housekeeper at the Royal Station Hotel about the job and Ricky left to take some photographs.

Jemma asked Emmett to man the office and told Irton to take the first shift watching Jodie. 'Bobbie's got a police inquest to attend for another case – and I'm going with her.'

'Of course, lass.' Irton rose but moved towards the kitchen rather than the exit. 'I'll just have another cuppa before I go. You know those lazy actress types. They never rise before eleven.'

'No. I want you to take your post now. I've already said I want twenty-four-hour surveillance on Jodie, starting now. If she *is* in a clandestine relationship, she's smart enough to change her habits to trick us.'

He stopped in his tracks, glowering. For a moment, Jemma thought he'd refuse to co-operate, and she felt Bobbie stiffen beside her. Then he just grinned, buttoned up his coat and left, muttering something about 'slave drivers' beneath his breath.

Jemma exhaled and reached for her own hat and coat. She hoped managing this case wouldn't always be as exhausting as this.

Bobbie chuckled when they stepped out into the bright street. 'Hannah got it wrong. They're not funny enough to be Laurel and Hardy. They're more like Tweedledum and Tweedledee – but not as pretty.'

Chapter Sixteen

Dozens of people were already crowded into the public gallery at York Magistrates' Court by the time Jemma and Bobbie arrived, and an expectant buzz hung over the courtroom. A smart middle-aged man in a black suit shuffled along to let them squeeze on to the end of one of the wooden benches. These were the last seats.

'Thank you,' Jemma said to the gentleman beside her. 'If you hadn't moved across, we'd have been left standing.'

He glanced behind at the crush of people on the benches. 'Yes, it's quite a turnout, this, for old Lance. I doubt there'll be this many people at his funeral.'

Jemma nodded and understood his cynicism. The public gallery was full of reporters. It was easy to recognise them, as most clutched notepads and pens in their inky fingers. *But who were the rest?* Friends and family of the deceased, perhaps? Or just nosy members of the public?

'Half of this lot are just ghouls,' the man continued. 'They've turned up to wallow in the gory details of the murder.'

'Were you a friend of Mr Richards?' she asked cautiously. 'It must be painful for you if you were.' He was a good-looking man in his late fifties. He was slim, with a healthy sun-tanned complexion and a fine head of thick silver hair.

'Yes. I worked with him for years. We are – sorry – *were* old pals.'

Jemma fought hard to temper her curiosity and keep her face sympathetic. 'I'm sorry for your loss, Mr—?'

'Alcott. Ben Alcott. I'm one of the curators at the Yorkshire Museum.'

'What was Mr Richards like?'

He turned and appraised her coolly out of a pair of intelligent grey eyes. 'Lance was a decent man. Very sharp – and funny. But he didn't suffer fools gladly and always spoke his mind.'

Jemma didn't have time to react to this unexpected praise for Richards. Bobbie grabbed her arm and pointed out Anthony's lawyer down in the main court area below.

Mr Pearson looked worried and was fidgeting with his papers. D.S. Fawcett sat behind him. In stark contrast to the lawyer, the police officer sat back with his arms folded and yawned. The case was solved as far as he was concerned.

Jemma desperately wanted to question Ben Alcott further, but the coroner arrived. Everyone fell silent when he explained that the purpose of the inquest was to open an investigation into the death of Lance Samuel Richards and try to establish how, when and where his death had occurred.

The first witness called to the stand was the dead man's father-in-law, Mr Yardley, who'd identified his corpse.

'That can't have been pleasant for him,' Bobbie murmured.

The elderly man returned to his seat, visibly shaking. He sat down next to a woman of about forty, who wore a sombre black suit and satin blouse. Face powder couldn't disguise the dark circles beneath her eyes and the lack of colour in her cheeks. *Ida Richards, the dead man's estranged wife?*

The next witnesses were the man who'd found Lance Richards's body in the alleyway and the police officer who was first on the scene. The officer ponderously described the horrific injuries to the dead man's skull and the journalists beside them took frantic notes. The officer also said he knew the body had been moved, due to the lack of blood at the scene.

Jemma glanced at the man beside her to gauge his reaction, but Ben Alcott's gaze was fixed on the drama below. His face was expressionless.

The police doctor who'd carried out the post-mortem arrived at the stand to give his testimony and the journalists leant forward in anticipation of some juicy quotes. He didn't disappoint them.

'The deceased's injuries were consistent with a single massive blow to the frontal bone of the skull with a heavy curved – or rounded – wooden object. There were splinters of wood left in the wound. His left eye socket was shattered, and the depressed skull fracture crushed his brain against the back of the skull and tore it, causing massive bleeding and nerve damage. Death would have been inevitable.'

The courtroom gave a collective shudder.

'The location of the injury on the frontal bone suggests the person wielding the murder weapon was taller than Mr Richards or standing in an elevated position.'

Jemma held her breath. Lance Richards had been described as five foot ten inches tall and according to Bobbie, Anthony Gill was about five foot seven.

'In your opinion, would a woman have been strong enough to deliver this fatal blow?' the coroner asked.

The doctor thought for a moment. 'In my experience, sir, women come in all sorts of shapes and sizes.'

A barely suppressed titter rippled round the courtroom. The coroner frowned.

'If she was elevated,' the doctor continued, 'and used gravity to her advantage, it's possible a woman may have administered this blow – and so might a small man.'

'And you're convinced the murder weapon was made of wood?'

The doctor nodded. 'The wooden fragments we extracted from his skull suggest this. Some of them were deeply embedded.'

'Have you any suggestion about what type of object was used to kill the deceased?'

The doctor shrugged. 'A massive wooden club, perhaps? The surface was definitely curved.'

The proceedings were wound up quickly after this. The coroner declared Lance Richards had been murdered by person or persons unknown and adjourned the inquest pending further police inquiries.

They trooped down the stairs and Bobbie dragged Jemma to the main area of the courtroom to introduce her to Mr Pearson. He was putting a large sheaf of papers in his briefcase when the women approached. He didn't look happy.

'There's been an unfortunate development, Miss Baker. Yesterday, the police went over the Castle Museum accounts and discovered the sum of £223 has gone missing. They've found it transferred into an account in Anthony's name.'

Bobbie was stunned. 'What? Are you saying Anthony has been cooking the books?'

The lawyer ran his hand through his thinning hair in exasperation. 'Yes. It's irrefutable, I'm afraid. Anthony has stolen money from his employers.'

'But… but *why?*'

'I don't know – and neither does Dora. Anthony has plenty of savings. I'm driving back to Armley Gaol now to confront him. This only adds to the case against him, I'm afraid.'

'But this doesn't make him a murderer,' Jemma protested. 'A thief, yes. But not the murderer of Lance Richards.'

'Unfortunately, that's not the end of the matter. The police suspect Richards tried to extort money from Anthony and Anthony stole the money to pay him off.' He handed them a sheet of paper.

It was a short list of names – with Anthony Gill's at the top, followed by *Violet Rodgers* and *Mary Kitson Clark*. Next to the top two names was written: *£223?* Mary Kitson Clark had *£50* written next to hers with a question mark.

'What is this?' Bobbie asked.

'It's a copy of a list the police found among the betting slips in Richards's lodgings. They didn't think anything of it at first. But now they've gone over the Castle Museum accounts and discovered the sum of £223 is missing, they've decided this is too much of a coincidence. They believe Richards blackmailed Anthony for £223 – and that this is motive for murdering him.'

'£223?' Jemma said. 'It's rather an odd amount – very distinctive. Most people prefer to work in round numbers like £200, or £250.'

'Dora and I are shocked,' Mr Pearson continued. 'We can't imagine what Anthony thought he was doing.'

'Unfortunately, there's more,' Bobbie said awkwardly. 'Yesterday, when I spoke to their neighbour Mrs Elgin, she told me Anthony often drives off into the night while Dora is away at work. She thinks he's got a woman.'

The lawyer's lips tightened with anger, and he snapped his briefcase shut. 'So, he's a liar as well as a thief? I shall drive over to Leeds immediately and have it out with Anthony. He's got to tell us the truth. How can he expect us to help him if he's keeping so many secrets?'

'But what about the two women on the list?' Bobbie asked. 'Are the police investigating them too, for the same reason? Surely, everyone on this list is now a suspect?'

'I believe they plan to interview the women today. I'll leave that list with you. If you'll excuse me, I need to go.'

He walked away and the two women sat down in a couple of chairs to talk. The courtroom was nearly empty now.

'I don't understand,' Bobbie said. 'What's happening?'

'I'm not sure yet.' Jemma pointed to Violet Rodger's name on the list. 'You said you had something to tell me. Was it about Violet Rodgers?'

'Gosh, yes. I'd almost forgotten!' Bobbie brushed a stray lock of her frizzy hair from across her face. 'I went over to Haxby about an hour after I left you last night. I found her home quite easily. She's well known in the village. It's in a quiet, rather remote little spot. Pretty little place. A short while later, she returned from work – laughing and joking with a dashing Polish army officer on her arm.'

Jemma smiled and thought of Don Hudson. 'Ah, the mysterious fiancé. I suppose she's not the first woman in this country who's had her head turned by a man in uniform – and she won't be the last.'

'Exactly, but when I went back again this morning – in the hours before I joined you in the office – I watched him leave.'

'Ahh.'

'Yes, *ahh*. She was still in her dressing gown and kissed him goodbye on the doorstep.'

'Naughty lady,' Jemma said, smiling.

'If her employers got wind of this affair, it would damage her professionally.'

'Exactly. York Corporation are one of the stuffiest employers in the city. She'd be out of her job before she could blink.'

'If Lance Richards knew about this, he may have tried blackmailing her...'

Jemma finished Bobbie's sentence for her. '...which gives her a strong motive to murder him.'

Bobbie nodded and the two of them sat in silence for a moment, turning this latest development over in their minds.

'Anthony is besotted with Violet,' Bobbie said, 'and Lance liked to tease him. Richards worked with the pair of them. He's bound to have noticed that Anthony was sweet on his lady boss. If Richards did know about Violet's indiscretions with her soldier, perhaps he used this information to taunt Anthony. If he threatened to expose her to their employers, it would explain Anthony's furious outburst on the day of the murder. He might have been protecting Violet.'

Jemma shrugged. 'Possibly. But we must remember Anthony has also been stealing from the museum funds and it looks like Lance was blackmailing him too. Was this the cause of their argument? To be honest, it's all supposition, Bobbie. We need either Anthony – or Violet – to tell us the full truth about what really happened. I bet Violet heard more of the argument than she claimed. And despite what the coroner said about women and the murder weapon, we've got to keep Violet on our list of suspects.'

'Where do we go from here?'

Jemma rose to her feet and picked up her handbag. 'We need to get back on track. Let's pay the staff at the Yorkshire Museum a visit. I'd also like to meet Mary Kitson Clark – preferably before the police interview her.'

Chapter Seventeen

Curious to find out how their other case was progressing, Jemma and Bobbie took a detour down the private drive of the Royal Station Hotel. The sun had bobbed fitfully in and out of the clouds all day but when they approached the hotel it obligingly illuminated the yellow-brick Victorian façade until it gleamed like honey.

Five storeys high and topped with soaring chimneys, the hotel was at least a quarter of a mile long. It overlooked extensive gardens and the minster beyond. A glorious view – one that Jodie had spurned for a smaller room at the back.

A vast array of expensive motor vehicles was parked along the road in front of the building, jealously guarded by uniformed chauffeurs whose buttons glistened in the sunlight as brightly as their precious cars. Jemma recognised Jodie's Rolls-Royce parked between a sporty Mercedes and a Jaguar.

A blond young man with a neatly clipped moustache, peaked cap and sunglasses stood polishing the silver winged woman on the bonnet, the famous *Spirit of Ecstasy*. *The replacement chauffeur*, Jemma thought.

He grinned at the women as they passed, and drawled out a 'Good mornin', ladies' in an American accent.

Bobbie didn't hear him. 'Good grief!' she exclaimed. 'What on earth's going on?' She quickened her pace towards the large crowd gathered outside the porticoed entrance of the hotel. There were so many of them, they spilled over the road and on to the grass edge of the garden beyond.

Jemma returned the chauffeur's greeting and hurried after Bobbie towards the crowd. The people ranged from young women like themselves to starry-eyed matrons and flushed older men. Everyone was smiling and chatting, and every single pair of eyes was fixed on the glass doors of the hotel entrance, which were flanked by two impassive and uniformed doormen.

They heard one elderly man ask his neighbour, 'Did you see her in her last film?'

'Yes,' he replied, 'wasn't she brilliant!'

'I think they've come to sun themselves in the loveliness and sparkle of Jodie,' Bobbie whispered to Jemma.

Jemma rolled her eyes and smiled.

Some of the crowd obviously expected a long wait. They'd brought folding chairs and picnic hampers and passed sandwiches and sweets to each other.

One of York's buskers had left his usual spot in the city centre and was using his guitar to serenade the crowd with a faltering version of one of Jodie's most popular hits from her film *The Midnight Girl*. His playing was indifferent, but the crowd tapped their toes and swayed with the beat.

Ricky was on the other side of the hotel entrance, leaning against one of the cars and chatting to another pressman, who also held a camera. Irton stood, smoking, against a black Citroën further down the street.

'She's here!' someone yelled. The crowd gave a collective squeal of delight and surged forward. The two doormen moved to stop them swamping the actress. The busker ramped up the volume and everyone craned their necks when the glass doors swung open, and Jodie appeared.

Radiant with smiles, the actress paused at the top of the steps to wave and blow kisses to her admirers. When the crowd erupted into cheers, her huge blue eyes sparkled with happiness. She wore a short Russian sable fur coat, which shimmered with light. The diamond and ruby bracelet dangling from her gloved wrist glinted in the weak sunlight as she waved. A red casque hat, decorated with a bow and a feather, was perched cheekily on top of her gleaming blonde hair and matched the bright red satin of her tight-fitting skirt.

Tall, willowy and perfectly toned by years of strenuous dance practice, Jodie walked down the steps with the grace of a goddess towards her Rolls-Royce. Reverentially, the crowds parted to let her pass. She was flanked by two men, one of whom was the British film producer Nigel Lansdowne.

Ricky followed them, snapping away on his camera.

'Isn't she gorgeous?' Bobbie had flushed with excitement and one of her hair pins sprang out. She pointed to Jodie's other companion, a handsome dark-haired man with violet eyes and the longest black eyelashes Jemma had ever seen. 'Ooh!' she squealed. 'That's Stephen Howard, the famous actor!'

Above the noise of the crowd, they heard Ricky call out, 'Mr Howard! Mr Howard! *Yorkshire Evening Press* – are you here to act with Jodie? Or are you her latest beau?'

The group stopped abruptly, and a ripple of shock ran through the crowd.

Stephen Howard paled, but Jodie just laughed and turned to face Ricky. The crowd fell as silent as a theatre audience.

'You're a cheeky fellow, Mr Yorkshire Evening Press,' she said sweetly. 'But let me tell you something.' She paused for dramatic effect, her eyes scanning her audience to make sure she had their attention. She was on stage – and she knew it. 'I never date actors. They've got greasepaint in their veins instead of blood.'

It wasn't true, of course. Any of it. But the crowd roared with laughter at her wit. 'Good old Jodie!' someone yelled.

'Nice reply, Jodie!' Ricky said. 'Now strike a pose for the paper, darlin'!'

Laughing, Jodie dropped her right hip and stuck her left hand on the other, elongating her slender legs. She tipped her head coquettishly and Ricky snapped away furiously, while the crowd shouted and cheered.

And then she was gone.

The Rolls-Royce pulled out from the kerb and drove off towards the city centre. A few seconds later, the black Citroën, with Irton crouched over the wheel, pulled out and followed it down the road.

'Wasn't she wonderful?' Bobbie exclaimed.

Jemma smiled. 'Yes, that was quite a performance. Do you—' She stopped abruptly as she saw a stooped, scruffy elderly man at the back of the crowd. A man she'd rather hoped she wouldn't ever have to see again.

'What's the matter?' Bobbie asked.

'That's Will Sharrow over there. What on earth is he doing here?'

Bobbie craned her neck to catch a glimpse of their local rival. Sharrow also ran a private inquiry agency in York, and he'd clashed with Jemma once before when they were both investigating the same blackmailer.

'Where is he?' Bobbie asked.

Jemma pointed.

Sharrow stared wistfully down the road after Jodie's Rolls-Royce. Then he turned and disappeared into the milling crowd.

'Perhaps he's a fan?' Bobbie suggested, with a wink. 'I'm not surprised. She's even more beautiful in real life than on the cinema screen!'

Jemma gave her a sharp nudge in the ribs. 'Get control of yourself, Bobbie – she's only a flawed woman like the rest of us.'

'But she's not, is she?' Bobbie said dreamily, as they turned to leave. 'She's a goddess!'

Chapter Eighteen

It was only a short walk to the museum, but Bobbie chattered about Jodie all the way there. By the time they'd paid their entrance fee to the botanic gardens and set off along the broad sweeping path up to the main building, Jemma was heartily sick of hearing about the actress's graceful walk, her wit and stylish dress sense.

But when the pale, elegant façade of the city's oldest museum, with its elaborate portico and tall Doric columns, loomed above them, Bobbie fell quiet and turned sulky.

A uniformed attendant stood behind the reception desk in the entrance hallway. Jemma went over to speak to him while Bobbie stood glowering at a large marble statue of the Roman god Mars.

Ahead of them, a pair of tall double doors led into the lofty central hall, illuminated by a skylight. Crammed full of display cabinets and glass cases, the room was dominated by the fossilised skeleton of a giant elk that stood on a central plinth. Its antlers must have been ten feet wide. A cleaning lady in a turban was flicking a duster over the cabinets but there didn't seem to be any other visitors. Tuesday afternoon must be one of the quieter times at the museum.

The attendant scratched his head when Jemma asked to see Mr Collinge, the museum's keeper. 'I ain't sure where he'll be. He might be in the Hospitium. You'll have to ask Miss Kitson Clark. She's in the workroom.'

The attendant called the cleaner over. 'Can you take these ladies to see Miss Kitson Clark?'

'As if I haven't got enough to do!' the woman grumbled, but she beckoned to them to follow her into the central hall.

They squeezed through the narrow aisles between display cases crammed with ancient artefacts. Everything was labelled in tiny handwriting or faded typewriter print, much of it in Latin. Protruding glass cases were hung on the walls, full of stuffed birds and mammals.

The cleaning woman walked slowly and limped, keeping the weight off her left hip. The silence in the room was oppressive and Jemma smelt the dust and the decay.

'Dead things,' Bobbie muttered beneath her breath. 'It's full of dead things.'

The cleaner's arthritis may have been a problem but there was nothing wrong with her hearing. She glanced over her shoulder, smirking. 'You ain't seen nothin' yet, lass. Wait till you get to the geological room.'

Here, rows of ammonites jostled for space in long glass cases with the fossilised remains of a giant crocodile. At least, Jemma thought it was a crocodile, but it might be some sort of obscure dinosaur. Everything was blackened with age and a century of coal dust from the boiler.

The next room they entered was the small chamber that housed the famous Kirkdale Cave exhibits. When they'd come here on their school trip, their teacher had told them Kirkdale Cave was a crack in a rocky cliff face near Malton that had turned out to be a hyena den from over a hundred thousand years ago. There no complete skeletons among the dozens of fossilised bones (Jemma remembered being very disappointed about that). But, curiously, there were also the remains of elephants and a rhinoceros, whose dead and dying carcasses had been scavenged by the hyenas.

'Do you remember coming in here with Miss Colbeck?'

'I was baffled,' Bobbie admitted. 'I still am. I can't image how the Vale of York was ever warm enough for African animals.'

'You weren't the only one. Back in 1830, the scholars of the time struggled to explain the discovery. Many thought the bones had been washed there in the great flood of Noah's Ark.'

Bobbie scowled. 'Stop the bloody history lessons, Roxby – or I'll have to pull your pigtails.'

The cleaner led them through another door into a cluttered and dusty storeroom, stacked high with wooden packing cases of different sizes. There was one tall window, overlooking the abbey ruins. A young woman in slacks and a faded man's check shirt was bent over one of the cases, rummaging among the straw.

'Miss Kitson Clark? These ladies are lookin' for Mr Collinge.' The cleaner turned and left, and the honorary curator of antiquities straightened up and turned to greet them.

Mary Kitson Clark was one of the tallest women Jemma had ever seen and was built like a female Amazonian warrior. She was also decidedly grubby. Her smudged face was pleasant featured rather than pretty, and she had an unruly mop of light brown curls that were trying to escape from beneath her headscarf. She had the glowing complexion of a woman who enjoyed the outdoor life and Jemma suspected she would be equally at home on a hockey pitch, handling a full team of carriage horses or wrestling the skeleton of a Tyrannosaurus rex out of the mud.

'Oh, you've come about poor Lance,' Mary said in the clipped accent of the upper classes.

Violet Rodgers had mentioned that Mary had 'family money'. But apart from the large and expensive diamond engagement ring on her left hand, there was nothing about Mary's appearance to suggest a wealthy background.

'Yes, we're working for the solicitor of Anthony Gill.' Jemma showed her Mr Pearson's card. 'He's conducting separate inquiries to the police. Miss Rodgers at the Castle Museum suggested we spoke to Mr Collinge about Lance Richards's time here as an employee.'

A shadow clouded Mary's brown eyes and her smile faltered. 'Oh dear. Poor Mr Collinge has been very upset about Lance's murder. He's not a well man. But I suppose it was inevitable someone would ask questions, sooner or later.'

Jemma frowned. 'Haven't the police been here? I gather Mr Richards worked here far longer than at the Castle Museum.'

'No. I suppose it's because they've already caught the murderer – your solicitor's client.'

'Mr Gill claims he's innocent, which is why his solicitor has asked us to make inquiries on his behalf,' Bobbie explained. 'Would you mind answering a few questions?'

'I'm not sure how you think we can help, but I'll try. Justice must be served, I suppose.'

Bobbie seized her chance. 'You must have known him well – and known something about the people he associated with.'

Mary sighed. 'He wasn't popular among the staff, and poor Mr Collinge found him very trying.'

'What about Mr Alcott, your fellow curator?' Jemma asked. 'I thought he was a close friend of the deceased. We've just met him at the inquest.'

Mary waved her left hand dismissively in the air. 'Yes – but Ben is such a pleasant and *tolerant* kind of man. He's friends with *everyone*. Besides which, they shared a love of mountain climbing and caving. Hobbies like that tend to draw men together.'

'What about your own relationship with him?' Jemma asked.

Mary shrugged again but this time she broke eye contact with them and glanced down at her feet. 'Oh, we rubbed along. You know.'

Jemma took a deep breath. 'The police share information with Mr Pearson, and they've recently discovered lots of betting slips in Mr Richards's room. It seems he was a bit of a gambler. Do you know anything about this?'

'Good gracious! No, I don't.'

'They also found a list of names with a cash sum next to them. Yours was among them – and the sum of £50 was written next to it.'

Mary blinked and pulled back in alarm.

'Does this mean anything to you?'

'No, nothing,' she stammered. 'I've not seen or heard of Lance for months.'

Jemma and Bobbie waited patiently, hoping she might feel obliged to fill the silence with more information. But she didn't.

'So, he never asked you for money?' Bobbie asked.

Mary laughed bitterly. 'Gosh, yes. All the time once his wealthy wife left him. He was always trying to borrow money from the staff and made lots of barbed comments about my own family's wealth – and how I should share it around. Stupid things like that. But I just ignored him.'

'Did he ever try to blackmail you?' Jemma asked.

Mary briefly broke eye contact again before she recovered her composure and indignation. 'Good grief! *No!*'

'The police suspect he was involved in several shady activities.'

'Well, that doesn't surprise me. He made no secret of the fact he was broke.'

'Why did Mr Collinge find him trying?' Bobbie asked.

Mary sighed and rolled her eyes to the ceiling. 'Lance was a rude man and didn't care who he upset. He embarrassed Mr Collinge at several meetings of the Philosophical Society and once wrote in a memorandum that Mr Collinge was from the Society for the promotion of loyalty and subordination among the lower classes.'

Jemma saw Bobbie's eyes narrow. Brought up by her socialist father, who'd spent most of his working life as a union leader, fighting for workers' rights, Bobbie didn't like to hear about anyone patronising the working class.

'It wasn't true, of course,' Mary continued. 'Mr Collinge is a sweetie – he would never try to subordinate *anyone*. Everyone loves him, especially our employees who *are* from the lower orders, like the caretaker and the attendants.'

'That must have been upsetting for him,' Bobbie said through gritted teeth.

'Yes, it was. And poor Mr Collinge is quite old and in such frail health.'

'Can you take us to meet him, please?'

'Certainly. He's in the Hospitium.' She set off towards the door, then stopped and turned round. 'But you'll be gentle with him, won't you? Lance's murder is horrid. It's been a nasty shock – and Mr Collinge *feels* things so keenly.'

Mary's mood brightened when she led them out into the main rooms of the museum. 'That's our vertebrae room over there,' she explained, 'and this door leads to our lecture theatre, where members of the Philosophical Society give talks. In fact, we're holding one tonight. Mr Charles Allen will be talking about "Some Aspects of Pond Life".'

Bobbie blinked in surprise. 'You've not stopped the talks for the war?'

'No. Our motto is *Keep Calm and Carry On*. People need a distraction in these times, don't you think?'

'Yes – but *pond life*?'

Fortunately, Mary didn't hear the incredulity in her tone. 'Yes, it's a fascinating subject!'

'I can tell Mr Allen a thing or two about pond life,' Bobbie muttered. 'I've met several examples of the two-legged variety.'

Mary stopped dead and turned to face them, her face alight with excitement. 'How wonderful! Would you like to come along and meet him?'

She really must see a doctor about her hearing, Jemma thought.

'I'm sure Mr Allen would be delighted to talk to you,' Mary continued. 'We're always looking for new members for our society, especially younger people. Our members are quite *old*, you see, and you *seem* like a couple of intelligent young women.'

Bobbie opened her mouth to issue some scathing reply, but Jemma stepped in. 'Thank you for your offer. We'll think about it.'

Undeterred, Mary strode ahead out of the main door, chattering about the excellent talk they'd enjoyed the previous month about lamp shells.

Thankfully, Bobbie kept her opinion about those bottom-dwelling marine invertebrates to herself.

Chapter Nineteen

The timbered Hospitium that housed the museum's valuable collection of antiquities was the only medieval building left on the site from the days of the former abbey. As its name suggested, it had originally been used to house the wealthy guests of the abbot, most of whom arrived by river barges. Jemma glanced at its wooden roof as they walked down the hill towards it and understood why everyone, including Violet Rodgers, had been determined to remove its contents to safety. One incendiary bomb from the Luftwaffe and the entire building would go up like a fireball. There were metal buckets, sandbags and a reel of hose pipe stacked against the Hospitium's wall.

'It's closed to the public for the duration of the war,' Mary explained, as she led them up the rickety wooden staircase to the main entrance.

They paused for a moment at the entrance while their eyes adjusted to the gloom after the bright sunlight outside.

At first glance, it was just how Jemma remembered it from her childhood visits. A large Roman mosaic floor dominated the centre of the room, cordoned off with faded red rope, and like the main building of the museum, it was crammed with display cases, many of which were topped with rows of antiquated pottery jugs and vases.

But most of the display cases were empty. The hoards of silver Roman coins, the Saxon gold and ruby jewellery, the bronze statues and belt buckles had vanished. Just like the storeroom where they'd met Mary, the edges of the room were stacked high with packing cases and crates.

Bobbie wrinkled her nose. 'It still smells mouldy,' she whispered.

Jemma smiled and silently agreed. The cooking smells from six centuries of cauldrons bubbling over open fires and other suspicious medieval odours had seeped into the exposed beams of the towering roof and now wafted down to their nostrils on tiny draughts.

There were two men at the far side of the room. One of them was Ben Alcott. He was on his knees, rummaging around inside one of the crates. He'd removed his smart jacket and black tie and rolled up his shirtsleeves, revealing a pair of muscular arms. Sitting beside him, on another case, was a white-haired and painfully thin old man, clutching a clipboard and a pen. His frailty painfully reminded Jemma of her late father.

Ben glanced up in surprise when they approached. 'Ah, we meet again, ladies.'

But his welcoming smile soon disappeared from his handsome face when Mary introduced them and explained their business. 'You're private detectives? *Female* private detectives?'

'Now, now, Ben,' Mary teased. 'There's no need to be so surprised. Don't forget – we gals get everywhere these days.'

Jemma turned to Mr Collinge, who'd paled at the mention of Lance Richards. 'I'm sorry if we've distressed you, sir, but Violet Rodgers at the Castle Museum suggested we talk to you about Lance. I know it's not a nice subject, but an innocent man's fate hangs in the balance.'

'You think that Gill chap is innocent?' Ben asked sharply.

'He claims he is,' Bobbie replied.

'But the police have arrested him and seem convinced of his guilt. Why should we co-operate with *you*?'

'We're working towards the same end as the police,' Jemma said. 'All any of us want is to find out the truth and York City Police are undermanned. Like everyone else in the city, they're overstretched because of the war. I know this because my brother is Inspector Gabriel Roxby.'

There was a short silence and the three museum employees exchanged glances. It was Mr Collinge who broke the impasse. 'I've met your brother,' he said quietly. 'He was most helpful when the Hospitium was burgled recently. He helped us retrieve the stolen items. We'll be happy to help.'

Ben Alcott looked like he was about to protest but Mary silenced him with an almost imperceptible shake of her head.

'Have they been here to talk to you about Mr Richards?'

'Not yet.'

They asked the same questions as before. Did they know if Lance Richards had any enemies? How did he get along with his colleagues here at the Yorkshire Museum? And why did he leave?

Mr Collinge replied but the answers they received from him only confirmed what they already knew. Richards had been a 'satisfactory' employee. He had a tendency to be tactless and upset people. He chose to leave the Yorkshire Museum of his own accord and take up a vacant position at the Castle Museum. Mr Collinge hadn't seen him for months and knew little about his private life except that he'd separated from his wife.

'And what about you, Mr Alcott?' Jemma asked. 'You told me earlier you were a friend of Mr Richards. When did you last see him?'

He shrugged. 'The two of us went hiking and camping about a fortnight ago and I've not seen him since. Lance was good company and great fun. I can't think of anyone who hated him enough to kill him.'

'Did he ever talk about his colleagues at the Castle Museum? Anthony Gill, for example?'

He looked her straight in the eyes and replied, 'He never said anything about the Castle Museum except the work was boring and so were his colleagues.'

'Did he have any enemies?'

'I don't believe so.'

'What about money troubles?'

'He never complained about being short of cash.'

Mary Kitson Clark shuffled with discomfort at this blatant lie.

Jemma's lips tightened with frustration. 'A couple of final questions, if I may? You mentioned that dreadful robbery that occurred recently. Can you tell me what happened, please?'

Ben's eyes narrowed. 'How is that relevant?'

'I don't know,' Jemma replied cheerfully. 'But I'm curious, I read about it in the newspapers. I even saw an article about it in the *London Evening Standard* while I was down there last week.'

'Gosh, really?' Mary said, surprised.

'I'm not sure we can tell you anything that hasn't already been in the papers, young lady,' Mr Collinge said. 'It was well reported.'

'Look, it was a smash and grab by a couple of amateurs,' Ben snapped. 'And they knocked our poor caretaker unconscious.'

'Yes, poor fellow.' Mr Collinge pointed to a large gap in the row of display cases. 'They stole his keys, let themselves inside and smashed the display cabinet over there. Then made off with a selection of bronze belt buckles, some Saxon rings and an old Roman sword scabbard.'

'Will Mr Dunn make a full recovery?' Jemma asked.

'Yes. He hopes to come back to work next week. We've missed him.'

'The papers said the items they stole weren't valuable,' Bobbie said.

The two museum curators laughed, and even Mr Collinge managed a weak smile. 'Value is a relative concept in an antiquities museum,' he explained. '*Of course* they're valuable – just *not* as valuable as the treasures we'd already sent to the country for safekeeping.'

Jemma glanced up at the exposed wooden beams of the ceiling. 'I can see why doing that is a good idea.'

Ben snorted. 'As it turns out, we've probably been wasting our time. The Germans will be here within a week.'

'Oh, don't say that!' Mary pleaded.

He shrugged. 'I speak as someone who faces up to the facts. You've heard the news – we're in retreat. The Germans will be over the English Channel within a week.' He turned back to Jemma and said sharply, 'Those men who broke in were ignorant and opportunistic. They had no idea of the worth of *anything* in here. We told the papers the items stolen were of no particular value, and the thieves dumped them.'

Bobbie frowned. 'Are your display cases locked?'

'Yes. The keys are kept in our safe.'

'So why did they smash the glass cabinet if they already had the keys in their possession?'

'It's different keys,' Mary explained. 'Mr Dunn only has the keys to open the exterior doors to the Hospitium, the main museum building and the gates to the botanic gardens.'

'Did you get Mr Dunn's keys back along with the other items?'

'Yes, they were in the bag the police retrieved.'

'Did you change the locks once you realised the keys had been stolen?' Jemma asked.

'That's none of your business, young lady,' Alcott snapped.

Jemma changed the subject. 'In the newspaper reports, it said the stolen items had been recovered in the same large bag the thieves used to remove them from here. Where did they get this bag? I assume when they met Mr Dunn at the gates of the museum, they weren't carrying a bag.'

Alcott gave an exaggerated sigh. 'Oh, that's easy to answer. It was my fault, I'm afraid. The bag contained my camping gear, my sleeping bag and my spare clothes. When Lance and I returned from our last trip to the Dales, I drove straight to work and dumped my holdall in the back room.'

'I remember,' Mary said, smiling. 'You forgot about it, and it got a bit whiffy.'

He laughed. 'Yes, damp clothes. I've always been a bit slow to sort out my laundry. Anyway, when the thieves broke in, they found my bag, tipped out the contents and used it to haul away the items they'd stolen. It's embarrassing.'

'You weren't to know,' Mary soothed him.

'Have we finished?' Ben asked. 'Can we get back to work now?'

162

Jemma smiled and shut her notebook, 'Yes. Thank you for your help.' She gave Bobbie's arm a quick squeeze – their signal to remain quiet – then she turned to Mary. 'I think we'd like to take you up on your offer to join the Philosophical Society and come to the talk tonight. Can we sign up?'

'Oh, how wonderful!' Mary clapped her hands with delight and led them back to the main building to sign the forms. 'You won't regret it, I promise!' she called over her shoulder as she bounded along the path.

'I already am,' Bobbie hissed under her breath.

Chapter Twenty

Now she'd got Mary alone and in a good mood, Jemma offered to purchase an expensive catalogue of the museum's most priceless antiquities and also asked for Mr Dunn's address. Mary happily provided both.

Bobbie waited until they'd left the museum grounds and were on their way to the caretaker's home before she exploded.

'For God's sake, Jemma! Are you crazy? You've signed us up to spend a boring evening listening to some musty old professor droning on about bloody pond life! What the hell were you thinking?'

Somehow, Jemma kept her face straight. 'I need to keep out of the house. Gabriel's mad at me because of what happened with Tom.'

'What!' Bobbie stopped in the middle of the pavement, full of sympathy. 'Then why didn't you say something earlier? We could have gone out dancing! At least at De Grey's we'd mix with people our own age – men of our own age – not dusty fossils! God! I can't remember the last time I felt a bloke's arms around me! Or a kiss. What's a kiss?' she asked tragically.

'You might get more kisses if you weren't still mooning after a married man.'

Bobbie ignored her reference to Vince Quigley. 'Seriously, Jemma, my lips have forgotten their purpose in life.'

Jemma grinned, rolled up her new catalogue and tucked it under her arm. 'It's surveillance, Bobbie. We're getting nowhere questioning these people about Lance Richards. Tonight's gathering is an ideal opportunity to watch them in their natural habitat.'

Bobbie fell into step beside her. 'Mr Collinge seemed a decent old chap. I felt he was telling us the truth.'

'Yes, but Mary knows something about Lance Richards's surprise departure from the Yorkshire Museum – and she's not telling. And I don't believe her when she said Richards never tried to blackmail her. Meanwhile, Ben Alcott was far too defensive. He was pleasant when we met him at the inquest but he's on his guard now.'

Bobbie nodded. 'I don't believe him for one minute when he says Richards never talked about his work or colleagues at the Castle Museum. They've spent hours together tramping over the moors and he turned up at the inquest – so he obviously cares. I can't believe the police haven't been here to talk to them already. What is D.S. Fawcett playing at?'

'He thinks he's already arrested the murderer.'

'Why did you ask about the green holdall?'

'It's something that's been bothering me about the break-in.'

Bobbie gave her a sideways glance. 'You think it's too convenient, don't you?'

'Yes. I think the thieves knew the bag was already there. The whole thing is too damn convenient, especially when they returned the stolen goods *and* the keys.'

Bobbie blinked. 'Blimey! In that case, the robbery was an inside job! Do you suspect Alcott?'

'It might have been any of them. Any one of them could have told the thieves a large bag was lying around inside the Hospitium, waiting to be filled up with stolen antiquities.'

'But it doesn't make sense. The thieves stole a random load of rubbish. Ben, Mary and Mr Collinge are the curators and keepers of Yorkshire's finest treasures. Surely, if one of them *is* involved, they'd have told the thieves where the good stuff was kept?'

'None of it makes sense. Hopefully, once we've talked to Mr Dunn it'll become clearer.'

'Yes, let's see what one of the *lower orders* has to say,' Bobbie said waspishly. Then she sighed. 'Do you know what? This case gets curiouser and curiouser.'

Maud Dunn answered the door. A grey-haired middle-aged woman, her pale eyes were swollen with crying.

'I hope we've not called at a bad time,' Jemma said. 'We can always come back later.'

'No, you're welcome, lass. Come in. We need a distraction right now – and Charlie'll be pleased to know someone is takin' an interest. The police don't seem to be tryin' to catch those villains.'

She led them into a small sitting room where Charlie sat in a threadbare armchair in front of the electric fire in his dressing gown. He had a pristine white bandage wrapped round his head. The room was scrupulously clean, but the nicotine-stained ceiling suggested someone in this house was a heavy smoker.

A battered old wireless set in the corner blared out the sonorous tones of a BBC news presenter. Maud switched it off. 'These are a pair of lady detectives, Charlie. They've come to talk to you about the robbery.'

Charlie Dunn raised a bushy grey eyebrow that matched the bushy sideburns framing his thin, lined face. 'I didn't know they employed wimmen down at Clifford Street.'

'We're not police,' Jemma explained, 'but my brother is Inspector Gabriel Roxby.'

Charlie nodded and reached for his pipe and tobacco tin. 'I've met him. Decent fellah. Better than that Sergeant Fawcett, anyhow.'

'Take a seat, girls,' Maud said.

They sat down and Jemma explained their role in the Lance Richards murder investigation. 'The truth is, Mr Dunn, I think there's some connection between the attack on you and the murder of Mr Richards. It just seems too much of a coincidence that *two* museum staff were attacked within a few days. I can't quite put my finger on it – and I've no proof – but it might help if you tell me what happened that night.'

'I should have known there were summat wrong from the off,' Charlie said. 'They were damn rude about your brother. Disrespectful, like. And the fat one's uniform didn't fit him. Turns out, they'd hired those costumes from the theatre supplier on Coney Street.'

'I'm confused where the young boys come into this,' Bobbie said. 'If this robbery was planned in advance, how did the thieves know a group of young lads would be inside the botanic gardens?'

Charlie shook his head and scowled. 'The trespassin' happens most nights. The wall on Marygate is fallin' down. The young scamps just climb over it and mess about in the gardens. The lads in there had nothing to do with the robbery.'

'They could be valuable witnesses,' Jemma said thoughtfully.

'Are most of the museum staff aware of this crumbling wall?' Bobbie asked.

'Aye, the Philosophical Society says they've not got the money to repair it.'

'So, the two men who attacked you just used these trespassing youngsters as an excuse to get you to go down there with your keys because they wanted to rob the Hospitium?'

Charlie nodded. 'But it were three men.'

Jemma stiffened. 'Three?'

'Aye, I forgot about the chap who telephoned here.'

'I thought he was one of the imposters who met you at the gate.'

'No, he were different. Them two that coshed me were rough beggars. They spoke rough. But the chap who telephoned me here were posh. Educated – wi' a posh accent. I reckon he were the brains behind the outfit.'

'But the police and the newspapers have only ever talked about the *two* men they were looking for.'

'That's because I've only just worked it out.' Charlie gave them a small smile, revealing his crooked and yellowing teeth. 'My memory's been a bit funny since the attack.'

'He had a nasty bang on the head,' Maud chipped in from her seat at the back of the room. 'He were out like a stone for two days. We phoned the station and left a message for Sergeant Fawcett. But he ain't got back in touch with us.'

Charlie sat up straighter and scowled. 'The police ain't bothered. They've got the stolen goods back and don't give a damn about what happened to me.' He jabbed a gnarled and indignant finger at the

169

bandage on his head. 'You mark my words, lass, they're not interested in findin' out who did this.'

'That's distressing to hear,' Jemma said.

'Aye, well, mek sure you tell your brother. Fawcett needs a kick up the backside as far as I'm concerned.'

Jemma shuffled uncomfortably and decided it was time to go. She'd no love for D.S. Fawcett and everything she'd heard about the police today suggested the man was either bone idle or downright incompetent. She rose to her feet and Bobbie did likewise. 'Thank you so much for your help, Mr Dunn. This is interesting new evidence. Very helpful. I'll be sure to tell Gabriel.'

'It's no trouble, lass.' Charlie sighed and gave a mournful glance at the radio. 'We needed the distraction anyway – especially after the news.'

'What news?' Bobbie asked.

'Haven't you heard?' Maud asked. 'The King of the Belgians has surrendered. That's another ally gone.'

Bobbie staggered slightly. Jemma reached out to support her.

'Are you all right, lass?' Charlie asked.

Bobbie sank back down on to the battered old sofa. She'd turned pale. 'I need to sit.'

Jemma reached out for her hand. 'It's Frank, isn't it?'

'You need a cup of tea, lass,' Maud said. 'I'll fetch you one.' She hurried out of the room.

Charlie sucked on his pipe and watched Bobbie through a haze of blue tobacco smoke. 'Have you got someone out there?'

'My brother, Frank. He's—' Bobbie's voice broke, then she straightened herself up. 'He's in the Green Howards.'

And she's got her old flame Vince to worry about, too, Jemma thought. Vince was stationed on the south coast with the Royal Engineers, only thirty miles across the sea from the rampaging Nazis.

'Green Howards, eh?' Charlie said. 'Same as our two lads.'

Jemma winced. No wonder Maud Dunn had been crying. *And what about Maisie's son, Harry?* He was trapped out there with the Yorkshire Light Infantry. This was the last thing her sister-in-law needed after Tom's accident. 'What does it mean, exactly? This Belgian surrender.'

Charlie regarded her calmly, but his voice was strained when he spoke. 'It means that now the Krauts have smashed both the Dutch and the Belgians, there's only us and the French left to fight – and God only knows how long the French will last. Meanwhile, there's over one hundred thousand of our boys – my boys – and her brother – trapped over there with their backs to the sea. God only knows how they'll get the poor sods home.'

A scalding hot cup of tea put the colour back in Bobbie's cheeks. But when they finally took their leave, she leant against the house wall and breathed deeply. 'Don't worry,' she said, 'I'm just enjoying the fresh air after the tobacco smoke.'

Jemma wasn't convinced. 'You should take the rest of the day off. Go home to your parents and spend some time with them. They must be worried sick too.'

Bobbie shook her head. 'No, they've got each other. I need to work to keep my mind off it. Besides which, they still think I'm waitressing, and restaurant staff can't just go home because they've had a bit of a shock.'

Jemma was surprised. 'Haven't told your parents about Smoke & Cracked Mirrors yet?'

Bobbie shook her head.

'Why not?'

'Because they've got a nasty habit of wrecking my life. The less they know, the better. I lost my job at the library and my fellah when my dad disgraced himself and got banged up in prison.'

'You can't keep blaming him for that,' Jemma said gently.

'Can't I?'

Jemma tugged on the sleeve of Bobbie's smart and fashionable new coat. 'But what about the money? You earn far more now. You've had a telephone installed in your home. How do you explain this – and your new clothes – to your parents?'

Bobbie shrugged. 'I just told Mum I'd had a promotion to restaurant manager. It explains the long hours we work. Mum accepted it – and the extra board I give her – without comment.'

'You're a crazy woman – but a kind one.'

Bobbie grinned. 'No, *they're* the crazies. Anyway, where to now? Shall we pay Lance Richards's landlady a visit, and his ex-wife?'

Jemma glanced at her watch. 'You'll have to go without me – but come back with me to Grape Lane and get the car. I want to check in at the office and I must go to the hospital to see Tom. I'll use the bus.'

She fished the car keys out of her bag and handed them to a delighted Bobbie. Driving Jemma's car was still a novelty for Bobbie; she never had to ask her twice to go somewhere in the car.

'It was an odd thing Mr Dunn just told us about the third man, wasn't it?' Bobbie said, as they set off back to the office. 'That's an extra bit of evidence against Ben Alcott. He's educated and speaks posh.'

'So does Mr Collinge – and no doubt Lance Richards had an educated accent.'

'Lance Richards? But he's dead!'

'True, but he was alive at the time of the break-in at the Hospitium. He had money troubles, which is always a good motive for robbery – and he might have known his mate Ben had left his camping gear in the Hospitium.'

'Blimey! Do you think his fellow thieves turned on him when the newspapers reported they'd stolen a load of worthless items?'

'Maybe. They might not have believed him – there's no honour among thieves.'

'We need to know more about the people Lance Richards mixed with,' Bobbie said thoughtfully.

Chapter Twenty-One

There was no sign of Emmett when Jemma walked back into the office but there were plenty of signs that he'd been there. The air was thick with cigarette smoke and an overflowing ashtray now littered her desk, along with several used cups and dirty plates. The tiny kitchen was in an even worse state, with dirty cutlery, bits of food and crumbs scattered everywhere. Grumbling, she rolled up her sleeves and cleaned up.

Emmett's absence was a mystery and added to her sense of frustration. According to her schedule, Emmett was supposed to stay here until five o'clock before taking some time off and relieving Ricky outside Jodie's hotel in the early hours of the morning.

But when she picked up the last dirty dinner plate from her desk, she found a scrawled note beneath it.

Hannah came. She got the job. Starts tomorrow. She nicked this while they showed her round. Remind me to keep my hand on my wallet while she's in the room. Emmett.

Below his note was a dog-eared floor plan of the luxury suites at the Royal Station Hotel with the fire exits marked. In one of the suites, room 504, Hannah had printed: *Jodie.*

Jemma's sharp eyes spotted something immediately – a connecting door from room 504 to room 505 next door. *Who?* she wondered.

But Hannah was one step ahead of her. In the space on the map for room 505, she'd printed: *Max Glazer.*

Jemma chewed her lip as she tried to work out the significance of this. When she arrived at the hotel, Jodie had requested a change of room – and been given an adjoining suite with a connecting door to the American impresario who'd managed her career in the United States. Did she deliberately ask for this suite because she wanted easy access to Max Glazer? Was Glazer her mysterious lover?

No doubt the two of them needed some privacy to talk business – but they didn't need adjoining suites to get privacy.

Jemma decided to think it over. Despite the glaring evidence laid out before her, she didn't think Jodie was this stupid and careless.

There was a small, badly written notice in the corner of the window of Lance Richards's boarding house that read: *No Blacks, Latins, Slavs or Jews, By order of Mrs Daisy Rainbow, proprietor.* Bobbie's lips tightened with disgust when she knocked on the door.

Mrs Daisy Rainbow was nowhere near as cheerful and colourful as her name. Thin and angular, she wore a greying rayon blouse and a scowl that would have turned milk sour. She sniffed suspiciously down her long nose when Bobbie explained her business.

'I've already told the coppers everythin' I know! Have you any idea how upsettin' this is for a poor widow lady? And how damagin' this murder is to my business? How will I rent Mr Richards's room out again now he's been murdered? Who'll want it? All I'm tryin' to do is earn a crust!'

Bobbie pulled a ten-shilling note out of her purse, held it out to the woman and watched the avaricious gleam brighten her dull eyes. 'I'm so sorry for your loss, Mrs Rainbow. I understand how difficult it must be for you. I've been authorised to pay for information about poor Mr Richards. Will this help?'

The woman sniffed again, snatched the note out of her hand and stuffed it into her skirt pocket. 'You'd better come in.'

She led the way through a dank hallway that stank of cat urine into her own private sitting room. It was stuffed with mismatched, uncomfortable furniture and hadn't seen a decorator since the 1920s. The soft furnishings were the same shade of grey and grubby pink – with a bit of clashing purple and orange thrown into the mix for good measure.

Suddenly, a large orange fur cushion transformed itself into a hissing ginger cat. It leapt up from the couch, took a swipe at Bobbie's stockinged leg and ran out of the room.

'Ouch!' Bobbie rubbed her leg and glared at the run in her stocking.

The landlady waved Bobbie towards the lumpy sofa vacated by the cat. 'Don't mind him. He don't like strangers.'

Bobbie sat down and pulled out her notebook. She asked Mrs Rainbow about the last time she'd seen Lance Richards.

'It were the night he were killed.' The woman puffed out her flat chest proudly. 'The police said I were the last person to see him alive apart from his murderer. He were just leavin'. I caught him in the hallway when he were tryin' to sneak out the door.'

Bobbie frowned. 'Sneak out? Why?'

'It were the rent – he were three weeks behind wi' it again.'

'That must be upsetting for you.'

'Damn right, lass. Who's gonna pay me the brass I'm owed now he's dead?' She eyed Bobbie's handbag and purse hopefully.

'What kind of mood was he in when he left?'

'He were bouncin' as usual,' the woman replied. 'Full of charm, big smiles and promises about gettin' me the brass he owed. When I asked him fer the rent and he just winked and said he'd get it fer me next week. Said he were expectin' a big windfall. That he were about to come into a lot of brass.'

'Did he mention where this money was coming from?'

'Naw, I just thought he planned to sponge it off his wife.'

'Did he tell you where he was going?'

'He didn't say owt about that, but he had his camping gear wi' him. A big bag and a rope coiled over his shoulder.'

'A rope?'

'The one he used fer rock climbin'. I thought he were off wi' his pal, Ben, fer another of their campin' and rock climbin' weekends.'

'But it was only Wednesday.'

The landlady shrugged. 'I'd forgotten the day.'

Bobbie chewed her pen thoughtfully. There'd been no mention of a rope and a large bag at the inquest and D.S. Fawcett hadn't shared this information with Mr Pearson. The police had not found these items with the dying man. So where were they? And who was Richards going to meet? Ben Alcott claimed he hadn't seen him for nearly a fortnight.

'Who were his other friends besides Mr Alcott?'

The landlady shrugged. 'It ain't my job to keep track of my lodgers.'

'Did he have a favourite pub?'

'Not that I know.'

'Did he ever bring friends back here? What about women?'

Mrs Rainbow scowled. "'Ere! What are yer suggestin'? I run a *respectable* house, I do – and I knew he were still married.'

'Can I search his room, please?'

The landlady's scowl deepened. 'The police already have.'

Bobbie reached for her purse again and handed over another ten shillings.

Grunting with satisfaction, the woman led her up the narrow staircase with a worn and threadbare carpet whose original colour had been lost beneath the filth.

Lance Richards's room was cold, dreary and stank of mould. The faded wallpaper was peeling away from the walls and there was a nasty damp patch beneath the grimy window. The bed, with its greying sheets and threadbare blankets, was unmade and his belongings were scattered everywhere.

'The police made a mess,' Mrs Rainbow informed her.

Bobbie picked her way over the piles of clothes and discarded shoes on the floor and sifted through a pile of papers left on the scratched surface of the dressing table. An old programme for Ripon Races, a few betting slips and a couple of pools coupons. There was nothing among them that told her anything new. Carefully, she pulled out the stiff drawers. Grimacing with distaste, she rifled through his undergarments and the other odds and ends men seem to shove in drawers.

At the bottom of his sock drawer, she found an old wallet made of cracked leather. It was empty apart from an expired membership card for York racecourse – and a membership card for the British Union of Fascists.

Bobbie's mind flashed back to Dora's comments about how Richards made Anthony uncomfortable singing the praises of the Germans and the Austrians. She set her face straight and turned back to the landlady. 'Was Lance a member of the BUF?'

The landlady broke eye contact and shrugged. 'Aye, he used to be – when it were runnin'. The government have banned it now.'

'It seems such a shame to clamp down on free speech like that,' Bobbie said slowly. 'The BUF are true patriots – they're the only ones who've told the truth about this unnecessary war since the start.'

The woman's eyes glittered with interest. 'Bit of a convert yourself, are you?'

'Absolutely. I've a brother out in France with the BEF. He's risking life and limb. But for what? For Poland? What does Poland matter to good honest English men and women? He's being used as cannon fodder in a war that should never have happened.'

Mrs Rainbow chuckled. 'I see yer not afraid to speak out.'

Bobbie nodded. 'My dad lost his job recently – to a Slav. How is that fair? And where's it going to end? This country is being overrun with refugees from Europe – Gillygate will be taken over by the Jews next.'

Mrs Rainbow nodded. 'Yer right there. Filthy scum, those refugees. They shouldn't let 'em in. You should come along to the meeting tonight. You'd fit right in.'

'Does the BUF still meet in York?'

'Aye – but it's had to change its name. There aren't many of us left. A lot of folks are too scared to come because of the commies – and the free day trips have stopped. Shame that. I enjoyed them free trips to

Scarborough. It's called the Tuesday Club and it meets at seven. There's a meetin' tonight.'

Bobbie hesitated for a fraction of a second, knowing this would make her late to meet Jemma. But this was an ideal opportunity to learn more about the kind of people Lance Richards mingled with. 'I'd like to go.'

Mrs Rainbow nodded. 'They hire a back room in The Dog and Duck near the castle. They're a decent bunch of folks. But keep the details to yerself, like. There's a lot of them commie agitators about. We're a peaceful bunch and don't like trouble.'

Tell that to the Jews on Cable Street, Bobbie thought.

'I'll be there.' She replaced the card in the old wallet, put it back in the drawer and forced a friendly smile on to her face. 'I'd better leave you in peace now, Mrs Rainbow. Thank you for your help.'

Bobbie felt like she needed a good wash once she left Mrs Daisy Rainbow's boarding house – and it wasn't just the dirt and grime of the place that made her feel like this.

She wasn't sure what she'd stumbled across – or how it fitted in with Richards's murder – but every instinct told her this was a major discovery. Violence and the BUF went hand in hand.

She glanced at her watch. She just had enough time to dash out to Heslington to see the dead man's widow, the woman with the cast-iron alibi. But she'd telephone Jemma first, to let her know she'd be late at tonight's meeting at the museum.

As she climbed into the car, she rolled her eyes as she thought of the evening ahead. A lecture with a load of dusty old fossils discussing pond life, preceded by an uncomfortable hour spent with the bottomscaping pond life of the local fascists. This wasn't how twenty-three-year-olds met decent blokes.

'You need to get yourself a better social life, girl,' she muttered as she switched on the ignition.

Chapter Twenty-Two

Ida Richards lived with her elderly father in a large detached Victorian villa. Brown-brick, with an elaborate wrought-iron porch sheltering the entrance, it was set back from the road behind a long garden full of mature shrubs. As Bobbie wound her way along the path beside the beautifully manicured lawn, she compared Richards's damp and dirty lodgings with this pleasant house in the leafy suburbs.

A maid led her inside a spacious drawing room, whose floor-to-ceiling French windows were flung open to the sun-kissed garden. She waited nervously, unsure whether the widow would want to talk to her.

But she was in for a pleasant surprise.

Mrs Richards greeted her with a smile. 'I know Mr Thomas Pearson. His legal practice has done a lot of work for me in the past. How can I help you?' She'd changed out of the sombre black clothes she'd worn for the inquest into a pair of old slacks and a jumper and there was some colour in her cheeks.

Bobbie sat down, relaxed, and pulled out her notebook. The maid went to fetch refreshments and cheerful birdsong drifted into the room through the open doors, along with the scent of honeysuckle. What she'd imagined would be the most awkward interview of the day was turning out to be the most comfortable. 'This morning's inquest must have been difficult for you,' she said.

Ida grimaced. 'It was awful listening to the doctor describe Lance's injuries. Please understand, Miss Brown, that although Lance and I had separated, I wouldn't have wished a death like that on my worst enemy – never mind my husband of twenty years.'

'Which is why it's so important we leave no stone unturned and find out what happened to him,' Bobbie said.

'The police seem pretty convinced it's Anthony Gill.'

Bobbie nodded. 'Yes, they do. He had a bad argument with Mr Richards and threatened him. But apart from Anthony Gill, can you think of anyone else who might have wanted to kill him?'

Ida shook her head. 'Lance upset a lot of people, but I can't think of *anyone* he's wronged *that* badly. Not someone who would resort to murder. But we separated six months ago, and I don't know what he's been up to.'

The maid arrived with a tray and while she poured the tea, Bobbie took the opportunity to examine Ida more closely. The woman's soft brown curly hair was dyed at the temples to cover the grey, but she'd retained her youthful complexion and had excellent skin. Her wide-set features suggested she must have been a beautiful woman in her youth. Bobbie estimated she was a good ten or twelve years younger than her deceased husband.

'I understand the police have already interviewed you.'

Ida nodded. 'Yes, they weren't here long. They just wanted to know where my father and I were during the night Lance was attacked. We were at home playing bridge with our neighbours.' She glanced up at the maid and smiled. 'Alice confirmed that neither of us left this house after the Broughtons went home.'

Bobbie smiled as she sipped her tea. Even Lord Peter Wimsey would have trouble breaking that alibi. The maid left and Bobbie asked, 'Who were Lance's friends outside of work?'

'Well, there's Ben Alcott, of course. We met Ben and his wife, Ursula, on an archaeological dig out in Salzburg. The men became friends immediately, but I never cared for Ursula. They enjoyed hiking and mountain climbing together.'

'What about his other hobbies, Mrs Richards? Was Lance a member of any groups or social clubs?'

'He had a few casual acquaintances with whom he went to the races here in York and in Ripon, but I can't remember their names.'

'And his political affiliations? Was he a member of any political party?'

Ida shrugged. 'He flirted with Oswald Mosley's party for a while when he returned from Austria. Politics bore me, Miss Baker. I came across too much of it when I lived on the Continent, and although there are some lovely Germans in the world, I found the intensity – and can I say arrogance? – of their ruling elite scary and quite unfathomable. I never understood how people can hate strangers so much. Why people can't just live and let live with their neighbours?'

'I agree. Was Mr Richards sympathetic to the Nazis and their brand of fascism?'

Ida shrugged again. 'He was when we lived among them.'

'The separation must have been difficult for you – it can't be easy to end a marriage.'

'Yes, it was. But I'd reached the end of my tether.'

Bobbie remained silent for a moment, hoping Ida would elaborate. When she didn't, Bobbie changed tack. 'When did you last see Mr Richards?'

'About five weeks ago, when he came here pestering me for money.'

'I understand he was always short of money. I met his landlady this afternoon and she said as much.'

Ida grimaced again. 'Mrs Rainbow is a dreadful woman – but she's quite right. Lance was hopeless with money. Apart from the lure of the racecourses and the dog tracks, he was full of dreadful get-rich-quick money-making schemes that never came to fruition.'

'That must have been difficult for you.'

Ida sighed. 'I know we're not supposed to speak ill of the dead, but Lance was lazy. He wanted to be rich – but wasn't prepared to work for it. It took me a long time to realise what kind of man he was.'

'It's hard when you love someone.'

Ida gave her a curious glance. 'You sound like you're talking from experience, Miss Baker.'

Bobbie swallowed hard and nodded. 'Yes, I've been disappointed by a man who didn't turn out to be what I expected. He's married to someone else now.'

Ida leant forward and patted her hand compassionately. 'I know it's hard – but you're probably better off without him, my dear. It's better to have found out the truth early about his true nature and saved yourself a lifetime of disappointment.'

Bobbie drew back, slightly confused. She'd never thought about Vince like this. 'What was Mr Richards like when you were young?'

Ida smiled. 'Oh, Lance was a real charmer. He was older than me and very debonair. He swept me off my feet with flattery and breathtaking promises and whisked me around the Continent.' Her eyes misted with sadness as she reminisced. 'He worked on archaeological digs in Egypt,

Rome and Mesopotamia. We mixed with some amazing people, had a glittering lifestyle and a cosmopolitan circle of friends.'

'What went wrong?'

Ida sighed. 'His employment never seemed to last long. He made a lot of mistakes through carelessness – and fell out with co-workers. The constant shifting from one place to another became wearisome and he became difficult to live with and cynical. He rubbed everyone up the wrong way.'

Bobbie nodded sympathetically.

'He used to take out his resentment and disappointment on me. It was never *his* fault. And then—' Ida's voice broke, and Bobbie watched her struggle with her next words.

'And then I found out about his first affair.'

'I'm so sorry.'

'I was devastated but he promised never to do it again, so I forgave him. We moved to Cairo, leaving his mistress behind.'

'But he had another affair?'

'Of course he did.' Ida looked down at the wedding ring she still wore on her left hand and twisted it sadly. 'A leopard doesn't change its spots, my dear. It made me ill, very ill. My father persuaded me to come back to York and he bought me the house on Tadcaster Road.' Her cheeks flushed with embarrassment when she added, 'We didn't have any money of our own. Lance had frittered it away.'

'But you took him back once more?'

'Yes, it wasn't long before he lost his job in Cairo and came back to York with his tail between his legs.' She fell silent.

'Was this when Mr Richards found employment at the Yorkshire Museum?'

'Yes. His pal Ben helped him get the job.'

'Do you know why Mr Richards left and moved to the Castle Museum? I can't seem to get a straight answer from anyone about this.'

'But of course I know what happened! That was the final straw for my marriage.' She leant forward, frowning. 'But you must be discreet with this information, Miss Baker. A woman's reputation depends on it.'

'I will,' Bobbie lied. She'd no intention of keeping quiet about anything if it had a bearing on her investigation.

'I can trust you, can't I?'

'Of course.'

'Lance sexually assaulted the female curator there, Miss Mary Kitson Clark. He cornered her when they were alone in the Hospitium.'

'What?' Outside, the sun had gone behind a cloud and, along with the shadow, a slight chill seemed to fill the room. 'Did he rape her?'

'It wasn't quite rape – but it was close enough. She managed to escape.'

'Did she go to the police?'

'Good heavens! No! She didn't want anyone else – especially her fiancé – to know anything about it. He's one of the Duggens. Part of the big land-owning family out at Thirsk. The poor girl's afraid he'd call off the nuptials if he found out she'd been manhandled by Lance. But she did come round to my house to tell me about it. She felt I ought to know what my husband was capable of. It was the final straw. I threw him out.'

'Do the museum staff know about this?'

'Mr Collinge does. Mary confided in him, and he took her side. Lance was persuaded to leave and take up the vacant position at the Castle Museum.'

'So, the staff at the Yorkshire Museum closed ranks to protect Mary's reputation,' Bobbie said thoughtfully. 'But what about Violet Rodgers at the Castle Museum? She's a single woman too – and just as vulnerable as Mary Kitson Clark. Does she know the truth?'

'I'm afraid you'll have to ask her,' Ida said. 'I've no idea.'

'Don't worry, I will.' Bobbie suddenly felt very protective of Violet Rodgers and irritated with the staff at the Yorkshire Museum. 'Did you tell the police any of this?'

Ida shrugged. 'They never asked.'

Chapter Twenty-Three

There were only a few minutes left of visiting time when Jemma arrived at the hospital, and she quickened her step. The bitter smell of antiseptic brought back the distress and horror of the night before. Her chest tightened with tension as she approached Tom's ward.

Maisie was already there, sitting beside the metal bed, holding his hand. She looked strained – but she was smiling.

And down in the bed, dreadfully pale and lost in his oversized regulation pyjamas, Tom was staring up at his mother.

Jemma's heart lifted with relief. 'Oh, Tom – sweetheart! You're awake!' She bent down to kiss him.

Tom smiled up weakly from his pillow.

'He came round at lunchtime,' Maisie explained. Emotion made her soft hazel eyes shine. 'He's still in a lot of discomfort but the doctors think he'll make a full recovery.'

'Oh, thank goodness! Bless you, sweetheart – we were so worried about you. How do you feel?'

Tom's voice sounded croaky. 'My head hurts – but I'm happy to see Mum.'

'We both had a little cry when he came round,' Maisie admitted.

Tom squirmed. 'Mum, *don't*.'

Jemma gave Tom a conspiratorial wink. 'You must be mistaken, Maisie. Big lads like Tom don't cry. It must have been the medicine they've given him. It made his eyes water.'

He rewarded her with another smile. 'Mum says I've to thank you for findin' me.'

'I just wish I'd got there sooner, Tom – and Mr and Mrs Wright helped too. Your friends Davy and Jim were worried sick about you.'

'He'll have a massive scar when they take the bandage off,' Maisie added. 'Quite a war wound to show the other boys.'

'Ooh, I bet Davy and Jim will be impressed,' Jemma said.

Tom smiled again.

Jemma turned to Maisie. 'Does Gabriel know Tom's back with us?'

'Yes, he was here when Tom woke up.' Maisie hesitated and then added awkwardly, 'He's started callin' Gabriel "Dad".'

Jemma squeezed her hand. They were still a new family, feeling their way around each other. 'And so he should. That's the best news I've heard all day.'

'Gabriel's gone to make enquiries,' Maisie continued, 'Tom's been able to tell us a bit about what happened. You were right, Jemma – he was attacked, by a man who'd broken into the barn.'

A bolt of icy horror shot through Jemma. She'd suspected it but was shocked to hear it confirmed.

The blood drained out of Tom's chubby and freckled cheeks. 'I don't want to talk about it, Mum!'

Maisie leant forward and gently stroked his face. 'It's all right. You're safe now, darlin'.'

Jemma forced herself to smile. 'Don't you worry about a thing, Tom. Your dad will soon catch the man who did this. He always gets his man.'

Jemma tried to imagine the rush of pride and emotion her brother would have felt when he heard Tom call him 'Dad' for the first time.

Gabriel would be tearing York apart, looking for the man who'd hurt his stepson. The vicious thug didn't stand a chance.

The nursing staff bustled into the ward in their starched aprons and caps and announced visiting time was over.

Tom became distressed, which triggered off a flood of tears in Maisie. Jemma said her goodbyes and walked out into the corridor to let Maisie take her leave of her son.

When Maisie appeared, Jemma put her arms round her and gave her a hug. 'It must be so hard for you.'

'I'm better now than I was last night when you called.' Maisie dabbed at her eyes with her hankie, and they set off for the exit. 'I'm just so glad he's all right. The nurses said he had a terrible night. He kept driftin' in and out of consciousness and screamin'.'

'Screaming?'

'I don't know what that bloke did to him, but he's terrified.'

'Has he been able to describe him?' Maisie shook her head. Her expression was grim. 'No. Accordin' to Tom, the barn door was already forced when he got there. He didn't see the bloke at first, he was hidin' in the shadows. Then he appeared out of nowhere, started yellin' at Tom and hit him with a piece of scrap metal.'

Jemma's hand flew to her mouth in horror. 'But why? Why attack a child?'

'I don't know.' Maisie's eyes flashed with anger. 'But I tell you this, Jemma. Once Gabriel tracks down this bastard, he'll have a lot more to worry about than the police when I get my hands on him.'

Gabriel was at home when they arrived back at the cottage. He was standing in the kitchen in his uniform, plating up three portions of fish and chips. 'This seemed like a good idea, today.'

Maisie flew into his arms and Jemma backed out of the kitchen and went up to her room for a while to give them a few minutes alone. When she returned, they were sitting at the kitchen table, shaking vinegar over their chips.

'The doctors think Tom can come home tomorrow,' Maisie said.

'He'll be better off at home with us,' Gabriel reassured her. 'He'll recover quicker.'

'I'm going out with Bobbie later,' Jemma said, hoping the prospect of some time alone would please them.

'Are you stalking someone?' Gabriel asked.

'No, we're going to the Yorkshire Museum to hear a talk from the Philosophical Society about pond life. It's Bobbie's idea.'

Gabriel choked on a chip. Once he'd recovered, he said, 'So that's where you're going. She telephoned earlier to say she might be late – something important has cropped up.'

Jemma nodded and wondered what it was.

'By the way,' Gabriel continued, 'I'm sorry I shouted at you this morning. I was just—'

She held up her hand to stop him. 'You don't need to apologise. I'd have done the same if it was my son.'

'What happened at the barn this afternoon?' Maisie asked. 'Did you find anything?'

Gabriel frowned and shook his head. 'I got a team of officers together – but we didn't find anything that looked like the weapon. There's so much junk in there. There were bloodstains where Tom fell, but there's no obvious sign of the weapon used to attack him. It would help if he could remember what it looked like.'

'Has the attack affected Tom's memory?' Jemma asked.

'Yes,' Maisie replied. 'But he did notice the man wasn't wearin' gloves.'

'If we can track down the weapon, we can get fingerprints.' Gabriel turned to Maisie. 'We've started house-to-house inquiries in the area. Thanks to the Wright family, half of Clifton already know a child has been attacked. The local community are being very helpful.'

'That's wonderful.'

He took her hand in his. 'York Police are stretched because of this museum murder investigation, but when I was down at the station, several of the lads volunteered to help out in their spare time.'

Maisie's eyes filled up with tears. 'People are so *kind.*'

'We'll catch this bastard, Maisie. I promise you.'

Maisie gave him a watery smile. 'I'm so sorry, Gabriel. This is our honeymoon week. You shouldn't have had to set foot in Clifford Street, never mind start an investigation into who attacked my son.'

'*Our* son,' Gabriel reminded her.

Jemma waited until some of their emotion had subsided before asking, 'While you were at the station, did you find out how this murder investigation is progressing?'

Gabriel nodded as he speared a chip. 'D.S. Fawcett is doing a good job. This is confidential, of course, Jemma – but he's uncovered evidence that suggests our main suspect was being blackmailed by the victim.'

'That's a strong motive for murder.'

'He's also following up reported sightings of the suspect's car on the Driffield Road.'

'Doesn't he have an alibi?' Jemma asked innocently.

'No. He claims he was at home that night, but a neighbour saw him drive away about nine o'clock and he has a distinctive Bentley. A couple of farmers – one at Stamford Bridge and another at Garrowby – claim they saw the Bentley drive past just before it got dark. Fawcett led a team up there this afternoon to question the people on the outlying farms to see if anyone else saw anything suspicious. But so far he's drawn a blank.'

'It's a remote area,' Jemma said, making a mental note to tell Bobbie about this. 'Does D.S. Fawcett think this is where he attacked Mr Richards? I'd heard a rumour the body was moved and just dumped in an alleyway.'

Gabriel shrugged. 'Yes, it was moved. But Fawcett doesn't know where the attack took place. He's been through the suspect's car with a fine-tooth comb but it's scrupulously clean, without even a speck of dandruff.' He paused to take another mouthful of food. 'In fact, it's suspiciously clean – as if it has been scrubbed to within an inch of its life. What bloke cleans his car like that?'

Jemma hid her smile. The police obviously didn't understand Anthony Gill's obsession with cleanliness and order.

'The suspect remains uncooperative and has been lying through his teeth to the police since he was arrested.'

'What about the murder weapon?' Jemma asked.

Maisie dropped her cutlery on to the table with a clatter. Tears were coursing down her face again. 'Gabriel, Jemma... I'm so sorry. I know this is normal for you two – but not *tonight*, please. Not while Tom...'

Gabriel was out of his seat in a second and had his arms round his wife.

Muttering an apology, Jemma guiltily pushed back her chair, gathered up her plate and took it to the sink. She kicked herself for her insensitivity. Brought up by their police sergeant father, discussing bloody murder at the supper table was second nature to the Roxbys. But Maisie had been a Roxby for less than a week and discussing Lance Richards, who'd died from a head injury like the one Tom had suffered, was too close to home. But for the grace of God, Tom might also have died.

After she'd rinsed off her plate and cutlery, she gathered up her handbag and left for the Yorkshire Museum.

Chapter Twenty-Four

Bobbie dashed home, unrolled her thick hair and plaited it. She put on her shabbiest coat and slipped a pair of fake spectacles into her handbag. On her way out of the house she stole her mother's old-fashioned funeral hat with its little veil from the hat stand. She wanted to make it as hard as possible for anyone she knew to recognise her. Attending a BUF meeting was not something to be proud of.

The Dog and Duck was a dilapidated old pub in a grimy back street in the shadow of the castle. The terraced houses were nearly all boarded up, a sure sign the street had been earmarked for demolition. She winced at the handwritten notice stuck in the corner of the window next to the entrance: *It's the policy of this pub not to allow Jewish customers.*

The inside of the pub was as gloomy and grimy as its exterior and she was glad when the barman directed her to the meeting room at the back of the building. But her relief was short-lived. She had to go back outside and down a dank narrow passageway that took her past the foul-smelling outside lavatories.

A brawny doorman stood outside the dilapidated meeting house in the back yard. He listened impassively to her explanation that she was meeting Mrs Daisy Rainbow. Through the open door behind she saw a dirty room with flaking plaster walls stained brown by decades of tobacco smoke. A small stage stood at one end, with a podium.

The doorman beckoned over a scrawny young man in an ill-fitting suit. He had the worst case of acne Bobbie had ever seen and lank hair slicked back with so much oil it looked soaking wet. He was about her own age, and she wondered how he had managed to avoid conscription.

He gave her a beaming smile that did nothing to improve his appearance and told her that new members were always welcome. 'The name's Ronald, by the way,' he said as they shook hands. 'Any pal of Daisy's is a mate of ours.'

'I'm Bobbie. Thank you. Where shall I sit?'

'With me, of course!' He pointed to a row of chairs. 'Daisy sometimes don't make the meetin's, so I'll look after yer and show you the ropes, so to speak.'

Bobbie nodded her thanks. They shuffled along to the seats he'd indicated in the centre of the row. *Is this what happens in this clandestine organisation?* she wondered. *Do they provide new members with a 'minder' who watches them until they can be trusted?*

'Yer in fer a real treat tonight, Bobbie,' he said once they'd sat down. She winced at the sour, ferrous smell emanating from his oily hair and his clothes. *Was there a hint of stale blood?* A quick glance at the reddish-black dirt beneath his fingernails confirmed her suspicion. He worked either in a morgue, a butcher's or at the local slaughterhouse. 'We've got a great speaker – one of the best. No one speaks the truth betterer than him.'

'Who is he? Where's he from?'

'Now, now, Bobbie,' he said, laughing, 'yer know we don't use our real names or mention our jobs since the government banned us.'

'So how do I know you're a butcher's boy from that shop on Coney Street?' she said with an innocent smile.

His eyes widened in surprise. 'Who told yer that? And they're wrong anyway – it's on Nunnery Lane. Who told yer?'

'It might have been Mrs Rainbow—'

He nodded with relief.

'Or possibly Lance Richards, her poor lodger,' she added, hoping he might know the name.

But he wasn't listening. 'I bet *Bobbie* ain't *your* real name?'

'No, it isn't,' she said with another smile.

He patted her hand in delight and looked chuffed with himself. 'I thought not! It's a lad's name. You're far too pretty to be a bloke!'

'You're too kind. So, what about this speaker?'

'He just calls hisself the General. As you know all about me, Bobbie, you'd better tell me about yersen, to make it fair. Are yer married?'

Bobbie hesitated a moment, unsure how to proceed in this bizarre situation. 'Yes. I'm married to the strongman at Corrigan's Circus. I'm a trapeze artist – but only on Tuesdays and Saturdays. On the other days I tame the lions.'

He howled with laughter, leant towards her and squeezed her thigh suggestively. 'We'll get to know each other proper, once the meetin' is over,' he promised. 'I can see yer quite a laugh, Bobbie.'

Fortunately for Ronald, he removed his hand before she slapped him. And she was spared the necessity of replying because they had to stand up to let an elderly couple squeeze past to the seats adjoining theirs. There were now about seventy people in the room. Bobbie was saddened to see so many fascists in York – and felt even glummer when she remembered Daisy had mentioned that most people stayed away these days. *Just how much support did this vile movement have?*

The other upsetting thing was how ordinary they all looked. Part of her had expected them to be horned, with forked tails, but they weren't. The women outnumbered the men, of course, because most of the blokes had been called up for active service, but these ordinary middle-aged men and women might have been her neighbours and the younger women may have once been her classmates.

'There's no sign of Daisy,' Ronald said, and gave her a suspicious glance.

She put on her brightest smile. 'No. Perhaps she's still upset about what happened to her lodger, Lance Richards.'

Ronald nodded, scowling. 'Aye, it were bad, that were.'

'Was he a friend of yours?' she asked sweetly.

'Aye, I knew old Lance. He came once or twice but I ain't seen him around fer a while.'

Bobbie was about to ask more questions when a greying middle-aged man (whom Bobbie thought ran a large haberdashery in the centre of York) walked over to the podium on the stage and cleared his throat to get their attention. The audience fell silent.

'Ladies and gentlemen, thank you so much for coming to our meeting tonight in this momentous week! As you know, the British army is outnumbered and surrounded and will soon be destroyed.'

Bobbie stiffened.

'While it gives none of us any pleasure to contemplate the bloody and unnecessary sacrifice of lives we'll soon witness in northern France, we must take comfort from the fact that we – we who have been vilified and imprisoned for our beliefs – will finally be justified for speaking out against a war that should never have happened.'

A murmur of approval went around the room.

'A war that should never have begun. A needless, senseless war. A war that is part of a Jewish conspiracy to dominate Europe that can be traced back to King Solomon!'

'Aye, lad. Aye,' murmured the elderly man beside Bobbie.

'But you've not come here tonight to listen to me. Let me introduce you to a man who can explain it so much better than I can – our General.'

The audience broke out into spontaneous applause and Bobbie stifled a gasp when a tall, athletic, silver-haired man in the full black shirt uniform of the BUF, complete with its banded collar and gleaming silver belt buckle, climbed confidently up the stairs on to the stage.

It was Ben Alcott, the curator from the Yorkshire Museum.

Bobbie shrank back down into her seat, grateful for her semi-disguise. His eyes scanned the audience, but they didn't linger on her.

'Good evening, fellow patriots!' Alcott began. Several in the audience greeted him back. 'And welcome – on this momentous day. The day this ridiculous war – started by our ridiculous government and promoted by the press, who are under Jewish control – finally comes to an end. How right we were to oppose it!'

The crowd cheered but Alcott held up his hand to silence them. His face turned grim and his voice bitter. 'Yet for saying this – we're called fascist sympathisers.'

The audience growled.

'Agitators!'

Another growl.

'And madmen!'

A yell of fury resounded round the room that nearly brought the crumbling plaster of the ceiling down on their heads.

Alcott held up his hand again to silence them. 'But I ask you, ladies and gentlemen, is Hitler mad?'

'No!'

'Was it a madman who restored Germany to one of the foremost nations in the world in only seven years?'

'No!'

'Is this a madman who now leads his forces across Europe, smashing everyone who opposes him?'

'No!'

'You're right, my friends! It's not Hitler who's mad – nor us! Hitler knows who the real enemy is. He knows it's the Bolsheviks and the Jews. He offered us peace – but our foolish government spurned it, using Poland as the excuse.'

'Aye, lad. That's right,' muttered Bobbie's neighbour.

'But what is Poland to us, ladies and gentlemen?'

'Nowt!' someone yelled.

'That's right, my friend, it's nothing! Nothing at all!' Alcott banged his fist on the podium in anger. 'And now *our* sons and *our* brothers are cornered—' He paused for dramatic effect before lowering his voice. 'And the only thing our pathetic government can suggest is a National Day of Prayer.'

There were jeers and growls of derision.

'I tell you what, my friends – it's too late for prayer to save their backsides!'

Another cheer.

'Meanwhile, refugees are flooding to our overcrowded country and the government is *welcoming* them. Dutch, Belgians, Latins and Slavs. And Jews. Thousands upon thousands of Jews. The streets of York will be unrecognisable soon!'

The crowd erupted with fury and Bobbie found herself transfixed by Ben Alcott, like a rodent caught in the stare of a snake. The silky tone of his educated voice dripped poison into the ears of his audience. He was mesmerising. Horrifically, dangerously mesmerising. And a quick glance along her line of seats confirmed it was the women in the crowd who cheered and jeered the loudest.

'But thankfully, my friends, the Germans will be at the gates of the city within the week!'

A huge cheer erupted, and Alcott raised his hand to silence them. 'And who will be at Bootham Bar and Skeldergate to greet them?'

'We will!' the crowd screamed.

'And then my friends, my fellow patriots, justice will be done. The Germans will soon round up this foreign scum – along with our traitorous government – and dispatch them back to the ghettos where they belong.'

A wave of nausea swelled up inside Bobbie. She gulped but the air in the room was stale and stank of body odour and tobacco – not to mention the ferrous tinge of the young man next to her.

No longer caring about anything, the murder of Lance Richards or his vile mate, Alcott, Bobbie rose to her feet and fought her way back along the tightly packed row towards the exit. Ronald called her name, but she ignored him.

She almost fell outside, but even here, with the nearby stinking privy, there was no fresh air. The doorman glared at her as she scurried back down the alleyway.

The soft rays of the late evening sunshine bathed the dilapidated street. She paused for a moment to get her breath and glanced nervously back over her shoulder. No one had followed her.

Desperate to put as much distance as possible between herself and the repugnant crowd, she hurried to the relative peace and calm of the large grassed area in front of the Castle Museum and the court building.

Whipping off the fake spectacles, she sank down on to a bench beneath one of the trees, grateful for its dappled shadow and the cheerful birds singing above her. Before her, the crenelated walls of the old Norman keep of York Castle rose into the cloudless sky.

As her breathing calmed, her shock turned to anger.

How dare they? How dare they dismiss the sacrifice made by the young men like her brother so lightly? How dare they praise that German madman? And how dare they think they were so bloody superior?

Her eyes focused on the ramparts of the castle and the irony of its proximity to that meeting of bigoted fascists hit her with a vengeance. Now her anger turned to fury.

Every school child in York – even those who loathed history lessons as much as Bobbie – knew the tragic story of York Castle.

One night back in the twelfth century, the terrified Jewish population of York sought refuge in the wooden keep to escape an angry mob. It was set alight, and they burned to death. One hundred and fifty terrified Jewish men, women and children perished in that burning building. It was the blackest hour in York's long and auspicious history. And it happened within one hundred yards of where that braying mob now cheered for the destruction of the rest of the city's Jews – and every other innocent refugee in the country.

Why were people so consumed with hate?

And what were they going to do if the Jerries did arrive? Would they help them repeat history? Would the city's Jews be herded into the castle keep? Would they stand there screaming with hate, waving their pitchforks, and set it alight?

She felt sick with disgust. They had to be stopped. *But who would stop them?*

Only the government can control extremists.

You need politics to fight politics. And politicians. They were the power. And women were politicians too; there'd been women in parliament for the past twenty years… it was somewhere she could make a difference.

For the first time in her life, Bobbie understood her father's attraction to the Labour Party.

Her father. Her loving but badly flawed father… she felt a desperate need to go home.

She found her parents hunched around the wireless set. He dad went out less and less to the pub these days. His fear for his son kept him at home listening to the news broadcasts.

'Big' Bill Baker was half the man he used to be since his shameful stint in prison last year and he seemed to have shrunk into himself. But tonight, he sat up straight, gripping the chair arms in his huge fists, and he had some colour in his sallow cheeks.

Her mother sat on the opposite side of the hearth, knitting. She smiled kindly as Bobbie entered and her face creased into dozens of lines. *She looks so old*, Bobbie thought, with a twinge of sympathy and love.

'Blimey, our Bobbie,' said her father. 'You look like you've been to a funeral.'

'Why are you wearing my hat?' asked her mother.

'I think it's pretty,' Bobbie lied. She bent down to give them both a kiss.

Her parents blinked, surprised by this unusual show of affection. 'What's got into you, lass?' her father asked. But their attention turned back to the wireless and the dull, sonorous tones of the new prime minister.

'What's happening? Any news?'

Her father was taut with excitement. 'There's been an appeal for recruits to report to the naval reserve or their nearest fisheries officer. They want engineers and second hands for motorboats and yachts.'

Bobbie frowned, sank on to the sagging sofa and removed her hat pins. 'What does this mean?'

'Boats, lass. Boats. They're goin' to send boats to get our lads back.'

Bobbie's mouth fell open in confusion. 'But how do they get troop carriers so close to the beach?'

'It's little boats. Fishing cobles. Ships like that. It's a rescue armada.'

'Fishing cobles!' *Would it work?* 'Do we have enough?'

Her father shrugged. 'I've no idea, but Mr Churchill and the admiralty are hopeful.'

'But there's hundreds of thousands of our boys over there… and they'll be strafed by the Luftwaffe…' Her voice trailed away. It was impossible. Impossible…

'It'll be a miracle.' Her mother smiled. 'A proper miracle. But God's on our side, Bobbie.'

Bobbie thought back to the braying crowd she'd just left. 'I hope so. I'd hate to think he was rooting for the enemy.'

Her mother reached over and squeezed her father's hand. 'We'll see our Frank again soon, Bill. You'll see.'

Bobbie sent up a silent prayer that her mother was right. Her father was already a broken man after his imprisonment last year. If anything happened to Frank, it would finish him off.

'Dad? What will happen if there's an invasion by the Jerries and we're overrun?'

Big Bill Baker snorted. 'It'd take them some time to subdue us. Then the likes of me would be lined up against a wall and shot.'

'Is that because you're a socialist – a member of the Labour Party?'

'Yes. There's no shades of grey with them fascist pigs. Socialists are commies in their eyes.'

'Dad, when you go to your next meeting, will you take me with you?'

'But you've no interest in politics, our Bobbie!' her mother exclaimed in surprise.

'I've changed my mind. And if you're going to be lined up and shot against a bloody wall for doing what's right, Dad – I want to be stood next to you.'

Chapter Twenty-Five

Jemma enjoyed her short walk through the botanic gardens. The path meandered in the shade beneath the boughs of several tall and exotic flowering trees. The warm evening air was heavy with the beautiful scent of blossom. Above her head, playful squirrels scampered around the branches, which were heavy with yellow tulip-shaped flowers. Occasionally, yellow petals floated down on the breeze. A steady stream of well-dressed, mostly middle-aged people were making their way along the path towards the museum's entrance.

Ricky suddenly appeared out of nowhere, grinning from ear to ear. 'Well, if it isn't my favourite lady!'

Jemma grabbed his jacket sleeve and dragged him around the thick trunk of a tree, away from curious eyes.

'Steady on, Miss Marple!' he laughed. 'I know I'm an attractive man but I'm too old to be dragged into a bush!'

'We're not supposed to be seen together, remember?' Jemma hissed. 'Why aren't you watching Jodie? It's your turn.'

'Don't worry, boss lady. Irton's coverin' for me while I do some official business for the *Evening Press*.' He tapped the Leica strung round his neck on its leather strap. 'I understand there's quite a shindig happenin' at the museum for the good and the glorious tonight. All York's toffs are attendin'.'

Jemma sighed. 'I don't know why I bothered with that schedule if you and the others intend to change it every two minutes.'

'Don't fret, Miss Marple. We've got it covered between us – and those guys are professionals. Besides which, I've got some news for you. You need to polish your dancin' shoes. The delectable Jodie is doing her bit for the war effort. She's hired De Grey's on Thursday night and will be entertainin' airmen from the local air bases – and I've got you an invitation.'

'Jodie is entertaining the troops?'

'God, no, lass. Not the troops. She's no Vera Lynn. Only the top brass are invited. Air force officers and so forth.'

Jemma smiled. 'Is Don behind this?'

'Of course. As soon as I told our friendly Canuck about our latest case – in strictest confidence – he told me to tell you that you can go along to the party as his guest. But we'll have to change your precious schedule again though,' Ricky added, his eyes wide with mock tragedy. 'There's no point in Emmett sittin' outside in a car all evenin' while you're swayin' to the beat on the dance floor only a few feet away from our actress.'

Jemma's smile broadened. 'I guess I'll just have to grin and bear another change. Thanks, Ricky.'

'Oh, and I've some other news for you too. Well, it's not news as such – just an idea. I nipped out to Jodie's new house in Bishopthorpe. You know the one I mean, the place she's bought for her family?'

Jemma nodded.

'I had a chat with some of the neighbours, who told me it's unoccupied while the builders do it up, but it's part furnished. While I were there, some bloke drove up the drive and let himself into the house with a key.'

'Was it one of the builders?'

'No. They'd already gone home. Besides which, he were in a shirt and tie. I didn't get a good look at his face – but I've jotted down his car registration number. It strikes me this place might be a sweet little love nest if our actress ever wants to escape from pryin' eyes...'

'Thanks Ricky. That's a good point.'

'Right, I'll see you later. We'd better go in separate.' Ricky strolled ahead, whistling, while Jemma followed.

It was the first time Jemma had ever been inside the Tempest Anderson Hall. The imposing lecture theatre was added to the Yorkshire Museum during the Edwardian era, and it had an opulence she didn't expect. Hundreds of plush red velvet seats were banked up away from the stage. Close to the high ceiling, a line of windows ran across the far wall. The blackout curtains were already drawn, and the hall was lit by a series of beautiful crystal chandeliers that blazed with light.

A loud buzz of polite conversation emanated from the dozens of people milling around at the front of the stage. Ricky was among them, photographing individuals and groups and scrawling their names in his notebook.

Jemma's heart lifted when she spotted her flamboyant and eccentric neighbour sitting on her own in the middle of a row. She hurried to join her. 'Hello, Fanny.'

A broad smile lit up the old lady's crinkled face as Jemma approached. Fanny had discarded the mock-mourning she'd donned for Gabriel's wedding and now wore an emerald-green turban on top of her greying head, complete with a large peacock feather. A fringed Chinese silk shawl was draped over her narrow shoulders. Beneath the vivid greens and turquoises, she wore a plain white silk blouse and beige slacks, which, for once, weren't splattered with paint.

'Jemma! How delightful to see you! I didn't know you were a member of the Philosophical Society.'

'I've just joined. Bobbie too. She may arrive later. We think we need to better ourselves.'

Fanny's grey eyes gleamed with amusement. 'Well, you've chosen a funny place to start. Tonight promises to be dreadfully dull. Are you sure you're not here in a professional capacity with your delightful little detective agency?'

Jemma laughed. 'There's no kidding you, is there, Fanny? But if it'll be so dull, why are you here?'

'Oh, I've been a lady subscriber of this society for years. My agent told me to join and mingle. One hundred and fifty of Yorkshire's wealthiest families support this society; many of them buy my paintings.'

'I'd heard it was a well-heeled crowd. So come on, tell me who's who.'

Fanny, who loved to gossip, laughed and pointed to two men at the podium in the centre of the stage.

One was hunched, heavily whiskered and bespectacled, and wore a crumpled jacket with patches on the elbows. The other was in his early forties and had slicked-back hair, a side parting and a high forehead. He wore an expensively tailored suit with a neatly folded handkerchief in his breast pocket. 'The hairy chap is Mr Charles Allen, our speaker for tonight. His companion is our president, the Earl of Feversham.'

'Blimey!' said Jemma. 'We *are* rubbing shoulders with the cream of British society. It's a pity Bobbie isn't here. It sounds like the place for her to find a rich husband.'

Fanny chuckled. 'That's been tried before – and it isn't always a successful strategy. Do you see the lovely young woman at the corner of the stage, with the heart-shaped face, the mink stole and the prominent cheekbones?'

Jemma followed her gaze to a glamorous blonde with slanting Slavic green eyes. She was laughing and flirting with a tall dark-haired man, who seemed familiar.

'That's our impoverished Hungarian countess, Anna Léna von Hatvan. She was desperate for a British husband when they started rounding up foreign nationals. It was the only way for her to stay out of an internment camp. No single man under ninety was safe.'

Jemma laughed. 'What happened? Did she find herself a rich British husband?'

Fanny pointed to a scowling young fellow on the edge of the crowd. A good ten years younger than the thirty-something countess, he looked uncomfortable and tugged at the stiff collar of his shirt in the same way Jemma's nephew had struggled with his formal clothes at the wedding. 'He's her new husband. She scooped him up from the street in the end. No one knows who he is. Desperate times lead to desperate measures.'

Jemma's attention returned to the tall dark man in his early forties who was standing with the countess. 'Isn't that Baron Stokesley?'

Fanny leant forward and examined his profile. The baron had half turned away from them. 'Why, yes, I do believe it is. The committee won't be pleased to see him here.'

215

'Why not?'

'He nominally supports the museum and the society. But he's also an avid collector of fine art and antiquities himself. Castle Stokesley is full of them. There's been a couple of times when he's abused his position within the society. After hearing on the members' grapevine about some newly discovered rare and exquisite artefacts, he's jumped in first and shamelessly outbid the museum before whisking the treasure off into his private collection.'

'Ah, that doesn't seem fair. Surely Yorkshire's priceless treasures should be available for everyone to see?'

Jemma scrutinised their debonair employer carefully. He was smiling down at the countess, but the smile didn't reach his eyes. They were smouldering with something she couldn't read. Was it irritation? Impatience? Boredom? Everything from the sharp lines of his Savile Row suit to the gold watch glinting on his wrist and his rigid square jawline suggested immense power, wealth and brutal self-control.

'And that, my dear, is Violet Rodgers – the first female curator of the Castle Museum.'

Jemma turned and watched Violet glide into the room on the arm of one of the handsomest men she had ever seen in a uniform. Her petite figure and dark colouring contrasted with his clear, fair complexion and his beautiful head of thick blond hair.

'Her fiancé is Lieutenant Władysław Włoch of the 6th Armoured Regiment of the Polish 2nd Corps,' Fanny said. 'They make a lovely couple, don't they?'

Jemma nodded. Lieutenant Włoch would give Flight Lieutenant Don Hudson a run for his money as the best-looking man in the allied forces.

'They plan to marry and return to Poland after the war,' Fanny continued.

'But what about her position at the Castle Museum?'

Fanny shrugged. 'Violet's not daft. She knows she'll be replaced with a man on twice her salary as soon as the war is over.'

'That seems so wrong.' Jemma's eyes widened with surprise when a tall, elegant and beautifully dressed and coiffured woman strolled over to join Violet and Władysław. 'Good grief, is that Mary Kitson Clark?'

It was. Mary had discarded her slacks and oversized man's shirt and now wore high heels, a chiffon cocktail dress and a smattering of diamonds at her wrist and throat. She towered over the diminutive Violet.

But behind her stood an athletic giant of a man with chestnut brown hair and bulging biceps, who towered above everyone.

'That's Ian Duggen, her fiancé,' Fanny explained. 'He's one of the Duggens from Thirsk, another one of the wealthiest families in England. He also plays rugby for England.'

Duggen had the healthy tan of a man who enjoyed outdoor sport, but a badly healed broken nose distorted the symmetry of his broad face. Jemma wondered how much extra material his tailor had had to use in his jacket to get it to stretch over his barrel of a chest.

'Don't be misled by his appearance,' Fanny continued. 'He's a pussy cat, a gentle man.'

Jemma watched the two couples and saw the friendship and affection between them. Both men were obviously devoted to their women.

She made a mental note to tell Bobbie to add both Władysław Włoch and Ian Duggen to her list of suspects. They needed to know where these men were on the night of the attack on Lance Richards. If Richards had blackmailed either of the two women, then their fiancés had ample motive to kill him. And both Władysław and Ian Duggen were powerful young men.

'And there's poor Ben Alcott, another curator at the museum,' Fanny said.

Alcott had joined Baron Stokesley and the countess. He looked flushed and was wiping the perspiration from his brow with his handkerchief. The evening was warm but Jemma sensed he'd had to hurry to get here on time. His tie wasn't properly knotted either, as if he'd dressed in a hurry. He glanced towards Jemma, said something to Baron Stokesley, and the peer's intense gaze also turned her way. They were talking about her. Her eyes met the baron's, and an involuntary shiver ran down her spine.

'Why *poor* Ben?' she asked.

'Oh, it's terribly tragic. His wife, Ursula, was interned at the start of the war.'

Jemma turned towards her in shock. 'She's German?'

'Oh, gosh, yes. And what's more, she's got familial connections with half of the Nazi High Command. She's spending the war in some dreadful camp on the Isle of Wight. Poor Ben was devastated when they took her away. Oh, look, they're about to start the lecture.'

But they never got to hear Mr Charles Allen speak. The next second, a piecing, shrieking wail rent the air that turned their blood to ice in their veins.

It was an air raid.

Everyone stood up and made their way towards the exit. The nearest shelter was next door, in the grounds of the city library.

As they reached the end of their row, Fanny turned back to Jemma and winked. 'Such a shame old Hitler's spoiling it for us. I was *so* looking forward to a night wallowing in British pond life.'

Ricky swore with irritation when the air-raid siren went off. No doubt it would be another bloody false alarm.

He was damned if he was going to spend the rest of the night in some ruddy shelter with a load of nervous toffs. Besides which, air raid or not, he was on a deadline. He had to develop these photographs for his editor – and relieve Emmett in a couple of hours.

Once he left the museum, he turned sharp right towards the Marygate exit. The night was closing in, and the botanic gardens were shrouded in the soft shadows of twilight.

'You're goin' the wrong way, mate!' someone yelled after him. 'The shelter's this way.'

He ignored the bloke and kept on walking. He wasn't the only one; ahead of him he saw a couple also making a dash for Marygate.

He'd almost caught up with them when he reached the Abbey Gatehouse. Ricky got a glimpse of the man's face when he stopped and turned towards the woman. The next second Ricky came to an abrupt halt, dodged behind the buttress of the medieval stone arch that linked the gatehouse to the church and flicked the cover off his Leica.

The man had gathered the woman into his arms for a passionate embrace.

'Ooh, you naughty, naughty boy,' Ricky muttered to himself, smiling.

The bloke turned and disappeared down the street, but the woman remained where she was. She pulled out her powder compact, checked her make-up and rearranged her love-tousled hair. Ricky had no idea who she was, but he knew she wasn't the bloke's wife.

The next second, another man ran past him. He joined the woman, and they hurried towards a parked car. Ricky whipped out his notebook, jotted down their registration number and watched them drive away.

He'd no idea what he was going to do with the photographs he'd just taken. But he knew they were dynamite. Celebrities behaving badly always sold papers. Once he'd identified the woman, one of the foreign tabloids would pay him handsomely for those shots.

'Nice one, Ricky, mate,' he said to himself. What with his commission from Jemma at Smoke & Cracked Mirrors, this had turned into a lucrative week.

And just to end a perfect evening, the damn siren stopped and the all-clear sounded.

Chapter Twenty-Six

Wednesday, 29th May 1940

A light mist descended on York just after dawn and swirled around the medieval streets, muffling the sounds of the waking city. It would clear later when the day warmed up, but just before eight o'clock, when Jemma carefully picked her way over the cobbles of Grape Lane, visibility was limited to a few feet. The lecture at the museum had been abandoned after the air-raid alarm and Jemma had walked home to Clifton with Fanny and enjoyed an early night.

Set back from the busy thoroughfare of High Petergate, Grape Lane was a little oasis of calm and Jemma was usually the first business owner to arrive. Today was no different. Every shop door she'd passed was closed and the blackout curtains and blinds were still drawn. There was no one else around.

Except there was.

As she stood beside the brass plaque inscribed with the name of her agency, her door key poised in mid-air, she heard the sound of heavy male footsteps walking towards her.

Then the hairs on the back of her neck stood up as the man suddenly stopped, hidden by the mist. An ominous silence fell on the street. Even the pigeons who nested in the eaves of the roof opposite fell quiet.

She swallowed hard. 'Hello. Is there someone there?'

A deep and menacing chuckle floated out of the mist. As her key slipped in her sweaty hand as she fumbled with the lock, it became a menacing laugh.

Jemma hurled the door open and slammed and bolted it shut behind her. She waited on the doormat, her ears straining for sounds – any sound – outside on the street. But the only thing she heard was the blood thumping in her own ears.

She took a deep breath and forced herself to calm down. This was ridiculous. *When did she become so stupid?* It was too early in the morning for drunks, but the city was swamped every day with bored and cheeky airmen from the bases. No doubt one of them had just had a laugh at her expense.

A delivery van rumbled over the cobbles. Throwing open the door, she stepped outside with her arms folded in defiance. The van disappeared into the mist, and she was left alone on the street. Completely alone.

Whoever it was had gone.

A pigeon fluttered across the road to its roost and started cooing with its mate.

Cursing herself for her stupidity, Jemma went back inside and picked up the post from the doormat.

There were two letters. One of them was a large brown envelope with no stamp and her name written in Ricky's untidy scrawl. The other was postmarked *Kent* and addressed to Bobbie. *Vince Quigley.*

Jemma tutted and rolled her eyes as she climbed the stairs to the office. Grabbing her drawing pins, she unpacked the photographs Ricky had provided and went to her noticeboard.

Ricky had taken photographs of Jodie's maid, her secretary and her agent and scribbled their names on the back. But the one he'd taken of the chauffeur – Toby Hainsworth – was useless. Hainsworth was still wearing his sunglasses and his face was obscured. She made a mental note to tell Ricky to try again.

The photograph of the mysterious visitor to Jodie's new family home was the most intriguing. His face was partially hidden, but he was obviously young, probably about Jodie's age, and smartly dressed. Ricky had written his car registration number on the back. She pinned the photo to the board, wrote out the number on a label and pinned it next to him.

Jemma's heart skipped a beat as footsteps hurried up the stairs towards the office, but it was only Bobbie. She burst into the room with her usual early-morning brightness and enthusiasm and headed for the kettle in the kitchenette. 'How's Tom?'

'Much better. He's awake and coming home today. The hospital phoned Maisie and Gabriel last night to tell them they'd release him today.'

There was a rattle of crockery from the kitchen. 'That's great news!'

'The nurse also said Tom had remembered something. The bloke was holding a broken metal statue of a woman when Tom first saw him. Tom turned to run and the man hit him from behind.'

Bobbie winced. 'The poor little mite.'

'Apparently, it was a statue of an ugly woman with wings and no feet.'

'Good. If it's hideous, it should be easy to find.'

'Gabriel's going back to the barn today to see if it's still there. He hopes there'll be fingerprints.'

'Let's hope so. They need to catch the bastard.'

'By the way, Gabriel said attempts by the police to trace the movements of Anthony's car have failed so far, but it was seen driving along the Driffield Road on the night of the murder, around Stamford Bridge and Garrowby.'

'Garrowby? That's the back of beyond. What the hell was Anthony doing up there?'

'I think you should take a drive up there yourself, Bobbie. Go about nine – the same time Anthony took his mysterious little jaunt.'

'I will. Does Gabriel know we're investigating this case?'

Jemma shook her head. 'There hasn't been time to tell him. He and Maisie are distracted with Tom.'

'I think you should mention it to him soon, Jemma. This is the first time one of our investigations has coincided with a police inquiry. He'll want to know in case there's a conflict of interest.'

Jemma shuffled uncomfortably and changed the subject. 'So, what kept you away from the pond life last night?'

Bobbie reappeared with the teapot and cups on the tray. The two women sat down in the armchairs and exchanged information about their respective evenings.

'So,' Jemma said archly, 'Lance Richards was a lazy womanising fascist with wandering hands. That's four damn good reasons to murder him, for a start.'

'The BUF meeting was horrible, Jemma. The way they cheered and jeered – the way Ben Alcott talked – it was disgusting.'

Jemma nodded sympathetically. Despite anglicising their name and making a valuable contribution to the British economy with their chain of wireless repair shops, Michael's family had been the victims of cruel racist slurs and mindless vandalism ever since they arrived in England back in the twenties. It had got worse since the start of the war. 'Can we add Ida Richards to our short list of suspects?'

Bobbie shook her head. 'She's got a good alibi – and the doctor at the inquest was almost certain it would have needed the strength of a man to deliver that fatal blow.'

'Hell hath no fury like a woman – especially a betrayed woman. But you're right. Move on from her. You need to find out where Ian Duggen and Władysław Włoch were on the night of the attack on Richards. If Richards *had* been blackmailing either of their women, they've got a strong motive to kill him.'

Bobbie scowled at a memory and her eyes glittered with hatred. 'To be honest, Jemma, I'd love to discover it was Ben Alcott who killed Richards. That man needs removing from society. I don't care if he's bitter because his wife has been interned – he's dangerous. You should have seen how he worked that crowd.'

Jemma smiled at her passion. 'I agree. It would be the prefect resolution to this case. But he's a red herring, Bobbie. He was Lance Richards's best friend – the only person who liked him – and as far as we can see, had no motive to murder him.'

Bobbie still looked angry, so Jemma added: 'If it's any consolation, Sir Oswald Mosley was arrested and interned last week. I saw it in the newspaper when I was in London.'

Bobbie rallied. 'Good. That's the head chopped off his odious organisation. I hope he rots in jail.'

'What do you plan to do next about our murder case?'

Bobbie gave a wan smile. 'It's tough going and personally, I think that at the moment we need some divine intervention from our patron saint of private investigators, Saint Father of Brown. But in the absence of his assistance, I'll speak to both Violet and Mary Kitson Clark again. Now I know about their little secrets, I'll apply some pressure.'

The telephone rang. It was Mr Pearson. Bobbie took the call and told him about their discoveries so far.

'Anthony has admitted stealing that money,' she told Jemma when she replaced the receiver. 'But he won't tell Mr Pearson *why* he did it. All he says is that it was a moment of madness.'

'Does he understand how much trouble he's in?' Jemma said, annoyed. 'The police think Richards was blackmailing him – that's motive for murder.'

'Oh, yes, he knows about this. He claims Richards didn't try to blackmail him. But he's not surprised the man found out about the stolen money. He was always in Anthony's room, rifling through his desk.'

'This persistent refusal to talk puts Anthony in a perilous position. To be honest, Bobbie, he's beginning to irritate me. By the way, there's a letter for you from Vince on my desk.'

Bobbie's face lit up with excitement. She grabbed it, tore open the envelope and returned to the armchair to read it.

'Why is he writing to you *here*?'

'I thought it was for the best. I don't want my parents asking questions.'

'That's the problem with clandestine affairs,' Jemma said pompously. 'You end up mired in secrecy and twisting yourself through hoops to keep your secret.'

'We're not having an affair. We're just friends. Old friends.'

'What do you expect to happen when he comes back to York, either on leave or at the end of the war?'

Bobbie shrugged and didn't glance up. 'I expect he'll go back to his rich and sluttish wife.' Then she raised her intelligent brown eyes and scrutinised Jemma's face. 'And what about you, Jemma? What will you do when Special Branch finally track down Michael and bring him home? Will you leave the agency and go back to being just a housewife?'

Jemma gasped. 'I was never *just* a housewife. Michael and I ran a wireless repair shop and an electrical store together.'

'A business that no longer exists. What will you do? Most husbands prefer their women to give up their jobs and look after them and the home. Will you close Smoke & Cracked Mirrors?'

'I've no idea,' Jemma snapped. 'If Special Branch do find Michael, I assume they'll hand him over to the military police for questioning. He might have to spend some time in a military prison.'

'You'll have to think about the future at some point.'

'What future? A bomb could land on our heads today and kill us. How can anyone think of the future?'

They heard Hannah's footsteps on the stairs outside. Jemma moved over to the desk, removed her typewriter cover and tried to calm down. Bobbie's questions had rattled her. What would Michael expect? What care would he need if he was injured? And where the devil would they live?

Now Maisie and Tom had moved into the cottage, it was crowded. Maisie's older son, Harry, would also stay there when he came home from the army, and Jemma knew Maisie would love to move in her elderly father so she could care for him. There just wasn't enough room for her and Michael to live in the cottage as well, especially not in her tiny attic bedroom with its single bed.

She pushed these worrying thoughts out of her mind and turned, smiling, to concentrate on Hannah.

Chapter Twenty-Seven

Hannah sank into a chair on the other side of the desk, still wearing her old check coat, and turned down the offer of a cup of tea. 'I ain't got long, Jemma. My shift at the hotel starts in twenty minutes.'

Jemma pulled out the hotel floor plan Hannah had provided the day before. 'I'll be quick. Thanks for this. But I don't want to read too much into it. I can't imagine Jodie being so stupid as to request a suite with an adjoining door to her lover's room. She knows we watch her every move and she's not daft. This suite is closer to the staff staircase to the attics. I assume her maid, Dinah Grey, sleeps up there?'

Hannah nodded her greying head and sniffed. 'All her staff sleep up there. You're right. Maybe she just wants her maid to be closer. The hotel staff say she's a demandin' employer. She runs her maid ragged.'

'Still, we can't rule out Max Glazer entirely. Has he brought a valet with him from the States?'

'No.'

'Then his suite should be empty when he's not there...' Jemma tapped the floor plan thoughtfully. 'Can you get into his room and have a snoop around? You know the score. Go through his private letters and see if there are any incriminating notes from Jodie. With her maid on constant guard, we can't search Jodie's room to look for evidence, but there's no harm in approaching this from the other direction.'

Hannah nodded and looked at her battered wristwatch. 'I need to go. I'll do what I can.'

Emmett arrived next, beaming from ear to ear. 'Mornin', lasses.' He threw his hat on to the hat stand by the door and lowered his burly frame into the armchair opposite Bobbie. 'You'll be pleased to know,' he said smugly, 'I've cracked the case and got the evidence the baron needs to divorce Jodie.'

'What?'

'We've got him. I took a photo of Jodie's lover last night. I gave the film to your man, Ricky, to develop when he took over the shift from me last night. He's just dropped some copies off now. I told the King me and Irton didn't need no help from you lasses – that we'd crack this case on our own.'

Jemma bit back her angry retort. 'What happened? Who is he?'

'Don't know – yet. Irton's outside the hotel now, waiting for him to reappear. Now we've got our mark, we'll soon get his name.'

'Where's this photograph?' Bobbie demanded.

Irton reached into his inside coat pocket. 'She gave this bloke a right big hug on the steps of the restaurant last night. A real clincher it were – and it's on film.'

'But this doesn't make sense,' Jemma protested. 'She must have known you were there.'

Emmett shrugged his broad shoulders and pulled out a small brown envelope. 'She'd gone to this restaurant wi' her mum. We saw the old biddy leave about eight thirty, and then Jodie came out with this bloke and gave him a hug.'

'Were they kissing?'

'On the cheek, yes. But it were only a matter of time before the tongues came out. She didn't give a damn whether we saw her or not.'

Jemma shook her head. This was wrong; all wrong.

He rose to his feet and came across to the desk with the envelope. 'He took himself off and climbed into another car. She let her chauffeur drive her back to her hotel.'

'Did you get his registration number?' Bobbie stood up and followed Irton across to the desk.

He snorted in disgust and pulled out his notebook. 'What do you think I am, lass? Some kind of amateur?' He flicked open the notebook to the right page.

Bobbie snatched it off him and dashed to the noticeboard. 'It's the same car Ricky saw yesterday at Jodie's house in Bishopthorpe!' She jabbed at the photograph Ricky had taken of the mysterious visitor to the house. 'Is this the same bloke?'

Emmett glanced at the noticeboard, scratching the scar beneath his eye. 'I can't rightly say. I can't see his face. But the hat and coat look the same.'

'Let's see that damn photograph.'

He proudly laid the black-and-white image on the desk between the two women. It was a brilliant shot of the actress in a compromising clinch with a man. But the minute Jemma saw the man's face, she laughed.

Bobbie was less amused. 'Oh, for pity's sake!' She stormed back to the board and jabbed her finger at a photograph in the top left-hand corner. It was the group shot of Jodie with her mother and siblings. 'Didn't you or Irton look at this bloody board yesterday? It's her *brother*, you idiot! You've taken a picture of Jodie hugging her own brother!'

Emmett's thick neck flushed with embarrassment.

'He must have joined her and her mother for the meal after visiting the new house,' Jemma said. 'If you'd bothered to familiarise yourself with this board, you'd have recognised him immediately.'

'I guess that's why Mr King wanted us in on the case,' Bobbie snapped. 'To stop you goons making a fool of yourselves and him!'

Emmett headed for the door. 'Now, now, lass. Anyone can make a mistake. There's no harm done.'

'Don't do it again!' Bobbie yelled as he disappeared down the stairs. She reached for her coat. 'We've been saddled with a right pair of idiots. I'll see you later.'

Jemma laughed and was about to agree with her when the telephone rang again.

Bobbie waved a goodbye and disappeared down the stairs.

It was Terence King on the telephone. Jemma's heart sank at his abrupt tone.

'I'll come straight to the point, Mrs James. I've just spoken to Baron Stokesley and he's not happy with you.'

'Good grief, why?'

'He was at some social event last night – and someone pointed you out to him.'

Ben Alcott, Jemma thought.

'Apparently, you'd spent the whole afternoon at the museum, asking questions about some robbery. He wants you to drop it and concentrate on finding evidence of his wife's adultery.'

'But…' Jemma spluttered. 'Emmett was watching Jodie. We've got a schedule drawn up. And I've got other cases to investigate.'

'Look, Mrs James, the baron is paying us a lot of money and he gets to call the shots. Do I make myself clear?'

'Absolutely.'

'To be honest, we're already on thin ice. I've disappointed him with my lack of results so far, and he wasn't pleased when I told him I'd involved a ladies' private detective agency. This man's a misogynist; he believes the only place for a woman is in the home.'

Jemma grimaced. 'Will he cancel the contract and employ someone else to shadow his wife?'

There was a short pause. 'Not yet. We've got another chance. But don't mess it up. How's the investigation going?'

She decided not to mention Emmett's blunder. She told him about the adjoining suite with Max Glazer. 'I think it's too obvious to be true but my operative, Hannah, plans to have a snoop around Glazer's room.'

'Glazer, eh?' King said thoughtfully. 'He wasn't my first choice for her lover in the office sweepstake. In fact, I've got ten bob on that film producer, Nigel Lansdowne. Let me know how it goes.'

'I will. We're also keeping an eye on Jodie's new home out in Bishopthorpe. We've realised it would make quite a cosy and private little love nest.'

'That's a good point.'

'Jodie's giving a private show for the officers from the local air bases on Thursday. I've got myself on the guest list. I suspect her inner circle will be there. It's an ideal opportunity for one of us to watch her when she's more relaxed and less guarded. She doesn't know who I am.'

'Good. Okay, it sounds like you've made a decent start. If it's any consolation, Mrs James, I don't share the baron's view of women. My female operatives bring an intuitive subtlety to our investigations that often gets good results. Just keep me informed about anything you discover.' He rang off abruptly.

Jemma felt wretched when she replaced the receiver. She knew she'd only just avoided being sacked.

She was also angry. It was unreasonable for Baron Stokesley to expect her and Bobbie to drop their other cases and just concentrate on his. But this was a man who expected everyone to jump when he snapped his fingers – especially women.

Once again, she wondered what it must be like to be married to such a man.

She had a strong suspicion she'd be happier if she was working for the other party in this nasty divorce case.

Chapter Twenty-Eight

Violet Rodgers's dark eyes were shrouded in suspicion when Bobbie arrived in her cluttered office. Violet stood up and didn't offer her a chair. Her carmine-tinted lips were pressed together in disapproval.

'What can I do for you? I can only spare you a few minutes. I'm busy and short-staffed. I've lost two of my employees this week, in case you'd forgotten.'

Bobbie ignored the jibe. 'I presume you've also had a visit from the police about these two new pieces of evidence?'

'Yes, they were here yesterday afternoon.'

'Did you know anything about Anthony stealing £223 from the museum?'

'Of course not! It was a horrible shock! And totally out of character.'

'So why is your name on the list found in Lance Richards's lodgings next to a figure of the same amount?'

'I can't explain it.' Her eyes shifted away from Bobbie for a split second. She wasn't good at lying.

'Did Lance Richards try to blackmail you?'

'Absolutely not! Why on earth would Lance blackmail me?'

'Perhaps because he'd found out Lieutenant Włoch of the Polish 2nd Corps has been staying overnight at your home. '

'What!'

'Maybe he thought you might hand over £223 if he promised not to tell your employers.'

Violet turned pale, sank into her chair and pulled a packet of cigarettes and an ashtray out of the bottom drawer of her desk. For the first time, Bobbie noticed the dark shadows beneath her pretty eyes. She looked like she'd hardly slept.

'You've been spying on me.' It was more a statement than an accusation. 'That's disgusting.'

Bobbie shrugged and sat down in the chair opposite. 'It's my job.' She waited a moment while Violet lit her cigarette. 'Look, Miss Rodgers, unlike your employers I don't care what you choose to do in your own time – unless it impacts on this case. I also know Lance Richards was an unpleasant, lying, cheating ratbag. I've spoken to both his wife and to Mary Kitson Clark. I know what he was capable of and how he treated women. It wouldn't surprise me if he had tried to blackmail or intimidate you in some way.'

'You've spoken to Mary?'

'Yes – but it was Mrs Richards who told me how her husband almost raped Mary. Did you know about this?'

Violet grimaced at the word *rape* and nodded.

'Did Richards ever try anything like that with you?'

She shook her head. 'No. Mary and I are good friends – she'd warned me about him before he started work here. Lance never tried to assault me – and I made sure he didn't get the opportunity. He tried to usurp my authority many times, but I stood my ground and he backed down.'

Bobbie hesitated for a minute, watching her closely. 'Did he know that you and Lieutenant Włoch and were… intimate?'

Anger flashed in Violet's eyes. 'Who says we're *intimate*?' she snapped. 'Władysław is based in Bradford. He has to have somewhere to stay when he visits, and there are *two* bedrooms in my cottage.'

'That wouldn't matter to a man like Richards. I understand he was very crude.'

The irritation faded from the curator's face, and she sighed wearily. 'He made suggestive comments all the time – especially in front of poor Anthony. He did it to tease him.'

Bobbie nodded. 'Yes, I've already noticed Anthony was fond of you. It must have embarrassed and upset him. Were they arguing about you on the afternoon of the murder?'

'I don't know – but I hope not.'

'Miss Rodgers, where were you and Lieutenant Włoch on the night of Lance Richards's murder?'

'Good grief! Surely you don't think we had anything to do with it?'

'It doesn't matter what I think – it's what the police think that matters.'

'All they wanted to know about was the stolen money! I told them I don't know anything about it – which I don't. I've no explanation for why my name was on the list next to the sum of £223. I had nothing to do with the theft.'

'But that's not how it looks. It looks like you and Anthony were in this together – or that Lance suspected you were. Anthony complained to me about how Lance was always in his office. He must have gone through Anthony's ledgers and found out about the stolen money. Maybe he put the question mark next to your name because he wasn't sure whether you were involved or not.'

'I wasn't involved.'

Bobbie remembered a comment Jemma had made. 'And why £223? This is an unusual amount of money – not a round number. It seems significant. Why £223?'

Violet turned away for a moment and hesitated. 'Are you and your agency honour bound to share any information you uncover with the police?'

'Quite frankly, Miss Rodgers, I wouldn't even share a bus with D.S. Fawcett if I had the choice.'

The corner of Violet's red lips twitched into a small smile. 'You might not have the choice soon. He knows your agency is investigating the case. Mary told him yesterday when he questioned her about Lance's infamous list. Fawcett isn't pleased.'

Bobbie shrugged. 'He was bound to find out sooner or later. And to answer your question, I have to report back to Anthony's solicitor. He'll decide what we share with the police.'

Violet sighed and flicked ash into the ashtray. 'This is only a thought, a suggestion – and I might be wrong.'

'Tell me.'

'The day before Anthony stole the money, I was at a meeting with the corporation and asked them for £223 to improve the staff quarters and amenities of the museum. I'd spent hours meticulously gathering quotes from builders and tradesmen. The corporation refused. I came back here and complained to Anthony about how mean they were. I was very upset.'

It was Bobbie's turn to roll her eyes. 'So, the daft beggar stole the money for *you*?'

Violet nodded. 'I suspect he did. I swear to you, Miss Baker, I'd no idea what he'd done until the police told me about the missing money. Anthony's dishonesty has upset me – and it wasn't until last night I made the connection. I'm probably wrong...'

'I doubt it. Anthony is a very precise man. You needed £223 – so he got you £223.'

'I'd rather the police didn't know about this.'

'They'll work it out soon enough – or someone at the corporation will. I assume someone takes minutes at these meetings?'

Violet nodded.

'Then someone will spot the coincidence. The amount stands out. I know it's embarrassing to admit your employee had a crush on you, but if I were you, I'd contact the police and tell them – soon.'

Violet frowned, unconvinced.

'You also need to think about poor Anthony. He's gallantly trying to save you from embarrassment, but he's suffering in prison. You've no idea how grim it is in Armley Gaol. He's under a lot of pressure to explain that money. The police will get it out of him in the end.'

Violet stubbed out her cigarette. 'I'll think about it.'

'So, where were you and Władysław on the night of the attack on Lance Richards?'

'We were together – at my house.'

'All night?'

Violet shuffled uncomfortably, then nodded.

'So, you've no alibi – apart from each other?'

'No, I suppose not – not if you put it that way.'

'I'm just showing you how the police will think if they expand their investigation. Look, as far as I can see you've not broken any laws, but whether you like it or not, you're about to get dragged into the centre of this case – so brace yourself.'

'Not if you track down the real killer first.'

'What?'

Violet stared at her with a hopeful, beseeching look on her elfin face. 'I've no faith in the police, Miss Baker. You've found out more in two days than the police have in a week. Please hurry up and find Lance's real killer.'

Chapter Twenty-Nine

Bobbie felt conflicted as she walked back outside into the sunshine and headed for the Yorkshire Museum.

She had a grudging respect for Violet and was touched by the curator's faith in her own investigation skills. But she had to remember that Violet or Władysław Włoch may have had something to do with Richards's death.

Mary Kitson Clark was working at the desk in Mr Collinge's office, an impressive but dusty room. There were wooden Victorian shutters at the tall window and a round servants' bell next to the fireplace. But the most unusual feature was the balcony running around the upper half of the high-ceilinged room, which gave access to a series of glass-fronted bookcases crammed with ancient leather-bound tomes. It was reached by a vertical wooden ladder. Bobbie felt dizzy thinking about all that knowledge hovering above her head.

Mary sat behind a huge and cluttered desk in front of the tall window. She frowned when Bobbie was shown in. 'I thought I'd answered your questions yesterday.'

'I need to ask you again if you've any idea why your name was on the list found in Lance Richards's room.'

Mary replaced the top of her fountain pen and laid it down on the desk. The enthusiastic and friendly woman had vanished; she was more guarded now. 'No. I told you this yesterday. I haven't seen him for months.'

Was it Bobbie's imagination or did her clipped cut-glass accent seem more pronounced than normal? She looked for other signs of nervousness and watched a faint flush creep up Mary's neck.

'He'd written the amount of £50 next to your name.'

Mary lowered her eyes as if studying the papers in front of her. 'After you left, I had a little think. I wondered if he was about to approach me again to ask for a loan. Like I told you, he was always trying to scrounge money from his work colleagues. Perhaps he thought to approach me—'

'That's highly unlikely, after what he did to you.'

'I beg your pardon!'

'I've talked with Mrs Ida Richards,' Bobbie said gently. 'She told me how he assaulted you.'

Mary's face reddened with embarrassment and distress. 'That wasn't her information to share! It has nothing to do with Lance's death!'

'It's a murder inquiry, Miss Kitson Clark. I'm afraid everything is relevant.'

'My reputation and my life would be ruined if this ever came out! My career – maybe my engagement! I'd be a laughingstock! Reviled!'

'I understand and I'm dreadfully sorry about what he did to you. It's distressing and I know you must have suffered – especially if you felt you couldn't tell your fiancé. But I need to know if Richards tried to blackmail you. He was desperate for money. Maybe he thought if he threatened to tell Mr Duggen, you'd pay him to keep quiet.'

'Don't be silly!' Mary snapped. She threw her hands out in frustration and her fountain pen flew to the floor. 'Ian would have killed Lance if he'd ever found out what he did! And the nasty little coward knew it.'

Bobbie paused and Mary's hand flew up to her horrified face when she realised what she'd just said.

'Where were you and your fiancé on the night of the attack on Mr Richards?'

'I was at home, with my parents.'

'And Mr Duggen?'

'He was at home too, at his family estate with his father. Look, Miss Baker, we had absolutely nothing to do with this murder.'

Bobbie left shortly afterwards. Mary was distressed and adamant that she and Duggen were innocent. There was nothing more to learn there today.

She needed some time to think and decided to take a stroll through the botanic gardens. The weather was warm and there were few other people around. Squirrels scampered playfully across the lawns and the gentle breeze rustled the leaves of trees, bringing down to her the perfume of their flowers. It was an oasis of calm in the bustling city centre.

As she strolled, she thought about the complicated relationships between the two female curators and the murdered man. Richards was a threat to the happiness of both women and either one of them – or their fiancés – might have flown into a passionate rage and attacked him for his vile behaviour and to silence his nasty mouth.

Did the murderer intend to kill him – or was it an accident?

She shrugged. This was irrelevant. Richards was left with life-threatening injuries. The murderer must have known he'd die soon and probably wouldn't regain consciousness to name his attackers.

But who out of the two young women and their fiancés was most likely to have committed such a crime? There was only one way forward now. She needed to try to break one of their alibis.

She sighed when she remembered the remoteness of Violet's tiny cottage. The lack of neighbours would make it difficult to find anyone who'd seen either Violet or Włoch leaving her home.

But she had to start somewhere.

Go with the most obvious suspect.

The coroner had been clear about the tremendous force needed to wield the wooden murder weapon and English rugby players tended to be some of the strongest men in the country. Last night, Fanny had told Jemma that Duggen was a *pussycat* and a *gentle man*. But apart from the sheer size of his biceps, Duggen also had the strongest motive to attack the damn man.

She'd reached a large and beautiful shrubbery, which blazed with colour. Shaded by the towering trees, islands of mature rhododendrons and fiery red azaleas were dotted around a rectangular central pond. The rhododendrons were heavy with pink and purple blossom but there was a sad air of neglect and decay hanging over this glade. It was full of discarded litter. Thistles and weeds sprouted everywhere, even through the gravel of the path, and the pond smelt rancid and was cloudy with algae. No doubt most of the gardeners had been recruited into the forces.

She heard the faint crunch of gravel behind her. She spun round and her heart missed a beat. The breeze ruffled the foliage and lower boughs of the trees, and among the shifting dappled sunshine and shadow, she thought she saw a shape flit behind one of the large rhododendrons.

It's nothing, her common sense told her.

But there's a murderer on the loose, her imagination replied. *And he, or she, probably knows you're after them.*

Suddenly, this isolated spot turned sinister and the pond looked deadly.

She dashed out of the shrubbery towards the main building of the museum. The windows were large and there were people inside. No one would accost her in such an exposed place where anyone might be watching.

Her heart rate didn't return to normal until she finally reached the street, where the pavements bustled with shoppers. Cars, military vehicles and delivery trucks rumbled across the cobbles. She paused for a moment to catch her breath and curse her imagination. *It's broad daylight, for heaven's sake!*

Shaking her head at her own stupidity, she turned towards the office on Grape Lane. She'd collect the car, drive out to Thirsk and find someone to confirm, or deny, Ian Duggen's alibi.

As she passed an empty shop's doorway, she heard the clanging bell of a police car. She glanced over her shoulder and was surprised when the vehicle screeched to a halt beside her.

A dark-suited officer climbed out of the passenger seat. 'Oi you! Wait there!' He slammed the door and strode over. It was D.S. Fawcett.

The other pedestrians turned to stare. Bobbie blushed with embarrassment and braced herself for the confrontation. *They think I'm a shoplifter. A criminal.*

Fawcett shoved his scowling face into hers. 'You're one of those P.I. dicks, aren't you? Roberta Baker, isn't it?' His hair stank of Brylcreem and his breath of cigarettes.

'That's Miss Baker to you, officer,' she stammered.

'Don't you get cocky with me, bitch. You're the daughter of that drunken jailbird, Big Bill Baker. Troublemaking runs in your family.'

If he thought mentioning her father would intimidate her, he'd got it wrong. The blaze in her eyes now matched his own. 'My father's a political agitator,' she said through gritted teeth.

'Stop being a smart arse, bitch. You're a troublemaker – just like your dad.'

'How so, officer?' she asked sweetly.

'You've been interferin' in my investigation. You and that blonde bit you work with.'

'I'm sure Inspector Roxby will be delighted to hear you talk about his little sister like that.'

'I'm warnin' you – keep your nose out of my bloody investigation!'

'We can't. We're paid by the accused's solicitor. He thinks you need help to find the killer – and I agree—'

Fawcett grabbed her by the shoulders and forced her back into the gloomy doorway of the empty shop, pinning her up against the wall.

'What the hell are you doing? Get your bloody hands off me!'

'Don't you get hoity-toity with me, bitch. I know what you are,' he hissed.

Bobbie glanced frantically over his shoulder, looking for help. But the uniformed officer in the driver's seat of the police car was studiously ignoring his senior officer's behaviour and reading a newspaper. The other pedestrians scurried in the opposite direction – or crossed the road.

'You're a ballbreaker,' Fawcett continued, snarling. 'One of those damn bluestocking communist bitches who thinks she can do the job better than a man.'

If she hadn't been so scared, she'd have laughed in his face.

Suddenly, a large burly shadow appeared behind Fawcett in the doorway, blocking out the daylight.

It was Emmett.

'Morning, Derek. Havin' a lover's tiff, are you?' Emmett's voice was calm, and his words pleasant, but Bobbie saw the suppressed anger in his eyes.

Fawcett let her go and spun round in surprise. 'Emmett! What the devil are you doin' here, mate?' He glanced back at Bobbie, flustered. Like most bullies, he valued the respect of his brutish peers. Roughing up women probably wasn't part of their code.

'I'm savin' you from a bollockin' from your inspector, I think,' Emmett said.

'I've just explained to this lass that we lads don't need any help from bloody women to solve our murders.'

Emmett nodded sagely, his broad face impassive. 'Aye, I heard. Shall we get a cup of tea, Miss Baker? Use them nice china cups of yours?' He held out the crook of his arm.

Fawcett blinked and stepped away. 'You're workin' together?'

Emmett didn't reply.

Normally, Bobbie wouldn't have touched Emmett with a bargepole, but she knew he was trying to get her away from Fawcett. Knights in shining armour came in all shapes and sizes.

Smiling graciously, she took his arm and threw a withering glance of hate back over her shoulder at the stunned police officer.

Chapter Thirty

Jemma spent the morning in the office and took a telephone call from another potential client, who suspected her husband was having an affair and needed someone to shadow him. Reluctantly, Jemma turned the work down. Baron Stokesley's threat to throw them off the case had alarmed her.

She was due to relieve Irton at two o'clock. Just after midday, he called from a phone box on High Petergate to let her know Jodie and Max Glazer were having lunch there at a restaurant.

'Are they on their own?' she asked.

'No. Her secretary, Mr Johnson, is with her. It looks like a business meetin'.'

'I'll meet you there at two and take over – but I'll need your car. Bobbie needs mine for another case.'

There was some muted swearing at the other end of the line, but eventually he agreed.

She winced when she slid into the passenger seat of Irton's black Citroën. The vehicle stank of male sweat and cigarette smoke and was littered with food wrappings. She tried not to think too closely about the suspicious stains on the seat beneath her skirt.

Irton nodded curtly and handed her a pair of binoculars. 'If you look through the window, you can just see 'em at the back of the restaurant. Glazer's got his briefcase with him and has been showin' her some papers.'

'You're right. It sounds like a business meeting, rather than a lover's tryst.'

'Aye. I'll be off. I'll leave you the binoculars. Don't damage my car.'

Once he'd gone, Jemma pulled her hat low over her face and took his place in the driver's seat. Soon afterwards, Jodie and the two men left the restaurant. They climbed into her Rolls-Royce and drove back to the Royal Station Hotel.

The building was still surrounded by a crowd of Jodie's fans, who squealed with delight when she arrived. Jemma parked the car and joined them.

Jodie wore a smart crimson belted coat today over a red-and-black check skirt. A small black cloche balanced cheekily on her gleaming blonde hair. Max Glazer went straight inside, but Jodie lingered among her fans, smiling and signing autographs. Tall and lithe, she towered above most of them in her red patent heels. Her pleasure in their adoration was genuine.

Jemma froze with shock when she saw her rival, Will Sharrow, among the crowd.

The scruffy and stooped private eye pushed his way closer to Jodie's side, trying not to attract her attention. Alarmed, Jemma moved closer to get a better view. *What on earth was he up to?*

As Jodie waved and turned away to go back inside the hotel, Sharrow reached out and slid an envelope into her coat pocket.

Terence King's words rang in Jemma's ears. *Lord Stokesley is running out of patience, and I'm worried he might try a shot in the dark and embarrass himself – and us…*

Jemma had a split second to make her decision. She'd no faith in Sharrow. Whatever he was up to, it wouldn't be good for her and Terence King.

She barged to the front of the crowd, knocking aside a woman. 'Check your pockets, Jodie! Don't give your coat to your maid!'

Apart from an indignant squeal from the woman she'd knocked into, a stunned silence fell on the crowd.

Jodie froze, framed in the centre of the doorway with a tall, uniformed doorman standing either side. She turned slowly to face Jemma, her features impassive. Her huge baby-blue eyes flicked over Jemma's face, then her gloved hand slid into her coat pocket. If her fingers discovered the envelope, nothing registered on the actress's face. She shrugged, turned away and strolled inside.

'What the devil are you up to, lass?' a man in the crowd demanded.

'You nearly knocked me over!' the woman complained again.

Ignoring the man, Jemma apologised profusely to the woman and retreated to her car.

But Sharrow was waiting for her beside the vehicle, his fists curling and uncurling at his side. 'You interfering bitch!' His voice cracked with distress and there were tears in his small brown eyes. He glanced away in a desperate effort to regain control of his emotions. 'Why don't you just leave it alone?'

'I'm sorry, Mr Sharrow. I don't know what the baron asked you to plant on Jodie but that's not how I, or Terence King, operate. We'll get the evidence he needs to divorce her, but we'll make sure it's legitimate and will stand up to scrutiny in a divorce court.'

'You sanctimonious little...' But he turned abruptly and took a few steps. Then he turned back and spat out his parting words: 'It's all right for the likes of you and King – creaming the profits off the business away from the rest of us!'

Jemma heard his desperation. *Was his business in trouble since she'd launched Smoke & Cracked Mirrors?* Maybe York wasn't big enough to support two private inquiry agencies.

He looked old and exhausted as he sloped off. A pang of pity flicked through her breast. This was no job for an old man. She'd never forgive Sharrow for the terror she'd experienced when he locked her in his office during an air raid, but she still felt compassion for the man.

Then another horrible thought hit her that pushed her sympathy for Sharrow aside.

Not only had she just thwarted the baron's independent attempt to frame his wife – but she'd also blown her own cover with Jodie. The actress had had a good look at her face.

But it didn't matter now, did it?

Once Sharrow reported her interference, the baron would sack both her and Terence King.

She put her head in her hands and screamed silently in frustration.

Hannah knew Max Glazer had gone out for lunch with Jodie, but she didn't get a chance to sneak up to the suites on the fifth floor until after two o'clock. Mrs Higgins, the housekeeper, refused to let the junior chambermaids up there and she kept a firm eye on the movements of her staff. Only the most trusted and experienced chambermaids serviced the rooms of the wealthiest guests. And none of the staff was allowed to use the lift.

Grabbing a pannier full of cleaning cloths and fluids, Hannah trudged silently up the back stairs on her soft-soled shoes. She was out of breath and her arthritic knee ached by the time she reached the elegant high-ceilinged, plush-carpeted corridor. 'I'm getting too old for this malarky, Archie,' she muttered breathlessly to her dead husband.

She knocked on Max Glazer's door, and when there was no reply, she whipped out the master key she'd 'borrowed' from Mrs Higgins's collection and let herself in.

The brown and cream marble suite was spacious, beautifully decorated and furnished in the art deco style. Glazer's briefcase wasn't there so she rifled through the drawers of the sitting room and then moved into the bedroom.

There was a novel beside Glazer's bed and a pack of American playing cards in the drawer of his bedside table. She knew they were American because of the one-dollar price tag on the front. The blue cardboard box was open and fraying at the edges. A few of the cards fell out on to the carpet.

Hannah scooped them up and sat back on the bed's sumptuous silk quilt in shock. They were explicit photographs of two naked men embracing. 'That's a funny Jack of Clubs, Archie,' she muttered.

Reluctantly, she pulled out a few more of the pornographic images. 'Well, if that's what he's into, Archie,' she muttered, 'I can't see how he'll be botherin' our Jodie.' She slid one of the cards into her pocket to show Jemma, and, feeling soiled, went into the bathroom to wash her hands.

The sound of the running water masked the sound of Glazer's return.

She nearly dropped the towel with shock when she heard the voices of the two men who'd walked into the bedroom. The transatlantic drawl of Max Glazer was unmistakable, but her eyes widened further when

253

she recognised the nervous laughter of Joseph, one of the hotel's young waiters.

She picked up her cleaning items and stood her ground defiantly.

When the two men fell silent, Hannah's stomach churned. No one paid her enough to be a witness to what she suspected was coming next. She threw open the bathroom door and walked out.

Joseph stood, his waistcoat flapping open, inches away from the flabby bald American. Glazer was undoing the buttons on the lad's shirt. They leapt apart when she appeared.

'Goddamn it, woman!' Glazer spluttered.

Joseph gulped like a goldfish.

'I won't tell any folks you two was here – and what you were up to,' she said, 'if you don't tell folks I were here.'

Glazer recovered his wits first. 'I'm not sure what you mean, ma'am. There's nothing untoward happening here.'

'If you tell Mrs Higgins I were here, then you'll be telling that to a judge.' She turned on her heel and left.

Back in the plush corridor, her first instinct was to flee, but when she passed the door of Jodie's suite, she heard the faint sound of male laughter.

One of the hotel's 'Do Not Disturb' signs dangled from the doorknob.

Hannah stood still, her ears straining, and she heard it again. The soft, deeper chuckle of a man mingled with Jodie's laughter.

Hannah weighed up her options. She'd been caught by Glazer in his suite and although she'd offered the two poofters her silence, she knew Glazer would complain to Mrs Higgins. Her days at the Royal Station Hotel were numbered. The management wouldn't believe her word over that of the wealthy American and the hotel probably couldn't care less what he got up to in the privacy of his suite. Besides which, she still had to get back downstairs and replace the master key without being spotted. Her chances of achieving all this – and keeping her job – were remote.

'In for a penny, in for a pound, Archie,' she said as she knocked on Jodie's door.

All she needed was a glimpse of the man. Just one glimpse.

The laughter stopped. A moment later, the door opened a crack and Jodie peered out, frowning. It was impossible to see into the room behind her, but Hannah got a good look at the actress. Jodie's luscious blonde hair was down and rolled over her shoulders in thick waves. She was swathed in a shimmering oyster silk dressing gown and there was a glass of bubbling champagne in her hand. 'What do you want?'

'I need to clean the bathroom, miss.'

Jodie's beautifully manicured nails pointed to the 'Do Not Disturb' sign. 'Can't you read?'

'No. Sorry, miss, I can't.'

'There's nothing wrong with the bathroom.'

'Would you like me to fetch you a cup of tea?'

Jodie's face creased in disbelief. 'No, I wouldn't. Go away, you annoying little woman. I'm sleeping.' She slammed the door in Hannah's face.

'Aye, lass, we know you're sleepin',' Hannah muttered to herself, 'but who the hell with?'

Her mind flicked over the list of Jodie's potential suitors. She knew Nigel Lansdowne, the film producer, was also a guest at the hotel. His room was on the floor below.

'I might as well be hanged for a sheep as a lamb, Archie,' she muttered as she hurried towards the stairs.

Chapter Thirty-One

Jemma started with surprise when Hannah threw open the passenger door of Irton's car and slid into the passenger seat beside her.

'I ain't got long. I've still got a job – just – and I've got to go back inside. But you need to know Jodie's entertainin' a bloke in her suite in her nightie, and it ain't Glazer, or that Lansdowne fellah. Besides which, he's a poofter. They'll probably sack me tonight.'

It took Jemma a few minutes to unravel this outburst and to establish that Jodie was swanning around in a negligée, not a nightie. Eventually, the full story of Hannah's snooping came out.

'I went down to Lansdowne's room and knocked on the door. He were a bit surprised when I offered to clean his lav, but at least he were there. So, it ain't him who's cavortin' wi' Jodie up on the top floor.'

Jemma gave Hannah a beaming smile. 'This is the best news we've had all day. You've eliminated Glazer as a potential lover – and probably Lansdowne as well.'

'I might lose me job.'

'Never mind. What about that actor, Stephen Howard?'

'The bloke she were swannin' around wi' yesterday? He ain't a guest at this hotel. Dunno where he'll be.'

'What's the second-best hotel in York, Hannah?'

'Dean Court Hotel.'

Jemma smiled thoughtfully. 'We should leave no stone unturned. It sounds like Jodie will be busy for a while. I'll nip back to the office and telephone the Dean Court. If he's not staying there, we've lost nothing. But if he *is* a guest and he's out of the hotel…'

'Then we might have our mark.' Hannah was already halfway out of the car.

Jemma smiled with relief when she turned the ignition. At least now they had something positive to report back to Terence King. Things were looking up.

Back in the office, Jemma was surprised to find Bobbie and Emmett sitting in the armchairs, having a cosy chat over a cup of tea.

'I thought you were watching Jodie,' Bobbie said.

Jemma dumped her handbag down on the desk and reached for the telephone. 'There's been a development. Do either of you know where the actor Stephen Howard stays while he's in York?'

'Aye,' Emmett replied. 'I had a smoke wi' Jodie's chauffeur last night. He let slip he'd dropped Howard off at the Dean Court Hotel yesterday.'

'Thanks.'

Jemma made the call to the hotel, claiming to be Howard's sister. She asked to speak to him.

'I'm afraid Mr Howard isn't in his room right now,' the receptionist told her. 'He dropped off his keys at reception this morning and hasn't been back since. Shall I take a message?'

'No, thank you, I'll try again later.' She replaced the receiver thoughtfully. Howard hadn't arrived at the Royal Station Hotel while she'd been watching the entrance, but that didn't mean he wasn't already there. He may have arrived early, while Jodie was still in the restaurant.

Laughter from the other side of the room made her glance up. Emmett was chuckling at something Bobbie had said.

'You two are enjoying yourselves,' she said. 'What's going on?'

'I had an unpleasant brush with D.S. Fawcett – and Emmett came to my rescue. I hope you don't mind, but I've told him about our museum case.' She recounted the events of the morning.

Jemma was furious with Fawcett. 'I can't believe what he did! Are you hurt?'

'No, I'm fine.'

'I'll tell Gabriel tonight. Fawcett needs disciplining!'

'No, don't,' Bobbie pleaded. 'I don't want a fuss. Now Fawcett knows Emmett is on our team, he'll leave us alone.'

Jemma's lips tightened and she was about to insist, but realised Bobbie was adamant. She turned to Emmett instead. 'How do you know Fawcett?'

The big man put down his teacup and scratched his scar. 'It were before the war on a joint operation between Leeds Police and the York City force. We were after a nasty gang of bog-dwelling Fenians who were threatening to bomb both cities. He weren't a bad bloke back then.'

'Well, he's a thoroughly unpleasant character now.' Jemma's gaze returned to Bobbie. 'You must have been scared silly.'

'It was scarier in the botanic gardens! I thought someone was following me.'

Jemma gasped. *Bobbie had been followed, too?*

Bobbie turned to Emmett as a thought struck her. 'That wasn't you, was it? You weren't behind me in the museum grounds?'

Emmett chuckled. 'No, lass. I've got better things to do. I were walkin' up the street when I saw the police car dash past. I recognised Fawcett when he jumped out. But it took me a few minutes to realise it were *you* he were roughin' up.'

'By the way, Mr Emmett,' Jemma said, 'when you were talking to Jodie's chauffeur, did you learn anything?'

'Only that he's a Yank called Hainsworth. He used to drive fer her over in the States. When her British chauffeur left, she brought him over.'

'Is he corruptible? Can we bribe him for information?'

Emmett shook his head and reached for his hat. 'No, he's devoted to the lass. He's got summat wrong wi' one of his eyes and thinks he needs an operation. She's promised to pay for it fer him. Anyhow, I'm off for a bit of kip – I'm doin' the night shift later.'

Bobbie stood up and shook his hand. 'Well, thank you again, Mr Emmett. I don't know what I would have done if you hadn't arrived. I'd already sent up a prayer to the patron saint of private detectives.'

Emmett's eyebrows shot up in surprise. 'I never knew we private dicks had a patron saint!'

'He's called Saint Father of Brown,' Bobbie continued blithely. 'He was martyred at a place called Chesterton.'

Jemma hid her smile. Bobbie obviously didn't intend to let her newfound friendship with Emmett stop her from ragging the man.

'Well, fancy that! Irton'll be pleased to hear it. He's a left-footer and is allus fiddlin' with his beads. Good day to you, lass.' A thought struck him as he left and he turned back, frowning. 'Fawcett may have a point about this museum murder of yours. If you lasses are right, and there's a killer still on the loose – you might end up his next victims. I'd carry a weapon if I were you.'

'Well, that's a cheerful thought,' Bobbie said once he'd left. She went over to the coat stand and lifted down her hat. 'Nice to think we might be caught in the middle between an enraged policeman and a brutal murderer.'

'Emmett may have a point,' Jemma said thoughtfully. 'I'm sure someone was following me first thing this morning.'

'What happened?'

Jemma told her. 'It was probably just my imagination.'

'Maybe. But we're stirring up a hornet's nest, Jemma. I think we're close to unmasking the real killer.'

Jemma shrugged. 'We'll just have to catch this murderer before he catches us. Where are you going?'

'I'm off to Thirsk for an hour or two to try and crack open Ian Duggen's alibi. Then I'm driving out to Garrowby tonight to try and find out what Anthony was up to.' Bobbie gave Jemma a cheery wave as she left.

Jodie's Rolls-Royce was still parked outside the hotel when Jemma returned, and there was no sign of her chauffeur. *Had she given him the afternoon off?*

She hoped the actress was still inside, but she may have left in a taxi while Jemma was back at Grape Lane. For the first time, she saw the advantage of doubling up the shifts. If Ricky had been with her, he could have stayed by the hotel while she dashed to the nearest telephone. But for this level of surveillance, they needed more staff.

She opened her copy of *Lord Edgware Dies* and settled down for a long, boring wait.

As the afternoon dragged on into early evening, the only event of note was Max Glazer leaving the hotel in a taxi. There was no sign of Nigel Lansdowne, Stephen Howard or the actress herself. Jodie's crowd of admirers outside the hotel gave up and drifted home for their suppers. A glorious sunset of soft pinks and the purplish hues of wild clover blossomed and flared over the soaring towers of the minster. But even this failed to relieve the tedium.

Emmett was half an hour late and by the time he took over she was stiff and weary. She buttoned up her coat and climbed gratefully out of the car and into the gloom of early evening.

Judging from the noise, York city centre was already full of drunken revellers. A couple of airmen swaggered down the road and slurred a cheery 'Good evening, miss!' in her direction. She smiled when they touched their caps in mock salute.

Bootham was quieter but far darker, especially under the trees. But she'd walked home before in the blackout, and she was sure-footed. A bus with its dimmed headlights rumbled past and a couple of cars, but apart from a man walking his dog there was no one else around.

When she approached Clifton, she once again got the unnerving sense she was being followed. She spun round. But there was only a young couple walking hand in hand on the other side of the road.

Stop it, Jemma, she chided herself. But she quickened her pace.

Her pulse calmed as she approached the noisy Grey Mare public house, where a couple of men stood talking by the door. But her relief didn't last for long.

Clifton Green was pitch black.

Throwing common sense out of the window, she broke into a run, dodging in and out of the shadows of the trees.

And so did the person following her. His heavy tread pounded behind her.

She pelted up the garden path and had her hand on the door handle when she heard the shot.

Yelping with fear, she fell into the house and slammed the door shut behind her. For the second time today, her fingers shook as she rammed home the bolt.

What the hell had just happened? Had someone just tried to shoot her? No. It must have been a car backfiring.

Gabriel suddenly came out of the kitchen and into the hallway.

'For God's sake, Jemma! What's happened?'

'Nothing,' she stammered. 'I just got a bit spooked by the dark.' She was reluctant to admit she'd probably just led a murderer back to their home.

He regarded her coldly and she sensed his suppressed anger. 'Come in here. I want to talk to you.'

Oh God, what now? She took off her hat and coat and followed him into the kitchen, which smelled of Maisie's delicious cooking.

He pointed towards a plate of food on the kitchen dresser. 'We've saved you some supper.'

'Thank you. What's the matter? Is it something to do with Tom? Is he all right?'

'Tom is much better. Maisie's upstairs settling him down for the night. No. The problem is *you*, Jemma. I saw Detective Sergeant Fawcett this afternoon.'

'Ah.'

'He told me you and Bobbie are interfering in his murder investigation.'

'That's not fair. We're officially investigating the case on behalf of the innocent man Fawcett has locked up in Armley Gaol.'

Gabriel's blue eyes turned to ice and his face hardened like granite. 'Innocent? Have you been promoted to the bench now, Jemma? Are you judge and jury?'

'No, I'm sorry, I said that wrong.' Her heart was still pounding from her fright outside and she struggled to form coherent sentences. 'His solicitor believes him to be innocent. He's employed us to find evidence to prove it.'

'In other words, you're trying to find a murderer – for financial gain. I'm not happy about this, Jemma. You were quizzing me for information about the case last night.'

'I'm sorry. We've always talked about your cases over tea.'

'And I've always trusted you to be discreet with the information I gave you. But not any more. You can't be trusted. You've changed since you set up this agency, Jemma. Your scruples have gone out of the damn window.'

'Gabriel, I'm sorry. I know I should have told you, but what with Tom…'

'Don't use Tom as a bloody excuse.'

He shook his head in disbelief and turned away. She'd have preferred it if he'd yelled at her; his disappointment was harder to bear.

'It's a conflict of interests, Jemma,' he said as he moved towards the door. 'And it probably won't be the last.'

'Yes, I know. I'm sorry.'

His next words took her breath away. 'It might be better if you moved out. I need to know I can talk about my work, in the privacy of my own home, without it being used by you for your financial gain.'

Jemma sank down into a chair at the kitchen table. She felt wretched. Absolutely wretched.

She didn't know what had upset her the most: the silent anger of her seething brother and his threat to throw her out – or the nutcase outside who may or may not have tried to shoot her.

She glanced at the plate of food but realised she'd lost her appetite. Should she telephone Bobbie and warn her? Tomorrow. Bobbie was somewhere out in the wilds of the countryside right now.

She went into the front parlour and closed the door behind her. The room was pitch black. Crossing cautiously over to the window, she pulled back the blackout curtain.

The moon had risen and bathed the village green in silvery light. Every shape she saw was silhouetted, black on black. Her eyes flicked over the familiar curves and lines of the garden, the trees and the old water trough on the green beyond.

Nothing. Nothing out of the ordinary. He'd gone.

She left the parlour and quietly opened the front door. From the muffled voices emanating from Tom's bedroom upstairs, it sounded like Gabriel was reading his stepson a story.

The warm evening breeze lifted her hair and filled her nose with the scent of honeysuckle.

Cautiously, she took a few steps back down the garden path, where the moonlight bounced off the trees and shrubs, throwing familiar shadows.

And then she saw it. The gleam of metal halfway up the trunk of a flowering cherry tree.

Returning to the hallway, she pulled her lockpick out of her handbag. One of its spiky arms was a small blade. Back in the garden, she carefully eased the gleaming metallic object out of the tree trunk and gasped when it fell into her hand.

It was a bullet.

Closing and bolting the door, she cast an anguished glance up the stairs. Her natural instinct was to scream and belt upstairs into the strong and protective arms of her big brother. But not now. Not after what had just passed between them.

She braced herself and walked into the kitchen. She'd deal with this herself.

She pulled open the drawer in the old dresser containing the German Luger pistol their father had brought back as a souvenir from the last war. Tipping out the box of ammunition, she loaded the gun and dropped it into her handbag.

The next time that fiend came for her, she'd be ready.

Chapter Thirty-Two

Bobbie peered out of the car windscreen. Her eyes strained against the encroaching night.

Cursing the blackout regulations that meant she was only allowed to use a single masked headlight, she dropped down a gear and slowed the vehicle to a snail's pace. The road markings had stopped back in Stamford Bridge. It was becoming harder and harder to follow the twisting road as it wound its way through this vast expanse of open countryside and isolated pockets of woodland. She wondered what would happen if she had an accident out here in the middle of nowhere. Probably no one would find her until morning – and only then if a milk lorry or farm tractor happened to rumble past.

Still, at least I'm on the right track, she thought, in a desperate effort to cheer herself up.

It had taken her a while, and several bone-rattling trips down rutted farm tracks, to locate the farmer at Stamford Bridge who claimed to have seen Anthony's Bentley on the evening of the murder.

'What's to do, lass?' he'd asked when he answered the door. A burly man with bulging arm muscles and huge hands, he stood in his stockinged feet on the doormat and gave her a friendly smile.

Bobbie explained her business and he nodded sagely.

'Aye, ah saw that car when ah were finishin' off t'haymakin' in t'top field. Them awd Bentleys are good cars. Me da used to own one.'

'Have you seen it before?'

'Can't say ah have, lass. But ah were talkin' to Bert Adams from Garrowby in't Drover's Arms last night – and he sed he'd seen it afore.'

'Garrowby? That's further down the road towards Driffield, isn't it? When was this?'

'He didn't say.' He gave her the address of Bert Adams's farm. She thanked him and hurried back to her car.

The squat, dark shape of the Adams farm was set back off the main road about fifty yards away. She decided to walk rather than risk Jemma's suspension on another farm track. She pulled off the road into a muddy lay-by next to a large wooded area.

The moment she opened the car door, the strong smell of rich earth, rotting vegetation and manure filled the car. She listened for a moment to the rustling leaves of the trees and the unmistakable sound of some small nocturnal mammal scurrying through the undergrowth. A dog fox barked, and down in the valley sleepy sheep bleated and called their lambs to their side. *So much for the peace and quiet of the countryside*, she thought with a smile.

But what the devil was Anthony doing out here on the night of the murder?

The moon slid out from behind a cloud and illuminated the area in its soft silvery light. She was just about to set off to the farm when she heard the sound of a car engine behind her. She walked around the other side of her vehicle for safety. Traffic fatalities had doubled since the introduction of the blackout, and she didn't want to become one of those statistics.

A dark-coloured Austin crawled out of the gloom and crested the brow of the hill. A pale-faced man clutched the steering wheel, his eyes fixed on the vague outline of the road ahead. It was the only other vehicle she'd seen for the past half an hour.

Curious, she walked after it for a few yards and watched it descend the hill. Halfway down, it slowed and turned off the road on to a rough track bordered by a high wire fence that glinted in the moonlight.

Bobbie frowned. The farmer back in Stamford Bridge had told her the Adams's farm was situated in an isolated spot. It was a couple of miles to the next village and had no neighbours. *So where was the car going?*

She climbed back into her own vehicle and followed the car. As she turned off the road on to the unmade track, the weak light from her single headlight illuminated a battered wooden sign dangling in a lopsided manner from the rusting wire fence. It read: *Garrowby Gravel Quarry.* Other signs shouted a warning – *Danger!* – and informed her that *Trespassers will be prosecuted.*

The moon went behind a cloud, and she slowed to a crawl once more. Somewhere ahead lay an old quarry and she'd lost sight of the other vehicle. The last thing she wanted was to bump into it in the dark and shunt it over the edge of a dangerous pit. She bounced along the rough track for about a quarter of a mile before she turned a corner and saw the car.

It was parked against the curved face of the quarry, and it wasn't alone. Two other cars were parked in front of it.

Bobbie pulled over, killed her own engine, and waited for the driver to emerge.

Nothing happened. All three vehicles were silent and still. Were they were waiting for something? *But what?* Another five silent minutes passed.

Confused, she climbed out and walked cautiously towards the parked vehicle. The only noise was the wire fencing, which shivered and strained in the slight breeze.

She reached the driver's door, peered inside and recoiled with shock when she saw the driver huddled across the back seat beneath a blanket. He stared back at her, his moonlit face white with surprise and annoyance.

Bobbie smiled. Suddenly, it all made sense. 'I'm sorry to bother you,' she called out, 'but I need to ask you some questions.'

This man was a trekker – one of the thousands of terrified people who abandoned their warm beds every night to sleep in their cars away from the built-up areas and the threat of air raids. But they were often ridiculed and abused across the country for their apparent cowardice.

Everything fell into place. When his sister worked her night shifts at the hospital, Anthony Gill became a trekker too. Dora had told her Anthony was scared of the air raids and Mrs Elgin told her he left with a thermos flask. No wonder Anthony wouldn't admit where he'd gone on the night of the murder.

Bobbie sensed the driver's fear as he reluctantly sat up and wound down his window. She heard his embarrassment as he gruffly asked what she wanted.

'My name's Miss Baker – I'm a private detective working for a solicitor. We're trying to find out about a man who drives a dark green Bentley. I was wondering if you'd ever seen it up here?' She described Anthony's car.

The man nodded. 'I've seen it around a few times. He doesn't come every night though.'

'What about last Thursday?'

He shrugged. 'I don't know. I get so little sleep these days I hardly know what day of the week it is.'

Bobbie thanked him and left him to his uncomfortable night's rest.

She moved across to the other two cars to make the same enquiry. The drivers were cagey and reluctant to talk but eventually they both confirmed they'd seen Anthony's car parked here on the odd occasion, although neither remembered him on the night of Lance Richards's murder. Bobbie managed to wheedle the names and addresses out of the trekkers and made a note of their car registration numbers.

Anthony still didn't have an alibi, but two farmers had seen him driving towards this disused quarry on the night of the murder. And if these trekkers were called as witnesses, they would be able to confirm that Anthony spent several nights a week up here hiding from the Luftwaffe. The nervous, stubborn and proud little man wouldn't be pleased to have his embarrassing secret revealed – but persuading him to admit the truth was Mr Pearson's problem, not hers.

Satisfied with her night's work, she slid into the car, backed up and drove home. She'd still not tracked down the murderer of Lance Richards – but they were one step closer to seeing Anthony a free man.

Chapter Thirty-Three

It was just after ten o'clock when Irton squeezed his bulk into the passenger seat of the Citroën parked outside the Royal Station Hotel.

'I got you these.' He tossed Emmett a packet of Woodbine cigarettes. 'It's the real stuff – none of that blasted Turkish tobacco.'

Emmett reached for them gratefully and ripped open the packet. 'Cheers, mate. That's good of yer. I'm missin' proper Virginia leaf.'

'Anythin' bin happenin'?'

'No. Glazer came back about twenty minutes ago but there's bin no sign of our actress. Plenty of comin's and goin's around here, though. Looks like the army top brass are havin' a knees-up inside. There were some fun and games this afternoon, mind you.' He told Irton what had happened. 'So, it looks like Stephen Howard is our mark,' he concluded. 'That old biddy, Hannah, did well.'

'She's got form, you know,' Irton said.

Emmett raised his eyebrows and glanced at him in surprise.

'I got bored earlier, so I gave O'Reilley a ring. He checked them out.'

'Bored?'

'There's nowt to do in this damn town,' Irton complained.

'There's pubs.'

'Full of squaddies and bleedin' airmen. I'd give anythin' for a quiet pint with me dog in the Railway Arms right now.'

'So, what did O'Reilley tell yer about Hannah?'

'She did some time thirty years ago for burglary. She were also suspected of a heist where a safe were cracked, but nowt were proved.'

Emmett sniggered. 'They say the quiet ones are the worst.'

'The two bosses are clean. But that Jemma is sister to Inspector Roxby of the York police – and she's married to a deserter. A Ruskie.'

'Blimey, I wonder if the King knows this?' Emmett paused for a moment. 'I came across our old mate Derek Fawcett ragin' at Bobbie this afternoon. It turns out her old man's an ex-con.'

Irton rolled his eyes. 'Yet to look at 'em both – and hear them speak – yer wouldn't think butter would melt in their damn mouths. Why were Fawcett havin' a go at her?'

'They're helpin' a solicitor track down the murderer for that museum job.'

'Nice work if you can get it.'

Emmett shook his greying head. 'I think they've bit off more than they can chew. Someone were shadowin' Bobbie today. She were scared.'

Irton scowled. 'Don't get involved, mate. We've got a job to do. We're not here to babysit women.'

Emmett didn't get the chance to reply.

Jodie suddenly emerged through the glass doors, swathed in a sequined white evening gown and a silver fox fur. Diamonds glistened at her ears and throat. She was laughing and hanging on to the arm of a handsome dark-haired man in his mid-thirties, with a neatly trimmed moustache. The couple strolled towards Jodie's Rolls-Royce.

'Bleedin' hell! It's that playboy, Arthur Kerner! Her old boyfriend. When did he get in town?'

'Dunno. But if he were here this afternoon, it might have bin him she were entertainin' in her room.' Emmett switched on the ignition. 'You stayin' for a bit?'

Irton nodded. 'Might as well. There's nowt else to do round here.'

The powerful Rolls-Royce leapt away from the kerb, shot down the hotel drive and spun around the corner into Station Road. Emmett put his foot down and the Citroën roared after it.

Irton was thrown against the door when they spun out on to the main road. 'Bleedin' hell! The lad thinks he's at Brands Hatch!'

The Rolls overtook a bus and flew over Lendal Bridge as if the silver statue on its bonnet had suddenly sprouted real wings. Irton slapped his hand over his eyes when Emmett swerved round the bus, narrowly missing a cyclist on the other side of the road.

They were just in time to see the Rolls screech to a virtual halt and swing right into Coney Street. 'He'll never keep up that speed in this town,' Emmett said. 'It were built fer dray carts, not cars.' He put his foot down again and both men grimaced as the vehicle bounced violently over the cobbles. Ahead, the Rolls took a sharp left.

'The bastard's tryin' to shake us off,' Irton muttered.

Emmett swung the wheel but had to brake sharply when a crowd of drunken airmen staggered and meandered erratically across the narrow road.

Irton rolled down his window and hollered at them to get out of the bloody way. A lively exchange ensued, most of it carried out in Anglo-Saxon rather than the King's English. During the altercation, one of the uniformed airmen kicked Irton's precious car. Furious, he was halfway out of the door before Emmett dragged him back inside. With one foot still engaging the clutch, he put his foot down flat on the accelerator. The powerful engine screamed a warning. The next second the vehicle surged forward, and the airmen scattered.

By the time they reached the junction with Parliament Street, the Rolls-Royce had disappeared. Irton slammed his fist down on the dashboard in frustration and swore.

'Let's think this through,' Emmett said calmly. 'She were dressed up in silver high heels and it's too late fer eatin'.'

'You reckon she's gone out dancin'? With Kerner?'

'Aye.'

'According to the lasses at Smoke & Cracked Mirrors, De Grey's is the poshest dance hall in town. But it's open to the public on a Wednesday.'

Emmett nodded thoughtfully. 'Lady Jodie ain't in the habit of rubbin' shoulders wi' the public. There's also a ballroom at the Dean Court Hotel for the use of residents. Several of her crowd stay there, includin' that actor, Stephen Howard.'

'Let's check it out.'

Emmett decided to hide the car and parked a few streets away from the Dean Court. They pulled down their hats, put their coat collars up and marched briskly through the Minster Precinct. Completely blacked out, the great cathedral towered silently into the starry sky beside them.

The doorman took one look at their coats and scruffy shoes and tried to refuse them entry. But Irton flashed his old identification from Leeds City Police. 'We're on police business, lad. One of yer managers called us in.'

The doorman gave the identification a cursory glance and let them pass.

They strode across the expensive rugs on the gleaming parquet floor, through an oak- panelled corridor towards the sound of a big band playing Glenn Miller's '*In the Mood*'.

The double doors of the ballroom were thrown wide open. Inside, beneath a glistening chandelier, Jodie swirled elegantly around the dance floor in the arms of Arthur Kerner. At a far table, Stephen Howard and Nigel Lansdowne sat laughing with a group of other women and men. They recognised Jodie's brother and sister – but not the other attractive blonde woman with slanting Slavic eyes.

'She's up to somethin' tonight,' Emmett said. 'She wouldn't have tried to lose us if she weren't.'

They found a couple of comfortable armchairs, discreetly shielded by a large aspidistra on a plinth, and ordered whisky from a passing waiter. It was delivered to them on a silver tray.

An hour and a half later, the tempo of the music slowed and the dance concluded with Billie Holiday's '*I Wished on the Moon*'. The guests drifted out of the ballroom, but it was another twenty minutes before Jodie and her party emerged.

The two private detectives shrank back into their seats. The group drifted to the base of the magnificent staircase and stood laughing among themselves. They'd had a lot to drink. The mysterious blonde woman was the loudest and spoke with an Eastern European accent.

'You keep Jodie in sight,' Emmett said. 'I'll sneak back to the car and start the engine in case she drives off somewhere else.'

He slipped outside and frowned when he realised there was no sign of Jodie's Rolls-Royce. Shrugging, he trudged back to the Citroën and drove it closer to the hotel entrance. Irton would find him.

A few minutes later, Irton slid into the passenger seat beside him. 'We've got her, mate,' he said smugly. 'You were right. There's definitely summat goin' on. Kerner picked up his room keys from reception and she's gone upstairs with him to his suite. They've called for champagne.'

'Another party?' Emmett asked.

'I dunno. They were alone when they went upstairs. But if she stays the night wi' him –we've got her. Kerner will have had to register her as his guest. We'll have evidence for the baron.'

Emmett grinned and the two men settled back for a long wait, grateful that the chiming bells of the minster had been silenced for the duration of the war.

They took it in turns to snatch some fitful sleep.

Once more a light mist tiptoed into the sleepy city to herald the arrival of dawn, but it soon dispersed. As the birds stirred in the nearby trees, Irton shook Emmett awake. 'Come on, I'm bloody freezin' and 've had enough of this. Let's see if she's still there.'

Emmett rubbed the sleep out of his eyes. 'She's not left?'

Irton shook his head. 'There's been no sign of her – or her bloody car.'

The two men climbed stiffly out of the vehicle and entered the deserted hotel.

The only people around were a chubby elderly man in a smart suit at the mahogany reception desk and a cleaner mopping the parquet floor. Judging by the puffy black circles beneath his eyes, the bloke at the desk had been on duty all night.

'Are you the manager?' When the man nodded, Irton slipped him a ten-shilling note across the desk.

'We need your help, mate. We're lookin' for an actress called Jodie, otherwise known as Baroness Stokesley. We believe she kipped down here last night, and we need you to check your hotel register.'

The manager's tired eyes widened and the lines at the corners of his mouth crinkled into a knowing smile. 'That's most generous of you, sir.' He picked up the ten-shilling note and pocketed it. 'Are you the gentleman Miss Jodie calls Adolf? She said you might pay us a visit.'

Irton and Emmett froze. 'Is she still here? Did she stay the night?'

'Oh, no, sir, definitely not. After the party in Mr Kerner's suite, she left in the early hours.'

'Don't play games with us,' Irton growled. 'We've been watching all night; we know she ain't left this building. You're bound by law to register your guests – we need to see your register.'

'I'm happy to show it to you, sir.' The manager reached for a large black leather-bound book and passed it across. 'But I can assure you, Miss Jodie left. I watched her go myself. She gave me a dazzling smile and a cheery wave. It quite made my night.'

Irton snatched the register out of the hands of the manager and scanned through the relevant page. He threw it back in frustration. 'Nothing,' he snapped at Emmett. 'The damn woman has tricked us again.'

'How?' Emmett asked. 'How the hell did she get out without us seein' her?'

The manager grinned at their frustration. 'Oh, that's easy. She made a special arrangement with us to leave via the back stairs and through the kitchen entrance.'

'Did she leave alone?'

'Only with her chauffeur. The Rolls was waiting for her in the delivery bay around the back of the hotel.'

'Where did she go?'

'She didn't say.'

'And you're happy to take part in this deception, are you?' Irton snarled. 'A respectable hotel like this.'

The manager shrugged and smiled happily. 'Well, she's our Jodie, isn't she? She's a darling.'

Chapter Thirty-Four

Thursday, 30th May 1940

Despite her determination to be brave, Jemma slept badly.

It didn't help that she was twice woken out of her fitful sleep by Tom shouting and screaming in the bedroom below. The first time he called out, she was half out of bed before she heard Maisie hurry across the landing towards her son.

It was difficult to get back to sleep. Her mind went over and over the shooting. The attack must relate to the museum murder. The murderer clearly resented their involvement in the case.

Had it been a warning shot?

Probably. The gunman had aimed wide to scare her. A second dead body connected with the museum mystery would be too obvious. Even the dim-witted D.S. Fawcett wouldn't have been able to ignore that. Fawcett would have been forced to widen his investigation. This would be the last thing the real murderer would want.

The second time poor Tom woke up the household with his nightmare, her mind returned to Gabriel's suggestion that she move out. She knew it made sense, but it had still been a shock. This was her family home. The place of sanctuary where she'd fled when her husband was declared missing. It hurt to think Gabriel wanted her to leave.

She knew his moods and tempers and suspected he'd soon relent. But he was right; everything would have to change once she got Michael back. She remembered how Bobbie had questioned her about the business earlier in the day and felt a wave of grief at the thought of leaving Smoke & Cracked Mirrors. She *liked* the way her life was now, especially her thriving little business.

Her biggest fear – but the most likely scenario – was that Michael would turn out to be injured and need nursing. *Was she capable of this? Nursing?*

Like most young women, her wedding vow *to love and to cherish... until death us do part* had been glibly uttered while she stood next to a fit and handsome young man at a church altar. The last thing she ever expected was that she might be forced to care for an invalid a mere twelve months later. But thanks to this damn war, young women all over the country were facing this grim reality. Every day, injured troops were sent back from Europe.

She sighed, turned over and drifted back into another fitful sleep. When the first rays of dawn crept through a crack in her curtains, she gave up trying and got up. She knew she'd be shattered at the dance tonight at De Grey's. But exhausting long hours went hand in hand with this job.

She was surprised to find Emmett in the office. He was fast asleep, sprawled across one of the armchairs with an empty teacup and an overflowing ashtray on the coffee table beside him.

He jerked awake and rubbed his eyes. 'Your man Ricky's taken over the watch. I thought I'd come in and report.'

She swept the dirty crockery and the ashtray off the table. 'Has something happened? I'll put the kettle on while you tell me.'

Despite her exhaustion and her irritation, she burst out laughing when Emmett described how Jodie had tricked them.

Emmett blinked his sleepy eyes with surprise. 'You ain't mad? The King would've thrown a tantrum.'

She poured the boiling water into the teapot and smiled. 'I've got a healthy respect for Jodie's intelligence. She'd run rings round any man – even Terence King himself.'

'Kerner's arrival has scuppered our theory that Stephen Howard is her lover.'

'Yes, it has. He's the motor-racing playboy, isn't he? He's probably come to York for her benefit party at De Grey's.'

Emmett yawned. 'It's like two steps forward and one step back with this damn case.'

Jemma nodded thoughtfully, passed him a cup of tea, and sat down in the other armchair. 'It might be time to refine our operation.'

Emmett managed a small smile and tapped his china teacup. 'Ooh, refinement.'

'Now we know Max Glazer is out of the picture – and probably Nigel Lansdowne – we can focus on Stephen Howard and Arthur Kerner. We need another vehicle and more staff. If we shadow them as well, they might lead us to something.'

'Like what?'

'Well, if we discover one of them buying flowers for Jodie—'

Emmett shook his head. 'Half the damn country buys flowers for Jodie.'

'What about jewellery? If either of them steps into a jeweller's, purchases a bracelet and scribbles a loving note to go with the gift, we've got our evidence. One of these men has *got* to be her lover, so inevitably we'll be led back to Jodie at some point.'

'I think I can see where you're comin' from,' Emmett said thoughtfully. 'And if they make arrangements for some secret tryst, she'll be the one jumpin' through hoops to arrive secretively – like she did last night. So, it'll be a lot easier for us to just follow the blokes.'

Jemma nodded. 'I doubt either of the two men will be as alert as Jodie. She's been playing cat and mouse with you guys for months and she's good at it. All we need is for one of the men to make a mistake, and we might get the evidence. I'll be at De Grey's tonight, which might throw up some more clues.'

'It's a good job she don't know who you are.'

Jemma grimaced. She'd forgotten about her rash behaviour with Jodie and Will Sharrow the previous day. 'I'll have a think about this today and look again at our schedule. We can hire another car but I'm not sure what we'll do about the extra manpower.'

'Talk to the King.' Emmett drained his tea, rose and put on his hat. 'He might send up another couple of blokes and a car.'

Once Emmett had gone, Jemma left a message with D.S. Marlowe's office, asking him to ring her back with an update on the search for Michael.

Next, she phoned Terence King's office. She remained standing while she made the call in the hope it would make her sound more authoritative.

King listened carefully and without comment as she relayed the events of the previous day, although he did chuckle when she told him about Hannah and Max Glazer. 'A friend of Dorothy, is he? That's interesting.'

King was also surprisingly calm about the Will Sharrow incident. 'I suspected the baron might have employed another agency. The man's desperate for results.'

'He'll be furious with us when Sharrow tells him about my interference.'

'He might not. Sharrow won't be keen to admit he failed – he may simply try something else.'

'I also drew attention to myself. Jodie saw me.'

'I wouldn't worry too much about it, Mrs James. You were standing in her crowd of admirers. She'll think you were a concerned fan who'd spotted Sharrow put something in her pocket – and if you turn up tonight at her party on the arm of a handsome Canadian airman, so what? You're just another citizen of York, out for a good time.'

Jemma sighed with relief and moved the conversation along. She told him about her idea to shadow both Kerner and Stephen Howard as well as Jodie. 'Hannah is convinced she's about to lose her job at the hotel, so we'll have an extra pair of hands, but we need more staff and another car for the next few days.'

'Leave it with me. I'll see what I can do. But I think you should turn the screws on Glazer. If you tell him you know he's a queer – and threaten to report him to the police for sodomy – he'll sing like a canary. I'm sure he'll tell us everything we need to know about our favourite starlet.'

Jemma recoiled and said nothing.

King chuckled. 'It that a problem for you, Mrs James?'

Yes, it was a problem. Blackmailing Max Glazer for information because of his homosexuality might get them results, but what about her own integrity? Gabriel had accused her last night of having no scruples. *Exactly how far was she prepared to sink for this job?*

She made up her mind. 'I'm not comfortable with that, Mr King. It's blackmail – it's against the law.'

He chuckled again. 'Don't worry. I'll get Irton to do it. Ask him to give me a call. How are the pair of them doing, anyway?'

'They've been helpful and supportive,' Jemma said quickly.

'They don't give you any trouble, I hope?'

'No.'

'So, you're getting along well?'

'Yes. Everything's fine – as long as you don't expect me to take responsibility for their literary education.'

King burst out laughing. 'That sounds like a good story.'

'Stories are the last thing they know anything about.'

He chuckled again and said, 'You'll have to tell me about it sometime, Mrs James – over dinner, perhaps?'

Her knees went weak at the thought. She clutched the edge of the desk for support. 'That… that would be lovely.'

He rang off and Jemma took a few minutes to compose herself after this unexpected flush of excitement. *You silly woman,* she chided herself. *Isn't your life complicated enough? The last thing you need is a crush on Terence King.*

Bobbie bounded up the stairs, burst into the office and threw her hat on to the stand.

'I've got a damn good idea where Anthony was on the night of the murder! And unless Lance Richards was also a trekker, it's unlikely our client is guilty. The two of them were probably twenty miles apart that night.'

She sat down and told Jemma the full story. 'I'll telephone Mr Pearson now, although what he'll say when he finds out I've investigated his client's movements, I don't know!'

Jemma shrugged. 'You were only following up on a lead we got from the police – and, unlike them, you got results. If Mr Pearson has any sense, he'll ignore his client's wishes and share this information with D. S. Fawcett. If Richards *was* with Anthony at the quarry on the night of the murder – then it's a potential murder scene. They need to examine it.'

Bobbie moved across to the telephone, frowning. 'Do you think the missing rope might be at the quarry? I can't imagine why anyone would climb around a deserted quarry in the dark… but that damn rope has got to be somewhere. Anyway, what's new in the divorce case?'

'Arthur Kerner has arrived at the hotel and the two of them gave Irton and Emmett the run-around last night. Oh, and by the way, something happened on my way home…'

But Bobbie was already dialling Mr Pearson's number and Hannah arrived breathlessly at the door. Jemma ushered Hannah into the kitchenette while Bobbie was on the phone.

'I'm sorry, Jemma. I've lost me job. Both Jodie and Nigel Lansdowne complained about me.'

'Not Max Glazer?'

'No. Not him. Mrs Higgins sacked me this mornin'. I managed to keep these though.' She tossed the housekeeper's set of hotel keys on to the draining board by the sink. 'They might come in useful.'

Jemma smiled. 'Don't worry, Hannah, you did well. I'll put you on the observation rota with the others.'

'I did get a bit of gossip afore I left. I don't know what's gone on, but Jodie has sacked her maid and sent her packin'. No one knows why.'

Jemma glanced up sharply. This was interesting news. She'd suspected that the maid was in Sharrow's pay. It was the only thing that made sense. Most women like Jodie would hand their coat to the maid to hang up. Checking the mistress's pockets in case she'd forgotten anything would be automatic. Sharrow and the baron must have bribed the maid to go through the pockets, find the incriminating letter and then take it to the witness box in the divorce court. It was a desperate ruse – and not necessarily one that would stand up to scrutiny in court, but Baron Stokesley and Will Sharrow were desperate men.

Bobbie appeared at the doorway to the kitchen. 'Did I hear you say Jodie has sacked her maid?'

Hannah nodded, and a curious expression settled on Bobbie's face.

'What are you thinking?' Jemma asked.

'That this is an ideal opportunity for a female detective agency. You should apply for the job, Jemma.'

Jemma shook her head. 'She knows who I am, and I know nothing about being a lady's maid! I come to *you* for fashion advice.'

'It might take a week before she finds a replacement,' Bobbie said. 'In the meantime, Jodie still needs to dazzle the world with her appearance and clothes. She's constantly in the eye of the camera and she's got this posh party at De Grey's tonight. You must give it a go.'

'*You* could do it,' Jemma said. 'She's not seen you – and you're the stylish one in this room.'

'But what about my other case?'

'We'll swap – I'll take over the museum murder.' Jemma's heart lurched as she said the words. Gabriel would be furious. But at least it might keep Bobbie safe from the murderer if she was with Jodie. The actress had excellent protection.

The three women stood silently while their brains toyed with this dramatic idea.

'It will be tough to pull it off. How will we even get into the hotel to speak to her?' Bobbie asked.

'I'll tek you in through the back,' Hannah said. 'Not everyone knows I've been sacked yet.'

'This might work…' Jemma said. 'It's a slim chance – but it might work…'

Bobbie spun on her heels and dashed back into the office. 'I need a reference – or three.' She pulled off the typewriter cover and sat down at the machine. 'Let's do this, Jemma – what have we got to lose?'

Bobbie typed out two forged references, put them in her handbag and snapped it shut with a decisive click. Then she pulled out her powder compact, applied another coat of lipstick and double-checked the pins in her hair, while barking out instructions to Jemma at the same time. 'Mr Pearson wants us to continue checking out the alibis of Ian Duggen and Władysław Włoch. Oh, and if you've got time, try to track down that butcher's boy – Ronald – on Nunnery Street. He's a spotty, greasy little fellow with dirty hands. He knew Richards and if you charm him, he might tell you some more about Richards's cronies. But for God's sake tell him you're married! He's another one with wandering hands.'

She pinned her elegant brown hat with its sculptured felt bow at a rakish angle on her head and stood up. She glanced down at her feet and smoothed down her dress. 'I wish I was wearing my best shoes – but at least this is my best coat and hat.'

'You look great, Bobbie – good luck!' Jemma called as the two women left.

Chapter Thirty-Five

The usual crowd of Jodie's admirers loitered around the hotel entrance. Among them stood Ricky, with his camera around his neck. Bobbie had an idea. 'You carry on round to the staff entrance and wait for me, Hannah. I'll join you in a minute.'

Bobbie strolled over to Ricky and casually asked: 'Is she inside?'

His long, scarred face creased into a frown. 'Yes, she's there. I thought we weren't supposed to be seen together?'

'This won't take a minute.' She pulled out a slightly bent cigarette from the bottom of her handbag.

'I didn't know you smoked.'

'I don't. This is for emergencies only. Get out your matches. Make it look like I'm asking you for a light.'

He fumbled around in the pockets of his fraying jacket for his matches.

'I need you to do something for me,' Bobbie continued. 'Get inside the hotel, go up to Jodie's suite and wait for me there. We'll cause a disturbance to bring her out of her room. I want to talk to her.'

His eyebrows shot up with amusement as he struck the match and held out the flame towards her. 'That sounds like fun.'

'Can you get inside?'

He winked. 'Leave it to me, lass. I can get into Fort Knox if I need to.'

Bobbie raised her voice, thanked him for the light and hurried towards the staff entrance at the rear of the building. With Hannah by her side,

Bobbie breezed swiftly into the hotel. Hannah led her to the staff staircase.

Bobbie shot up the stairs to the top floor, ignoring the curious glances of the other staff. She was breathless when she finally arrived in the plush corridor with its elegant art deco mirrors and wall lamps that resembled scallop shells.

Ricky was already there, lurking behind a large aspidistra on a marble plinth.

'How did you get in?' she whispered. Their feet sank into the thick carpet as they walked towards the door of Jodie's suite.

'Simple. I told one of them doormen I needed the lav and slipped him a few shillings.'

Once they reached Jodie's door, Bobbie spun round on Ricky. 'Get away from there, you sneaky rat! Leave that door alone!'

'You what?'

Bobbie reached over and hammered on the door to Jodie's suite. 'I said: stand back, you scoundrel! Don't think I don't know what you're doing!'

A light went on in Ricky's eyes. 'I weren't doin' anythin', missus! Honest, I weren't!'

'You can tell that to the management!'

The door to Jodie's suite swung open and her secretary stepped outside, a thickset, jowly man in spectacles and a pinstripe suit. Bobbie remembered his name from Jemma's board in the office: Johnson.

'What's happening out here?' he demanded.

She pointed a finger at Ricky. 'I've just found that… that photographer snooping around Jodie's door – I think he was trying to pick the lock!'

'I weren't! She's just an interfering busybody.'

'There are no photographers allowed inside this hotel. I don't know how you got in, young man, but I'm phoning the management.' As Mr Johnson turned to go back inside, Bobbie rushed to his side. 'Please don't leave me out here with him! He's a brute and has threatened me.'

The secretary hesitated for a second and glanced at Ricky's scowling face. Then he ushered her inside the suite and shut the door behind her. 'You'd better disappear fast,' he called over his shoulder to Ricky.

Mr Johnson moved over to the telephone on a cream sideboard and phoned down to reception for assistance.

They were in the living area of the suite, a luxurious peach and cream paradise, full of marble pillars and tables, with silk soft furnishings. Huge baskets and vases of flowers adorned every surface, and their scent filled the room.

Jodie was sitting on a peach velvet chair by the window, next to a small table scattered with papers. She was wearing a simple aquamarine tea dress that emphasised her large baby-blue eyes. Earrings of the same vivid blue flashed in her earlobes and a matching dress ring glittered on her hand. Her beautiful hair was brushed but unstyled and tumbled down over her shoulders. She put the lid on her expensive tortoiseshell fountain pen and said calmly, 'Good gracious. What on earth's going on?'

'I came up to see you, Your Ladyship,' Bobbie stammered, 'but I found one of those blooming photographers trying to pick your door lock. I thought you needed to know he was here.'

The actress's eyes glinted with amusement. 'How sweet of you. But why were *you* loitering outside my door?'

Bobbie took in a deep breath. 'My name's Roberta Baker. I've a friend in this hotel. One of the staff. They told me you'd lost your maid. I've come to offer you my services. I've been a huge fan of yours for years, and I'm a trained lady's maid.'

The smile never faltered but Jodie's eyes narrowed. 'This friend of yours? It wouldn't be one of the chambermaids, would it?'

Bobbie feigned confusion. 'No. It's Little Laurie Tipton – the chap who mans the lift. He's a neighbour of mine, he lives on Tanner Street. You must have noticed him?' It was a risk to mention Laurie but if she slipped him a quid on her way out, he might back her up.

'Ah, yes, the cheerful little chap with the stunted growth.'

'That's the one.' Bobbie whipped her references from her handbag and held them out. 'I've got these references. When I left school, I was a parlourmaid for Lady Norton in Gargrave, but she trained me up to be her maid. After that, I went to work for Mrs Raleigh at the Blayton Estate in Derbyshire.'

'I've never heard of either of them,' Jodie commented. Bobbie's stomach lurched. She hadn't thought of this. As Baroness Stokesley, Jodie had mixed with the British upper classes for years and was probably on first-name terms with most of them. Her nervousness heightened when the actress reached out her elegant hand, took the references and scanned them.

'Lady Norton and Mrs Raleigh are quiet, elderly ladies; they rarely went up to London. I had to come back to York to nurse my poorly mother but she's much better now and I'm looking for work. I thought I'd have to work at Rowntree's... or become an ATC vehicle mechanic.'

'You can drive?'

'Yes, Your Ladyship. Both my previous ladies lived remotely so I learnt. I was delighted when Little Laurie said you had a vacancy. I'd love the opportunity to work for you, Lady Stokesley.' Bobbie squeezed the handle of her handbag for reassurance. She was running out of things to say.

Mr Johnson put down the telephone receiver and joined the two women. He eased his bulk into the chair opposite Jodie and picked up a file from the table. 'I'm afraid you're out of luck, Miss Baker. We've already sent for a replacement maid for Her Ladyship to our agency in London.'

Bobbie's heart sank but Jodie held up her elegant hand to quieten her secretary; she was still reading the references. 'Let's not be too hasty, Lionel. It might take days to interview and recruit a new maid.' She looked up at Bobbie and scanned her from the tip of her hat to her toes. Her sharp eyes eventually settled on Bobbie's hair.

'I like your hat. Do you style your own hair?'

'Of course, my lady.'

Jodie rose elegantly to her feet. Close up, the actress was surprisingly tall. 'Let's have a trial. Come with me into the bedroom and do mine.'

'I must protest, Your Ladyship!' Mr Johnson exclaimed. 'We know nothing about this young woman.'

Jodie dropped the references into his lap. 'Then write to her former employers and find out if she's genuine.'

Bobbie struggled to contain her excitement. It would only be a matter of days – possibly a week – before her lies were uncovered, but a week was a long time in the world of private detection.

'But the London agency plans to send you some women to interview,' Mr Johnson protested.

'Yes – and the last two we've had from the agency have proved to be rather treacherous. Come with me, Miss Baker.'

The adjoining bedroom was in the same feminine shades of peach and cream as the sitting room, with several large, gilded mirrors. But it looked like Hitler had dropped a bomb in it. A shimmering evening gown, stockings, shoes and other items littered the floor. A fur coat was flung in the corner. The dressing table was scattered and smeared with make-up and half a dozen pots of cream and bottles of expensive French perfume, most of which had lost their lids and stoppers. Among them glittered a selection of random earrings and a diamond bracelet. An inlaid wooden jewellery box sat amid the chaos with its lid open, spilling out more diamond bracelets and a ruby necklace.

Jodie followed her gaze, scooped up the jewellery and replaced it in the box. 'Let's remove temptation, shall we?' She carried the box over to the safe in the back of the wardrobe and shielded her hands from view as she twisted the dial.

Bobbie noticed the two used champagne glasses on the bedside tables. Jodie had been entertaining someone in her bedroom.

'I'm not the tidiest woman in the world,' Jodie admitted. 'I trust I can rely on your discretion about anything you see or hear in this suite?'

'Of course, my lady.'

Jodie sat down on the cushioned stool at the dressing table and gathered up a selection of jewelled hairpins from the detritus on the surface for Bobbie to use.

Over the next ten minutes, Bobbie almost forgot why she was there. She stood behind her idol in a floral scented boudoir, styling her silken tresses. She'd had plenty of experience styling Jemma's hair, which was of a similar soft texture, and her fingers confidently rolled and pinned Jodie's hair. *This makes up for the dreary hours shadowing suspects*, she thought to herself with a smile. Not to mention the grim trip to Armley Gaol and being pushed about by D.S. Fawcett.

'Can you sew?' Jodie asked, as Bobbie pushed in the last of the hairpins and applied hairspray.

'Yes, my lady.' She couldn't – but Jemma could.

Jodie turned her head from side to side, examining her reflection in the mirror. She stood up and pointed to the gown on the floor. 'There's a tear in the hem of that gown. I caught my heel in it last night. You can fix it. I also need you to pull out my dark green silk evening gown and iron it ready for tonight's benefit at De Grey's. You can lay out a selection of accessories to match and I'll make my choice this evening.'

Bobbie frowned. 'Dark green, ma'am? Are you sure?'

Jodie caught her eye in the mirror and raised an arched eyebrow. 'Is there a problem, Miss Baker?'

'I'm sure you know best, my lady. It's just that the carpet and walls in De Grey's are forest green.

Jodie let out a delightful peal of laughter. 'So, you think I'll fade into the wallpaper? Quite right, Miss Baker. And thank you for remembering. It's some years since I last danced in De Grey's. In that case, let's have a change of plan. Prepare my red chiffon gown and the white silk stole with the scarlet and gold peonies.'

Bobbie held the hand mirror up behind Jodie to show her the back of her hair.

The actress nodded with satisfaction. 'If your references are genuine, you can have the position while I'm up in Yorkshire. Mr Johnson will sort out your pay and accommodation. Obviously, you'll have to move into the hotel. I keep long and erratic hours. I trust your mother is fully recovered and you can leave her now?'

'Yes, my lady!' Bobbie grinned in delight. 'But I'll have to pop back home to tell her and collect some items.' *And she needed to update Jemma about her success.*

'You can call me "Miss Jodie" and I'll call you "Baker". Once you've completed those tasks I've already set, pull out my trunks and start packing.'

'Packing, my lady – sorry – Miss Jodie? Are we leaving?'

'Absolutely. I'm sick to the back teeth of being pestered by photographers, over-enthusiastic fans and private detectives. Tomorrow, we'll move out to the country estate of my good friend the Countess von Hatvan.'

Chapter Thirty-Six

Jemma was sitting at her desk, doing administration, when D.S. Marlowe rang her back. He asked her abruptly what she wanted.

'I wanted to know if there'd been any developments in your hunt for Michael?'

'It's only been a few days since we last spoke, Mrs James.' She heard the irritation in his voice.

'Yes, but that bus stop below the bridge—'

'I've already checked it out. It's on the route to Towcester and Northampton. We've expanded our search for your husband to Buckinghamshire and Northamptonshire.'

'Good, good...' she murmured. *Why did Towcester ring a bell?* Then she remembered – or at least, she thought she did. 'My brother has an old friend with the police in Northamptonshire, Superintendent Jim Jones – perhaps he might be able to help?'

'The police in both counties are already assisting us, Mrs James. We're doing everything we can.'

'Thank you. I'm sorry to bother you.' She replaced the receiver and rubbed her tired eyes. Damn this exhaustion. Something still niggled about Towcester. *What was she missing here?*

Bobbie thundered up the stairs, flew into the office, grinning, and dropped a large parcel on the desk. 'I've got the job!'

'That's brilliant news! Have you got time for a cup of tea?'

'Absolutely not! But you'll have to help me. She's ripped a dress and I told her I can sew. Will you fix it and give it back tonight? We're leaving York tomorrow, by the way. To go to her friend's estate in Beningbrough.'

Jemma's face fell. 'Beningbrough? That's six miles away and remote. It won't be so easy to keep tabs on her out there.'

Bobbie's grin widened. 'Then it's a good job we've now got someone on the inside.'

'Who's her friend?'

'It's that Hungarian countess, Anna Léna von Hatvan.'

Jemma's frown deepened. 'Fanny pointed her out to me at the museum talk. The woman seemed chummy with Baron Stokesley. I'm surprised Jodie trusts her.'

Bobbie shrugged and turned to go. 'I'll telephone you every evening with an update when I can get away. Probably between six and eight o'clock. Got to dash. I need to go home and pack. I'll tell my parents I'm staying with you for a few days. See you later!'

Jemma waved her off, unwrapped the beautiful gown and explored the damage. The silk was as delicate as gossamer and still smelt of the actress's perfume. It would have to be hand sewn and her sewing basket was at home.

She sealed up the parcel and reached for her car keys.

Gabriel and Tom were sitting at the kitchen table eating tinned-pilchard sandwiches. Tom's bandaged head with its unruly mop of red hair was bent over his plate as he wolfed down his food. He still had dark rings beneath his eyes, but he had some colour in his freckled cheeks.

'Hello, Tom. It's lovely to see you up and about. How do you feel?'

'Much better, thank you, Jemma,' he mumbled with his mouth full.

'That's good to hear.'

'Maisie's just out at the shops,' Gabriel told her. His tone sounded friendlier.

She filled the kettle and lit the gas. 'I've popped home because I need to do some sewing. I'll clear away the table when you've finished and get out my stuff.' She walked across to the cupboard in the dresser where she kept her sewing basket. The catalogue from the Yorkshire Museum lay on top of the basket. When she bent down and reached inside, it slithered to the tiled floor and fell open.

Jemma picked it up, glanced at a grainy black-and-white photograph on the open page and froze.

It depicted a bronze statue of an ancient Greek mythological creature called a harpy. Half woman, half eagle, it had a scowling tortured face and huge wings. Below the rounded feathered breast were two stumps where the statue's deadly talons had broken off. The wings were in better condition.

'Good grief.' She turned to Tom and placed the catalogue on the table in front of him.

'Tom, was this the statue the man used to hit you?'

The colour drained from Tom's face again. 'Yeah.'

'And it was part of your collection of scrap in the barn?'

He didn't reply.

'Where did you boys find it?'

Tom threw down his crusts and jerked his chair back. Jemma hastily stepped out of the way.

'I can't remember! I told you I can't! Leave me alone!' He stormed out of the room.

Gabriel called after him and half rose to his feet. Then he grabbed the catalogue. 'What the hell is this, Jemma?'

'It's an ancient Greek statue that was brought here by the Romans.'

Gabriel read the text, frowning. 'But it doesn't make any sense. If the museum has lost one of their statues, they'd have reported it.'

'They've been packing up valuable artefacts like this for months to send to safety in the country. Maybe they don't know it's lost.'

Gabriel's frown deepened. 'After lunch, I'll get my coat, go back to the barn and see if it's—'

He broke off as the front door slammed and Maisie came into the kitchen. She dumped her wicker shopping basket on the table, sank wearily into a chair and pushed back an escaped tendril of her long auburn hair.

'What's the matter, love?' Gabriel asked.

'There's something goin' on, Gabriel, and I don't know what to make of it.'

'What's happened?'

'I went to the chemist shop to get Tom somethin' to help him sleep better. And while I were there, I bumped into Kenneth Newby's mum.'

'That's one of Tom's friends, isn't it?' Jemma asked.

'Yes. And guess what? Mrs Newby were at the chemist's for the same reason as me. Just like Tom, their Kenneth has also been sufferin' from bad nightmares.'

Gabriel frowned. 'It must be a coincidence. It was the attack at the barn that set off Tom's nightmares.'

Jemma shook her head. 'No, it wasn't. Tom had a nasty dream on the night of your wedding, after you'd left for Scotland.'

Maisie's frown turned into a scowl. 'There's definitely somethin' wrong, Gabriel. I can feel it. Kenneth is a sensitive lad – more sensitive than those Wright twins – but what happened to our Tom wouldn't have upset him that badly.'

Gabriel pushed the museum catalogue towards Maisie. 'Actually, we've just uncovered another mystery. Tom says the statue the man used to hit him looked just like this harpy.'

Jemma handed Maisie a cup of tea, but her eyes were fixed on the photograph. 'Dear God! It's the scrap they've been collectin', isn't it? They've got hold of somethin' they shouldn't. What the hell have they done?'

'Let's not jump to conclusions,' Gabriel soothed. 'Tom's a good lad. He knows right from wrong.'

Maisie's mouth set in a determined line. 'The difference between you and me, Gabriel, is that while you've only been a parent for five minutes, I've spent twenty years bringin' up two lads and suspicion is my middle name. I'll speak to Tom.'

She picked up the catalogue and went upstairs. Jemma and Gabriel heard the murmur of low voices. Then Tom started shouting at his mother, screaming to be left alone.

Maisie didn't shout back, but when she came downstairs her face was like thunder. 'He's admitted it's the statue, but he won't say where they got it.'

'Why?' Jemma asked.

'He'll have sworn a pact of silence with his bloody pals. They're thick as thieves, those lads. There's only one way to deal with this. I'll telephone Mrs Newby and Mrs Wright and ask them to bring their lads round here. We'll have it out with all four of them at once. Gabriel, you'll need to put on your uniform.'

'Oh, no, Maisie!' he pleaded. 'I'm trying to be his father – not some heavy-handed copper!'

She gave him a withering glance and walked out to the telephone in the hallway.

Jemma gave her brother's arm a reassuring pat and whispered, 'I wasn't married for long myself, Gabriel, but I've some advice: I think it's better to do what she says.'

'What? Always? For the rest of my life?'

'Absolutely.'

Maisie asked the mothers to bring the Wright twins and Kenneth Newby round to the Roxbys' as soon as they'd finished school.

In the meantime, Gabriel went back to the barn and searched it again. There was no sign of the harpy.

'Should we notify the museum?' Jemma asked her brother when he returned empty-handed.

'Not yet. Let's see what the lads have to say.'

The boisterous curly-haired twins, Jim and Davy Wright, looked sulky and chastened when they arrived. They were also extremely grubby, and their school uniforms were stained. Kenneth was cleaner. The smallest of the four pals, he was thin and delicate-looking, like his pale-haired mother. He was also nervous and close to tears.

The three boys sat fidgeting uncomfortably on the sofa, avoiding eye contact, while their grim-faced mothers stood behind them.

Jemma hovered in the doorway while Gabriel – in full uniform – took one of the chairs by the hearth. He looked calm but the serious expression on his face had a sobering effect on the boys. Eventually, Maisie managed to persuade Tom to come downstairs. He threw himself sullenly into the chair opposite Gabriel. His round face was deathly pale beneath his freckles.

Gabriel cleared his throat. 'Right, lads, as you know, a terrible crime has been committed. A vicious and evil man attacked Tom. It's important we catch this man before he hurts someone else. The police need your help.' He paused.

The four boys said nothing.

'It's good to help the police,' Mrs Newby urged her son. Kenneth's lower lip quivered.

Gabriel opened the museum catalogue and showed them the photograph of the harpy. 'Tom told us this was the statue used as a weapon by the man who attacked him. It's a statue of a harpy and we think it belongs to the Yorkshire Museum.'

All four boys stared down at their toes.

'I suspect the man who attacked Tom was looking for it when Tom disturbed him in the barn. That's why he's taken it away with him. It's very valuable.'

Gabriel paused again and there was more strained silence. His tone hardened. 'The police need to know where you got it from, lads. How did a statue from the museum end up in your barn?'

Davy Wright shrugged. 'Can't remember. Folks give us boxes of junk all the time.'

'I'm sure they do,' Gabriel said patiently. 'But it's unlikely this statue ended up in a box of junk. Come on, lads. It's time to tell the truth. How did you get it?'

'We didn't steal it!' Kenneth blurted out.

'I'm sure you didn't, son. I know you're good lads.'

'Will we go to prison?' Jim asked.

'Of course you won't!' Maisie reassured them. 'You're not criminals – you've been the victim of a crime. A horrible, horrible crime.'

Tom glanced up at Gabriel. 'Is Mum right? Is that different, Dad?'

Gabriel nodded. 'Yes, very different.'

The strain in the room caused by Gabriel's calmness and gravitas was palpable. Even Jemma felt like she ought to confess.

The Wright twins still looked conflicted. Jemma suspected Kenneth would be the one to break first. But she was wrong.

'We didn't do nothin' wrong!' Tom blurted out. 'It were just lyin' there… on the grass.'

The twins reacted angrily.

'Snitch!' Jim exclaimed.

'Yer promised to keep yer gob shut!' Davy added.

Tom rounded on his friends. 'Aye, well, it weren't you two who were hit on the head with a harpy!'

The three boys glared at each other, and the adults held their breath.

Then Kenneth giggled. 'Hit on the head with a harpy. That's funny, that.'

It broke the tension. Soon all four boys were giggling.

'Where did this happen, son?' Gabriel asked. 'Where did you find it?'

'Down the side of the museum. I picked it up and took it to the barn.'

'When was this?'

'On the Wednesday night before the wedding.' He glanced at Gabriel, embarrassed. 'Sometimes we climb over the broken wall on Marygate and go explorin' in the museum grounds. Folks leave newspapers on the benches. We collect those too.'

'It's good at night,' Jim said. 'It's quiet and spooky.'

'Too spooky that night,' Davy said gloomily.

All four boys suddenly fell silent. Everything from nervousness to downright distress suddenly flickered across their faces at the memory. Jemma felt alarmed – and sensed the other adults did too.

What the devil had happened?

'So, this statue was just lying there on the grass down the side of the museum,' Gabriel said slowly. 'Did you see anything else while you were there?'

Silence.

'Was there anyone else around?'

'There was other stuff,' Tom said. 'It were strewn everywhere. Broken boxes.'

'We didn't do it,' Jim insisted. 'It were like that when we got there.'

Kenneth finally burst into the tears that had been bubbling close to the surface since he arrived. 'And we didn't kill the bloke either! He were already dead!'

Chapter Thirty-Seven

It took some time and a lot of patience for the shocked adults to calm Kenneth down and reassure the boys that no one thought they were murderers. All the mothers moved closer to their sons. Maisie crouched down beside Tom's chair.

Eventually, the boys told them the whole story. They described how they'd broken into the botanic gardens, wandered up the side of the museum by the Tempest Anderson Hall, and found a scene of carnage. There was a large-wheeled trolley stacked with wooden crates. But some of them had been shattered and had spilled out their contents. Once their eyes had adjusted to the shadows cast by the building, they realised that a dead man was also sprawled among the wreckage and the splintered wood. He lay in a pool of blood with his head bashed to a pulp.

Maisie gave Tom a hug. 'Dear God, what on earth have you lads stumbled across!'

'We didn't tread on him, Mum!' Tom protested. 'We didn't go near him.'

'How did you know he was dead, sweetheart?'

'He were so still. But his eyes were open. He were staring up at the stars. We didn't know what to do.'

'I still see him,' Kenneth confessed, with a sob. 'Every night in my dreams.' Mrs Newby put her arm round her son.

'Me too,' Tom said quietly. 'I dream about him too.'

'Tell us what happened next,' Gabriel asked gently.

Tom's next words sent a chill down the spine of every adult in the room. 'Another bloke came out of the side door of the museum and yelled at us. He said we were murderers and he'd have us!'

'We legged it,' Jim said. 'The bloke chased us for a bit then gave up and went back.'

'We're not murderers,' his twin added. 'Someone else had done him in.'

'I've never run so fast, Mum!' Kenneth said. 'It was horrible!'

'Do you think he's the man who attacked you in the barn, Tom?'

'I'm not sure,' Tom said. 'It were dark at the museum – and dark in the barn too. I didn't get a good look at him either time. But he had the same posh voice.' He gulped back his emotion. 'When I went in the barn, he just stepped out of the shadows with the harpy in his hands. Then he yelled that I was a thief and a murderer – and he hit me when I turned to run.'

'You'd got something he wanted,' Gabriel said grimly. 'He must have been desperate to get back the statue. He'd tracked you boys down to the barn.'

Maisie hugged Tom again. 'You should have told us, darling.'

'I were frightened, Mum.'

'It ain't Tom's fault,' Davy said. 'We swore a pact to stay quiet, Mrs Roxby. He couldn't say owt.'

'We thought we'd go to prison,' Kenneth added.

'No one is going to prison,' Gabriel said firmly. 'But we still need your help to track down the man responsible. Not only did he attack Tom, but it looks like he'd killed the man you found.'

Jemma started. 'Good grief! I've just remembered something. That's the night the museum curator, Lance Richards, was attacked.'

She dashed into the kitchen to their pile of old newspapers and found the edition of the *Yorkshire Evening Press* she wanted. The lead story reported the attack on Lance Richards and his photograph was on the front page. She took it back into the parlour and held it up for the boys. 'Was this the man you saw lying on the ground?'

Kenneth grimaced and looked away. The other boys frowned and shrugged.

'His face were a mess, Jemma,' Tom said, 'but maybe.'

Gabriel took off his cap and ran his fingers through his curly white hair. 'Good God. What the hell has happened here?'

'It's too much of a coincidence for it *not* to be Richards,' Jemma said. 'The lads must have disturbed a burglary that went horribly wrong. Richards was desperate for money and thoroughly unscrupulous.'

Gabriel gave her a sharp glance. 'Let's not jump to conclusions. Maybe Richards was just in the wrong place at the wrong time, like the boys. Perhaps he saw something was wrong, went to investigate and was attacked for interfering.' He turned back to Tom. 'Remind me again, son, how did the statue of the harpy end up in the barn?'

'I were holdin' it when he chased us off. We'd picked up a few pieces of scrap before we saw the bloke. The harpy came with me when I ran. I forgot to drop it.'

A wary expression crossed Maisie's face. 'Lads, what else did you pick up from the stuff scattered on the ground?'

There was a mass shuffling of feet.

'There were a few tanners lyin' around,' Davy said vaguely.

311

'Sixpences?' Mrs Wright's voice sharpened. 'Empty your pockets, son – and the rest of you.'

The boys protested but eventually a curious collection of bits of string, boiled sweets covered in pocket fluff, an empty matchbox containing a dead centipede, used bus tickets and a small vole's skull were placed on the coffee table by the sofa. Among the pile were copper pennies and tuppences – and several tiny, gleaming silver coins. Most showed the blurred image of an emperor's head and had Latin inscriptions around the side.

Jemma flicked through the museum catalogue. 'They're Roman denarii. Two thousand years old.'

Mrs Wright groaned and rolled her eyes to the ceiling. 'Oh lads, what the hell have you done?'

'Are there any more?' Gabriel asked.

'Only those we spent in the sweet shop,' Jim admitted. 'Mrs Hogarth who runs it has bad eyes. She thought they were tanners.'

This was too much for Mrs Wright. 'You little sods!' For a moment, it looked like she was about to box the ears of both of her sons, but Gabriel held up his hand to calm her.

'Did you take anything else?'

'Yes,' Davy said. 'I had hold of a battered old metal bowl when we ran. It were dented and had most of its stones missin' – only one blue one left. No one would want it. I put it in with the other scrap.'

'Is it still in the barn?' his mother asked.

'Yes. That bloke who attacked Tom didn't find it. I've kept it safe, Mum.'

The other adults in the room turned to Jemma expectantly.

312

She flicked through the catalogue, found a photograph, and showed it to the boys.

'Yes, that's it!' Davy said.

Jemma cleared her throat and kept her voice neutral. 'I think Davy has taken the Ormside Bowl into the barn for scrap. It's an embossed gilt drinking vessel used by a Saxon church. The historians suspect the church was looted by the Vikings because the bowl ended up in a Viking grave. The catalogue describes it as the museum's greatest treasure. It's both beautiful and priceless.'

Mrs Wright groaned and put her head in her hands. 'You thievin' little sods. God only knows what your da will say when he gets home!'

'It weren't stealin', Mum! The stuff were just lyin' there – honest! It were scrap. It's a battered old bowl!'

Mrs Newby turned an anguished face to Gabriel. 'Inspector Roxby, will there be any charges brought against the boys?'

Gabriel shook his head.

'But the trespassing and the coins?' Maisie whispered.

Gabriel rose to his feet. 'We'll forget about that – although I'll have to send an officer to Mrs Hogarth's to try and get those denarii back. No, the lads are helping with police inquiries now. That's good enough for me. I need to make a phone call and I want Davy to show me this bowl. Then we'll go to the museum and the scene of this crime.'

Davy looked delighted. 'Will we go in a cop car?'

'No, Jemma will drive us.'

Davy turned to his mother. 'See, Mum! We're helpin' the police with their inquiries!'

'We need to recover the bowl,' Gabriel continued. 'People dig up Roman coins every day in York, but that bowl sounds unique. It'll be the evidence we need to confirm the boys' story and mount an inquiry. Once it's recovered, we'll go to the museum.'

Ten minutes later, Gabriel and Jemma led the Wright twins out to Jemma's car. They hadn't planned to take Jim but where Davy went, Jim went too. Kenneth was staying to play with Tom.

'I've told D.S. Fawcett to take some officers to the Yorkshire Museum,' Gabriel told Jemma as he climbed into the passenger seat. 'I've also instructed them to rouse the keeper, Mr Collinge, to let him know we're on our way.'

Jemma nodded and switched on the ignition. 'This has got to be something to do with the burglary at the Hospitium.'

'That was a botched job carried out by a couple of ignorant thugs.'

Jemma shook her head. 'There were *three* of them. The caretaker, Mr Dunn, has now remembered that the man who telephoned him had a posh voice – just like the voice Tom described. Mr Dunn is adamant it wasn't one of the two rough men who coshed him at the Hospitium.'

'Why don't the police know about this?'

Jemma shrugged as she pulled out into Bootham. 'Mr Dunn left a message for D.S. Fawcett at the station, but he didn't get back to him.'

Gabriel rolled his eyes to the roof of the car. 'You'd better tell me what else you and Bobbie have uncovered.'

She told him everything. Including how Fawcett had threatened Bobbie and how she'd been followed and shot at the previous night on her way home.

By the time she'd finished, Gabriel was struggling to contain his anger with Fawcett, with her – but most of all with the gang who'd threatened and hurt his family. It was only the presence of the two young lads in the back of the car that kept him from exploding.

Jemma shivered when they entered the gloomy and dilapidated barn. The memory of the other night when she'd found Tom flooded back. She wondered how Tom would feel when he walked into this place again. *Would he even cross the threshold?*

But her anxiety lifted when the Wright twins finally unearthed the tiny Ormside Bowl from beneath a pile of old pans and a broken kettle. She gasped, distracted by its beauty.

No bigger than a cereal bowl, its gilt outer shell was skilfully embossed in a vine pattern and the engravings on the silver interior were exquisite. The fact that such a beautiful object had narrowly avoided being melted down for scrap to help the war effort made it even more precious. She felt protective of the tiny object. But then again, she reasoned, the Ormside Bowl had survived fifteen centuries and a string of Viking raids. It was a great survivor.

She placed it carefully into a cardboard box full of cotton wool that she'd brought for the purpose. Then the group left the gloom of the cluttered and cobweb-strewn barn for the car.

Chapter Thirty-Eight

The museum and botanic gardens had already closed for the day, but they were expected, and a gardener opened the main gate to let them drive inside. They parked behind the police car that was outside the museum.

The old building faced the sunset and was bathed in the soft evening light. Gleaming like honey, it looked out from its promontory over the peaceful city. Three squirrels scampered playfully across the lawn and birds twittered above their heads in the exotic trees. It was hard to believe such a peaceful place had been the scene of violence and death.

D.S. Fawcett stood with another officer by the great columns at the porticoed entrance. His handsome face was contorted by a scowl when he saw Jemma.

'Stay with the boys for a moment while I have a word with Fawcett,' Gabriel said grimly.

But the twins weren't prepared to wait around while the grown-ups talked.

'We'll show you where it happened, Jemma,' Jim said. They led her across the front of the building, towards the ruins of St Mary's Abbey. Leaving the path, they wound their way through the scattered piles of old medieval stone and went down the side of the Tempest Anderson lecture theatre.

'It were 'ere,' Jim said.

Jemma glanced at the windows above, which glinted in the early evening sunshine. One of them belonged to the curator's storeroom where she and Bobbie had first met Mary Kitson Clark.

She examined the ground. The carnage described by the boys had been cleaned up. The thieves had done a good job. But there were still one or two large splinters of wood on the grass and her sharp eyes spotted a glint of silver in the shadow of the building. Another Roman denarius.

She heard voices and turned around. Gabriel, D.S. Fawcett, Mary Kitson Clark and Mr Collinge were coming towards them. The elderly curator looked drained and ill. He leant heavily on a walking stick. Mary hovered protectively at his side. D.S. Fawcett looked sullen and glum. Jemma hoped he'd had the sharp end of Gabriel's tongue.

'There must be some mistake, officer,' Mr Collinge protested as they approached. 'There's nothing missing. All our precious artefacts are now safe at our secret hiding place in the country.'

Silently, Jemma handed Mary Kitson Clark the cardboard box containing the Ormside Bowl.

Mr Collinge looked like he was about to collapse when Mary opened the lid and showed it to him. She led him to a section of ruined abbey wall, where he sat down. He was speechless with shock.

'I found it, sir!' Davy told him gleefully. He pointed. 'It were lyin' just there. Is there a reward?'

'Don't push your luck, son,' Gabriel growled.

Davy grinned and shrugged. Then, their job done, the twins ran off to climb on the abbey ruins.

'But it doesn't make any sense!' Mary exclaimed. 'The Ormside Bowl was shipped away to the country, along with several other precious artefacts, last Tuesday.'

'Obviously not,' Gabriel said calmly. 'It never left the building, and a gang of thieves came back on Wednesday night to remove it. It looks like the boys disturbed a burglary.'

'We know your statue of a Greek harpy was also stolen,' Jemma said, 'along with several Roman coins.' She showed them the denarius she'd just found in the grass, along with the large splinters of wood. 'I've just found this down here. It's further proof that the story the boys told is true.'

Mary took the coin from her, and her broad face paled. 'Good grief, it's probably part of the Henwood Collection. We shipped it to the country at the same time as the harpy and the Ormside Bowl.' Her face twisted with confusion. 'But Mr Alcott designed us a foolproof system.'

'Alcott?' Gabriel asked. 'Who's he?'

'One of our other curators.'

'And Lance Richards was his best friend,' Jemma added.

'Our contact in the country has confirmed that all the artefacts arrived safely,' Mary continued. 'The custodians of the treasures of Yorkshire are aware of their responsibilities.'

'What's your system?'

Mr Collinge found his voice. 'Every antiquity is wrapped separately and placed in a case – sometimes with others. Each case has a packing note, with a brief description of the contents. They're all signed by me and an independent verifier.' He pointed a shaky finger towards Jemma. 'Mrs James came across me, and Mr Alcott, doing this in the Hospitium the other day. Once the crates were placed in our lorry, it was locked with a key, which remained in my possession. The second key was with our host or hostess into whose care the crates had been entrusted. When they arrive, the crates are opened, and the contents checked by two witnesses before they're resealed. They told me everything had arrived safely.'

Gabriel's face clouded with confusion. 'That sounds… thorough.'

'So how did these baubles come back and end up out here on the lawn?' Fawcett asked sharply. 'Along with a dead body?'

Mr Collinge winced at the word *baubles* and shrugged his thin shoulders. 'I've no explanation.'

Something stirred in Jemma's memory. 'Were the packing notes on a pad and numbered sequentially?'

'Yes.'

'Why is this important, Jemma?' Gabriel asked.

'It's something Michael and I used to do when we ran the wireless repair shop and electrical store in Middlesbrough.'

Fawcett snorted disparagingly. 'A wireless repair shop!'

Jemma ignored him. 'When a delivery arrived, the first thing we did before we unpacked it was to check the small number at the bottom of the pages were sequential. It was too easy for unscrupulous delivery drivers to remove the odd box or package from the lorry. If the sequence of numbers was broken, we knew a box was missing. Did Ben Alcott build this check into your system?'

Mary and Mr Collinge looked at each other and Jemma saw their faces drop before they shook their heads.

'So, if Jemma is right,' Gabriel said, 'the crates containing this bowl and the harpy never went on the van. Who supervised their dispatch?'

There was a slight pause. Then Mary said, 'It was Ben. The rest of us were caught up in a meeting. Ben had hired the lorry and the drivers, but it came early.'

'That was convenient,' Jemma said archly.

'Ben left the meeting and went alone to organise the dispatch of the crates with one of our museum attendants.'

'So, Ben would have told him and the lorry driver which crates to load – and which ones to leave behind?'

'Of course.'

Jemma felt her brother stiffen beside her and saw the concern deepen in Mary's face every time Alcott's name was mentioned. They were rapidly coming to the same conclusion she'd already reached. 'Were these items crated up and left in your storeroom upstairs before they were dispatched?'

'Yes.' Mary pointed up towards the window. 'They were in the room up there.'

Everything suddenly fell into place. 'I think I know what happened.' Jemma handed the wooden splinters to Gabriel. 'I've a strong suspicion these will prove to be the same type of wood found in the skull of Lance Richards. If you give them to the doctor who carried out the autopsy on the curator, I think he'll confirm it.'

'Lance?' Mary exclaimed. 'What has he got to do with this?'

'I believe he was part of the gang who robbed your museum,' Jemma said. 'He was desperate for money, unscrupulous and probably bore a grudge against you and Mr Collinge for the way you removed him from his cosy job here at the museum.'

Mary blushed but said nothing.

'I think he arrived here with at least one other man last Wednesday night to steal a selection of your artefacts, which were deliberately kept off the lorry the day before. They lowered them out of the window to a trolley below with the rope Lance Richards took out of his lodgings on the same night.'

'That's tommy-rot,' Fawcett snapped. 'Why lower them when they could just as easily carry the stuff downstairs and out the front door? The grounds are shut to the public at night.'

Jemma pointed to the twins, who were climbing the abbey ruins. 'The caretaker told us there'd been gangs of young lads roaming these grounds at night for weeks and it's quieter – and probably darker – around this side of the building.'

Fawcett scowled. 'Why'd he tell you – a member of the public – and not the police?'

'I'm not a member of the public,' Jemma replied sweetly. 'I'm a private investigator who has been legitimately employed by the solicitor of the man you've wrongly accused of murder to investigate the death of Lance Richards.'

Fawcett opened his mouth but snapped it shut again and turned sulky when he caught Gabriel's eye.

'Don't jump to conclusions, Jemma,' Gabriel warned. 'Anthony Gill worked with Lance Richards at the Castle Museum and might have been part of the gang. And he refuses to explain where he was that night.'

Jemma snorted. 'Gill loathed Richards. And besides which, he's a trekker and was on his way to Garrowby Gravel Quarry to sleep out there. Ask his solicitor. You've already got the name of two farmers who saw his car driving towards Garrowby that evening. And Mr Pearson has the names of another two trekkers who will confirm Anthony regularly spent the night up there with his cocoa.'

Gabriel and Fawcett gaped at her.

'There's a big problem with your theory, young lady,' Mr Collinge said. 'The caretaker and I are the only people with keys to this building. These thieves wouldn't have been able to get inside.'

'That's where the so-called bungled burglary in the Hospitium comes into this mystery,' Jemma replied. 'When those thugs attacked your caretaker, it wasn't an attempt to steal anything. The gang simply wanted his keys. They copied them, tossed the originals back in the bag with the items they'd pretended to steal and dumped the whole lot where it would be found.'

'Surely you changed the locks?' Gabriel asked, shocked.

Mr Collinge and Mary shuffled uncomfortably. 'We tried, but it wasn't easy or cheap to get a replica lock and key for the six-hundred-year-old door of the Hospitium. Once the originals were returned, Ben said we should stop trying and just risk it. We were about to ship out the most valuable artefacts anyway.'

'Oh, he did, did he?' Fawcett growled. 'It seems to me this Alcott fellah has been pullin' the wool over your eyes from the start.'

'The thieves smashed up the place and stole a few items,' Jemma continued. 'But this was to throw the police off the scent and make it look like a bungled robbery.'

Gabriel gave Fawcett a scathing look. 'It worked.'

'That robbery was always about getting the keys to the main building,' Jemma continued. 'They weren't interested in the items they took from the Hospitium; they wanted the valuable items you'd got crated up in the storeroom above.'

'Very clever,' Fawcett snarled, 'but this doesn't explain why the gang killed Richards. Clearin' up the mess and disposin' of the body would have delayed them.'

Jemma smiled and looked up at the window. 'I think you'll find it's a case of *Murder in Mesopotamia* – or perhaps not.'

'What the hell's that?'

'*Murder in Mesopotamia* is a clever novel by Mrs Agatha Christie, in which the victim was murdered while looking out of her bedroom window by a heavy object falling from the roof. In the novel, it was dropped deliberately. But I'm not sure Richards was deliberately killed. I think he was looking up when one of the crates landed on his head by accident. It was dark and they were rushing. Perhaps the rope was poorly tied and a heavy crate slipped. Richards was familiar with ropes and an experienced mountaineer – and so was his mate Ben Alcott – but his fellow thieves might not have been.'

Fawcett shook his head. 'The coroner at the inquest said Richards died from a blow to the head by a wooden club.'

'No, he didn't. He said Richards had a dent in his skull caused by a heavy rounded object *like* a wooden club. A wooden crate containing a heavy curved object dropped from a great height would have had the same effect – and left that dent and those splinters of wood in his skull.'

Fawcett snorted and jabbed an irritated finger in the direction of the rounded Ormside Bowl. 'Well, it weren't that diddly little thing, if that's what you were thinkin'.'

Mary's eyes widened and her hand flew to her mouth. 'Oh my God – the marble bust of Constantine the Great! Don't tell me that's been stolen too! It's twice life-size and heavy. I can barely lift it with both arms.'

'The bust is Roman – the head from a marble statue commissioned about the year 306,' Mr Collinge added. 'Constantine was crowned emperor, here in York – or Eboracum, as it was known back then – when his father, the previous emperor, suddenly died in Rome. It's part of the only statue of an emperor known to have been erected in Roman Britain. It's rare and hugely significant.'

He rose decisively to his feet and leant on his stick. 'We need to telephone our custodian in the country immediately. We need to do a full inventory of what's missing.'

'Hold on a minute,' Fawcett said, 'there's a bigger crime happened here than the loss of a lump of old stone. I've got a murder to solve – and this is lookin' more and more like an inside job to me.'

'Surely you don't suspect one of us!' Mr Collinge said, aghast. 'Everyone who works in this profession knows that these items – the Ormside Bowl and the harpy – are so rare and famous, they'd never be able to sell them.'

'Unless they were destined for a private collector,' Jemma said thoughtfully. Her mind shifted to Baron Stokesley.

'No one in this country could even put them on *private display* without someone noticing,' Mary said.

'Maybe they're not destined for exhibition in this country,' Jemma continued. 'Lance Richards was a member of the BUF with known sympathies with Nazi Germany. His mate, Ben Alcott, even more so.

His wife has connections with the Nazi High Command. From what I've read, Hitler is the biggest thief of art and valuable artefacts in Europe.'

Mr Collinge and Mary were horrified. 'Ben's part of the BUF?'

'York City Police have chased those thugs in the BUF out of the city,' Fawcett said smugly.

'No, you haven't,' Jemma said. 'They still meet regularly at The Dog and Duck pub near the castle. They call themselves the Tuesday Club now. My colleague, Bobbie, went to one of their meetings this week.'

Fawcett's face went puce with anger.

Jemma just shrugged. 'This is only a theory,' she said, 'but Ben Alcott was the speaker at the meeting. He seemed convinced the Germans were about to goose-step their way into this city. What better way to show your loyalty to an invading army than to present the Führer with a collection of Britain's most exquisite treasures?'

'That's fanciful tommyrot!' Fawcett snapped. 'The Nazis will never get past the beaches... our lads will slaughter them on the shingle...' His voice died out and no one replied.

Gabriel turned to Mr Collinge. 'If it hadn't been for the boys stumbling across this burglary, when would the theft have been discovered?'

Mary and Mr Collinge exchanged worried glances.

'Probably not until after the war was over and our hosts sent back the crates.'

'Good grief.' Gabriel rolled his eyes. 'By which time the thieves would have been long gone. Right, Fawcett, get a couple of officers up here to tape off this area and examine it for clues. My sister has done enough work for York City Police this week. It's time we did our own job – and did it properly. In the meantime, where's this Alcott fellow? His name's cropped up a lot.'

'He's taken a few days off,' Mary said. 'He's gone hiking in the Dales.'

'Does he have a vehicle big enough to transport crates of stolen artefacts and the body of a dying man?'

'Yes,' Mr Collinge said. 'He has an old van.'

Chapter Thirty-Nine

Bobbie spent a happy afternoon packing Jodie's clothes into trunks and suitcases. Never had she seen such a gorgeous array of sumptuous fabrics. The actress owned a leopard fur coat, several short-sleeved merino wool jumpers and numerous mulberry silk undergarments that made Bobbie blush. She spent five minutes just holding up each of Jodie's fur stoles, admiring the lustrous sheen, and letting them slither through her fingers onto the bed.

Jodie was out at De Grey's, rehearsing her dance routine for the show. When she returned, Bobbie helped her into her red off-the-shoulder chiffon gown, which exposed the angel wings of her collarbones. Then she restyled her hair, copying an old photograph Jodie provided.

Jodie smoked a cigarette in a long holder while Bobbie worked on her hair, watching her in the mirror. 'Where did you go to school, Baker?'

'Miss Colbeck's School for Girls.'

Jodie raised an elegant eyebrow in surprise. 'The private school? How did a lass from Tanner Street end up there?'

'I was a scholarship pupil.'

Jodie laughed. 'That must have been difficult at times. Were you bullied?'

'They tried – but I fought them off.'

'I bet you did.'

'I made a good friend at Miss Colbeck's – we're still best friends today.'

Jodie shrugged and frowned. 'Friends come, friends go – especially if your marriage breaks down. Mine have deserted me in droves since I left Stokesley.' She sighed, then added, 'You must have been clever. I was always rather hopeless at lessons.'

'Ah, but you had an amazing talent for something else – your dancing,' Bobbie regretted her words the minute they left her mouth. Her comment was spontaneous, but it made her sound like a starry-eyed fan rather than a servant.

Jodie took it as her due. 'Do you have a young man?'

Bobbie shook her head. 'I'm between men at the moment. Resting – like you actors do between films.'

Jodie flicked her ash into the crystal ashtray and smiled wryly. 'We all need a rest from them, now and then.'

'Your friend whom we're visiting – the Countess von Hatvan – did you meet her at school?'

'Good lord, no! Anna Léna was educated by a private governess and went to a Parisian finishing school while I was still playing hopscotch in the school yard on Priory Street. No, I met her through my marriage to Stokesley. They share a fascination with old and decrepit works of art.'

Bobbie frowned as she rolled the last curl around the tongs. *If she's more his friend than yours, why are we going there?*

Jodie was still watching her expression in the mirror. 'I take it from your frown that you're not a fan of Rembrandts and antiquities, Baker?'

'Absolutely not,' Bobbie replied with vigour. 'History was my least favourite subject at school. I find a lot of the historical stuff in York quite creepy – especially in the museums. What about you, Miss Jodie?'

'I'm the same about museums. As for art, I'm an art nouveau fan myself. I've several original paintings by Alphonse Mucha and glassware by Lalique. I've also had a stained-glass window designed in the style of Louis Tiffany. Stokesley said this was childish.'

Bobbie smiled. 'Well, I haven't a clue who these folks are, miss, but I'm sure your paintings are beautiful.' She removed the tongs, patted the curl into place and held up the hand mirror behind the actress's head. 'There, what do you think? Are you happy with this?'

Jodie twisted her head to each side and nodded with satisfaction. She passed Bobbie a platinum necklace set with diamonds and rubies, which Bobbie fastened at the back of her elegant neck.

'You might have to find some courage tomorrow if you don't like creepy old places, Baker. The Countess von Hatvan lives in a mouldy old building that used to be a convent.'

'A convent? For nuns who've forsworn contact with men? Don't worry, Miss Jodie, I'll fit right in.'

Jodie laughed. She stubbed out her cigarette, rose from the stool and reached for her jewelled clutch bag. Bobbie helped her into her mink stole.

'Don't wait up for me tonight, Baker. I'll be late.'

When Jodie left for De Grey's, Bobbie tidied up the suite then took a walk to their agency office on Grape Lane. She checked no one had followed her and let herself in with her key. She made a cup of tea and wrote out a quick report for Jemma. But she was restless, excited, and wanted to chat. She suspected Jemma had already left for De Grey's with Don but decided to telephone her anyway.

Jemma answered the call.

'Why aren't you out with Don?'

'I'm not going, Bobbie. I've cancelled. Apart from being shattered, there's been a development at this end – we've solved the museum murder.'

Bobbie nearly knocked her tea over in surprise. 'Good God, Miss Sherlock! That was fast! I give you my murder inquiry – and five minutes later you've solved the blooming case!'

She sensed Jemma smiling at the other end of the line. 'I had some help from a gang of ten- year-old boys.'

Jemma told her all about it. 'Mr Collinge eventually confirmed there's half a dozen priceless antiquities missing – including the bust of Constantine. Ben Alcott is also missing – along with his van. He was supposed to be driving to the Dales for a walking holiday but when the police went round to his home, most of his wardrobe was empty. His landlady told them he said he'd be gone for a week or two and he left with a suitcase rather than a rucksack. His tent is still in the house. There's a warrant out for his arrest. The police are now convinced he's the mastermind behind the robbery.'

'So, where does this leave poor old Anthony?'

'The charges against him for murder have been dropped – but once he's released from Armley Gaol, they'll probably rearrest him for the theft of the money from the museum.'

'Well, that's a great result – of sorts. I guess our job there is done.'

'Yes, I'll telephone Mr Pearson first thing in the morning. I'll be able to concentrate on our divorce case now.'

'Will Tom and the other boys be all right? They've had a shocking experience.'

'They seem relieved and cheerful. No doubt they'll be heroes among their school chums by the end of the week for assisting the police in a murder case. That'll take their mind off the horror they've seen.'

'And what about Don? How did he react when you stood him up?'

'Pleasantly, and like a true gentleman. He did get a bit upset, though, when I begged him to take Ricky along to spy on Jodie instead of me.'

Bobbie burst out laughing. 'I can just see them dancing the Lindy Hop together at De Grey's. Oh Jemma, poor Don – you'll have to make it up to him... he's been a good friend to us.'

'I will. How's it going at your end?'

'Great. I've managed to bluff my way through it so far and sent Madam Jodie out to the dance looking like a Hollywood starlet. She's surprisingly friendly and seems a bit lonely – although there is one thing that puzzles me.'

'What's that?'

'She's not particularly close to this Hungarian countess. I'm not sure why we're going there. It seems an odd, spontaneous decision.'

'Watch her closely,' Jemma advised. 'Jodie's not spontaneous, she's a very clever woman who thinks things through. Oh, and Bobbie, be careful. Ben Alcott is still out there, and the police have discovered he owns a gun. Gabriel thinks he might be the one who fired at me last night. Just telephone me tomorrow night, so I can check you're all right.'

'I will.'

———

'Either Irton or Emmett will be parked nearby if you need them. Even though we've got you on the inside, we need to keep up the shadowing, so she doesn't get suspicious. I'm repairing Jodie's dress now. I'll drop it off at hotel reception for you tomorrow morning.'

'Thanks, Jemma – and well done.'

Chapter Forty

By the time Jodie surfaced at noon, Bobbie had already heard from the other hotel staff about her tremendous success at De Grey's. Although none of them had been present, the staff canteen was buzzing with tales of her brilliant singing and dancing. Apparently, the air force personnel had been wowed, and there would be photographs in tonight's newspaper. Several baskets of flowers arrived at reception for the actress. But due to their impending departure, Jodie had already left instructions that they were to be sent to local charities.

Clearly exhausted, the actress was silent as she breakfasted in her suite. Bobbie hurried to finish the packing.

The country estate of the Countess von Hatvan lay on the banks of the River Ouse, north of the city. Bobbie travelled in style and comfort in the front of the Rolls-Royce next to the American chauffeur, Toby Hainsworth. Jodie sat quietly in the back, flicking through a film script.

Bobbie glanced back over her shoulder as they pulled out. Irton's black Citroën trailed them at a discreet distance, with Emmett at the wheel. Then she relaxed into the plush leather seat and enjoyed the trip.

As they neared Beningbrough, the sky clouded over and it started to drizzle. They turned off the main road on to a narrow lane lined with hawthorn hedgerows, which wound its way through mile after mile of flat arable fields dissected by dykes.

She peered through the rain-spattered window looking for a public telephone box, but she barely saw a farmhouse, never mind a village.

The only vehicles on the road were farm tractors and military vehicles and several times they had to pull over to let a truck pass.

On one of these occasions, Hainsworth pointed with his gloved hand to a set of chimneys rising above the trees in the distance. 'Beningbrough Hall is over there, ma'am. It's owned by Lady Chesterfield but there's a load of air force men billeted there.'

'Which explains all the military. You seem well informed for a foreigner.'

He smiled, revealing his brilliant white and even teeth. 'I look at maps and listen to gossip.'

'Is there a village?' she asked.

'No, ma'am – but there's several farmhouses down here at a junction. The convent lies just beyond it.'

Bobbie felt a glimmer of unease; she hadn't expected this level of isolation.

Despite the dullness of the weather outside, Hainsworth still wore his sunglasses. She remembered the eye condition he'd mentioned to Emmett and wondered how much it impaired his vision. *Not very much*, she decided after he'd deftly swung the big Rolls round a few more sharp corners.

As they drove through the junction with the cluster of farmhouses, she saw a small post office nestled among them. *Good. At least they might have a telephone.* The last thing she wanted was to use the one in the convent and be overheard.

Finally, they reached a small lodge next to a huge set of closed rusting iron gates. A battered van was parked next to the house and smoke curled out of the chimney, but there was no one in sight. The front garden was overgrown and full of weeds and the window frames and door needed a new coat of paint.

'Wait here a moment, Hainsworth, until the lodge keeper opens the gates,' Jodie told him.

But the lodge keeper didn't appear and Hainsworth had to climb out and open and shut them himself.

On the meandering drive up to the convent, he skilfully avoided a large number of potholes and the low-hanging boughs of the trees, which needed coppicing.

Bobbie had expected the convent to be a romantic collection of honey-stone medieval buildings, perhaps overgrown with ivy or sweet honeysuckle – but it was nothing of the sort. An austere brick Victorian building loomed ahead of them. It looked more like a workhouse than a country estate and, like the gatehouse at the end of the drive, it was in a poor state of repair.

The inside of the building was as grim as the outside. The draughty hallway was panelled in dark wood and gloomy and the stair carpet was threadbare. There were no heating radiators and ugly fireplaces dominated every room. *It must be freezing in winter.*

The middle-aged housekeeper who greeted them looked miserable, but she was polite. 'Good afternoon, Your Ladyship. The countess will be down in a moment.'

Jodie gave her a beaming smile, pulled off her gloves and hat and handed them to Bobbie.

'Thank you, Mrs Grimshaw. I'll wait for her in the sitting room. Please can you tell Hainsworth and Baker where to take our luggage.'

She swanned off into a large room at the side. Bobbie caught a glimpse of more dark oak panelling and a lumpy red sofa.

Mrs Grimshaw glowered at Bobbie and Hainsworth. 'Lord knows where I'm to put you!' She led them up the staircase to the first floor. There were a lot of dark oil paintings on the walls above the panelling and several ghastly statues and works of art dotted around on window ledges and random plinths. In Bobbie's opinion, they did little to improve the appearance of the house.

The housekeeper gestured towards some Egyptian pieces. 'The mistress's art collection is priceless, so make sure you don't break owt.'

'No, ma'am,' Hainsworth said.

Bobbie just raised a disparaging eyebrow behind the woman's back. It rose even higher when the housekeeper took them upstairs and pointed to two bedrooms. 'That's the mistress's room – and there's the master's.'

Bobbie remembered Fanny had told Jemma the countess had married her husband last year to avoid internment as a foreign national. The separate bedrooms for the newlyweds suggested this had been an arrangement of convenience rather than a love match.

The housekeeper opened a door almost opposite the countess's bedroom. 'This is Baroness Stokesley's bedroom. You two will have to sleep upstairs in the attics.'

Hainsworth gave her one of his gorgeous smiles. 'I'm sure it'll be fine, ma'am.'

'Well, I hope so. We're not used to havin' visitors. I'm not sure what the countess were thinkin' of when she invited you.'

Jodie's room was far smaller than her suite at the hotel but agreeably furnished, with colourful cushions, curtains and rugs to soften the austerity of those depressing dark panels. Feminine knick-knacks adorned the dressing table and it had a pleasant view from the window over the countryside. Bobbie's room, however, must have once been a nun's prayer cell and contained little more than an uncomfortable iron bed and a rickety old table with a cracked bowl and jug of cold water for washing.

She and Hainsworth carried the luggage out of the Rolls-Royce and up to the bedrooms.

On one of her return trips from the car, Bobbie saw the countess coming down the stairs. A glamorous blonde in her mid-thirties, she had wonderful cheekbones and slanting Slavic green eyes. But her face was spoilt with a scowl, which magically disappeared once she turned into the sitting room.

Bobbie hovered by the half-open door and heard the two women greeting and kissing each other.

'Jodie, darling! How lovely to see you! Welcome to my humble little home.' The woman had a strong Eastern European accent, but her grasp of English did credit to her private governess.

'You too, Anna Léna. Did you enjoy the show last night?'

'You were magnificent, darling, absolutely magnificent. That audience had never seen anything like it! But why aren't you still in York, basking in your well-deserved glory?'

'Oh, I'm sick of it, Anna Léna. I'm constantly pestered at the hotel. Apart from Adolf and his cronies who follow me everywhere, there's the press – and the fans. And I was even pestered by one of the hotel chambermaids!'

Bobbie heard the wood and springs creak as someone sat down on the lumpy sofa.

'How shocking! I hope you complained.'

A lighter clicked and the smell of cigarette smoke drifted out into the hallway.

'I did. But I needed to get away for a while into the peace of the countryside – and I remembered your kind offer…'

One the countess never thought she'd take up, Bobbie decided.

'Absolutely, darling – and that's one thing we can provide. My humble little home may lack the luxury you're accustomed to, but we've plenty of peace and quiet. *A few days* here will do you good.'

Bobbie grinned at the emphasis the countess put on the words *a few days*.

'Where's Horace?' Jodie asked.

'Out somewhere… I suppose. He finds it *too* quiet here. I think he thought being married to an aristocrat would be more exciting.'

Jodie laughed softly. 'I don't suppose he'll stay around for long.'

'Hopefully not.'

'Still, he got you out of a fix when he married you.'

'He was well paid, darling. It nearly broke me, handing over that money.'

'Are you strapped for cash again? Would you like me to give you fifty? And I'll take you and Horace out for dinner tonight. Nigel is still in town; we'll ask him to join us.'

The countess's voice lifted with delight. 'Thank you, *darling*. I'll take you up on *both* offers – although the fifty will only pay for my cocaine for a week.'

Jodie chuckled. 'You really should stop that dreadful habit, Anna Léna.'

Bobbie heard the floorboards creak above her head and Hainsworth's tread on the landing. She moved towards the stairs.

Once she'd unpacked and hung out Jodie's cocktail dress for the evening, she explored the rest of the house. There only seemed to be two staff: the countess's personal maid and the sulky Mrs Grimshaw, who was the cook as well as the housekeeper. Thin and plain, with lank brown hair, the countess's maid was Hungarian like her mistress, and spoke hardly any English.

The only telephone was on a small table in the hallway. She toyed with the idea of using it to call Jemma after Jodie and the countess had left for the restaurant, but decided not to risk it.

She wandered back up to her attic bedroom to get her copy of *The Man in the Queue* and glanced out of her window, which overlooked the garages at the back. The sun had come out and it promised to be a pleasant evening.

The Rolls was parked by the garages. Hainsworth had removed his jacket, rolled up his sleeves and was washing the country mud off the vehicle with soapy water and a cloth. Beside him stood another man, speaking with some animation and pointing to the car. Presumably this was Horace, the countess's husband.

Bobbie opened her tiny window but only heard their laughter, not their words.

Hainsworth looked hot from the exertion of washing the car. He took off his sunglasses for a moment to wipe the sweat from his face.

Bobbie gasped as excitement and shock surged through her body. The next second, she reached for her pocket camera.

Everything suddenly fell into place.

'Oh Jodie,' she whispered. 'You clever, clever girl!'

Chapter Forty-One

Jodie took a long time dressing for dinner that evening and was thoughtful and silent. Bobbie got the impression she was deliberately dawdling and that something was bothering her.

So, it should, lady, Bobbie thought with a smirk. *I know your secret.*

Jodie caught her smile. 'You seem happy.'

'Yes, Miss Jodie. I'm very content with my new role.'

'You're easy to please.' Jodie smiled and pointed to a sealed letter on the dressing table. 'Be a sweetheart and pop this in the post box for me tonight, please. There's a post office down the lane.'

'Yes, Miss Jodie.'

There was a tap on the door and the countess swanned into the room in a delicate lace dress, a lustrous string of pearls and a cloud of French perfume. 'Are you nearly ready to come down, Jodie? We don't want to be late.'

'I'll be with you in a moment, Anna Léna. Please wait for me downstairs.'

The countess left and Jodie rose and went over to the door. She watched the countess descend the stairs. 'Stay here, Baker, and tidy the room.'

Bobbie blinked and glanced round the spotless bedroom, wondering what she'd missed.

Suddenly, Jodie reached down, took off her silver high heels and glided silently out of the room, carrying the shoes with her.

Cautiously, Bobbie followed. She peered down the corridor and watched the actress tread noiselessly down the threadbare carpet and disappear into the countess's bedroom.

Bobbie followed her, grateful for her soft-soled shoes and the half-open door. There was a large free-standing cheval mirror just inside the room, which reflected the actress's movements. Jodie was pulling out the drawers of her hostess's bedside table and rifling through the contents.

Bobbie retraced her steps, deep in thought.

Her beloved crime novels were full of high-class kleptomaniacs who toured country houses stealing the family silver and other valuables. But Jodie was rich, and the countess seemed to be as poor as the proverbial church mouse. Jodie wasn't stealing; she was looking for something.

Then she remembered Jemma's comment that the countess was *close* to Baron Stokesley and an idea leapt into her mind.

The one thing the Stokesleys wanted more than anything else in the world was to get rid of each other.

Did Jodie suspect the countess was having a secret affair with her estranged husband? If so, this peculiar visit was an ideal opportunity to find evidence to divorce him.

It made sense – but how did she manage to stay so calm in the presence of her husband's mistress? A new wave of respect for Jodie, mingled with sympathy, flooded through Bobbie. If her suspicions were correct, then the woman's acting skills were phenomenal.

Jodie and the countess left for their evening out in York a few moments later.

As soon as the Rolls disappeared down the drive, Bobbie popped Jodie's letter into her handbag and set off for the post office. The sun still blazed in the sky above, but she didn't need the sunshine to lift her spirits. She was grinning from ear to ear.

Jemma and Terence King would be delighted with her latest discovery. She knew she needed better photographs of the American chauffeur than the long-distance shots she'd taken from her attic bedroom – and a couple of him and Jodie together were needed. But at least they now knew what – and whom – they were dealing with.

She marched down the overgrown drive, enjoying the peace and the cheerful birdsong, and was only vaguely aware of the lodge keeper sitting in a deckchair in the distance. He was in overalls with his cap pulled low over his face, reading a newspaper.

It's so quiet out here, she thought. So different from the city. No traffic, no people – only the birds and the distant lowing of cattle.

'Good evening,' she said cheerfully as she passed the lodge keeper.

He put down the newspaper and smiled to return her greeting.

Then the smiles drained from both their faces and Bobbie froze in her tracks.

It was Ben Alcott.

'Mr Alcott…' she stammered. *Perhaps he didn't know there was a warrant out for his arrest?*

Then she saw the front page of the evening newspaper in his lap. It was split into two. On one side it reported Jodie's triumph at De Grey's and on the other, the audacious theft at the Yorkshire Museum. Alcott's photograph, with the caption *Wanted for Questioning*, was side by side with a radiant Jodie swirling across the dance floor like Ginger Rogers.

Run! her instincts screamed, but her feet seemed glued to the spot. She glanced up and down the deserted lane, frantically looking for Emmett in the Citroën. But he'd followed Jodie's Rolls back to York when it turned out of the drive.

A slow, unpleasant smile crept across Alcott's face. He rose to his feet and pulled a black Webley revolver out of the pocket of his overalls. 'This is an unfortunate meeting for you, Miss Baker.' He levelled the gun at her stomach.

Unable to run, defiance was the only thing left. 'Why? Do you plan to kill me like you did your best mate, Lance?'

Alcott laughed. '*That* was an unfortunate accident.'

'Taking a pot shot at Jemma wasn't.'

He shrugged. 'It was a warning.' His eyes flickered down towards the newspaper then back to Bobbie with an ice-cold glare that was more terrifying than anger. 'Unfortunately, it seems I was too gentlemanly on that occasion. I assume it was your friend who solved the case. The stupid police were too busy barking up the wrong tree.'

'Of course it was Jemma.'

'I should have killed her when I had the chance.' He raised the gun and added quietly, 'I won't make the same mistake again.'

Bobbie scanned the lane again. *Please God... where's a bloody military truck when you need one? A farmer...? Even a bloody farmer on a tractor...*

Alcott followed her anguished glance. 'Yes, you're right. This is too public a place for an execution.' He stepped closer. 'Move inside the house – now.'

Don't move, her instincts screamed. *If he gets you inside, you're dead.*

But it was hopeless. He grabbed hold of her arm, slammed the gun into the back of her neck and shoved her forward.

'You murdering fascist bastard!' she screamed.

He stopped, spun her round and punched her in the face to shut her mouth. Then he hauled her inside. Sobbing and clutching her jaw, she fell through the doorway. Before her eyes adjusted to the gloom, he'd wrenched open a small door beneath the stairs and shoved her inside.

For a split second, she thought he'd pushed her into a pitch-black broom cupboard.

Then she realised there was nothing beneath her feet.

It was the stone staircase down into the cellar.

Pain seared through her head, shoulders, hands and wrists as she crashed against the rough wall and bounced down every. Single. Stone. Step.

She collapsed in an unconscious heap at the bottom.

Chapter Forty-Two

Everyone, apart from Emmett, had attended the staff meeting at the agency office on Grape Lane that morning.

Hannah made them a cup of tea while they exchanged information. Despite the excitement of the night before at the museum, Jemma had slept well, satisfied that they'd done a good job for Anthony Gill and secured his release.

Ricky had gone along with Don to De Grey's and taken photographs for his newspaper. 'I had my eye on her – but there weren't anything special to see. That old boyfriend of hers – Kerner – were there. So were Glazer, that film producer Lansdowne and the actor Stephen Howard.'

Jemma winced and wished she'd been there. She was sure she'd have noticed a glance, a touch or a light caress that would have told them what they needed to know.

'She gave a good performance for the air force lads and their wives,' Ricky continued. 'She sang a few songs with Howard and there's a rumour she's about to make a film with him.' He tapped his Leica, satisfied. 'I got a few shots for the *Evening Press*.'

'Did she dance with anyone in particular?'

'After the show, she danced with everyone – including most of the air force top brass.'

'Glazer's left town,' Irton informed them. 'I collared him yesterday and threatened to tell the police he'd seduced that young hotel waiter. He agreed to meet me at eight this mornin' with some information – but he never showed. When I asked at the hotel reception, they said he'd already left town and was takin' the next flight back to the States.'

Jemma sighed with relief to hear the attempt to blackmail Glazer had failed. 'Never mind, there's been a fortunate development in this case.' She updated them about Bobbie's new employment as Jodie's maid.

Hannah and Ricky looked impressed and even Irton raised an appreciative eyebrow. 'That lass has done well. That'll take some of the pressure off us.'

'Not necessarily.' Jemma explained how she wanted to extend the shadowing to the men and pushed a revised copy of the schedule towards them. 'Unless Mr King sends up some more operatives, there's only five of us to watch Kerner, Lansdowne and Stephen Howard. I don't think Lansdowne is romantically involved with Jodie; his interest seems to be purely business – and he definitely wasn't in her suite the other afternoon. So, we'll just concentrate on Howard and Kerner for the moment. Hannah can share my car.' She slid the keys across the desk. 'You take Kerner today, Hannah.'

'I hope you know how to use the accelerator, lass,' Irton said. 'That boy racer drives like a madman.'

Hannah gave him a haughty glare.

Irton turned to Ricky. 'Have you got some wheels, mate?'

The photographer laughed. 'I've got a bike – but I doubt it'll keep up with Jodie's Rolls!'

Jemma remembered Ricky's shady dealings with the black market. 'Can you borrow one – and get some petrol for it?' Jemma asked. 'I know you've got a lot of mates who owe you favours.'

He nodded. 'I'll sort something out.'

'Good, you can follow Stephen Howard. An actor like him is always followed by the press. Irton, you relieve Emmett later. By the way, Bobbie says Jodie intends to leave York today and decamp to the country home of her friend, the Countess von Hatvan.' She slid three copies of the convent's Beningbrough address towards the others, along with directions on how to find it.

'Bloody hell, you're organised, lass,' Irton said.

Ricky's forehead creased into a frown, distorting the scar in his eyebrow. 'Why the devil is she goin' there?'

'We don't know. She told Bobbie she needs some peace and quiet...' Jemma broke off as Ricky's frown deepened. 'What is it, Ricky?'

'That woman is Stokesley's mistress.'

'What!'

He nodded. 'She ain't Jodie's friend. I saw Stokesley with the countess after the talk at the museum the other evenin'. They were snoggin' in the street when they thought no one were lookin'. Eatin' each other's faces, they were.'

Irton chuckled. 'So, the baron's already got his third wife lined up? The dirty beggar. No wonder he's desperate to get rid of the actress.'

Jemma's eyes shifted to Ricky's fingers. They were slowly stroking his camera case. She knew what it meant. 'I don't suppose you captured this romantic moment on film?'

'As it happens, I did. Ain't too sure what to do with the photographs, though.'

'No British newspaper will touch them,' Jemma warned. 'The baron's lawyer will slap an injunction on their publication the minute it's suggested.'

Ricky shrugged. 'There's always the Yanks.'

Now they'd been briefed, they rose to leave. 'I'd keep them photographs to yersen, mate,' Irton suggested. 'Stokesley will go mad if they become public.'

Jemma called Ricky back once the others had left. 'I'd like a copy of those photographs, please, Ricky. I'll pay you for them.'

'Why?'

'Insurance. The baron keeps threatening to sack us because we don't get results fast enough.'

'Bloody hell, Miss Marple! Don't tell me you plan to threaten *him*!'

'No. I don't do blackmail. But if necessary, I'm quite happy to jump ship and work for the other side.'

Once they'd left, Jemma made two telephone calls. Terence King was delighted to hear Bobbie was now in Jodie's employment and Mr Pearson was over the moon to hear the mystery of Lance Richards's death had been solved and the murder charges against Anthony would be dropped.

Jemma spent the day in the office, typing out invoices and dealing with a telephone call from another potential new client. Once she'd finished her work at six o'clock, she pulled out her novel to keep her company. If Jodie was dining out, Bobbie should find it easy to call between six and eight o'clock as arranged.

But by eight o'clock, when Bobbie hadn't called, she lost interest in her novel. She waited another hour, glancing nervously at the old grandfather clock in the corner of the room. Perhaps Bobbie had telephoned her home instead and left a message with Gabriel?

Maisie, Gabriel and Tom were in excellent spirits when she arrived back at the cottage. Gabriel was sitting in his old armchair by the kitchen hearth, puffing on his pipe. Maisie was fussing around Tom, giving him his supper.

'I've plated up some food for you, Jemma,' Maisie said.

Starving, Jemma sat down at the table and devoured the meal.

Tom's head was still bandaged but he had colour in his plump, freckled cheeks and was full of excited chatter. The strain seemed to have lifted from the whole household.

Despite her worry about Bobbie, Jemma did her best to join in with the light-hearted mood of the house and gave Tom an affectionate kiss when he went up to bed.

'We've not found Alcott,' Gabriel told her, once the boy had left the kitchen. 'But every force in Yorkshire is looking out for him. He won't get far. By the way, that bullet you gave me – the one you dug out of the tree – it matches Alcott's Webley pistol.'

'Will you charge him with my attempted murder when you arrest him?'

Gabriel shuffled uncomfortably in his seat. 'To be honest, Jemma, I'd like to keep you out of it as much as possible. I know this would be good publicity for your business, but the way you handled your investigation makes York City Police look like the Keystone Cops. Fawcett didn't investigate the burglary at the Hospitium properly and stupidly arrested the most convenient suspect for the murder. I don't want the public making comparisons with our investigation. We need to keep our credibility with the public; it's important they have faith in the police, even if at times we let them down. We've already got enough on this Alcott fellow to send him to prison for a very long time, without involving you.'

Jemma smiled. 'Of course.'

'And if we find any links with the Nazis – he'll hang. That said, I'm very impressed with how you solved this case. You did really well. If I could employ women at York City Police…'

Horrified at the thought, Jemma held up her hand to stop him. 'Thank you – but no thank you. I'm happy where I am.'

'I'd be grateful if you'd stay out of the limelight.'

'Of course I will.'

'In fact, I'm beginning to think Agatha Christie novels should be mandatory reading for my officers.'

She laughed.

'And a couple of other things. First, I want you to forget what I said the other night about moving out. This is your home and always will be.'

'Thank you – but I know everything will change once we find Michael. There simply isn't enough room for him here.'

'We'll cross that bridge when we come to it.'

'By the way, your friend who works for the Northamptonshire police, is it Superintendent Jim Jones?'

Confusion flickered across her brother's face at this abrupt change of subject, then he remembered. 'Yes, we were in the North Riding Constabulary together before I transferred to York. He's done well for himself down in Northamptonshire. Why do you ask?'

'D.S. Marlowe has expanded the search for Michael into Northamptonshire, and I remember we talked about your friend a few months back. I'm trying to remember what you told me. I think there'd been an incident… can you remember the conversation?'

Gabriel shook his head and laughed. 'I can't. Is it important?'

'I don't know. Something's niggling in the back of my mind.'

'Do you want me to phone Jim and let him know the situation about Michael and ask for his help?'

'Thanks, Gabriel. Marlowe said they'd already enlisted the help of the local police, but I don't suppose it'll do any harm if you called him.'

Gabriel smiled. 'I guess I owe you one, Jemma, after this week.'

'Now, what's the other thing you wanted to mention? You said there were a couple?'

A look of concern shifted across his face, and he took another puff of his pipe. 'You need to be more careful what type of work you take on, Jemma. No more murder cases. I want you to promise to stick to shadowing adulterers and finding lost kittens in the future.'

She gave him a wan smile and a slight nod of her head and rapidly changed the subject. 'It's not me I'm worried about today. Bobbie hasn't telephoned me tonight. She's undercover on a job and is supposed to check in between six and eight.'

Gabriel's jaw set. 'Oh, for God's sake! Not Bobbie as well! What sort of job?'

'It's just a divorce case, nothing dangerous. She's shadowing a suspected adulterer. But it's so unlike Bobbie.'

Gabriel relaxed and shrugged. 'She might not have access to a working telephone.'

'I suppose so. She's out in Beningbrough. It's very remote.'

Gabriel patted her hand. 'She'll turn up. Bobbie's one of the feistiest and most resourceful young women I've ever met. Adulterers don't tend to turn violent. And if they did, I wouldn't fancy their chances against Bobbie.'

Jemma smiled and enjoyed the mental image of Bobbie and Jodie tearing each other's hair out in a cat fight. In her imaginary scenario, the actress gave as good as she got. She kissed Gabriel good night and went up to bed.

But her smile drooped as she mounted the stairs and her anxiety returned.

Where the hell are you, Bobbie?

Chapter Forty-Three

Bobbie woke up confused, shivering and in horrendous pain. She lay on the damp flagstone floor of the pitch-black cellar. Everything throbbed and her throat was parched.

She tried to move her limbs. They were all grazed and bloodied, but apart from her right shoulder and upper arm, everything worked. Pain seared through her body – along with a wave of nausea – as she pushed herself into a sitting position with her good arm. Her hair was matted to her forehead with blood, but the bleeding seemed to have stopped. Her mouth, jaw and nose were swollen and sore from Alcott's punch.

She fought back tears of self-pity and forced herself to examine her surroundings. As her eyes adjusted to the gloom, she saw a narrow strip of light above. It came from beneath the cellar door – and so did a murmur of voices.

Wincing, she felt for the steps with her good arm… and was surprised when her fingers located the handle of an enamel cup. She lifted it and sniffed the liquid inside. But one sip reassured her it was water. She swept her good arm around until she found her handbag on the floor beside her. It contained aspirin. She took a few tablets and drank the water.

Obviously, Alcott didn't intend to kill her just yet.

Not trusting herself to stand up, she dragged herself back up the cellar steps on her bottom. Every movement sent a new wave of pain searing through her shoulder.

The voices belonged to Ben Alcott and a woman, and they appeared to be arguing.

'What the hell were you thinking?' Alcott demanded.

'I didn't invite them!' the woman yelled back. 'They just turned up!'

The Eastern European accent of the countess was unmistakable. For a moment, Bobbie was surprised – then she remembered that Alcott was hiding out in *her* lodge. The damn woman was broke, with a passion for ancient art and antiquities and an expensive drug habit to feed. Of course she was involved in the robbery at the museum.

'And what about those goons in the black Citroën? You told me this place was deserted – that's why we picked it. The bloody place is crawling with people!'

'Don't worry about the men in the car. They just follow Jodie everywhere. I'll make sure she – and they – aren't here when the lorry turns up.'

'You do realise the woman's a private investigator, don't you? She's with the same outfit who investigated Richards's death.'

The countess lowered her voice and Bobbie didn't catch her next comment, but she knew it was only a matter of time before they connected her with Emmett and Irton and the shadowing of Jodie.

She only caught a few snippets of Alcott's reply, but those she heard made her shiver again. 'Hull docks… Let them deal with her… drugs…'

A pair of high heels clicked over the flagstones towards the door. The door handle above Bobbie's head twitched. The countess obviously wanted to see Alcott's captive for herself.

Alcott joined her. 'It's locked and the keys are in the kitchen drawer. She fell down the stairs and is unconscious. I've just been down to check on her and left some water. She's still breathing but she'll be out until morning.'

'Fell? Or was pushed?' the countess asked. 'I haven't forgotten that you assaulted that child. Now every policeman in the county's looking for you.'

'It was time to get out anyway. And what was I supposed to do? Let the damn woman run back to York and tell the police I'm here?'

'It's another mistake, Alcott. Richards's accident was bad enough. They won't be pleased with this bungling.'

Who the hell were *they*?

'I'm not taking the blame for this,' the countess continued, 'but they'll have to know. Once more, you've compromised the whole operation.'

'If you hadn't invited half of York into your house none of this would have happened!'

Her captors moved away from the door into another room, still arguing.

Bobbie sat quietly, nursing her injured arm and trying to make sense of what she'd heard. Thanks to the water and aspirin, the throbbing in her head had subsided. It was easier to think.

Hull docks suggested someone – or something – was going on a boat trip to the Continent. *Alcott?* Probably. *The stolen artefacts from the museum?* Probably. *Or her?* She fought back a new wave of fear.

She knew only too well where Alcott's loyalties lay and had a strong suspicion the destination was Germany – probably via newly conquered Holland. Special Branch would have investigated the Hungarian bitch's loyalties and contacts at the start of the war, but they must have missed something, and her arranged marriage had enabled her to stay at large.

Was this outrageous robbery an attempt to curry favour with the Germans before they invaded Britain? An insurance policy to show their loyalty and a devious way to gain a hefty amount of cash into the bargain?

She heard footsteps outside in the hallway. The front door opened and closed as Alcott showed the countess out. He switched off the hall light and went upstairs to the bedrooms.

So, where were the stolen artefacts from the museum?

She glanced back down the cellar steps. If they were down there, then there had to be a light switch somewhere. Praying it wasn't outside the locked door, she rose to her feet and used her left hand to feel along the rough walls. Relief shot through her when her fingers closed on the switch.

The weak glow from a single naked light bulb now illuminated her prison. Feeling less woozy, she carefully walked down the steps.

Brick-built, with damp, flaking walls, the cellar was stacked high with junk and wooden crates, which looked oddly familiar.

Bobbie knew she had to explore but the first thing she needed to do was support her throbbing arm and shoulder. There was a rusting old pram in one corner containing a few mouldy old blankets, which smelt rank. She wrinkled her nose in disgust as she used her teeth to grip and her good hand to tear the cloth. Eventually, she managed to fashion a triangular sling from the rotting material and slid it over her head.

Next, she looked for something to use to defend herself against Alcott. She knew it was a vain hope – the man had a gun. But no one was drugging her and shoving her on to a lorry bound for the Hull docks without a fight.

She eventually found a small rusty axe beneath a pile of gardening tools and old paint tins. If she found the courage, she would hurl it at him when he came for her.

But for the moment, it had another use. Using the edge of the axe, she prised open the lid of one of the packing cases. With only one arm, it took her ages. She was sweating by the time it popped free.

Inside, packed carefully in straw and sawdust, was a large, gleaming marble bust. It was too heavy to lift out, but the slight reddish-brown stain on the top of the head told her exactly what – and who – it was. 'Hello, Mr Constantine,' she said to the old Roman. 'I see they've repacked you since you did the world a favour and dispatched Lance Richards.'

Her voice sounded strange, and she knew chatting to a murder weapon was the sign of a madwoman – but it comforted her.

'The pair of us have had a few adventures this week, haven't we?' She patted the emperor's bust affectionately. 'Don't you worry, old man. I'll get us both out of here and back to where we belong. I'll rejoin the world of the living – and you can go back to the dusty fossils.'

Chapter Forty-Four

Saturday, 1ˢᵗ June 1940

Before the others arrived at the office, Jemma found the convent's telephone number in the directory and put through a call. 'Hello,' she said to the grumpy woman on the other end of the line. 'I'm the sister of Miss Roberta Baker – Baroness Stokesley's maid. Can I speak to her, please?'

'No, you can't,' the woman snapped.

'Well, can I leave her a message?' she stammered.

'No. Baker ain't here. She's run off.'

'What!'

'Aye, and your thievin' sister has taken fifty quid of her mistress's money, too.'

'That's not possible!'

'Tell that to the police.' The woman slammed down the receiver, leaving Jemma in a state of shock.

Instinctively, she dialled Bobbie's home and asked if she had popped back to fetch the book she wanted? During the short conversation that followed, Jemma discovered that neither of Bobbie's parents had seen her since she left home two days before.

She didn't tell Mrs Baker her daughter was missing and managed to end the conversation without frightening the woman, but she felt guilty when she replaced the receiver. Bobbie's mother had always treated Jemma with kindness, and she hated lying to her.

She stumbled into the kitchenette and made herself a pot of tea. Her hands shook as she poured the water into the pot.

Hannah, Emmett and Ricky arrived together.

Ricky sank into one of the armchairs. 'Stephen Howard went to the restaurant with Jodie and the others last night. But this morning he checked out of the hotel and went back to London.'

'Good,' Jemma said. 'That's one less of them for us to worry about. The rest of us need to concentrate on finding Bobbie.'

Quickly, she explained to her shocked colleagues what had happened. 'There is no way Bobbie would have walked away from her assignment,' she finished firmly, 'and she's not a thief.'

'Then what the hell's happened?' Ricky asked.

'I don't know, but I've got a bad feeling about this.' Jemma turned to Emmett. 'Did you see any sign of Bobbie when you followed the Rolls to the convent yesterday?'

Emmett shook his head and his broad face creased with concern. 'She were in the car when it sailed up the drive with the rest of them. I never saw her again. Do you think it's got owt to do with the trouble you were havin' with your investigation into the museum?'

'I don't know. The countess has a connection to the museum but so do most of the aristocrats in Yorkshire. Emmett, I'm going to drive out to Beningbrough, and I want you to come with me. Ricky, please will you continue to shadow Lansdowne? Hannah – please stay here by the telephone in case Bobbie calls.'

'Have you told your brother Bobbie is missin'?' Ricky asked.

'Not yet. It's too soon for the police to mount a missing person enquiry. Let's try to find her ourselves first.'

The drive out to Beningbrough seemed interminable – and the emptiness of the vast fields and ditches of the landscape took on a sinister appearance. The blazing sunlight turned the crops in the fields into a rippling sea of gold, but the sight failed to cheer her up. *What if Bobbie had had an accident out here?* It would take forever to find her.

'How do you plan to handle this?' Emmett asked.

'I'll have to speak to Jodie herself. We need to know what happened at the convent. The servants – like the old woman who answered the phone – will only tell us what they've been told to say. And if Bobbie's been hauled off for theft by the police and is languishing in a police cell, I need to know where it is.'

'This might blow your cover.'

'It's probably already been blown. I've a strong suspicion Jodie's found out who Bobbie works for. That's why she's gone. But if they just hurled her out of the house and told her to walk back to York, I'll be very annoyed.'

'The baron won't be pleased if her cover's blown.'

Jemma shrugged and concentrated on a series of sharp bends. 'We did our best – and quite frankly, I don't care what Stokesley thinks. I just want to know Bobbie is safe.'

'If you plan to drive up to the convent,' Emmett continued, 'drop me off with Irton at the gate. Jodie already knows who I am, so it's best not to be seen with me. If you keep on sayin' she's yer sister, you might get away with it.'

Irton was parked in the shade of a group of oak trees about fifty yards from the entrance to the convent. She slowed and let Emmett out of the car before turning into the overgrown driveway. Thankfully, the large rusty gates had been left open.

Halfway down the narrow drive, she met Jodie's Rolls coming the other way, with the actress sitting in the back. Jemma slammed on the brakes and blocked their way. Climbing out of the vehicle, she marched towards them.

'Can you move your car, ma'am?' the chauffeur asked.

Jemma ignored him and moved to Jodie's window, which was rolled down to let in a breeze.

The actress wore a turquoise skirt suit with a matching felt hat, decorated with a tiny peacock feather. There was a film script spread out on her lap. She gave Jemma a filthy look. 'What do you want?'

'Excuse me, baroness. This is a matter of some urgency. I'm looking for Bobbie Baker.'

'Aren't we all?' Jodie replied, laughing. But the laughter didn't reach her baby-blue eyes. There was anger there. 'Who are you?'

'I'm Jemma, her best friend. Do you know where she is?'

'Ah, the good friend she made at Miss Colbeck's School for Girls.'

'Yes,' Jemma stammered, slightly taken aback. 'There's a family emergency at Bobbie's house. I need to know where she is.'

'I see. How unfortunate. Well, I'm afraid I can't help you. Her dirty secret has been revealed, I'm afraid. A good friend of mine discovered it last night and gave her marching orders.'

'Her secret?'

Jodie smirked triumphantly. 'Oh, come on, *best friend*! Don't tell me you didn't know Bobbie's a private investigator – employed by my husband, Baron Stokesley.'

Jemma hesitated.

Jodie's eyes narrowed further. 'It's a ladies' detective agency in York, apparently – and her partner is a Mrs Jemima James. Jemima. Jemma. That'll be you, I suppose?'

It was pointless to deny it. 'Yes, it is. Look, Bobbie's not a thief.'

'She's left my employment with an envelope, addressed to my builder, that contained fifty pounds. When I telephoned him today, he hadn't received it.'

'What time did she leave and how did she get back to York?'

Jodie waved a dismissive hand. 'I've no idea. I'd told her not to wait up last night and she wasn't there this morning when I rose. My friend dealt with it.'

'Did someone give her a lift back to York?'

The chauffeur shrugged. 'I wasn't here, ma'am.'

The countess. It had to be the countess who was behind this. But if she was Stokesley's mistress, why did she betray Bobbie? Surely the woman would be desperate for the baron to get his divorce.

'Bobbie's disappeared and I think she may be in trouble.'

Hainsworth leant out of his window. 'That isn't Miss Jodie's problem, ma'am. The girl's lucky we've not contacted the police. Now kindly remove your car.'

Jemma's mouth fell open as she finally recognised his delightful Californian accent. She had a flashback to a pleasant afternoon in Clifton picture house, spent in the company of an extremely good-looking young actor with sun-kissed blond hair, a dazzling smile and a cheeky wink.

'The car, ma'am?' Hainsworth said, with growing irritation.

Jemma snapped back to reality and reached into her handbag. She tossed her business card through the open window. 'For what it's worth, Jodie, I wouldn't trust the countess as far as you can throw her. And if you hear anything about Bobbie's whereabouts – anything – please let me know. I'm desperately worried.'

Jodie made no effort to touch the card in her lap. She looked Jemma up and down impassively. 'You must care for her a lot.'

'I do.'

Jodie rolled up her window but as the glass rose, Jemma heard her say, 'Yes – it's a pity. I was getting quite fond of her myself...'

Jemma backed up her car to let the Rolls past, then she drove on to the convent. The grumpy housekeeper answered the door but slammed it in her face as soon as she explained what she wanted.

She drove back to the gates and hesitated there, looking for Emmett and Irton.

There was no sign of either of them – or the Citroën.

She slapped the steering wheel in frustration. Of course. Irton would have followed the Rolls the minute it turned out of the drive on to the road – that was his job. But she was disappointed in Emmett. She thought he liked Bobbie and wanted to help find her. But ultimately, they were professional P.I.s whose job was to shadow Jodie. Terence King's men – not hers.

Feeling very lonely, she tried to work out her next move. It was still too early to involve the police; they wouldn't look for a missing person until they'd been gone for at least twenty-four hours. She decided to work her way back to York, asking anyone she met on the way if they'd seen Bobbie.

She pulled up next to the lodge, walked up to the dilapidated house and knocked on the warped and peeling door.

She just had time to wonder why the curtains were drawn when the door swung open, and she found herself standing next to a man with a gun in his hand.

'Another one of you!' Ben Alcott exclaimed. 'Bleeding hell, it's like bloody Piccadilly Circus around here!'

Chapter Forty-Five

Jemma froze with fear and scrambled for the loaded Luger in her handbag. But Alcott pushed his gun against her forehead and wrenched the bag from her hands.

He forced her into the kitchen, tipped the contents on to the table and whipped away the Luger.

'Bobbie,' she croaked. 'What have you done with Bobbie?'

He didn't reply. He indicated she was to back into the hallway. The next thing she knew, he'd opened a small door and prodded her down the cellar steps, slamming the door behind her.

Relief swept through her when she saw Bobbie sitting on a packing case beneath a naked light bulb. But her relief was short-lived. Bobbie's face was bloodied, swollen and deathly pale and she was wearing a filthy sling. 'Dear God, what's he done to you!'

She flew to Bobbie's side and tried to hug her, but Bobbie winced and drew back. 'I think I've broken my shoulder, Jemma. It hurts like hell.'

Jemma crouched beside her and took her hand in her own. Tears of relief rolled down her cheeks. 'Oh, Bobbie, thank God you're alive! I've been worried sick.'

Bobbie gave a faint smile. 'Well, if this is a rescue attempt, Roxby, it's bloody pathetic.'

Jemma laughed and wiped her tears away on her jacket sleeve. 'I know I'm useless. I had my dad's old pistol – but I didn't get to it in time. The last thing I expected was for Alcott to open the door.'

Bobbie was strangely calm. 'You wouldn't have been able to shoot him, Jemma. You're not a killer. But I am,' she added grimly. 'And I've got this.' She held up the rusty axe. 'If you hadn't been in the way, I would have hurled it at him just now and killed him when he opened the door.'

Jemma smiled sadly. 'With your left hand and a blunt axe, sweetheart? I don't think so. You'd have probably just nicked his ear and given him a bad case of septicaemia.'

'Even that would have delighted me.'

'I'm just so pleased you're safe.'

'Mm, *safe* isn't the word I'd use, Jemma. We're in a bit of a pickle.' She told Jemma what had happened to her and what she'd learnt through eavesdropping on Alcott and the countess last night. 'I don't know what Alcott has planned for us, but I suspect it won't be pleasant.'

'I'm surprised he's not shot us already.'

'Too much blood to clear up,' Bobbie said calmly. 'As Agatha and Dorothy have shown us, disposing of dead bodies is not as easy as the murderers think. That countess won't want any trace of us here on her property to implicate her. No, if he's going to do it, it'll be on the quayside next to the docks. That way he can just kick our bodies over the edge into the Humber.'

Jemma grimaced, sat down on another packing case and tried to stay hopeful. Bobbie was white as a sheet from the pain. 'I'm not sure Alcott has got it in him to kill us. It sounds like Lance Richards's death was an accident.'

Bobbie shrugged her one good shoulder and touched her swollen jaw with her fingertip. 'Alcott's violent – as Tom and I can attest. He's also unpredictable, making a lot of mistakes and part of a nasty gang, some of the whom are even less scrupulous. Don't forget those thugs who knocked poor Mr Dunn unconscious. There's a lorry coming sometime today – probably tonight, when it's dark – to take away the stolen antiquities. I suspect we'll be part of the cargo.'

Jemma's hopes sank but she squeezed Bobbie's hand. 'Emmett, Irton, Ricky and Hannah will notice I've vanished – and my car's parked outside on the road. Don't give up hope, Bobbie. Someone will see it and rescue us.'

Bobbie gave a little laugh. 'Did you leave your key in the ignition?'

Jemma blushed. 'Yes, but even if I'd removed it – he's got my handbag.'

'Alcott will be hiding your car as we speak. Still,' Bobbie added more cheerfully, 'the good news is I've solved the mystery of Jodie's lover – it's that gorgeous actor, Budd Martin. She didn't leave him back in the States. Instead of *resting in between films*, he's popped over here to play at being her chauffeur. No wonder she wanted a suite closer to the stairs to the staff quarters in the hotel attics.'

Jemma smiled. 'I know. I've just worked it out.'

'Damn you, Miss Sherlock. You could have left this one for me to solve on my own!'

When Jodie's Rolls swung out of the convent's drive into the narrow road, Irton instinctively reached for the ignition. 'You comin' too?'

Emmett hesitated. 'I think we should stay and help Jemma.'

Irton scowled. 'I've told you before. We ain't here to babysit those lasses.'

'Aye, I heard. But if Bobbie is lyin' in a ditch somewhere, Jemma's goin' to need our help.'

'The King won't be pleased if Jodie gets away from us.'

Emmett shook his head, made his decision, and reached for the door handle. 'The King's got a soft spot for the blonde. You go – I'll stay.'

He climbed out of the car and instinctively, as a man who spent his life in the shadows, he moved into the dark shade of the trees that lined the road. Besides which, it was damn hot out in the sun.

While he waited, he pulled Irton's newspaper out of his coat pocket and read about the dramatic robbery at the Yorkshire Museum and the search for a man named Alcott. The lengthy report didn't mention the York Ladies' Detective Agency but he'd no doubt they'd played their part in solving this audacious crime; the charges had been dropped against their client. Those lasses got results. He took a long look at the photograph of Alcott and wondered if there was a reward for his capture.

He was so immersed in the newspaper, he didn't hear Jemma's car until it turned out of the drive and pulled up next to the lodge. She nipped out and went up to the door of the building. He folded the paper, slid it into his coat pocket and set off to join her.

A man answered the door, armed with a gun. It was the geezer in the photograph.

Emmett's hand instinctively delved into his pocket for his own gun.

But he couldn't get a clear shot. Jemma was between him and Alcott and within seconds the bastard had hauled her inside, shouting something about *Piccadilly Circus!*

He waited for the sound of a gunshot – and was relieved when it didn't come.

Sweat trickled down his forehead as his mind ticked over his options. He didn't like any of them.

He knew he needed to get help because Alcott wasn't working alone. That countess had to be involved; this was her property. And he'd no idea who else was in that lodge. If he burst in with his gun blazing, Jemma might get hurt in the crossfire – and no doubt Bobbie was in there too.

But the thought of leaving the women alone with a desperate murderer went against every chivalrous bone in his body.

The door opened again. Alcott came out and ran towards Jemma's car, still carrying his gun.

Emmett raised his own gun, trained on Alcott's legs – then hesitated. The countess might be inside with another pistol trained on the women. *Easy, fellah…*

Alcott slung the car into reverse and backed it out of sight down the convent's drive.

Get reinforcements! Emmett's common sense screamed. *Irton told you her brother is a copper.*

Sending up a quick prayer to their patron saint, Saint Father of Brown, he turned abruptly and ran towards the small group of farmhouses and the post office at the junction.

Dehydrated, starving and in chronic pain, Bobbie grew weaker as the hours ticked by. She slumped against Jemma, who put her arm around her to support her.

'My head's throbbing, Jemma.'

Jemma tried to distract her by reminiscing about their school days and some of the detective novels they'd both loved. She was careful not to talk too much about the future because, as each minute passed, she became less and less convinced they had one.

She took the axe from Bobbie, placed it by her side and tried to brace herself. If they were going to get out of here, *she* would have to be the one to use it – preferably before Alcott jabbed them with a hypodermic syringe full of sedatives.

Bobbie groaned and Jemma was wracked with guilt. 'I'm so sorry, Bobbie. I should never have involved you in this stupid detective agency. If I'd have thought for one minute…'

'Don't be silly,' Bobbie murmured. 'I've loved it. You took me away from a badly paid dead-end job and gave me a career – adventure – and a sense of worth.'

'A dangerous career.'

Bobbie tried to shrug with her good shoulder but winced instead. 'Don't blame yourself. It was always inevitable I'd die in the grounds of a nunnery. Besides which, if I remember rightly, it was *my* suggestion we set up Smoke & Cracked Mirrors. Stop claiming the credit for everything, Roxby. It's becoming a bad habit.'

Jemma gave a little laugh and said tentatively, 'If it's any consolation, darling, I've decided what I'll do if – when – I get Michael back and he's injured.'

Bobbie twisted her ashen face towards her.

'I'll keep the business, move us out into a flat and – if I need to – I'll pay for a professional nurse to look after Michael.'

A small smile flickered at the edge of Bobbie's mouth. 'People will talk. They'd expect you to do it yourself.'

'You sound like my sister.'

'God forbid!'

Jemma shrugged and stared down at the filthy floor. 'Someone will still have to work to pay the rent. And I'm damned if I'll give up our agency when we've both worked so hard – and suffered so much – to build it up. But you're right, people always criticise successful independent women and try to shove them back into the box of dutiful wife and selfless mother. Violet Rodgers and Mary Kitson Clark know this. So does Jodie. Sometimes we just have to stand firm and brazen it out.'

'Well,' Bobbie said. 'That's the best news I've heard all day—' She broke off and jerked with alarm when they heard a loud bang and shouting. Heavy boots clattered across the ceiling above.

Bobbie moaned, 'The gang's arrived. They've come for us.'

Jemma's throat went dry. She picked up the axe and rose to her feet. 'You stay where you are, Bobbie.' Gripping the weapon tightly in her sweating hands, she climbed the stairs.

She'd attack whoever opened the door. She had to. Their lives depended on it.

She heard Alcott yelling and winced. *Could she do it?*

She had to. Don't think. Just strike.

The key turned in the lock and the door handle twisted…

She raised the axe. Braced. Ready to strike.

The door swung open, and a large uniformed man – larger than Alcott – moved into the doorway.

'Drop that bloody axe, Jemma!'

She let go. It clattered down the stone steps behind her.

Sobbing, she ran into her brother's arms.

Chapter Forty-Six

The house swarmed with armed police officers.

Gabriel hugged her tight. 'Are you all right?'

She heaved great sobs of relief. 'Yes – but Bobbie's down there – she's hurt. How did you find us?'

'Your mate Emmett called it in. We sent some lads over the fields to the convent. Once they'd arrested the countess and her husband, we learned that Alcott was on his own here with you two.'

'Oh, Gabriel, I've been so scared!'

'I'll get Bobbie.' He hugged her again and passed her across to another officer, who helped her outside.

When she passed the kitchen door, she saw Alcott lying face down on the filthy tiles. One grim-faced officer stood over him with a gun while another snapped on the handcuffs. Alcott saw her and yelled out, 'You interfering bitch! This is all your fault.'

She had a strong urge to walk over and stamp on his face, but the officer saw the look in her eye, grabbed her arm and led her out.

Jemma sank on to a low wall, blinking against the strong sunshine. Someone handed her a flask of water. Now the scene had been secured, police cars appeared at the lodge. She felt a surge of satisfaction as one vehicle turned out of the convent's drive with the manacled and white-faced countess sitting in the back.

A few moments later Gabriel appeared, carrying Bobbie in his arms. He was sweating and looked a tad strained.

Bobbie, however, was in fine spirits and grinning weakly. 'Eee, Gabriel! It's just like the time when I was twelve and I fell off the swing in the park and hurt my leg. Jemma fetched you to carry me back to the house.'

'You've clapped on a few pounds since then, Bobbie,' Gabriel grunted. He took her to one of the police cars and gently placed her inside. 'This woman needs to go to the hospital, immediately.'

'Yes, sir.'

'Do you want me to come with you?' Jemma handed Bobbie the flask of water.

Bobbie grabbed it and drank deeply. 'No. Just tell my parents where I am. The police need you here, Jemma – don't forget to tell them about the bloody truck that's coming tonight.'

Jemma nodded – it made sense – but it felt wrong to watch Bobbie be driven away.

'They'll soon patch her up,' Emmett said at her shoulder.

She spun round and gave him a massive hug. 'I don't know how I can ever thank you for what you've done!'

Emmett blushed to the roots of his thinning hair. 'Steady on, lass, I'm a married man, I am.'

It was another half an hour or so before the stolen artefacts and antiquities were loaded into a police van and dispatched back to the museum.

Gabriel then ordered everyone out of sight. The police planned to wait in and around the house until the rest of the gang of thieves showed up with the lorry. Alcott and the countess hadn't had time to warn anyone before they pounced, and they were confident they could round up the rest of the gang – including those waiting at Hull docks – before nightfall.

At this point, Gabriel ordered Jemma back to York. The police had found her car hidden and abandoned in the thick undergrowth down the side of the countess's drive. It was badly scratched but still purred into life when Emmett turned the ignition key. He insisted on driving. 'I'll take you home.'

Jemma shook her head. She was desperate for a cup of tea but there were things to do. 'No. I need to call at Bobbie's parents. Then let's go back to the office. The others need to know Bobbie's safe.'

As they turned on to the road to York, they saw Jodie's Rolls pulled up next to a police officer. Emmett slowed down as they approached, and Jemma rolled down the window to listen. The officer instructed the actress and her chauffeur to return to York and book into a hotel; the convent was a crime scene and there was no access to it.

'But my clothes and jewellery are in there!' Jodie wailed.

'You'll have to wait, miss, until the scene is examined by the police.'

Jemma smiled and told Emmett to drive on. *Serves her right for not caring more about Bobbie*, she thought.

Back in York, Mr and Mrs Baker listened with open mouths and mounting horror as Jemma explained their daughter had been kidnapped and injured by the man the police wanted for the murder of the museum curator.

'What the devil was she doin' in Beningbrough?' her father asked. 'We thought she worked as a restaurant manager on High Petergate.'

'Bobbie will explain everything,' Jemma said quietly. 'She's wide awake and quite lucid. We'll drive you to the hospital.'

The office was crowded with people when they returned. Among them was Terence King, sitting in one of her armchairs with a cup and saucer in his hands. Her stomach did that silly fluttering thing again.

Hannah and Ricky rushed to her side, asking about Bobbie, and King rose politely to his feet. The tall, well-built professional man in the expensive suit seemed to dominate her cosy but slightly shabby office. Even Irton was there, lurking at the edges of the room.

Her legs wobbled, and she sank wearily into the armchair. She wasn't sure whether it was a reaction to seeing King or sheer weariness. The adrenaline that had kept her going for the past few hours had started to subside.

Hannah pushed a welcome cup of tea into Jemma's hand and she and Emmett explained what had happened. King said little, apart from asking a few questions, but she saw the concern in his intelligent dark-brown eyes.

'Jesus, Miss Marple,' Ricky exclaimed. 'You and Bobbie might have been killed!' He rose to his feet. 'If you're all right now, I think I'll go and see Bobbie in the hospital. I've left those photographs you wanted on your desk. I'll pick up some flowers on the way.'

'Aye, and mek sure you buy 'em from a shop and don't filch 'em from a graveyard,' Hannah said.

Ricky chuckled as he left. 'As if I would!'

Jemma smiled. Ricky and Bobbie sparred constantly, but she knew he had a soft spot for her friend.

Irton turned to Emmett. 'You did well, mate. Sorry I left you to it.' Jemma sensed he was less sure of himself around his boss.

Emmett shrugged and a slow grin spread across his broad face. 'I didn't need no help. I had the situation under control. Shame there weren't a reward out for catchin' that geezer, though.'

'Yes, well done, Emmett,' King said, 'and don't worry, there'll be a bonus in your pay packet this week.' He gave Irton a hard stare. 'It's good to know at least one of you had the best interests of our female colleagues in mind. The two of you can head back to Leeds now and take the rest of the weekend off.'

Jemma frowned. 'But what about Jodie? She'll be back in her hotel suite at the Royal Station Hotel by now.'

King shuffled uncomfortably and lit a cigarette. 'That's partly why I'm here, Mrs James. I phoned up this morning to tell you the job's over. But when Hannah answered the telephone and told me that Bobbie was missing, I thought I'd better drive over and see what I could do to help – and give you the bad news about the assignment in person.'

Hannah jabbed a finger in his direction and said, 'He cares, him.'

'That was kind of you,' Jemma said, 'but what's happened? Why has the baron sacked us? Surely the last thing he knew we'd just got Bobbie into Jodie's service. It was going well.'

'Jodie's goin' back to America,' Hannah interrupted. 'To work with that Glazer fellah.'

King took up the story. 'It's all over the London papers. Apparently, before Glazer left, he persuaded her to sign a Hollywood film deal. She'll be acting alongside her old flame, Budd Martin.'

Jemma smiled. 'Ah, Mr Martin…'

A smile flitted across King's scarred face, making him look years younger. 'Yes, your favourite actor with the dreamy eyes.'

'We'd heard a rumour Jodie was about to make a film for the BBC with Stephen Howard and the British producer, Nigel Lansdowne.'

King shook his head. 'It looks like the lure of Hollywood is too much for her.'

Or the lure of Budd Martin...

'The baron's decided to drop us from the job and employ Pinkertons in New York again. He's sure that once she's back in the States with Martin, they'll soon get the evidence he needs for a divorce.'

Irton shrugged. 'Ah, well, it were good while it lasted.'

'I'm sorry the contract turned out to be so short-lived, Mrs James,' King said.

Jemma just smiled. 'It's not *quite* over yet...'

King raised a curious eyebrow, but Irton distracted him.

'Shall we be off then, boss?'

King nodded and thanked his men.

'Can you stay for a moment longer, Mr King?' Jemma asked. 'I want to ask your advice about something.'

He nodded. 'Call me Terry.'

Jemma rose to her feet and shook Irton's hand. 'It's been an education working alongside you, Mr Irton.'

'Learnt a few tricks from us, have you, lass?' Irton asked smugly.

'Absolutely.'

She gave Emmett a genuine and heartfelt hug. 'We owe you,' she whispered in his ear.

Hannah also rose and gathered up her handbag.

'Come back on Monday,' Jemma told her. 'I've got more work for you – although it won't be so exciting.'

'Borin' is good,' Hannah announced firmly. She pulled her old check coat over her shoulders. 'You sure you'll be all right, lass?'

Jemma nodded and showed them out.

King visibly relaxed now his men had left. 'So, why isn't it over yet, Jemma?'

She noted his informality and decided she liked it. She reached across for the envelope of photographs Ricky had left on her desk and gave them to him. 'There's been a development, Terry, and I need to ask your advice.'

He gave a low whistle at the sight of their client in a deep and passionate embrace with the countess. 'Who is she?'

'She's a Hungarian countess called Anna Léna von Hatvan. She's part of the gang responsible for the museum robbery and owns the old convent where Alcott hid the antiquities and held Bobbie and I prisoner. At the moment, she's locked in a police cell in York. I suspect the police will throw the book at her – and there may even be a charge of treason laid at her door.' She explained the plan she had for the photographs and why she thought it would work. 'Will two hundred be enough?'

He burst out laughing. 'By God, you're a wily one, Jemma! But no – I'd ask for three hundred – not two. Obviously, fifty per cent of it is mine,' he added with a wink.

'You can have twenty per cent. Ricky took the photographs – and Bobbie and I've suffered for this case.'

'Thirty – and I'll take you out to dinner tonight. Irton told me the restaurant at the Dean Court is quite a swanky place. I'll throw a bottle of champagne into the deal. Interested?'

She smiled. Her heart was pounding with excitement, but she knew her limits. 'Perhaps tomorrow? I think I need to go home and get an early night. It's been a stressful and exhausting day. I was only seconds away from killing my brother with an axe.'

He laughed again. 'A wily *and* dangerous woman – who also happens to be gorgeous.' He reached for his hat, and they rose to their feet. He towered over her and gazed down fondly, emanating masculinity and strength.

He lifted her hand and gently kissed it. 'I'll pick you up at seven tomorrow. It's a pleasure doing business with you, Jemma.'

Chapter Forty-Seven

Sunday, 2nd June 1940

Jemma fetched Bobbie from the hospital just after ten.

An X-ray revealed that Bobbie *had* broken her shoulder. But apart from strapping her up comfortably, pumping her full of fluids and giving her strong painkillers, there wasn't much else the doctors could do. She was delighted when Jemma walked into the ward jangling the car keys.

Bobbie's face and hands were grazed, swollen and bruised and the pristine white triangular sling was large and depressing, but there was colour in her cheeks, and she was smiling. 'Are you ready for a little adventure, before I take you home?'

'Always, Miss Sherlock. Lead the way.'

Jemma drove to the Royal Station Hotel and the two of them walked straight into the light and airy marble-tiled reception area. They went across to an elderly female receptionist standing behind the gleaming teak desk.

'We'd like to see Jodie, please.'

The woman stared at them suspiciously over the rim of her tiny glasses. 'Miss Jodie only sees people by appointment.'

Jemma smiled and slid the envelope of photographs across the desk. 'Oh, I think she'll see us. Please send these up to her suite and tell her we're in the lobby.'

They walked towards a comfortable velvet sofa and Bobbie caught sight of herself in one of the many gilt mirrors filling the lobby. She grimaced. 'Crikey! I look a real mess! You've only brought me along to make Jodie feel guilty, haven't you?'

'Of course.'

Five minutes later, the receptionist came over and told them Miss Jodie would see them now. 'She's in her usual suite.'

'No need to show us up,' Bobbie said cheerfully. 'We know the way.'

Jodie had on the same turquoise suit she'd worn yesterday, and her big blue eyes narrowed with suspicion when they entered, but she asked them to sit down. The damning photographs of her husband and the countess were spread out on a low table in front of her. 'I'm pleased to see you found your friend, Mrs James – and I'm sorry you had such a dreadful experience, Miss Baker.'

'No thanks to you,' Bobbie muttered beneath her breath.

'I'm intrigued by these photographs you've provided. I assume you have the negatives and all other copies safe in your care?'

'Of course.'

'But I don't understand why you've given them to *me*? I thought you worked for my husband.'

Jemma smiled. 'I've decided to switch sides. I don't like him.'

Jodie laughed. 'Then you're unusual among our sex, Mrs James. Most women find him charming.'

'Not if they work for him, I suspect. I'm here to sell you these photographs, the negatives – and our silence on the matter, in exchange for three hundred pounds.'

Jodie gasped and beside her, Bobbie tensed with surprise.

'With these images, you'll be able to get the divorce you want from the baron,' Jemma added.

Jodie chuckled and shook her head. 'I'm afraid not, Mrs James. My lawyer made it quite clear that a random kiss is never enough. Photographic evidence for a divorce case has to be far more incriminating than this – and dreadfully seedy. Only a photograph of my darling husband actually in bed with another woman will suffice.'

'I'm not proposing you take these photographs to a divorce court, Jodie. I suggest you take them to your husband and *persuade* him to do the *honourable thing*. I'm sure once he sees these, he'll agree to let himself be photographed taking a prostitute to a hotel and let you divorce him on the grounds of adultery.'

Jodie's mouth dropped open in surprise, revealing her perfect teeth. 'But he's always refused to do this. Why would these photographs change his mind?'

'Because your friend, the Countess von Hatvan, is part of a gang of international thieves with links to the Nazis. Last night, York City Police rounded up the rest of the gang – and discovered their network and links to German antiquity dealers. Apart from numerous other charges relating to the robbery, the countess has also been charged with treason.'

Jodie sat back in her chair, stunned. 'Dear God! I didn't think it was as bad as that!'

'You can expect a visit from Special Branch soon. They'll want to know what – if anything – you knew about the woman. Meanwhile, if those photographs became public – sent to the press, perhaps? – your husband's reputation would be ruined.'

Jemma paused for a moment to let her words sink in. 'Baron Stokesley has been – wittingly or unwittingly – cavorting with a traitor.

I understand he previously declined to let you divorce him for adultery because he was frightened his invitations to the royal court and regimental dinners would dry up?'

Jodie nodded, fascinated.

'Well, if those photographs of him in a clinch with a traitor became public, then all that would happen – and worse. Even his London clubs would blackball him. He'll be shunned by society.'

Jodie burst out laughing. 'You've thought it all through, haven't you? You want me to *blackmail* Stokesley, make him agree to a divorce on *my* terms.'

'Absolutely. Although I don't think they call it blackmail within marriage – I believe it's known as a *compromise.*'

Jodie chuckled and reached for her handbag. 'Very well, but I'm not paying you three hundred. One hundred should suffice.'

'No,' Jemma said gently. 'We have to compensate Miss Baker for the injuries she received while she was a member of your staff.'

Jodie glanced guiltily at Bobbie. 'Very well, two hundred – a hundred each.'

'I'm sure Mr Martin will be delighted to hear you've finally found the means to get rid of your irritating husband. I imagine he'll happily chip in with another hundred. Although, please make sure it's pounds sterling and not dollars he provides.' Jemma glanced around theatrically. 'Where is he, by the way? Still sitting in the Rolls?'

A forced smile spread across Jodie's face and her throat flushed beneath her pearl necklace. She didn't look up as she pulled her cheque book out of her handbag. 'My, oh my. You are a clever little thing, aren't you, Mrs James?' She paused, then asked, 'What do you intend to do with this information?'

'Absolutely nothing. I know it would ruin you – and him – and your plans for your wonderful Hollywood film. I happen to be a huge fan of Mr Martin's and don't want to see that spoilt.'

Jodie smiled. 'You're not a fan of mine?'

Jemma ignored the question. 'I'm sure your film will delight millions across the world – and we live in a frightened world that desperately needs a distraction right now.'

'So, you're not blackmailing me?' Jodie asked with a small smile.

'No. I don't believe in blackmail. All I want is a decent payment for the photographs.'

'You're the woman in the crowd who warned me about the false letter that was shoved into my coat pocket, aren't you?'

'Yes. I believe in fair play.'

Jodie wrote them a cheque for three hundred.

They went back to the office for a celebratory cup of tea.

Bobbie whooped with delight and grinned from ear to ear. 'You bloody clever clogs! That was amazing, Jemma! You were so cool! How on earth did you manage to stay so calm and keep your face straight!'

Jemma grinned. 'Jodie's not the only actress in Yorkshire.'

'You were brilliant! What a fantastic end to an amazing week. The museum murder is solved—'

'—a murder that turned out *not* to be a murder, but an unfortunate accident.'

'The priceless antiquities have been returned to the Yorkshire Museum—'

'—which no one knew were stolen in the first place.'

'And the Stokesleys will get their divorce—'

'—albeit not in the way the baron hoped.'

'And to cap it all,' Bobbie finished, with a grand flourish of her good arm, 'the most celebrated actress in Britain has paid us a fortune to keep quiet about the fact she's sneaking around the countryside with her lover.'

Jemma giggled. 'But the best result, Bobbie, is thanks to us and the part we played in capturing Ben Alcott – Tom's stopped having nightmares. Now he knows his attacker is in jail, he's sleeping like a baby again.'

'That's excellent news.' Bobbie held up her cup. Jemma copied her and they chinked the cups together in a toast.

'To us. To Smoke & Cracked Mirrors. We've done well.'

Jemma drank her tea and smiled as her mind drifted forward to the evening ahead. 'Oh, there's something I didn't tell you. Terence King turned up here yesterday…'

The telephone rang.

'It's Sunday!' Bobbie complained. 'Don't our clients ever take a day off?'

Jemma picked up the receiver.

It was D.S. Marlowe. 'Mrs James?'

'Yes?'

'We've found your husband – he's alive. But he's not the man you knew, I'm afraid…'

Chapter Forty-Eight

Jemma travelled down to St Andrew's Hospital for Mental Diseases on the train with her mother-in-law, Sofia.

Her grief for her son and the shock and strain of the past few months showed on Sofia's pale, lined face and in her nervous hand fidgeting. The Nordic beauty of the Russian woman, with her finely chiselled bone structure, had faded. Her silver hair had thinned, her skin sagged from her jaw with unhappiness, and she was painfully thin. But hope still gleamed in her pale-grey eyes.

A hope Jemma didn't share.

For months now, Jemma had held on to a fantasy that Michael would walk back into her world, a whole and complete man. She imagined they would eventually pick up the pieces of their life together and move forward into the future. She'd even dreamt of starting a family…

But the reality of her situation now made her stomach churn with dread. She didn't know how she would react to seeing Michael – or what she would do.

As the train thundered down the track towards Northampton, her conversation with Marlowe played over and over again in her head.

'He had a terrible head injury when the police picked him up in Towcester,' Marlowe had said. 'It's healed on the outside – but he has brain damage.'

'How bad is it?' Jemma's hands shook as she held the receiver. 'Can he talk? Move? Walk?'

'Yes, he can do all of those things. But he can't – or won't – speak English. For the first few months, the doctors thought he was talking rubbish. When they finally got him a Russian interpreter – who understood a little of the Ukrainian dialect — they realised he's chattering to himself in Ukrainian, and he thinks we're at war with the Bolsheviks. He spends most of his time playing the piano in the ward and climbing trees in the grounds.'

Jemma swallowed hard and tried to adjust to the image of the man Marlowe was describing. 'Will he get better?'

Marlowe's pause told her everything she needed to know. 'You'll have to talk to the doctors about that. If it's any consolation, Mrs James, Special Branch and the military police no longer have any interest in AC James.'

It wasn't a consolation. They'd pursued Michael with a vengeance over the past five months. The fact they were now backing away was ominous.

'How did he end up in Towcester?'

'He can't remember that – or anything about the train crash. But we assume it was something to do with that bus stop below the bridge you mentioned. The police found him, begging for food on the streets of Towcester.'

Jemma froze with horror. She finally remembered her conversation with Gabriel last March – the one that had been niggling at the back of her mind.

They'd been talking about xenophobic attacks on foreigners – particularly on Michael's parents and their business. Then Gabriel had mentioned an 'old tramp' his mate Superintendent Jim Jones had found in Towcester:

The poor old fellow had lost his marbles and was speaking gibberish. He didn't know who he was, or how to speak English – all he can do is play the piano. They didn't know whether to imprison him as a foreign spy or send him to a mental asylum.

Somehow, in the retelling, her young husband had morphed into an *old tramp*.

She found the irony hard to bear. Unwittingly, she'd known the fate of her husband since March.

As the train rattled over the points, flashed through station after station and steamed south, Jemma desperately wanted to bury her head in her novel. But Sofia asked her to repeat her conversation with Marlowe. Sofia's spoken English and understanding of the language was good, but the story Jemma had relayed to her was so bizarre, she was convinced she'd misunderstood.

'Marlowe said the train crash at Bletchley had left Michael with a massive brain injury, and he'd developed chronic amnesia – and other problems.'

'And this amnesia, it is memory loss, yes?'

'Yes, but it's more complicated than that, Sofia. They think he's regressed to his childhood.'

'Regressed?'

'Gone back. He thinks he's a little boy again. He keeps climbing trees.'

'He always loved climbing trees when he was young. Does he remember me, his mother?'

'I don't know.' Jemma swallowed and turned to look out of the window at the rolling countryside as it swept past. It pained her to speak the next sentence. 'According to Marlowe, Michael doesn't remember me.'

Sofia sat back in her seat, aghast. Then she pulled herself together. 'But it's something, yes? That he remembers our war in Russia against the Bolshevik pigs? There is hope his full memory will return.'

Sensing Jemma's misery, she leant across the aisle and squeezed her hand again. 'You are a good girl, Jemma. Many young women wouldn't have grieved like you. When they were told their husband was missing, they'd have gone straight out and found another man. But you never lost the faith.'

You've no idea how close I came, Sofia.

It had broken her heart when she'd had to telephone Terry to cancel their dinner date.

The train slowed with a squeal of brakes and outside in the corridor, the ticket inspector shouted, 'Northampton! Northampton station!'

'Now you'll get your reward,' Sofia added in delight. 'Now we'll see Mykhail once more!'

Jemma fought back another wave of anxiety, gathered up their luggage and tried to share her mother-in-law's enthusiasm.

St Andrew's Hospital for Mental Diseases was far less foreboding and grim than most British asylums. Built of soft yellow stone and set in extensive wooded grounds, it looked more like a stately home than a hospital. Its mellow external appearance was reflected in the calmness of its interior. Yes, it stank of disinfectant, but the uniformed staff were compassionate and efficient and the whole place was scrupulously clean.

A white-coated doctor with thinning grey hair and spectacles introduced himself as Doctor Wood. He took them into his bland office. 'I thought we should have a little chat before you see Michael. It might help to prepare you. I'm afraid Michael was left with dreadful brain damage after the accident.'

He talked about Michael's damaged hippocampus and some theory of Freud's about regressive, infantile behaviour... an unconscious defence mechanism... the train crash... extreme trauma and stress...

But the medical terminology washed over the women.

'When will he get better?' Sofia demanded.

'Will his memory return?' Jemma asked.

Doctor Wood shuffled the papers in Michael's folder and broke eye contact with her. 'It's been nearly five months since his accident,' he said gently. 'His progress is non-existent. There is no guarantee any of his memory will return.'

'Of course it will!' Sofia exclaimed. 'We just need to get him home, yes? How soon can we take him home?'

He shook his head sadly. 'Michael may need care all his life – probably in an institution. You've a good institution in York, I believe, Mrs James – Bootham Park Hospital?'

Jemma grimaced and nodded. This former asylum had a mixed reputation and was close to where she lived in Clifton. As a child, she and her friends had sometimes scrambled up the wall to peer at the sad and disturbed patients wandering inside the grounds. Other children had thrown stones and called out names. The thought of Michael living there was heart-breaking.

'I can arrange for him to be transferred,' the doctor continued.

'No! No!' Sofia protested. 'Jemma and I can care for him! It'll be better for Mykhail.'

'It's up to you, Mrs James,' the doctor said to Jemma. 'You're his wife. The decision is yours.' He pushed his spectacles up his nose and looked at her expectantly. 'But I need to warn you that when the frustration mounts, he can be aggressive.'

The women stared at him in disbelief. *Michael? Aggressive?*

He stood up. 'Come and see him now. It may help you make a decision. He's in the visitors' lounge. We've kept the other patients away so you can have some privacy.'

They heard Michael before they saw him. As they approached the spacious sitting room that served as the visitors' lounge, the sound of a beautifully executed Tchaikovsky piano concerto drifted down the corridor towards them.

'He always was such a graceful player,' Sofia said, smiling. 'He learnt so young.' She rushed ahead into the room, calling out his name. She flew across the carpet towards her son, who rose in surprise from the piano stool and embraced his mother.

Jemma watched from the doorway. Michael's hands held Sofia's face, exploring every line and contour as his mother drowned him in a torrent of Ukrainian.

Jemma's eyes revelled in the sight of him. Her gorgeous husband. That lithe, athletic body, those clear blue eyes fringed with dark lashes. Her heart leapt with love and hope as his blond head bowed over Sofia. *If he remembered Sofia – then, surely, he would know her?*

He answered Sofia in an awkward stilting manner – but it was still his voice. The voice she never thought to hear again except in her dreams.

'He remembers me!' Sofia called in delight. 'But he's shocked at how old I've become! Come, Jemma – come here!'

Sofia stepped aside and Michael looked across the room at his wife for the first time.

Their eyes met – and Jemma's fairy tale ended.

Those gorgeous blue eyes, which had once twinkled with intelligence and wit and gazed at her with adoration… stared back. Blankly.

Mildly curious – but blank.

There was no love, no recognition. It was like someone had just switched off the light.

Fighting back the urge to cry, Jemma walked forwards and forced herself to smile. 'Hello, Michael,' she said. 'Do you remember me, darling?'

He didn't respond.

Sofia said something and Jemma heard her name mentioned.

Michael reached out. For a moment, she thought he wanted to hug her and was about to throw herself into his arms… then he picked up her hand and shook it formally. 'Mykhail,' he said and turned back to his mother, muttering something in Ukrainian.

The pain of the rebuff was so sharp, it was like he'd slapped her.

Sadness consumed Sofia's features. 'He said… he said… you're a very pretty lady, and he's pleased to meet you.'

Jemma's voice became shrill with desperation. 'Didn't you tell him I'm his wife?'

'He doesn't believe me – he laughed and said he's too young to be married.'

Jemma's heart sank and the last vestige of hope left her.

'Have faith, Jemma,' Sofia pleaded. 'Once we get him home, he'll remember everything.' She led Michael by the hand across the carpet towards a group of comfortable armchairs.

Jemma followed in a trance and finally saw the jagged wound on the back of his head. It was pitted with scar tissue, shiny red bald patches and tufts that sprouted at odd angles.

The next few minutes were excruciating. Jemma had never felt so lonely and so jealous in her life. As mother and son chatted, Michael gazed at Sofia with the adoration he'd once laid at her own door.

Sofia did her best to relay snippets of their conversation to Jemma and the doctor in English, but each bit of news only compounded Jemma's distress.

At one point Sofia dropped her voice and squeezed Michael's hand tighter. Whatever she had just said made him cry. Jemma watched in horror while he sobbed. She desperately wanted to put her arms round his broad shoulders and comfort him – but how could she touch a man who didn't know her?

Yet we've shared our bodies with each other and the most intimate moments of our lives…

Sofia fished her handkerchief out of her bag.

But Michael pushed her away so roughly she fell back in her chair. He stomped off back to his piano. The next minute he was hammering out *"The Ride of the Valkyries"* with such ferocity, it sounded like the mythical beasts were after him.

'What happened?' Jemma stammered. Michael's rough treatment of his mother had alarmed her.

Tears rolled down Sofia's cheeks and her face contorted with anguish. 'Mykhail thinks we're still in Kiev. He asked after his dog.'

'Dog? I didn't know he had a dog.'

'We had to leave it behind in Kiev when we fled. We had no choice. I've just told Mykhail the dog is dead. He loved his dog.'

Mykhail. Her husband wasn't Michael any more – he'd become little Mykhail again. She was married to a man-child. 'He thinks he's six years old, doesn't he?'

Sophia nodded. 'He doesn't remember anything about our escape to England or his life here.'

Doctor Wood suggested they left Michael to his piano and went back to his office.

They called out 'goodbye' in both English and Ukrainian, but Michael didn't glance round, compounding the misery of the women.

They were both crying when they sat down in the office. The doctor patiently let them deal with their grief before he brought out some forms and once more broached the subject of transferring Michael to the York asylum.

Sofia tried to protest but Jemma had made her decision. 'Let's do as Doctor Woods suggests. Let's get Michael back to York. Once he's in Bootham Park Hospital, the doctors there can examine him. Let's see what *they* say.' It was the only glimmer of hope they had – that another doctor may see something Doctor Wood had missed.

Sofia buried her head in her hands. 'Poor Mykhail! This is a tragedy! A tragedy for him! What a waste of his life!'

Yes, Jemma thought sadly. *And it's a tragedy for me too...*

Chapter Forty-Nine

Wednesday, 5ᵗʰ June 1940
York

A sharp rap on the front door woke Bobbie from her nap.

Alone in the house for the first time for several days, she'd settled down on the settee with her novel and nodded off. Her book clattered to the floor, and she jerked upright. Grumbling at the disturbance, she hauled herself up with her good arm and padded towards the front door in her slippers. She hadn't bothered to pin up her hair today and knew she looked a bit wild and scary.

But the young telegram boy standing on the doorstep in the navy-blue uniform and pillbox hat barely looked at her as he pushed a buff-coloured envelope into her hand and avoided eye contact.

Bobbie froze to the spot and stared at the dull envelope, addressed to her parents, as if it were a piece of poisoned meat. A telegram only meant one thing: news about – or from – Frank. She was seconds away from finding out if her brother was dead or alive.

'Yer supposed to read it and tell me if there's a reply, Mrs Baker,' the young lad said awkwardly. 'It's nine words for sixpence.' He couldn't have been more than fourteen. *Why on earth did they send children out to do a job like this?*

Bobbie leant against the door jamb to brace herself in case her legs gave way. Then she tore open the envelope.

'Coming home. Get the beer in Dad. Frank.'

She burst out laughing and burst into tears at the same time.

Incoherent with relief and joy, she waved the young lad away, closed the door and leant against the wall while she laughed, sobbed and snorted into her handkerchief.

He'd done it. Her ugly, bullish and bloody annoying big brother had scrambled off that French beach and survived the evacuation at Dunkirk.

The notoriously fickle *Luck of the Bakers* had held firm.

She went into the kitchen and placed the telegram in the centre of the table where her parents would see it on their return. Then she went into her room to tame her hair.

She couldn't sit still – and she'd no idea how long her parents would be. She needed to talk to someone. She'd get a bus to Clifton and go and see if Jemma had returned from Northamptonshire yet. With any luck, Maisie would also have had some good news about Harry…

The papers had been full of the success of the evacuation for the past two days, and last night she and her parents had heard the wireless newsreaders report extracts of Mr Churchill's stirring speech in parliament during the BBC news broadcast.

Their tiny island had had its miracle. Nearly four hundred thousand of Britain's sons had been rescued from the advancing German army by navy vessels and a flotilla of small boats manned by courageous civilians.

They'd hardly dared hope Frank was among them… but he was.

The sunshine flooded into the city, lifting the spirits of a jubilant population. Everyone seemed to be walking taller and smiling.

She spotted Mrs Dunn, the museum caretaker's wife, carrying a heavy shopping bag and hurried after her. 'Mrs Dunn? Do you remember me? I came to your house the other day.'

The woman's old, lined face broke into a beautiful smile. 'Why, of course I do, lass! What on earth have you done to your arm?'

'Oh, that's nothing. I fell down some stairs. I wanted to know if you'd heard anything about your sons and nephews?'

Mrs Dunn's smile spread even wider. 'Yes! They're safe! All four of them!' She raised her shopping bags to show Bobbie. 'Our Dan came home last night – he's eatin' me out of house and home already! What about your own brother?'

'He's safe.'

'Thank the Lord!'

Another woman joined them on the pavement – and then another. 'Isn't it wonderful!' one exclaimed.

'I can't believe it,' said the other.

'Neither can the bloody Jerries!' Mrs Dunn said, laughing.

'Mr Churchill says we'll fight them on the beaches.'

'Aye, that we will. We'll never surrender.'

More people, all strangers, gathered around.

'It's a bloody miracle!'

'My brother came back in a fishing boat.'

'It were a pleasure cruiser, for my son – tiny little thing, he said.'

'Our Fred's a wag – he told me he'd swum back across the flippin' Channel.'

The crowd burst out laughing.

Reluctantly, Bobbie dragged herself away from the jubilant crowd and boarded the bus.

But her happiness was tempered when Maisie answered the door and told her she'd still not heard anything about Harry.

Bobbie gave her a one-armed hug. 'I'm sure you'll hear from him soon, Maisie. They'd got hundreds of thousands of them out of France. It must be chaos down there on the south coast right now…'

Maisie managed a brave smile and pulled her hat over her flaming auburn hair. 'I was just goin' to get Tom from school. It's his first day back and he wouldn't go unless I promised to take him out for a treat afterwards.'

'Is he still not fully recovered?'

Maisie rolled her eyes and smiled. 'No, he's fine, Bobbie. But he's ten years old and will find any excuse not to go to school. Gabriel's workin' late so I'm takin' Tom to a tearoom for a bite to eat. After that, we're goin' to Clifton picture house at five thirty to see a film. You can wait here for Jemma. Make yourself a cup of tea, love. She should be back soon.'

Bobbie thanked her, waved her off and put the kettle on. The Roxbys' kitchen was familiar territory. She'd spent as much time here as at her own home during her childhood. But having one arm strapped to her body in a sling slowed her down. She was just lifting out a cup from the cupboard when the front door opened and slammed shut.

A grubby, unshaven and very attractive soldier in the khaki uniform of the King's Own Light Infantry strode into the kitchen and dropped his kitbag on to the floor.

He blinked at the sight of her, then grinned. Whipping his beret off his red-gold hair, he tossed it on to the kitchen table. 'Good grief! It's Vivien Leigh! What the devil are *you* doing in my mother's kitchen, Miss Leigh?'

Bobbie smiled back. 'You must be Harry.' He had a smattering of freckles (just like her own) that stretched across his broad cheeks. His brown eyes were laughing but the dark shadows beneath hinted at his exhaustion.

He snapped to attention and saluted her. 'Corporal Harold Langford at your service, ma'am.'

'You've just missed your mother – she's gone to fetch Tom from school and is taking him to the cinema at five thirty. They'll be so pleased to see you!'

'And me, them!' Still grinning, he pulled out a chair and sat down. 'But you have the advantage on me, lass. I know you're not my new aunty, Jemma – I remember her from Clifton primary school She's small and skinny with white hair and a flat chest.'

'She's grown a bit since then,' Bobbie said, smiling. 'I'm Roberta Baker – Bobbie – Jemma's best friend.'

'I prefer Vivien,' he said with a wink. He pointed to her sling. 'And what the devil have you done to your arm? It looks like you've had a worse war than me – and that'll take some beating!'

'The arm's a long story.'

'Well, I've got a forty-eight-hour pass – and I don't plan to waste a minute of it. If you speak quickly, I'll listen.'

She laughed. 'Would you like some tea?'

He nodded and she poured them both a cup. He gulped his down and she wondered if he was dehydrated as well as exhausted. She desperately wanted to ask him what had happened at Dunkirk but sensed his need for normality and distraction.

'Thank you, Bobbie. That tastes good. But what I need right now is a pint of good old English ale to wash the salt and grit of that bloody French beach out of my mouth. Do you fancy joining me?'

Bobbie glanced at her watch. 'I don't think the pubs are open yet.'

He waved a dismissive hand in the air. He had large hands, she noticed. Slightly calloused, with long, slender, artistic fingers. Jemma had told her he was an accomplished carpenter in civilian life, a woodworking artisan.

'A few of the lads have gathered outside The Grey Mare,' he said. 'They've persuaded the landlord to open early. Everyone seems to be in the mood for a bit of celebration – can't think why,' he added with a wink. 'So why don't you come with me? I'll buy you a port and lemon – then we can catch my mother and Tom before they disappear into the bowels of the cinema. Don't worry,' he added, when she hesitated, 'I'll get a wash, a shave and change my shirt first. One of Hollywood's best actresses deserves nothing less.'

She smiled, gazed back and almost drowned in the liquid pool of his warm brown eyes.

'Do you know what, Harry – that's the best offer I've had in weeks… but there's one condition.'

'Name it.'

'You don't mention pond life, anything historical or bloody museum antiquities.'

He burst out laughing. 'Dear God, lass! What kind of company do you keep?' He slapped his hand across his heart. 'On my life, Miss Bobbie Baker, I promise you those dirty words will never pass my lips. And if they do – you can wash my mouth out with soap.'

'Then I'll get my hat. Lead the way, Corporal Langford.'

Author's Note & Acknowledgements

The idea for a daring fictional robbery at the Yorkshire Museum formed in my mind after watching an episode of *Foyle's War* on TV.

At the start of the Second World War, every art gallery and museum in Britain packed up its most precious items and whisked them away to the safety of the countryside or put them down disused coalmines. I knew the British Museum in London had sent some of its treasures to the safety of Skipton Castle in Yorkshire, and I began to wonder what they did with the priceless antiquities owned by our own museum in York. Where did they go to escape the threat posed by the Luftwaffe?

I contacted Adam Parker, the Associate Collections Curator of the Yorkshire Museum, for help and soon found myself immersed in the fascinating world of the Yorkshire Philosophical Society (YPS). Adam was very helpful. He sent me wartime photographs of the museum exhibits, links to the annual reports of the YPS and a floor plan of the museum in 1940. He also gave me a guided tour of the museum and a private viewing of the exquisite – and oh so precious – little Ormside Bowl. Yes, it really exists – as do most of the other exhibits I've mentioned. The only exception is the ancient Greek harpy. I made this up because I liked the phrase *hit on the head with a harpy*. Like little Kenneth Newby, I thought it was funny.

At times, Adam found my excited chatter about the fictional robbery I planned for his museum deeply uncomfortable, which makes his help and advice even more generous.

Yet, despite my research, I didn't discover where the YPS sent their most precious antiquities during the Second World War. Their annual accounts talk vaguely of these precious objects being sent 'to the country' for safety. It didn't matter in the end. Knowing that the YPS was founded and run by one hundred and fifty of Yorkshire's wealthiest families, many of whom owned ancestral piles, I felt quite comfortable with the idea that our county's treasures were locked in the cellars of several sprawling country homes.

The YPS is still going strong and runs fascinating talks several times a year in the Tempest Anderson lecture theatre – although I haven't seen one on *pond life* on the agenda for several decades. I sincerely hope they enjoy my slightly tongue-in-cheek depiction of their society's history.

I also owe many thanks to Dr M. Faye Prior AMA, Associate Collections Curator at York's Castle Museum, for her help, and to Katie Brown, the Collections Manager at the Kirkleatham Museum in Redcar, who's an expert on the real-life Violet Rodgers.

Both Violet Rodgers and Mary Kitson Clark were real women and curators at York's museums during the Second World War, although Mary didn't take on this position until 1941. (I've fiddled slightly with the date to suit the timeline of the novel). I know it's always a risk fictionalising real women, who may have living descendants. But whenever my historical research uncovers clever and enterprising females who were pioneers in their field, I always want to include them. It was easy to find out information about Violet; less easy to uncover much about Mary Kitson Clark. So, I hope their descendants will forgive me for my liberal use of artistic licence, especially Mary's imaginary engagement to a rugger player called Ian Duggen. (In reality, she married an Anglican priest.)

The elderly and frail Mr Collinge was also the curator at the Yorkshire Museum, although he'd retired by the end of 1940, and Lieutenant Władysław Włoch was Violet's fiancé. They married after the war, when York Corporation replaced Violet with a male curator – and gave him twice her salary. Violet went to Poland with Władysław and continued her career there.

Jodie and Baron Stokesley are fictional characters but when writing about their marital breakdown and divorce, I drew on the real-life scandalous divorce of Baron Inverclyde and his famous actress wife, June. This was one of the most high-profile divorce cases of the 1930s and was sensationally reported in the British press. June later wrote about it in her autobiography, *The Glass Ladder*, which I thoroughly enjoyed.

Interestingly, I suspect I'm not the only crime writer to have found inspiration from this source. Two years after the Inverclyde divorce, Agatha Christie published *Lord Edgware Dies,* in which a famous actress *appears* to murder her wealthy and titled husband. I'm convinced Agatha was also inspired by Inverclyde v. Inverclyde.

The story of Jemma's husband, Michael, was inspired by the strange mystery of Andreas Grassl, 'the Piano Man', who was found wandering the streets of Kent in a soaking wet suit in 2005. Unable to speak or remember who he was, he spent his time playing a piano in a hospital ward until the frenzied British media launched a national campaign to solve the mystery of his identity.

If anyone is confused by the mention of Bletchley Wireless Manufacturing, it might help to know that code breaking was only *one* of the valuable wartime activities carried out at the top-secret institution at Bletchley. The site is now world-famous as the place where the Enigma Code was cracked. Churchill's 'Secret Army', otherwise known as the Special Operations Executive (SOE), also trained there at the start of the war. And yes, our multilingual Michael was destined for the SOE before his accident.

Incidentally, the winter weather in Britain in 1939/1940 was as bad as I've described. And there was a fatal train crash caused by snow at Bletchley train station in December 1939.

Most of the York hotels, streets and buildings I've included are real, with the exception of the old convent in Beningbrough. As everyone in York knows, the real convent is in the city centre on Nunnery Lane.

I would also like to thank my editorial team, Jenni Davis and Sandra Mangan; my brilliant cover designer, Lisa Horton, and my son's partner, Lorena Muscai, who took the lovely photograph of the Yorkshire Museum on the book cover. And I need to thank my father, Tony James, for his help with the railway scenes during Jemma's trip to Bletchley. Every historical novelist needs a dad who's a steam engine enthusiast and a walking encyclopaedia about the 19th century British railway network. Thanks, Dad.

Finally, to you, my readers. Thank you for reading my novel. If you enjoyed *Dancing with Dusty Fossils,* please leave a review. I would also like to encourage you to visit my website and sign up to my occasional newsletter. It's the best place to hear about forthcoming releases, writerly updates, competitions and special offers.

Karen Charlton

www.karencharlton.com

Bibliography

Martin Edwards, *The Golden Age of Murder* (HarperCollins, 2015)

June Hillman, *The Glass Ladder* (William Heinemann Ltd., 1960)

Peter J. Hogarth and Ewan W. Anderson, '"The most fortunate situation": the story of York's Museum Gardens' (Yorkshire Philosophical Society, 2018)

F. Dalton O'Sullivan, *Crime Detection* (O'Sullivan Publishing House, 1928)

Barbara J. Pyrah, *The History of the Yorkshire Museum and its Geological Collections* (William Sessions Ltd., The Ebor Press, 1988)

David Rubinstein, *War Comes to York* (Quacks Books, 2011)

Susannah Stapleton, *The Adventures of Maud West: Lady Detective* (Picador, 2019)

Van C. Wilson, *Alexine: A Woman in Wartime York* (Van C. Wilson, 1995)

Van Wilson, *Rations, Raids and Romance: York in the Second World War* (York Archaeological Trust, 2008)

Van Wilson, *The Changing Face of Clifton* (York Archaeological Trust, 2011)

ABOUT THE AUTHOR

In addition to The York Ladies' Detective Agency Mysteries, Karen Charlton is the bestselling author of The Detective Lavender Mysteries, which are set in Regency London and feature Bow Street's Principal Officer, Stephen Lavender, and his humorous sidekick, Constable Ned Woods.

A former English teacher, with two grown-up children and a small grandson, Karen lives in a remote North Yorkshire fishing village with her two cats and writes full time. She's a stalwart of the village pub quiz team.

Karen always enjoys a good mystery and loves historical fiction and historical dramas on TV. She's an avid reader herself and loves to hear from her own readers. You can easily contact her via her website. For the latest news about her fiction, her public appearances and some special offers, sign up for her occasional newsletter on the home page: www.karencharlton.com

THE DETECTIVE LAVENDER MYSTERIES
By KAREN CHARLTON

Welcome to the world of Stephen Lavender, a Principal Officer with the Bow Street Runners, and his loyal constable, Ned Woods, Regency England's most intrepid crime-fighting duo.

Follow their adventures through the six novels and the four short stories in this series, which starts with *The Heiress of Linn Hagh.*

Printed in Great Britain
by Amazon